GOAL!

D0492325

milkshakefilms

www.**goal**the**movie**.com

**Also available in the GOAL series,
written by Robert Rigby:**

GOAL: GLORY DAYS
Novel based on the characters
from the box office hit movies,
GOAL! and *GOAL II*

GOAL!

OFFICIAL TIE-IN NOVELIZATIONS
BY ROBERT RIGBY

TWO BOOKS IN ONE
GOAL! and GOAL II: LIVING THE DREAM

CORGI BOOKS

GOAL! COLLECTION
TWO BOOKS IN ONE – GOAL! AND GOAL II: LIVING THE DREAM
A CORGI BOOK 978 0 552 560405

First published in Great Britain by Corgi Books
an imprint of Random House Children's Books
A Random House Group Company

This collection first published 2009
Film materials copyright © Goal Limited, 2009
Text copyright © Robert Rigby, 2009

1 3 5 7 9 10 8 6 4 2

including:

GOAL!
First published in Great Britain by Corgi Books, 2005
Text copyright © Robert Rigby, 2005
Film materials copyright © Goal Limited, 2005

and:

GOAL II: LIVING THE DREAM
First published in Great Britain by Corgi Books, 2006
Text copyright © Robert Rigby, 2006
Film materials copyright © Goal Limited, 2006

Corgi Books are published by Random House Children's Books,
61–63 Uxbridge Road, London W5 5SA

www.kidsatrandomhouse.co.uk
www.rbooks.co.uk

Addresses for companies within The Random House Group Limited can be found at:
www.randomhouse.co.uk/offices.htm

THE RANDOM HOUSE GROUP Limited Reg. No. 954009

A CIP catalogue record for this book is available from the British Library.

Printed in the UK by CPI Bookmarque, Croydon, CR0 4TD.

EVERY DREAM HAS A BEGINNING...

milkshakefilms

GOAL!

**OFFICIAL TIE-IN NOVELIZATION
BY ROBERT RIGBY**

CORGI BOOKS

ACKNOWLEDGEMENTS
(GOAL! THE MOVIE)

GOAL! original story by Mike Jefferies & Adrian Butchart

GOAL! Screenplay by Dick Clement & Ian La Frenais

Producers Mike Jefferies, Matt Barrelle & Mark Huffam

Executive Producers Lawrence Bender & Peter Hargitay

Co-Producers Danny Stepper & Jo Burn

Associate Producers Allen Hopkins, Stevie Hargitay,
Nicolas Gautier & Jonathan Harris

Special Thanks to
FIFA
adidas
Newcastle United
FA Premier League

One

Life was better now. Santiago eased his lean, toned body back on the pool lounger and gazed out over the shimmering, clear water.

He adjusted his aviator glasses slightly as the afternoon sunshine beat down from a clear blue sky. Even the crucifix around his neck was hot against his brown skin.

All around was luxury – sheer southern Californian luxury. Palm trees swayed slightly in the warm, gentle breeze and water sprinklers played on manicured lawns, forming mini-rainbows as the sunlight caught the droplets. Beyond the pool, steps led up to a wide terrace and beyond that sat the sprawling mansion itself.

Santiago glimpsed the Aztec tattoo he wore proudly on the inside of one forearm and his thoughts drifted back. To before. To ten years ago . . .

He sees himself, a ten-year-old boy, dazzling his playmates in a game of soccer on a dust-dry patch of waste ground down in the poorest quarter of a poverty-stricken Mexican town.

Close to the makeshift pitch, tin shacks sit amongst overcrowded apartment blocks, their walls plastered with colourful graffiti. Washing lines stretch between the shacks and the soccer-mad kids' game is accompanied by a cacophony of salsa music, shouts, crying babies and the roar of traffic.

But the boys are oblivious to all this. They think only of their game as they scamper about in the dust.

Santiago is in a class of his own. He takes the ball on his chest, allows it to drop from knee to instep, and in a liquid-like movement he rounds another kid and slots the ball deftly between two beer crates serving as goalposts.

And then the memory, and the picture, shifts, like a television flicking from one channel to another.

Santiago is sleeping. He feels himself being shaken and he opens his eyes. His father, Herman, is staring down at him.

'Get your things, Santiago.'

The small boy scrambles from his bed, rubbing the sleep from his eyes. His grandmother, Mercedes, is lifting his baby brother, Julio, from the cot.

'Quickly, Santiago.'

The bewildered ten-year old grabs his photograph of the World Cup, which he long ago tore from an old magazine, and then dives beneath his bed for his one truly prized possession – his football.

The mental picture shifts again, fast-forwarding to the inside of a battered truck as it bumps along in total darkness. Santiago and his family travel in silence. Another family and a number of young men are also crammed into the ancient truck. Everyone has handed over the required number of dollars for this one-way journey.

A baby starts to cry. A match flares as a young man lights a cigarette, and in the sudden light Santiago sees nothing but frightened faces. He clutches his football even tighter.

When the truck stops, the weary travellers climb out onto a dirt road, and as the vehicle rumbles and wheezes away they are ordered to follow their two guides through a maze of cactus and sagebrush.

They reach the border. Searchlights, mounted on a US border patrol wagon, scythe through the inky darkness. The illegal immigrants run up an incline towards a gaping hole in the two-and-a-half-metre-high border fence.

Just as he reaches the gap, Santiago's football slips from his hands. It bounces away, downhill. He turns to chase after it, but his father grabs one arm.

'Forget it, it's only a stupid ball,' he hisses.

Santiago catches one final, fleeting glimpse of his beloved football before he is bundled through the gap in the fence and his father urges him to: 'Run! Run! Run!'

* * *

4

Ten years ago. A long time.

Santiago glanced at his tattoo once more and sighed. He heard footsteps, but before he could turn to see who was approaching, a heavy hand cuffed him, none too gently, across the back of his head.

'Get off there. You want to lose us this job? There's leaves to be cleared from the drive. Go get the blower.'

Santiago said nothing. He just got up, grabbed his T-shirt and shrugged as he walked away to carry out his father's orders.

Sure, life was better now. But not much.

Two

The pick-up truck was going east on Sunset Boulevard, heading downtown. Santiago and his father were crammed into the open back along with three more gardeners and an assortment of machines and gardening tools – including the leaf blower.

Santiago checked his watch, then unzipped a sports bag and began pulling out his soccer gear. He took off his T-shirt and slipped on a faded striped shirt. The other guys took little notice. It had been a long, hot, tiring day; they were saving their little remaining energy for pulling the top from a bottle of beer when they got home.

As Santiago took out his boots, with their

distinctive red and yellow laces, the old guy sitting opposite decided to show a little interest. 'How you guys doing this year?'

Santiago shrugged his shoulders. 'Two of our best players were picked up by Immigration. Maybe they'll make it back for the play-offs.' He checked his watch again. 'That's if we make it to the play offs. I'm late.'

By the time the truck pulled in at the kerbside, Santiago was changed and ready to play. He jumped over the tailgate and went running off towards the park.

Concrete flyovers towered over three soccer pitches and a baseball diamond, all of which were squeezed into an area surrounded by industrial units.

The match had already begun, and as Santiago arrived at the pitch-side, the *Americanitos'* coach, César, was prowling the touchline, a cigarette dangling from his lips. It was many years since César had played soccer; his pot-belly was too big for even the outsize pants he wore. But he knew a good player when he saw one.

'What's the score?' asked Santiago, waving

7

both arms towards the referee in an attempt to attract his attention.

'We're one down, and you're late. Get on there!'

The ball went out of play, and as César tottered off to fetch it, the referee came over to where Santiago was standing and pointed at his legs. 'I don't want anyone hurt. No shin pads, no game!'

Shin pads were a luxury Santiago had never quite managed to afford. But the problem had arisen before so he knew exactly what to do. Close to the pitch, a couple of overflowing garbage cans were almost hidden by a pile of discarded cardboard boxes. Santiago grabbed one and tore off two rectangular pieces. From a distance, they could almost have been shin pads.

He stuffed one into each of his socks and looked at the referee. 'OK?'

The ref shrugged and beckoned Santiago onto the pitch. 'Pitch' was a generous, if loose, description. It was rock-hard and almost grass-free, and the corner 'flags' were three oil drums and the remnants of an old pram.

But that didn't matter to Santiago. The game was all that mattered. The game was what he lived for.

He jogged to his usual position up front, smiling as he saw the relief on the faces of some of his team-mates now that their star player had made his belated entrance.

For a few minutes, Santiago felt his way into the game, moving with speed and grace, making deft lay-offs and taking up perfect positions the other *Americanitos* never quite managed to read or exploit. He was way ahead of the game, but not yet fully in it, so he dropped a little deeper.

Then he got his chance. One chance was usually all he needed. He made some space for himself and collected a hopeful punt out of defence. Almost casually, he rounded one lumbering defender, flat-footed another and then closed on the goal. From the edge of the box he curled a rising shot past the helpless and astonished keeper.

He could almost hear the legendary Mexican commentator, Andres Cantor, screaming, 'GOOOOAALLLLL!!!!!!'

* * *

Santiago worked a night job in a popular and noisy Chinese restaurant. He collected dirty dishes, shifted heavy cans and cartons, took out the trash, and sometimes washed the dirty dishes that the young waiters carried in from the restaurant.

He'd been there for more than six months and several times he had asked the boss if he could become a waiter, because waiters got better pay. The answer was always the same. 'No, you not Chinese.'

There was no arguing with that, but at least every night he worked, Santiago went home with a little more cash. A little more to add to the savings he stashed in an old trainer kept at the top of the wardrobe in the bedroom he shared with his young brother, Julio.

After the soccer match, Santiago was running late again. One of his team-mates gave him a lift in an old Ford Galaxy, and as they pulled up outside his home, he had barely enough time to take a quick shower, change his clothes and maybe grab a burrito as he left for the restaurant. He didn't like Chinese food – he saw too much of it.

He jumped out of the front passenger seat, slammed the door, shouted, 'Thanks for the ride', and walked up the incline towards the house, a single-storey building perched on a hillside close to the Dodgers' stadium.

In the small front yard, Santiago's father and another man had their heads under the raised hood of a pick-up truck. Herman gave his son no more than a fleeting glance as he passed by and went into the house.

The voice of a football commentator blared out from the TV set in one corner of the cluttered living room. The goals from a Real Madrid versus Barcelona match were being shown, and Santiago's grandmother was watching even more avidly than her younger grandson, who was sitting by her side. There were two soccer fanatics in the Muñez family, and as far as Mercedes was concerned, Santiago ranked number two.

She was up and out of her chair as Real scored their second goal. '*¡Mira! ¿Qué te dije?*' she said. They always spoke Spanish at home. 'See the difference since Beckham came back? No one crosses the ball like him.'

'Yes, I see,' answered Julio. 'You mind if I get on with my homework now?'

Santiago stood smiling in the doorway as his grandmother switched off the TV set and asked him her usual questions. 'How did you do? You play well?'

'Won, four–two. I scored a couple, should have got another.' Santiago nodded towards the window. 'What's the deal with Dad?'

'He wants to buy a truck of his own.'

'Why?'

'So you can work for yourselves. Your own business, Muñez and Son, eh?'

Santiago reached into his sports bag and brought out his asthma inhaler. He took a quick puff. 'That's his best plan for me? The rest of my life with dirt under my nails?'

Julio looked up from his schoolbooks. 'There's always plan B.'

'Yeah? And what's that?'

'The American Dream. We win the lottery, man!'

As Santiago was about to head for the bedroom, Herman came in from the front yard. He didn't look happy, but then he rarely did; life had never done Herman Muñez many favours.

'So what happened?' asked Mercedes.

'The guy wants too much money.'

Santiago made certain he didn't smile as he looked at his father. 'That's too bad, Dad.'

Three

Even when he was on holiday, Glen Foy took his football seriously. He couldn't help it. St James' Park, or a park in the San Fernando Valley. Shearer and co., or a bunch of seven-year-olds. Football was football. It was a serious business.

Glen was staying with his daughter Val, who lived in southern California with her husband and two young sons. And one of those sons, seven-year-old Tom, was out there on the pitch while his granddad and mum watched from the touchline, shouting their encouragement.

Only in Glen's case, it wasn't exactly encouragement. 'Keep your position, Tom! Stop bunching up, you're meant to be on the wing!'

'Dad!' said Val. 'It's not the Cup Final. They're seven years old.'

'Best to start 'em young.'

Glen's accent was an unusual mix of southern Ireland and the North-East of England. He'd lived in and around Newcastle for most of his adult life. At forty-eight, he'd put on a few pounds since his heyday, but still looked in pretty good shape, especially with his holiday tan.

On the far side of the pitch a group of young mums were reliving their cheerleader days.

'Go, Wild Cats, go!'

The young kids swept across the pitch like a swarm of angry bees, but Glen's grandson appeared to be on the periphery of most of the action.

'Come on, lad! Get in there!'

Val rested one hand on Glen's shoulder. 'Easy, Dad. To tell you the truth, I'm not sure Tom's heart is really in soccer.'

'Soccer,' muttered Glen disdainfully. 'Soccer. The game's called *football*.' He sighed and turned away. There was a senior game taking place on the adjacent pitch – a team of Hispanics taking on a tough-looking bunch of Europeans wearing the shirts of the Croatian national team.

One player immediately stood out. The young Hispanic picked up the ball at around the halfway line and then, with a deceptive burst of speed, eased his way past first one, and then another defender before sending a perfectly weighted pass across the field. Glen lost interest in the kids' match.

The young player was dictating the game, frequently making fools of the opposition, while at the same time making his team-mates look far better than they were.

Glen slowly edged his way along the touch-line, close to where a pot-bellied Hispanic guy with a cigarette dangling from his mouth stood bawling instructions to his team. But not once did Glen's eyes shift from the young player. Even when he didn't have the ball, he was good. The movement. The runs. The feints and dummies. He collected the ball, beat one player and was then hacked down by a crunching tackle from behind.

'Aye, aye,' whispered Glen. 'He won't like that.'

But the young player simply got to his feet and gave his opponent a withering look that said, *Is that the best you can do?*

The Croatian defenders lined up in a wall, following the shouted instructions of their goal-keeper. The young player waited calmly with his foot on the ball, gesturing to his team-mates to take up positions of their own.

When the referee blew his whistle, it looked for a moment as though the player would go for a cross. But then, effortlessly, and off just a couple of strides, he aimed for the goal. The ball curved around the wall and powered into the net, giving the stranded goalkeeper no chance.

'Bloody hell,' whispered Glen before he realized he was spontaneously applauding.

He walked up to the coach. 'Did you teach him to do that?'

The coach grinned through tobacco-stained teeth. 'God taught him to do that.'

'Bloody hell,' said Glen again.

The old bus stood in the parking lot shaded by a small stand of trees. Long ago it would have been a school bus, but instead of being towed off to the breakers' yard when its school days were through, it had been patched up and custom painted with vivid street scenes. As he waited, Glen studied the artwork and read the word *Americanitos* daubed on the side.

The *Americanitos* came ambling towards their bus in twos and threes, chatting about the game, the goals, the missed chances, the ruthless play of some of the opposition. The star player was alone, his boots with their distinctive red and yellow laces slung around his neck. Glen went straight up to him.

'You played a blinder.'

'A what?'

'You played very well,' said Glen with a smile. 'Brilliant.' He held out his hand. 'I'm Glen Foy. I used to play a bit myself.' As they shook hands, Glen nodded towards the boots. 'What's with the laces?'

The young player looked a little embarrassed. 'For my mother. The colours of Spain.'

'Oh, right. Still live there, does she?'

'I don't know where she lives.' He obviously

wanted to change the subject. 'So where did you play?'

'England.'

'England! You played for *England*?'

Glen laughed. 'No, lad, I played *in* England. Have you ever thought of turning pro?'

Most of the *Americanitos* had climbed onto the bus and some were staring out through the dusty windows, wondering what was going on.

'Pro teams here go for college kids. None of us went to college.'

'It's usually exactly the opposite in England; don't get many university graduates in the Premier league. Look, I bumped into a British agent I know on the flight out here. I'm gonna get him to check you out.'

He saw the player's doubtful look.

'I'm serious; I think you're worth it. I was a scout for four years after I stopped playing, so I know what I'm talking about.'

The bus driver had started up the engine and the team coach appeared on the steps. 'Hey, Santiago, come on! Some of us have homes to go to!'

'Santiago,' said Glen. 'Santiago who?'
'Muñez. It's Santiago Muñez.'
'And when's your next game?'
'Saturday.'
'Then I'll see you Saturday, Santiago.'

Four

Beautiful young women clad in Adidas tracksuits were gliding around the open-air Sky Bar at the Mondrian Hotel with trays of canapés and drinks. But no one ate too much or drank too much. It was all about being there. Seeing the right people, shaking the right hands. Being seen.

Barry Rankin was always highly visible, almost as high profile as some of the football stars he represented. Barry sat at a table on the terrace overlooking the city of Los Angeles with his cellphone at one ear. He was enjoying the brunch reception thrown by Adidas to promote their new range of sportswear, even though this particular transatlantic call was to one of his more demanding and troublesome clients. 'Gavin, abroad is not a good idea. Down the line, definite, but not now. Look, if you went to Real or Inter I'd make a ton of money, right? But I won't do that. I'm putting your interests first, Gavin. I'm thinking of you.'

Barry was speaking to Gavin Harris, one of his top clients and a Premiership player anxious to settle a move during the transfer window. Barry listened patiently as Gavin explained exactly why *he* thought he should be plying his trade in La Liga.

A girl carrying a tray was hovering nearby and Barry gestured to her for another drink – only his second. He lifted a glass from the tray, took a sip and resumed the long-distance conversation. 'But think of the drawbacks, Gavin. Foreign country, foreign food, and the only foreign food you like is curry. Believe me, you won't get a good vindaloo in Madrid. Look, you've got to trust me on this. I'm on to it and I'll have it sorted before the transfer deadline. Now, I've got to go; someone here I *have* to speak to. Say hello to Christina. Bye, Gavin.'

He ended the call and sat back in his chair. There was no one he *had* to speak to, but there were one or two people he wanted to have a few words with, including the blonde who had given him his drink. He stood up and was starting to stroll across the terrace when he felt a hand on one arm.

'Barry, is this a good moment to talk?'

Barry turned round, smiling his most welcoming smile. After all, it might just be Sir Alex Ferguson.

It wasn't. Barry was confronted with a face he knew from somewhere back in time, though he couldn't quite put a name to that face. But the smile remained; this could be business and Barry was always open for business. 'As good a time as any, er . . .'

'Glen. Glen Foy.'

'Of course, Glen. What you doing out here?'

'On holiday, staying with my daughter.'

'Nice. Having a good time? It's all a bit unreal out here, eh? Lala Land.'

Glen sighed. He'd had a feeling that this wasn't going to be easy. 'I phoned you, remember?

About the lad I saw playing. You really ought to take a look at him before you go back.'

'Of course I remember, Glen. But my life's a meeting, man. I hardly have time—'

'He's a young Mexican kid,' said Glen quickly, unwilling to be sidetracked. 'They played in second-hand strips on a pitch with gopher holes, but he was special. I'm telling you, he dazzled me, and I don't dazzle easy.'

Barry's phone rang. He glanced at the screen and chose to ignore the call. 'There's a lot of good young kids around, Glen. And not enough teams for them all.'

Glen had been expecting this; it was time to play his trump card. 'Last time I was dazzled, it was a young kid called Jermain Defoe. My lot didn't want him, and nor did you.'

Barry held up both his hands. 'Yeah, yeah, all right. Sore point.'

'The lad's playing at UCLA next Saturday. Two o'clock. Will you be there?'

Barry nodded, apparently convinced. 'I'll be there. Totally.' His phone rang and once again he looked at the screen to check on the caller. 'I have to take this one, Glen. Business.'

'You will . . . ?'

'I'll *be* there. Now relax. Grab a drink; get yourself some food. Chill.'

Five

The *Americanitos* bus was a lot fuller than usual as it trundled down Sunset Boulevard through glorious Beverly Hills. Today's match was in glamour land, and friends and girlfriends had come along for the ride, to breathe in the heady atmosphere, to feel part of it all. For one afternoon, at least.

Santiago sat at the back with his grandmother and brother. He was staring out through the window and looked nervous and edgy.

Mercedes looked plain angry. She'd been building up to saying something from the moment they boarded the bus, and both grandsons knew what was coming. 'Your father should be here to watch you.'

'It's just another game,' said Santiago with a shrug, sounding a lot more indifferent than he felt.

'It's not!'

Santiago turned to look at his grandmother. 'You know what he said when I told him about the agent?'

'I can probably guess.'

'He said, "Movie stars have agents. What does an agent want with you?" So I tell him. I tell him the agents sees me, he signs me, I go to Europe and make plenty of money and I come back and buy us a house on the west side. And you know what he says then?'

Julio had been reading a book, apparently not listening to the conversation. But he looked up and repeated the words they had all heard from Herman many times. ' "There are two types of people in this world. People in big houses, and people like us who cut their lawns and wash their cars." '

'That's exactly what he said,' said Santiago as his brother went back to his book. 'The only way he believes we can make things better is by buying a truck so we can have our own gardening business. Big deal.'

Mercedes sighed. 'Your father has had a hard life.'

Santiago glanced at his ripped jeans and faded T-shirt. 'And we don't?'

The pitch was good, better than anything the *Americanitos* had ever played on. The grass was in pristine condition and reminded Santiago of some of the lawns he spent hours cutting. And it wasn't just the pitch that was different. On either side there was banked seating for spectators and even a proper scoreboard.

On the far touchline, the Galaxy Reserves were getting their pre-match pep talk from no less than four identically tracksuited coaches. Nearby stood trestle tables loaded with electric fans, coolers packed with soft drinks and rows of plastic water bottles. To complete the picture, trim cheerleaders were going through the first of their perfectly drilled routines.

The *Americanitos* – and their girlfriends,

proudly dressed up for their day out in their tightest skirts and largest hooped earrings – simply gawped. They'd seen nothing like this before. This was another world.

César, cigarette dangling from his mouth as usual, looked at the anxious faces of his own players as they stared across at the tanned, athletic, all-American boys waiting to take the field.

He spat his cigarette out onto the ground. 'Hey, come on, you guys, we gonna beat ourselves here? OK, they look good, but that don't mean they play good. Get out there and show them what the *Americanitos* can do!'

César's rallying call was answered with a few half-hearted shouts of 'Yeah' and 'All right', but the portly coach feared that the Galaxy Reserves might have this game won before they even kicked the ball. Even Santiago looked nervous. But Santiago was nervous for another reason: this was the chance he had only ever dreamed of.

Further along the touchline, he saw a man standing up in the ranked seating. He was waving. It was Glen. Santiago waved back. Glen was here; that must mean the agent was here, too.

As his team-mates ran onto the pitch, Santiago kneeled down by his sports bag, turned his back and grabbed his inhaler for a quick, unnoticed hit. Only his family knew about the asthma: he preferred it that way.

Glen was sitting with his daughter, and as the teams lined up, his eyes were scanning the spectators for Barry Rankin. He was late.

The match had not started well for the *Americanitos*; they were already one down and were struggling to keep up with a clinical, well-organized side playing disciplined football.

It was plain to see the result of the Galaxy Reserves having four coaches. They were neat and efficient in defence, midfield and attack, and while no one stood out, as a unit they were impressive.

Santiago was playing a lot deeper than he preferred, trying to marshal the midfield, attempting to get something going.

If it was frustrating for Santiago, it was even

more so for Mercedes as she watched and fretted with Julio at her side. 'They can't keep possession. Santiago is too deep. Too deep. He should be up front.'

'If he goes up front he'll never get the ball,' said Julio.

On the far side, Glen was worried too, not only because Santiago was struggling to show his true ability, but also that there was still no sign of Barry Rankin.

There was a rare cheer from the *Americanitos*' supporters and Glen looked back from scanning the seating to see Santiago emerging from a tackle in his own half, the ball at his feet. He rounded an opposing midfielder and set off on a long run out wide. As he cut inside, a defender came thundering into the tackle. Santiago dummied him as though he wasn't there, went wide again and looked up for support. It was still on the way; there was no one to pass to.

As the full back bore down, Santiago shimmied inside and sent a left-foot shot from the tightest of angles screaming past the goal-keeper and in at the near post.

'Yes!' shouted Mercedes.

'Oh, yes!' bawled Glen. He turned to his daughter. 'You see! That's what I've been talking about. And that pillock Rankin isn't even here to see it! Can I use your phone?'

Barry Rankin had his eyes full elsewhere. He was stretched out on a lounger at someone's – he couldn't exactly remember whose – beach house, admiring the bikini-clad eye-candy draped around the pool. Music was pumping out from a CD player and Barry was enjoying a long, cool drink when his mobile rang.

Without thinking, he flipped it open and answered the call. 'Yo!'

He didn't get a chance to speak again for the next thirty seconds as Glen bawled him out for not being at the game.

When Glen finally paused for breath, Barry took his chance. 'Listen, Glen, listen. I did *not* forget. I've been in a meeting since breakfast.'

'A meeting with music!' shouted Glen.

Barry gestured for the nearest girl to turn down the CD a little. 'Just finished, mate,' he said into the phone. 'I'm grabbing a late lunch. Look, I'm having real trouble tying up this Gavin Harris deal.'

'But I've got a kid here who's special. Very, very special.'

'Yeah, I know, you said. Can you get me some video on the kid?'

'Video! Are you crazy? Forget it, Barry, and I hope you choke on your late lunch.'

Glen hung up and Barry was left holding the phone with no one to speak to, aware that the three closest girls were watching. He smiled and shrugged. 'Bad connection.'

Thanks mainly to Santiago's inspirational goal and his all-round performance, the game ended in a one–all draw. The *Americanitos* lifted their game in the second half and almost stole the match when, close to the end, their star man thundered a shot against the woodwork.

But a draw was a fair result, and as Santiago joined his grandmother and Julio at the touchline he saw Glen walking towards them.

'You played great, son.'

Santiago nodded his thanks. 'This is my grandmother, and my brother.'

'And you are the agent?' asked Mercedes quickly.

'No, Grandmother,' said Santiago. 'This man arranged for the agent to come.'

Glen wasn't looking forward to the next bit, but they had to know. 'And I'm afraid he didn't. He let me down. Said it was business, the usual excuses.'

He saw Santiago's crestfallen look and felt worse than he already did about raising the lad's hopes.

Mercedes was still optimistic. 'So he will come to the next game, yes?'

'I'm afraid not. He's going back to England tomorrow, and so am I. I'm really sorry, Santiago.'

Santiago reached down and picked up his sports bag. 'I guess my old man is right. You dare to dream, but that's all it can ever be – a dream . . .'

Six

be a farewell barbecue. The family,
rs, everyone gathered together out
d, having a good time, all wishing
ge at the end of his holiday. The
ere, and so were the neighbours,
f honour had gone missing.

side the house, perched on the arm
he family den. He was making a
hone call, waiting impatiently for
answered. Glen felt as though he
go down.

playing career, Glen had never been
abber, a genius who could bring a
feet with a flick, or a run, or

a stunning volley from outside the box. He was more a grafter, tenacious, the Mister Dependable who never gave up. And he wasn't going to give up now, not while there was still a chance. Slim, unlikely – but still a chance.

The phone was answered and a sleepy voice muttered, 'Hello?'

'Mr Dornhelm, it's Glen Foy.'

In Newcastle, Erik Dornhelm heard his wife sigh with irritation as his eyes cleared and focused on the digital clock. It read 03.32. 'Glen . . . ? Do I know you, Mr Foy?'

'I was your chief scout, when you first took over. You fired me – well, not exactly fired me; you wanted your own people. I understand that and I don't hold it against you.'

'You don't? So why are you calling me at three thirty in the morning?'

Glen smiled; at least he hadn't slammed the phone down. Not yet. 'I'm in California. I've seen a player here. I think he's a remarkable talent.'

'And who does this remarkable talent play for?'

'It's just local league, but the thing is, I'm on a plane back home tomorrow and I need you to make me a promise.'

Dornhelm's wife turned over and hissed, 'Erik!' as she pulled the duvet up over her head.

'Mr Foy,' said Dornhelm quietly. 'You're waking me up like this just so I can make you a promise?'

'Yeah. If the lad turns up on your doorstep, will you see him? Give him a run out, that's all I'm asking.'

Dornhelm laughed quietly. 'That's all, eh? And if I make this promise, can I go back to sleep?'

'Yeah, course you can, Mr Dornhelm.'

'Then yes, Mr Foy. Goodnight.'

He hung up and Glen smiled. Suddenly the steaks sizzling out there on the barbecue seemed a lot more appetizing.

Santiago and his family emerged from the church into the bright Sunday morning sunlight. The priest was standing by the door, dutifully shaking hands with every member of his flock as they left after Mass.

As Santiago walked down the steps he heard one short sharp burst on the horn of a Ford Explorer parked across the road. In the rear were the kids and Glen's luggage, and the man himself was sitting in the passenger seat, next to Val.

He waved as Santiago saw him, got out of the car and came hurrying across the road. 'I'm glad I caught you. I called your coach – he told me where to find you.'

'The agent?' said Mercedes. 'He comes to see Santiago after all?'

'Better than that,' said Glen. 'Santiago, if you can get yourself to England, Newcastle United will give you a trial.'

Santiago stared. 'Newcastle! Are you kidding me?'

Before Glen could answer, Herman grabbed Santiago's arm and spoke to him in Spanish. 'What is all this? You really think you can go and play football in England? It's *bullshit*.' He turned on Glen and reverted to English. 'Why do you fill him with ideas like this? Who the hell do you think you are?'

He walked away while everyone else squirmed

with embarrassment. Everyone but Mercedes, who turned to Glen. 'He is supposed to fly halfway across the world on something you say? This is a big thing you ask of Santiago.'

'I'm not *asking* him to do it; I'm saying he *should* do it. He's a special talent, and I hate to see special talent go to waste. The Newcastle manager has promised me that Santiago will get a trial. The rest is up to him.'

The Explorer's horn sounded again and they looked over to see Val anxiously pointing at her watch and then beckoning Glen to the vehicle.

'I'm gonna have to go or I'll miss my flight,' said Glen, reaching into a pocket and bringing out a card. He handed it to Santiago. 'That's got my home and business numbers on it. I hope I see you again, Santiago. I really hope so.'

Money. Cash. Dollars. As Santiago sat in his bedroom counting his savings that afternoon, he realized his father was right about one thing, at least: the whole world revolved around dollars. The need for them, the quest for them, and in his case, the lack of them.

He didn't have enough cash to get to England, but as he stuffed the dollar bills back into the old trainer, he made up his mind he would earn what he needed to make the trip. It would take a little time, but he'd do it.

Until now, Santiago had never quite known what he was saving for; it had just seemed like a good idea. Saving for something, someday. Now he knew exactly why. He had a goal. He was going to England. To Newcastle.

He was about to push the trainer back into its hiding place in the wardrobe when the bedroom door opened and Julio breezed in, a baseball in one hand and a catcher's glove on the other.

Santiago hurriedly put the trainer behind his back and sat down on his bed. 'Why don't you knock?'

'Because it's my room, too,' said Julio, sitting on his own bed. He threw the baseball hard into the glove. 'You got enough?'

'What?'

'Santiago,' said Julio, as though he were the one talking to *his* kid brother. 'Everyone knows you keep your money in that trainer.'

'They do?' Santiago pulled the trainer from behind his back and sighed. 'Can't anyone have a little privacy in this place?'

'Nope,' said Julio, transferring the ball back to his throwing hand. 'Are you going, then?'

'Grandma thinks I should.'

'And what about Dad?'

'I haven't asked Dad. There's no point.' Santiago got up and pushed the trainer back into the wardrobe. As he turned round, his younger brother threw the baseball towards him, just out of arm's reach. Santiago stretched for the ball, but it clipped his fingers and fell onto the floor.

Julio laughed. 'You'd better go. You're sure not gonna make it at baseball. How far is England?'

Santiago stooped down, picked up the baseball and tossed it back to his brother. 'Right now, about four hundred dollars too far.'

Four hundred dollars: small change to many of the rich folk Santiago worked for, but for him, it was a lot. He just had to get on with it. He started his moneymaking scheme that evening at the Chinese restaurant, firstly by asking the boss for every extra shift he could get, and then by employing his own special skills during his first break.

Two of his workmates stood watching in the alley at the back of the restaurant as Santiago effortlessly played 'keepy-uppy' with a football.

'Yeah, very pretty, Santiago,' called one of them. 'But that ain't gonna take my money.'

'Nor mine,' yelled the other young Latin American. 'And don't let it touch the ground. You said, without touching the ground.'

Santiago smiled, and lifted his head for a moment as he measured the distance. Then he flicked the ball a little higher with his right foot and just before it touched the ground he brought his foot through and sent the ball into the air. It came down exactly where it was meant to, into a rubbish skip more than twenty metres away.

'That's five bucks each,' he said as his friends dug into their pockets for the cash.

In the days that followed, Santiago worked harder than he ever had. He didn't mention his plan to his dad; he just cut grass, cleared leaves, dug flowerbeds and, most boring and exhausting of all, cleared brush; hacking away at dead undergrowth with a machete. Whatever the job, however tiring, he got on with it, without complaint. And every evening, as his day's pay was counted out into his hands, he mentally calculated how much closer he was to the four hundred dollars he needed.

His dad would watch, but say nothing.

Santiago's only relief from the gruelling routine was when he played for the *Americanitos*. That was never hard work; football was what he lived for.

He was usually dropped off outside the house after matches. And as he jumped from the bus after one weekend game, he noticed a pick-up truck parked close to the house. It wasn't new, maybe five years old, but it had obviously very recently been cleaned up and made to look its best.

At first, Santiago thought nothing of it, but then as he got closer he saw what was loaded into the back of the truck. The lawnmower, hoses, the leaf blower, garden forks and spades. Santiago recognized them all.

Then he realized. Then he knew.

He sprinted for the house, through the front door, past both his grandmother in the kitchen and his father, who was sitting watching television.

Santiago dashed into his bedroom and threw open the wardrobe door. His hands were trembling as he reached for the old trainer. It was still there, but as he pulled it down and looked inside, he saw exactly what he had feared. Nothing. The money had gone.

For a few moments Santiago stood perfectly still, trying to stay calm, trying to keep his breathing regular. Then, with the trainer still in his hands, he went back to the living room.

His father looked up from the television as he felt Santiago's eyes boring into him.

'You took it. How could you do it?'

'I paid forty-five hundred for the truck,' said Herman loudly, before Santiago had the chance to say any more. 'From you, I take twelve hundred, but I'm giving you half the business. That's a good deal!'

Mercedes came to the kitchen doorway. 'You took his money? You stole it?'

'Stay out of this, Mother!' said Herman, getting up from his chair.

'You knew what the money was for!' yelled Santiago, unable to stop himself from shouting. He threw the empty trainer onto the floor. 'Two more weeks and I would have had enough!'

'To chase your stupid dream!' Herman's face was red with anger. 'Big-time ball player in England! It's bullshit! And when you fail, how you gonna get back in this country without papers?'

'I won't fail! You think I should give up, just so I can do what you do!'

They were glaring at each other, eyes bulging, fists clenched. Herman took three steps forward, until his face was just a few centimetres from his son's. When he spoke, his voice was deep and low as he struggled to suppress his fury. 'What I do? I'll tell you what I do. In Mexico, I worked day and night to get us to America. When your mother walked out on us, I held this family together!'

'Leave my mother out of this!'

Santiago made to walk away, but his father

grabbed his arm. 'I worked. I made enough to get us this house. Now we have our own business, everything gets better.'

'For you!' said his son, shaking himself free. 'But not for me!' Santiago looked at his grandmother, who sighed and shook her head. They both turned away. Mercedes went back into the kitchen and Santiago returned to his bedroom.

His chest felt tight. His breathing was shallow. He pulled open the drawer in the bedside cabinet next to his bed and took out his spare asthma inhaler. He needed it. Badly.

Seven

Newcastle United chairman, Freddie Shepherd, looked happy. Barry Rankin looked happy. Gavin Harris looked happy. And Erik Dornhelm was making sure he looked happy.

He *was* happy. In the main. The club's new signing was good; there was no doubt about that. For £8.4 million he had to be good. As the second half of the season's push for that vital Champions League spot gathered momentum, a skilful, attacking, goal-scoring midfielder was exactly what the team needed.

Gavin Harris was all of that. And a bit more. He came with history; a playboy reputation. There had been several unwelcome appearances on the front pages of the tabloids to offset the many back-page reports of his artistry and match-winning performances.

Signing Harris was a gamble, but if it helped clinch that Champions League place, it was a gamble both Freddie Shepherd and Erik Dornhelm were prepared to take. Dornhelm was no pushover as a manager; he had a reputation, too, as a tough, no-nonsense disciplinarian.

Gavin Harris certainly looked the part as he sat on the podium, flanked by Dornhelm and Shepherd. His clothes were casual, but top-designer, exclusive, expensive casual.

The club had chosen to unveil their new signing in the conference room of one of Newcastle's top hotels. The three men were all smiles behind the bank of microphones jutting up from the table in front of them. Cameras flashed as photographers jostled for position and reporters fired in the usual questions.

Barry Rankin stood on one side of the podium. His smile was the broadest of all. He had worked hard to finally clinch this deal, harder than his client would ever know. Barry reckoned he deserved every penny of the percentage he would make on the Gavin Harris transfer.

'It's a great honour to be joining Newcastle United,' said Gavin in answer to a reporter's question. 'Alan Shearer has been a hero of mine for years. I'm very grateful to get the chance to play alongside him in the same team.'

Dornhelm nodded and kept smiling. So far so good: the new boy had said all the right things. Time to wind up the carefully staged event, while they were still ahead.

He got to his feet, holding a pristine black and white Newcastle United shirt with the name HARRIS already printed on the back. 'This is a very good day for the club. Gavin is a very gifted player; he should fit in very well with our set-up. I'm very pleased to present him with this shirt.'

Gavin stood up and both men held the shirt as the cameras flashed again.

Dornhelm may have been anxious to bring the event to a close, but some of the reporters had other ideas.

'Winning the league's out of sight, Erik,' called

one. 'What are your realistic goals for the rest of the season?'

'Qualifying for the Champions League. Top European football is essential for a club like this.'

Another reporter spoke up from the opposite side of the room. 'Then you'll need to start picking up a few more maximum points from the remaining games, won't you?'

Dornhelm was ready with the standard diplomatic answer about the quality of the opposition in the Premiership, but before he could reply, Gavin Harris spoke up. 'Shouldn't be a problem.' He looked at Dornhelm. 'Bring 'em on, eh, boss?'

Dornhelm's smile remained fixed, but he said nothing. In his mind, he could already see tomorrow's back-page headlines running along the lines of: COCKY HARRIS SAYS EUROPE IS NO PROBLEM.

At the side of the podium, Barry Rankin kept smiling as he let out a huge sigh of relief, very glad that the deal was well and truly done.

* * *

'Where's your father?'

Santiago stood with his T-shirt in one hand, ready for a quick shower before another shift at the Chinese restaurant. His grandmother and brother had obviously been waiting for him to arrive home and they obviously had something to say. 'He's gone to El Monte to get a part for his precious truck. Why?'

'Good,' said Mercedes, walking over to the old bureau on one side of the room. 'He doesn't have to hear this.' She opened the bureau, took out a large brown envelope and tipped the contents onto the table. 'Train ticket to San Diego. Bus ticket to Mexico City.'

Santiago almost dropped the T-shirt. 'Mexico City?'

'You can't fly to London from LA,' said Julio. 'You're illegal.'

Santiago looked from his grandmother to his brother and then back to his grandmother. 'What's going on here?'

By way of explanation, Mercedes picked up the third ticket lying on the table. 'This is your plane ticket. It's dated one week from now to give you time to get a passport.'

'Pass—?' Santiago finally realized exactly what his grandmother had done. 'How did you do this? Where did you get the money?'

Mercedes shrugged. 'I've worked hard all my life. I have savings.'

'*Had* savings,' corrected Julio. 'And she sold things, too.'

'What things?'

Mercedes glared at her younger grandson and then shrugged again. 'Things from the past. Don't worry, it's for your future.'

'Grandma, I can't—'

'Don't start telling me what you can't do. This is about what you *can* do, what you *must* do.'

Santiago looked at his brother. 'You knew all about this?'

Julio smiled. 'Of course I knew. You're the only one who doesn't know things around here. You have to go, I want the bedroom to myself.'

He was putting on a brave face; they all were, now that Santiago's dream of going to England was so close to becoming reality.

'But take a shower before you go,' said Julio. 'You smell real bad.'

'Tonight?' said Santiago to his grandmother. 'I'm going tonight?'

Mercedes nodded. 'Before your father gets home. You'd better get packed.'

Santiago went to his grandmother and brother, put his arms around them both and pulled them close. All three had tears in their eyes.

'Julio's right,' said Mercedes through her tears. 'You do need a shower.'

Eight

The immigration official at Heathrow Airport studied the photograph in the brand-new Mexican passport with great care. Then he lifted his eyes and studied Santiago's face with the same care and attention.

Santiago smiled self-consciously. His smile was not returned as the official went back to his close examination of the photograph. He looked up again. This time Santiago didn't smile.

'Purpose of your visit?'

'Excuse me?'

'Business or pleasure?'

'Oh,' said Santiago. 'Business. Yes, business.'

Santiago saw the raised eyebrows and realized

that his questioner was thinking that the young man facing him certainly didn't look like a businessman.

'I play football. That is, I hope to.'

The eyebrows lifted a little higher. 'For who?'

'For Newcastle United.'

'Is that right? One moment.' He turned away and beckoned to one of his colleagues. In the long queue behind Santiago, other weary travellers sighed and visibly sagged at the thought of another delay. Many were tired and irritable; their aircraft had landed more than an hour after its scheduled early-morning arrival time.

'This young man wants to play for your team, Mr Henderson,' said the official as his colleague joined him at the desk.

Santiago waited as the second man subjected him to another few seconds of close scrutiny. 'For Newcastle?' he said at last.

'Yes, sir,' replied Santiago nervously.

'You'd better let the lad in, then,' said the new arrival in a strong Geordie accent. 'We need all the help we can get.'

Glen Foy was hard at work. Since losing his scouting job, Glen had built himself a successful business devoted to another of his loves – classic cars. And while no old E-type Jaguar, Morris Minor or Triumph Herald could ever give Glen the same thrill as that first sight of an undiscovered footballing talent, he enjoyed his work.

He kidded himself that finding old vehicles for restoration wasn't *so* different from scouting for young players. Both jobs required a keen eye, the knack of assessing potential and the confidence to act quickly to beat off rivals. He knew he was kidding himself, but it helped: restoring cars was a job; football was in his blood.

Foy Motors – Glen hadn't thought for too long about the choice of name – employed three mechanics and a receptionist-cum-secretary, who shared an office with Glen. But the hub of the operation was the workshop, and whenever he could, Glen liked to go out there and get his hands dirty.

He was standing beneath an E-type on a hydraulic lift, checking out the exhaust system, when he heard a female voice shouting over the noise of men at work and the radio which was always switched on. 'Call for you, Glen!'

Glen wiped his hands on a convenient piece of oily rag, went to the office and picked up the phone. 'Hello, Glen Foy.'

'Glen, it's me, Santiago.'

'Santiago!' said Glen, genuinely pleased to hear Santiago's voice. 'How you doing, son?'

'I'm good, Glen. Fine.'

'This is a great line, you could almost be in Newcastle.'

'Not quite. I'm in London – Heathrow Airport.'

There was no reply, and for a moment Santiago had a terrible feeling that it had all been a mistake, that Glen had never really intended him to come to England. 'Glen? Glen, are you there?'

He heard Glen laugh. 'Course I'm here, lad. You took me by surprise, that's all. You did it: you came.'

'I want to play for Newcastle.'

Glen laughed again. 'Then you'd better find your way to King's Cross Station, lad.'

It took a couple of hours, but Santiago made it to Kings Cross. The station was heaving as thousands of travellers dashed to or from platforms, studied the huge departures board, queued for fast food, or streamed, like a trail of ants, down the stairs towards the maze of tube lines running deep underground.

Santiago's ticket to Newcastle used up a huge amount of his remaining funds, but he didn't care; the long journey was almost over. He walked onto the platform and climbed into the first carriage of the waiting blue-and-orange GNER train.

The trip to the North-East of England would take three and a half hours and Santiago was impressed as he threw his bag onto the luggage rack and settled back into the seat. He was going to travel in style: plenty of legroom, comfortable seat, even a little lamp on the table in front of him. He would relax and enjoy the ride as he took in the beautiful

English countryside he'd heard so much about.

The train pulled away and Santiago got his first real view of England: grimy North London streets and Victorian terraces. It wasn't quite what he had been expecting but he guessed it would get better once they made it to the countryside.

As the train snaked its way through North London, Santiago saw the brand-new Emirates stadium, soon to be the home of Arsenal, close to the track on his right. And then in the distance he could see Highbury, the famous old ground the club would be leaving. Football: it was everywhere in England.

A uniformed man came wandering along the carriage asking to see all tickets. He stopped and gave Santiago a slightly suspicious look as the young man dug into his jeans pocket and handed over his ticket.

'Did you wish to upgrade, sir?'

'Upgrade?'

The ticket inspector sighed. 'This is a standard ticket, you are travelling in first-class accommodation.'

'I shouldn't be here?'

'Not unless you are prepared to pay considerably more than you have for the privilege.'

'More?' said Santiago, horrified. 'No, I can't pay any more.'

'You'll find second-class accommodation in that direction,' said the ticket inspector, indicating towards the front of the train with his thumb.

Santiago grabbed his bag from the rack and passed straight through another carriage just like the one he had speedily vacated. He reached the buffet car and then the first of the standard carriages.

It was easy to see the difference; the compartment was crowded and the seats were much more cramped with a lot less legroom, but as Santiago took the first vacant seat he found, he felt comfortable enough. He was tired, and as the train gathered speed, he drifted off to sleep.

He woke with a start when he realized someone was poking him in the shoulder. For a few confusing seconds he thought he was at home, and that his father was waking him to go to work.

He opened his eyes and saw an elderly woman glaring down at him. 'You are in *my* seat, young man.'

Santiago shook his head, clearing his thoughts. The train had stopped at Peterborough and new passengers were moving about the carriage. 'Your seat? You own this seat?'

A man sitting on the other side of the aisle leaned across towards Santiago. 'There's no need to be cheeky. Give the lady her seat, there are plenty more further down the train.'

'But I didn't know—'

The woman brandished her ticket in front of Santiago's face. 'I have a ticket with my seat reservation printed quite clearly on it. If you look at the card at the back of this seat, you will observe that you are sitting in *my* reserved seat. Do you wish me to call the ticket inspector to get you to move?'

'No! No, no,' said Santiago quickly as he stood up and saw the card at the back of the seat. The last thing he wanted was another run-in with the ticket inspector. He grabbed his bag from the rack. 'I'm sorry, I didn't know.'

'They all say that,' said the woman, as Santiago moved even further towards the front of the train. He felt as though he was gradually walking to Newcastle.

Eventually, he reached a carriage where there were plenty of unreserved seats and he settled down for a third time.

The rest of the journey was uneventful and the view got a lot better. The train stopped at stations with unfamiliar names like Doncaster, York and Darlington, and after three hours it pulled in to Durham. As it moved away again, a voice came over the PA system to announce that the next stop would be Newcastle.

Santiago felt his heart quicken. At last. He was almost there, but he suddenly felt homesick. He missed his grandmother and his brother, and yes, he even missed his dad. Glen was a virtual stranger, but Santiago couldn't wait to see him.

The train cruised back to high speed, and as Santiago glanced from the window to his right, he saw the magnificent metal sculpture, *The*

Angel of the North, standing proudly beyond the hill running up from the trackside.

He couldn't judge how far away it was, but even from this distance it was stunning. Arms, or wings, outstretched, it reminded Santiago of a joyous footballer celebrating a cup-winning goal. In less than half a minute, *The Angel* had disappeared behind trees, but the image stayed with Santiago until the train began to slow down.

To the right of the train, rows of terraced house ran uphill, and away to his left, as the winter sky darkened, the young Latin American got his first sight of the sprawling city.

'The next stop will be Newcastle,' said the voice on the PA. 'Newcastle, next stop.'

The rhythmic sound of the wheels on the tracks changed suddenly as the train rumbled slowly across the River Tyne. Santiago saw another bridge to his left and to his right he counted four, no five, more bridges.

The sound of the wheels changed again and the train slid smoothly into the cavern of Newcastle Central Station.

Santiago pulled down his bag and followed

the other passengers down onto platform four. He walked through a short tunnel, just as Glen had told him, and then up a ramp to cross to the main concourse.

Glen was waiting, exactly as he had said he would be. 'It's great to see you, son,' he said, grabbing Santiago's bag. 'But why didn't you call me from the States to let me know you were coming?'

'I had to wait in Mexico for my passport. I only got it yesterday.' They were walking to the main exit. 'It's not OK that I'm here?'

'No, it's fine; you caught me a bit off guard, that's all. You can stay with me till you get sorted.'

At the main exit, a long queue of taxis stood waiting for passengers ready to be whisked off to various parts of the city. But Glen indicated to the left and they kept walking. 'Welcome to the Toon.'

'The Toon? What is the Toon?'

'This place. Where the Geordies live?'

Santiago was struggling to keep up with the conversation. 'What is a Geordie?'

Glen smiled. 'Someone who lives in the Toon. You've got a lot to learn, bonny lad.'

Glen lived at Tynemouth, in a neat semi-detached house on the promenade opposite the sands and the North Sea. He parked his Audi in the drive-way next to the well-kept front garden and they both got out of the car.

Santiago shivered as the bitterly cold north wind blew in from the sea. It was almost dark now, but he could just make out the grey water and angry white waves breaking on the shore-line. It sure didn't look like the Pacific over there.

Glen smiled as he took in Santiago's light, LA-style clothes. 'You're not exactly dressed for these parts.'

'I didn't realize it would be so cold.'

'Cold? This is what we call bracing. You wait till the weather turns bad! Come on, let's get you inside.'

The house was as well kept as the garden but seemed, to Santiago, neat and functional rather than lived-in and warm as he had imagined.

'You live here alone?'

Glen nodded. 'My wife died three years ago.'

'I'm sorry.'

'I miss her,' said Glen with a sigh. 'This place has never felt the same. That's why it was good to see my daughter out in your part of the world. I've got a son, too, but he lives in London and he's just got engaged, so I don't see him very often.'

Santiago unzipped his bag, took out a small statue and handed it to Glen.

'It is the Virgin of Guadalupe. My grandmother had this since she was a little girl, but she wanted you to have it. It will bring blessings on your house.'

'I'm very touched, Santiago,' said Glen, looking a little embarrassed. 'I'm not a very good Catholic, mind.'

'But my grandmother thinks you are a good man, and my grandmother is always right.'

Glen really was embarrassed now. 'Come on, I'll show you your room, and while you're getting settled in, I'll get us some food. I'd better warn you though, I'm no Jamie Oliver.'

'Jamie who?'

'Never mind,' grinned Glen. 'We'll get used to each other.'

Glen decided to play safe on the cooking front. He pulled two frozen shepherd's pies from the freezer and while they were heating in the oven he boiled some water for the accompanying frozen peas.

For the first time in a very long while he laid two places at the kitchen table, and when the food was ready he went to the stairs and called up to Santiago. 'Grub's up. D'you fancy a beer?'

There was no reply.

'Santiago?'

There was still no answer. Glen climbed the stairs and knocked gently on the bedroom door. *Still* no answer.

He pushed open the door and saw Santiago sprawled out on the bed, sound asleep. On the bedside table stood a framed photograph of the Muñez family. It looked as though it had been taken three or four years earlier; Glen recognized Mercedes and the younger Santiago and Julio. The two boys were standing on either side of a man Glen guessed must be their father,

Herman. He had his arms around his sons' shoulders and looked every bit the proud dad.

Glen tiptoed in, pulled a duvet over his sleeping guest, went back to the door and switched off the light. 'You wouldn't have fancied my shepherd's pie, anyway,' he whispered as he closed the door.

Nine

Santiago was standing by the front door, looking out towards the bleak, grey, forbidding North Sea, when Glen came down the following morning.

'Sleep all right?'

'I woke up early. I'm sorry about the food.'

'You didn't miss much. You can grab some breakfast when we get to the workshop?'

'Workshop?'

'The place where I work.'

'But I thought you worked in football.'

Glen smiled. 'Not any more, lad. But don't let that worry you. Come on, I like to get in early.'

They drove through quiet streets as the city

and suburbs eased into another day. The area around Foy Motors was rundown: rows of terraced houses, many of them boarded up and awaiting the bulldozers.

As they stepped from the Audi, Santiago saw the Foy Motors sign above the roll-up shutters.

'You fix cars?'

Glen unlocked the heavy padlock and pulled up the shutter. 'I restore old ones, give them a second lease of life. There's a café just down the road: my lads usually get in there for breakfast before they start work. You get yourself something to eat and we'll go to the club at about ten.'

The café was easy enough to find. It was filled with working men sitting in clouds of blue, cigarette smoke as they downed huge mugs of tea and fried breakfasts, and exchanged early-morning banter.

Santiago had no idea what to order, so when he saw the handwritten sign on the wall behind the counter offering 'Full Breakfast', he went for that. He sat alone at one of the few vacant tables, and ten minutes later a plate overflowing with bacon, sausages, eggs, beans, tomatoes and a foul-looking circle of something black with white flecks was placed in front of him.

He picked up his knife and fork, uncertain where to begin, then prodded the black stuff a couple of times to make certain that it wasn't still alive.

At the next table, three men wearing overalls with FOY MOTORS emblazoned on the back were talking football; everyone in the place seemed to be talking football.

The biggest and loudest of the three was sounding off about Newcastle's latest signing. 'I've heard that some of the players have a real problem with Harris. Don't like his attitude.'

'Not surprising, is it, Foghorn,' said the second man. 'Three clubs in five years should tell you something.'

The third man, older than the others, nodded wisely. 'He's better when he stays inside. If he's not in the mood he drifts out wide and gets lost.'

'Maybe he should stay lost,' said the aptly named Foghorn, who looked up from his breakfast and saw Santiago staring at him. 'What are you looking at?'

Santiago had been trying to understand the strange accents. 'I'm sorry, but you talk about football, yes?'

'There's nowt else *to* talk about.'

The older man was equally intrigued by Santiago's accent. 'Where you from, son?'

'Los Angeles.'

Foghorn was suddenly interested. 'Oh, aye? D'you know Charlize Theron? She's a cracker.'

Santiago grinned. 'Oh sure, she's over at my place all the time.'

The throwaway line went down well with the Geordies.

'You're a long way from home,' said the older one. 'What you doing up here?'

'I have a try-out for Newcastle United.'

'A trial!' Foghorn's voice boomed out through the café. 'Howay! I had one, you know. They offered me fifty grand a week and a house by a golf course. But I said no, I prefer being a paint sprayer. Isn't that right, Walter?'

Walter was the older man. 'Paint spraying's all you're good for, Foghorn.' He turned back to Santiago. 'Are you serious, lad?'

'Yes. Maybe today. Your boss, Glen, arranged it for me.'

'Did he now? He kept that quiet.'

'Aye, he did,' said Foghorn, leaning towards Santiago. 'If you're having a trial today, you'll need to run like a whippet.' He speared the black blob on Santiago's plate with his fork and transferred it to his own. 'You'd better give this black pudding a miss.'

Glen's car was behind a double-decker bus. It was all so strange to Santiago. The leaden sky, the grey city streets, everyone in heavy winter clothes. Nothing was familiar or reassuring.

The traffic moved slowly, held in a succession of traffic lights, as Glen edged the Audi through the busy, bustling city.

'What you have to understand, Santiago, is that football's a religion in these parts. In London, you've got any number of clubs, same in the Midlands. There's two in Manchester and two in Liverpool. But up here, it's just The Toon.'

After his conversation in the café and Glen's explanation, Santiago was beginning to understand the almost fanatical devotion of the Newcastle United supporters. 'You don't speak like people from The Toon.'

'I'm Irish. Came over to play thirty years ago and never left.'

'Why?'

'I like it here.' The car was moving slightly uphill. They reached a roundabout, and as Glen moved the vehicle away again he nodded to Santiago to look up ahead. 'There she is.'

Santiago's eyes widened and his mouth gaped open. Directly ahead was St James' Park. It dominated the skyline. Glen had said football was like a religion in these parts, and St James' Park stood there like a massive, modern cathedral: a towering structure of concrete, glass and metal.

'Not bad, eh?'

Santiago couldn't answer. He just stared.

Glen parked the car and they walked back to the stadium and down an approach road, which slid beneath part of the huge arena.

On the outer side of the high-roofed tunnel, lifts and escalators soared away towards the administration and hospitality areas of the stadium. Midway along the inner side were steps leading to double glass doors. The sign above the doors read: PLAYERS AND OFFICIALS ENTRANCE.

'We timed it right, said Glen. 'There's the man himself.'

Erik Dornhelm, dressed in an expensive suit and looking more like a high-powered executive than a football team manager, was standing on the steps, deep in conversation with another man. Glen took Santiago's arm and gestured that they should wait. As soon as the conversation ended, he urged his young friend forward and called to Dornhelm before he could continue up the steps.

'Morning, Mr Dornhelm. This is the young man I was telling you about. Santiago Muñez. From Los Angeles.'

Dornhelm showed no sign of remembering the late-night conversation. 'When was this?'

'When I called you in the middle of the night and you promised to give him a try-out.'

'I did?'

The throaty roar of a serious sports car engine

echoed through the tunnel, and all three men turned to see an Aston Martin convertible pull to a standstill. Gavin Harris emerged from the driver's seat, mobile phone at one ear.

'One moment, please,' said Dornhelm to Glen and he walked over to Harris, who instantly terminated his phone call.

'Morning, boss,' he said with a smile.

Dornhelm was in no mood for exchanging pleasantries, and Glen and Santiago heard every word exchanged between the Newcastle manager and his new midfielder. 'I'm sure you have a watch, and I'm sure it's a Rolex. What time does it say?'

Gavin didn't bother checking his Rolex. 'Yeah, sorry, boss. I called in at the hospital; dropped off a shirt for a sick kid. We should have had the PR people there – would have made a great photo.'

Dornhelm remained stony-faced. 'Gavin, this is bullshit. We have six journalists inside waiting to interview you; they have been waiting for fifty minutes. Get in there! And when you've finished with the Press, you train with the reserves!'

Gavin knew better than to argue. He just

nodded and hurried up the steps. Dornhelm returned to Santiago and Glen. 'Where were we?'

'I called you,' said Glen. 'About Santiago here.'

Dornhelm almost smiled. 'Yes, my wife remembers it well.' He looked at Santiago. 'Where do you play?'

'In Los Angeles,' said Santiago nervously.

'I mean, in which position do you play?'

'Oh. For my team I play up front. But I prefer midfield. That way I get to see more of the ball.'

Dornhelm studied Santiago for a few moments, appearing to weigh him up, and then nodded to Glen. 'Get him over to the training ground. Let's see what he's got.'

He walked up the steps and disappeared into the building through the glass doors. Santiago looked at Glen. 'My trial? It isn't here?'

Glen smiled. 'No, lad, you'll have to wait a bit longer before you make your first appearance at St James'.'

The training complex had been recently refurbished. A dozen football pitches clustered around a converted manor house with state-of-the-art training facilities, treatment and changing rooms, a restaurant and offices.

Santiago sat alone on a bench in the vast changing room. He was wearing training gear he'd been given and a brand-new pair of football boots. He tied the laces and thought to himself that a pair of boots like these would have cost him a month's wages back home.

He was nervous. He stood up and reached into his jacket pocket for his asthma inhaler. He took a quick puff and slipped it back into his pocket just as a tracksuited man of around Glen's age walked into the room.

'All set?'

Santiago nodded.

The new arrival held out his hand. 'I'm Mal Braithwaite, first-team coach.'

They shook hands and Santiago tried to look a lot more confident than he felt. Braithwaite wasn't fooled. 'Glen's told me all about you. We go back a long way, so I'm on your side.'

'Thank you, sir.'

'I'm not a "sir". I'm "coach". "Sir" is the gaffer and he's checking you out today.'

He saw Santiago's bewildered look and smiled. 'You ready?'

'Yes, si— coach, I'm ready.'

He followed Braithwaite from the changing room, crossing himself as he went.

Rain was falling steadily as they emerged into the gloom of the bleak winter's day. It wasn't what Santiago was expecting and certainly not what he'd been praying for as he crossed himself.

On a pitch nearby, two teams wearing coloured bibs were playing a practice match. Glen stood watching, his coat collar up around his neck. He winked at Santiago as Braithwaite whistled to one of the players to come off the pitch.

The game stopped for a moment as Braithwaite put an arm on one of Santiago's shoulders and pointed towards Gavin Harris, who was looking far from happy out on one wing.

'Midfield, on the right. Slot inside Gavin.'

Santiago pulled a bib over his head and jogged onto the pitch. The other players watched curiously as he moved alongside Gavin Harris, who totally ignored Santiago's nervous smile.

Close to the touchline, a big central defender wandered towards Braithwaite. 'Who's this, then?'

'Young Mexican lad. Be gentle with him, Hughie.'

'Oh, you know me, coach, I'll be as gentle as a lamb.'

Hughie Magowan was six feet two and tough as teak. He revelled in his hard man reputation and thought of every one of his numerous yellow cards as battle honours, campaign medals. He was nearing the end of a long and bruising career, and many Premiership strikers still bore the scars they had collected in their close encounters with Hughie Magowan.

These days Hughie spent most of his time adding experience and steel to the youth and enthusiasm of the reserve team; he only ever got a sniff of the first-team squad in an emergency. He would be little missed when he finally hung up his boots, but until then Hughie intended to carry on making his mark – literally.

The game resumed, the rain fell steadily, and the ball stubbornly refused to come anywhere near Santiago. He was uncertain as to whether he should go looking for it or hold his position.

Glen watched with growing frustration, and after five minutes Braithwaite called out to a young midfielder, who was playing a deeper, holding role on the same team as Santiago. 'Franny! Bring the kid into the game!'

The midfielder nodded and the next time he picked up the ball, he sent a long pass directly into Santiago's path. It wasn't a difficult ball, not for anyone used to British conditions. But as it skidded off the muddy turf, Santiago totally misjudged the bounce and the ball slipped away over the touchline.

Santiago felt as stupid as he had looked and a few of the players raised their eyebrows or exchanged 'He's useless' type glances.

Hughie Magowan was a lot more direct. He didn't mince his words, only opposition players. 'Bloody amateur,' he growled.

As the ball was recovered, Mal Braithwaite turned to Glen. 'Are you sure about him?'

'Give him a chance, Mal,' said Glen. 'He's not used to these conditions.'

The throw-in was taken and Glen saw Erik Dornhelm, now in a tracksuit and looking a lot more comfortable for it, come striding out from the changing rooms.

Carl Francis, the young black player known as Franny to everyone on the Newcastle staff, was doing his best to give Santiago another opportunity. He collected the ball from a defender and sent it, more gently this time, towards the newcomer. The pass could have done with more weight and Santiago was forced to run back towards his own goal to collect it.

An opposing forward came charging towards him and Santiago knew that the safe and obvious option was the simple pass back to his central defender. But he was out to impress. As the forward lumbered in, Santiago feinted to one side, swivelled and jinked away. The forward was left charging at air.

Mal looked at Glen. 'He's a funny one.

Awkward one minute and then he does something like that.'

Glen smiled and turned towards Erik Dornhelm. He wasn't watching; he was talking on his mobile with his back turned from play.

Santiago still had the ball. He moved diagonally across the pitch and delivered an inch-perfect pass to Gavin Harris. He didn't see what happened next. As Harris went for the shot, Santiago's legs were swept away as Hughie Magowan finally arrived with his late, late tackle.

'Welcome to Newcastle, *amigo*,' grinned Hughie as Santiago picked himself up from the mud.

Gavin's shot had been deflected off a defender for a corner. Santiago jogged into the opposition box, and Franny directed him to a position near the back post. He found some space and, as the ball swung across from the corner flag, he ran and jumped. Hughie was all over him like a rash; this guy could have fouled for England.

The ball went clear and the players swept from the box, leaving Santiago face down in the mud.

It didn't get much better. There was the occasional inspired touch or flick, but overall Santiago spent more time on his backside than on his feet as Hughie, along with a couple of the other defenders who joined in the fun, completed his introduction to old-fashioned, blood-and-thunder British football.

But every time Santiago went down, he got gamely to his feet, without complaint and ready for more. It was like nothing he had experienced before; a totally different game to the one he played and dominated back in the Californian sunshine.

Glen fretted on the touchline, painfully aware that Dornhelm appeared to have seen enough and was getting ready to leave. He was talking on his mobile again as he walked slowly along the touchline.

On the pitch, Santiago ran on to a bouncing ball. He flicked it over one defender's head with a move as skilful as one by Ronaldinho, and as Hughie charged in, he nutmegged the big man, hearing him curse as he sped away. Gavin Harris was lurking near the edge of the box. Santiago played a neat pass and kept running, and unselfishly Gavin turned the pass into a lovely one–two.

Santiago hit the ball on the run, and it curled goalwards and rattled the upright. As the ball was scrambled away, the assistant coach who was refereeing whistled for a foul.

Gavin Harris picked up the ball and placed it carefully for the free kick, ready to remind the manager and head coach exactly why the club had forked out £8.4 million for his services.

But it wasn't to be.

'Let the new lad take it!' yelled Mal Braithwaite.

Gavin shrugged and moved aside, in some way curious to see what the youngster would make of the dead ball opportunity.

The defenders formed a wall, Hughie in the middle, as the goalkeeper shouted his instructions.

On the touchline, Glen's thoughts went back to California and the stunning free kick he'd watched Santiago take against the Croatian team. The ball was closer to the goal this time, the angle less acute; it was an easier shot.

'Do it again, Santi,' breathed Glen. 'Just do it again.'

Santiago appeared to have exactly that in mind, setting himself up in a similar way, only a couple of strides from the ball.

The whistle blew, he took the two strides, pulled back his right foot – and felt himself start to slip in the mud. He was completely off balance, and as he slithered backwards to the ground, his foot connected with the ball and sliced it high and wide of the goal.

The miss was greeted with the inevitable jeers from the other players and Hughie came running out from the defensive wall, his smile as wide as the mouth of the River Tyne. He leaned down towards Santiago with his arm outstretched as though he was going to help him to his feet. But as Santiago reached upwards, Hughie drew back his arm and turned the outstretched hand of friendship into a dismissive wave of farewell. '*Adios, amigo.*'

'All right, that's enough,' shouted Mal from the touchline. 'Four laps round the perimeter.'

The other players set off on their warm-down

run, jeering, moaning and complaining about their slave driver of a coach. Before Santiago could get up and join them, Mal shouted again. 'Not you, Santiago. You get yourself down to the showers.'

As Santiago struggled up from the mud he saw Mal turn to Glen and shake his head.

They were back at Glen's house. The drive back from the training ground had been awkward, beginning in silence, with neither of them knowing quite what to say.

Santiago, bruised and battered, ran through the whole painful experience again in his mind, and when he came to the humiliating experience of the free kick, he felt himself redden with embarrassment.

'My legs wouldn't do what my brain was telling me,' he said at last. 'I'll be better tomorrow, I promise. I know I'll be better.'

There was no way Glen could let him down gently. 'There won't be a tomorrow, Santi. I'm sorry. I argued with Mal, but . . .'

His voice died away. There was nothing more

to say. Santiago had been expecting it anyway, but until the words were said, he had clung on to the hope that just maybe he had shown enough to be given one more chance.

It was over, almost before it had begun.

Glen felt the disappointment almost as acutely as Santiago. He *knew* what the boy could do; he'd seen that special talent with his own eyes. It was almost criminal to let such a talent go to waste. But what more could he do?

Santiago had been up in the bedroom for a while. Glen stood at the living-room window, watching the day darken and the North Sea remorselessly roll in against the shoreline.

He heard footsteps on the stairs and Santiago appeared at the doorway. 'My father believes people have a place in life. You work, you feed your family, you die, and it's foolish to think otherwise.'

Glen was still gazing out of the window, watching wave after wave wash onto the sand. 'Aye, my old man fed me the same line. Which is why he swept factory floors for his whole life.'

'Could I make a phone call please, Glen?'

Glen turned from the window. 'What for?'

'To my grandmother. To tell her I'm coming home.'

'No.'

'But . . . but it won't take long. And I'll pay for the call.'

'I mean, don't call her. Not yet. I want to make a call first.'

Ten

It was part of a manager's job, particularly the manager of a club like Newcastle United.

No club could exist and thrive without the loyalty of its supporters, so getting out there in the community went with the territory. Invitations had to be accepted to various school and hospital visits, meetings with local business-men, charity events and black-tie dinners.

At some functions, it was enough just to be there, to be seen, to shake hands and pass on a little titbit of information about the club that the listener thought they alone were hearing. Of course, they never were.

On other, more formal occasions, there were

speeches to be made, and while Erik Dornhelm was not one of nature's natural speechmakers, he took his responsibility seriously and always arrived with a few well-prepared words. His approach was simple: open with a little laugh – nothing sidesplitting, Dornhelm was no comedian – then get to the point and end with another football joke. Above all, keep it brief and don't bore them rigid.

Tonight was one of those occasions; the Northern Merit Awards. Two hundred people – the men in black tie, the women in evening dress – were gathered together in the splendid reception room of the Gosforth Park Hotel.

They were seated in groups of twelve at round tables heavy with gleaming silver and sparkling glassware.

Dornhelm was doing his best to appear completely interested as the wife of a local garage owner told him how her late father had once been a stalwart for Accrington Stanley and would undoubtedly have gone on to play for England if only the Second World War hadn't intervened.

'Of course, by the time it was over he was too old. Sad, isn't it?'

'Yes, very sad,' said Dornhelm, thinking that it was about time the main course arrived.

He looked up and saw someone heading for the table. But it wasn't a waiter. It was Glen Foy.

'Sorry to interrupt proceedings but at least I got here before the speeches.'

Dornhelm sighed with irritation. 'I am making one of those speeches, Mr Foy. This distraction is not welcome.'

'Yeah, well I wouldn't be here if you answered my calls.'

The other guests at the table had ended their own conversations; this was far more interesting.

'What do you want, Mr Foy?'

'Santiago, the kid. What happened today wasn't fair. The boy grew up in poverty and hardship; his only way out is his skill with the ball.'

Dornhelm picked up his wine glass and took a sip as Glen continued.

'He comes to England on my say-so, travels six thousand miles, he's got jet lag, he's nervous, and you put him on a muddy pitch in borrowed boots and then you spend most of your time on your mobile. It's not fair. It's not right.'

As Dornhelm glanced to his left, he saw that the woman he'd been speaking to was now staring at him reproachfully and shaking her head as though she agreed with every word Glen had spoken.

Dornhelm coughed. 'Your discovery seemed to be flat on his ar—' He looked towards the woman next to him. 'Flat on his back for most of the time.'

'There was one magic moment,' said Glen quickly. 'He took the ball on the bounce and—'

'I saw it!' said Dornhelm more loudly than he had intended.

Two waiters arrived and began serving the main course from silver platters.

Glen smiled at a woman seated across the table. 'Looks good. I've already eaten, but I'm told they do you very well here.' He looked back at Dornhelm. 'Listen, I know what I'm talking about. I was a scout, remember? And a good one. And I remember muddy days, watching young lads clogging each other all over the park. But just once in a while, you'd see one who'd lift your heart. Like this lad. Give him a month? That's all I'm asking. One month?'

Glen held his arms out from his sides, palms upwards, as though he was appealing to the other diners around the table for their support. He didn't need to; it had been quite a performance.

Dornhelm was aware that everyone, even his own wife, was staring at him, silently urging him to answer the right way. He picked up his wine glass and took a sip.

Off the living room at Glen Foy's house was a small alcove. It was like a shrine to football, and to Glen's career.

After Glen went out, saying he 'had a little business to do', Santiago watched television for a while, but soon grew tired of the endless 'reality' programmes. He'd had enough reality for one day. He left the set switched on and went into the alcove, where for the first time since his arrival he took the time to study the framed photographs closely.

The young Glen was easy to spot in the Newcastle United and Irish international team line-ups. There were more photos: Glen in different teams; Glen the tracksuited manager.

Santiago picked up a scrapbook and was soon engrossed. Black and white photographs, match programmes, faded newspaper cuttings. Santiago read every word and smiled each time he came to a mention of his friend.

The television was blaring out the theme tune to another programme and Santiago didn't hear the car pull up outside or Glen enter the house.

'That was all a long time ago.'

Santiago jumped as he looked up and saw Glen leaning against the wall. 'I'm sorry, I was just—'

'No problem. My wife did all that. I never got round to clearing it away.'

'You never told me you were major league.'

Glen smiled. 'Not for long enough though. I did my knee in.' He picked up a photograph of a Newcastle side from the late 1970s. 'Look at that. Shorts were shorter and hair was longer, and we didn't drive Aston Martins or Ferraris.'

'But you were still heroes.'

'Oh, yeah. Footballers have always been heroes, even in my father's day when they made eight quid a week and worked down the mine. Working people have always needed their football. It lifts them; it's something more to think about and talk about than the daily struggle of day-to-day life.'

He replaced the photograph on top of the cabinet. 'Go on a bit, don't I? But it's the reason I was so proud to put on the skipper's shirt.' As he spoke, he pulled open a drawer in the cabinet and took out a neatly folded Newcastle United shirt. He let it fall loose and Santiago spotted the number six on the back. 'Here,' said Glen, passing him the shirt.

'I cannot accept this; it is too special,' said Santiago, shaking his head.

'I'm not giving it to you, lad! I just want you to try it on, see what you look like in the black and white.'

Santiago's face fell. 'What's the point now?'

Glen smiled. 'The point is, I had another little chat with Erik Dornhelm tonight. I gave him a touch of indigestion, and he's given you a month's trial. So go on, try it on.'

Eleven

The training-ground dressing room was crowded with reserve squad players. Most were changed into boots and training kit; the younger ones anxious to get out and impress coaches and management, a few veterans, like Hughie Magowan, more intent on going through the motions and keeping their heads down.

A player like Hughie had nothing to prove. Everyone knew what he could do – or these days what he *couldn't* do. He was still, just about, an asset to the club. In an emergency, he had the know-how and experience to slot into the first team and do a passable job, as long as the opposing strikers didn't have the pace of a

Thierry Henry or a Jermain Defoe. And with the reserves, he could give the youngsters a genuine taste of what life would be like for them if and when they made it through to the big time.

But time was against Hughie, and he knew it. And he didn't much fancy the prospect of playing out a last couple of seasons in the basement divisions, or living on the reduced wages such a move would bring.

The dressing-room banter was centred on the recent first-team performances and the fact that Gavin Harris had hardly set Newcastle alight since his much-heralded arrival. Some of the older guys were mouthing off about his lack of effort and commitment to the team.

'Another glory boy,' moaned Hughie. 'Only in it for himself. He doesn't give a toss about which club he plays for; it's just the money for blokes like him.'

The younger ones listened and wisely kept their mouths shut, more concerned about getting a chance to make their mark before the end of the season and having their contracts renewed.

The door swung open and Mal Braithwaite

walked in with a nervous-looking Santiago and the reserve-team coach, Bobby Redfern.

'Listen up, you lot,' said Mal. 'Say hello to Santiago Muñez.'

'I thought we'd already said goodbye to him,' said Hughie, not bothering to join in with the general nods of hello and welcome.

Mal completely ignored Hughie's sarcasm. 'Santiago's from Mexico.'

'I'm from Los Angeles,' said Santiago. 'I was born in Mexico.'

Mal smiled. 'Oh, are you? Well, there we are then. Now you all know everything you need to know. And before the day's out I want all of you to let Santiago know exactly who you are.'

Hughie finished tying a bootlace and stood up. 'It'll be a pleasure, coach.'

Before Mal's 'get to know Santiago' instructions could really take place during another practice game, there was a meticulously planned, high-pressure morning of training, starting with a full warm-up, including gentle stretches and aerobic work.

Santiago could hardly believe he was actually

there, but the full reality of everything that had happened over the past few days hit him as he glanced across to the adjacent pitch to see Erik Dornhelm arrive with the first-team squad. He'd seen Gavin Harris before, but now he was getting his first look at the other big names.

He was like a kid in a sweet shop as his eyes darted from one player to another: Shearer, Given, Jenas, Dyer.

Bobby Redfern saw him staring. 'Hey, Muñez! Never mind that lot, get on with what you're meant to be doing!'

The second stringers went into phase two of training. Fifty-metre sprints, jinking through slalom cones, knee-lift runs through lines of tyres, dead ball and passing practice.

Santiago had always thought he was fit, but he had known nothing like this before. The *Americanitos* training nights had usually amounted to little more than a kickaround, with everyone crowded around one goal trying to beat the keeper, followed by a five- or six- or seven-a-side match, depending on how many players had bothered to turn up.

By the time the practice match started, Santiago was knackered, but he wasn't going to let anyone else know that. And the introductions Mal had spoken of might have been a pleasure for the others, but the new boy found them far from pleasurable.

Hughie Magowan was particularly 'welcoming'. His crunching tackles were meant to leave their mark. And they did. But each time Santiago went down he got up and got on with the game without complaint, and by the time Mal whistled for the end of the game, even Hughie was slightly, if reluctantly, impressed.

It was a long, hard first session, and when it was over Santiago only had time to shower and change before being whisked off for a full medical examination.

He was given a white hospital robe, a form on a clipboard and a clear beaker with his name written on it, then directed to a small room with instructions to get changed, fill in the form and fill the beaker. Santiago was getting used to following orders and a few minutes later he walked into the examination room holding the clipboard and his filled beaker in one hand, while the other clutched at the back of the hospital robe to prevent it from coming apart.

A young and very attractive nurse with dark hair pinned back was sitting at a desk, filling in a form. She looked up as Santiago entered.

When he smiled self-consciously at her, she didn't return the smile but simply stood up and took the clipboard and beaker from his outstretched hand.

'Sit there, please,' she said, nodding towards the examination table.

Santiago perched on the edge of the table and the nurse wrapped a strap around his arm as she prepared to take his blood pressure. She began pumping air into the valve but avoided Santiago's eyes as he smiled again.

'It may be a little high,' said Santiago.

'Oh. Why's that?'

'I didn't think the club doctor would look so good.'

'I'm not the club doctor, I'm the club doctor's nurse.' She released the pressure on the valve and the air hissed out. 'The club doctor will be along to examine you soon.'

The nurse was obviously unimpressed by footballers' chat-up lines. She made a note of the blood pressure reading. 'Did you fill in the paperwork?'

'Some words I didn't understand.'

The nurse picked up the clipboard and moved back to Santiago. 'Like what?'

'This one,' said Santiago, pointing at the form.

'Cardiovascular. It means heart problems.'

Santiago smiled. 'No, no.' He pointed at another word. 'And this one?'

'Respiratory. Do you have problems with your lungs, or breathing?'

Santiago hesitated. Of course he did. He had asthma. But he wasn't going to let that get in the way of his entire future. It wasn't a problem. It never had been.

'Well?' said the nurse.

'No, no way.'

'Fine. Step against the wall, please. I need to make a note of your height.'

Santiago moved across to the measure on the

wall, and the nurse had to stand very close as she took the reading.

'What's your name?' asked Santiago.

'Harmison,' said the nurse, showing Santiago her laminated name badge. '*Nurse* Harmison.'

'I mean, your first name?'

'You don't need to know that. You don't need to know where I live, or my phone number, what my star sign is, or what I'm doing on Saturday night. Now, sit on the chair, please. I have to take some blood.'

Santiago sighed and sat on the chair. 'Oh, man, I don't like those things,' he said as *Nurse* Harmison advanced with the needle raised.

'But you've got a tattoo,' said the nurse as she saw the Aztec symbol on his arm. 'Or is it just a rub-on transfer?'

'That was a gang thing,' said Santiago with a shrug.

'A gang? You were in a gang?'

'I'm from east LA, I had no choice. And once you're in, there's only three ways to get out. You get shot, you go to jail, or you're like me, you have a grandmother who kicks some sense into you.'

The young nurse looked hard at Santiago, and for a moment she almost smiled. Then she raised her eyebrows and went back to looking at the needle. Slowly and carefully, she eased it into Santiago's arm.

'Ay-ee!'

'Sorry, tough guy.' This time, she did smile. 'My name's Roz.'

That evening, over one of Glen's speciality frozen shepherd's pies, Santiago gave his host a full rundown of what had happened during his first day at the club.

Glen wanted to know the lot; he'd been thinking about his young protégé all day at the garage, hoping that the Newcastle coaches would begin to see the talent he'd spotted during those matches back in California.

'I think it went OK,' Santiago told him. 'Bobby Redfern didn't say I did good, but he didn't say I did bad, either.'

'What about Dornhelm, did he see you?'

'No, he was with the first-team squad all day. I don't think he even knew I was there.'

'Oh, he knew all right,' said Glen. 'And he'll know exactly how you did.'

By nine o'clock Santiago was feeling exhausted, his whole body aching after his first full day of training. But before turning in for an early night there was something he wanted to do. 'Glen, can I call my grandmother? She will want to know what happened today. I will pay for the call.'

'Of course you can call her, lad. Give her my best, and tell her that statue is standing by my bed.'

Nine p.m. English time was one p.m. in California. It was a good time to call. Mercedes was sure to be home, while Julio would be at school and Herman at work.

As Santiago spoke in Spanish to Mercedes from the cold, dark corner of North-East England, he could almost see and feel the sunshine of California.

His grandmother's questions about training were almost as detailed as Glen's had been, and when Santiago finally got through his story for a second time, he heard his grandmother laugh contentedly. 'We're proud of you, you know that, Santiago, don't you?'

'What about Dad, is he proud of me?'

There was a pause. 'You know your father, he doesn't talk about you much.'

'And what he does say isn't good, eh?'

Mercedes quickly changed the subject. 'Tell me about England. Do you like it? Is the scenery beautiful?'

Santiago thought back to his meeting with Roz Harmison. 'Oh, yes, Grandmother, some of the scenery is very beautiful.'

Twelve

Santiago slipped into the routine of day-to-day training as easily as he always thought he would. He even began to get accustomed to the biting cold and overcast skies.

Most of the reserve squad were welcoming and Santiago quickly struck up a friendship with another young player, a Liverpudlian by the name of Jamie Drew.

Even the first-teamers were friendly enough when they crossed paths with the second-stringers, in the changing room, or the canteen, or during a combined first team and reserves session in the gymnasium.

The gym was state-of-the-art, with an

impressive array of muscle-building and body-strengthening machines and equipment. Santiago had to be taught how to use the machines without injuring himself, but once he knew, he wanted to try the lot.

He was doing leg-lifts, strengthening his calf muscles, with as much weight as he could cope with.

His target was fifty. He reached thirty with no problem. Then it got tougher. Each lift got harder, and slower. He got to forty and kept going, counting down the last ten in Spanish. Sweat stood out on his brow, his eyes closed tightly to aid his concentration. Forty-five. He paused for a second and then went on. Just five more. He had to do it. Forty-six, forty-seven, forty-eight . . . forty-nine. It was agony. Fifty!

Santiago gasped as he let the leg weights sink back into position. He lifted his head and opened his eyes – Alan Shearer stood there watching him.

'Finished with that, son?'

'Oh! Oh, sure. Sorry.'

'No problem.'

Santiago climbed unsteadily off the machine and watched as Shearer took the seat and began adding more weights. Ten pounds, then another ten, and then another. He began his own exercise, making it look as easy as a stroll in the park.

Santiago, calves aching, went over to Jamie, who was working on another machine.

'Alan Shearer,' said Santiago.

'What about him?'

'He spoke to me.'

Jamie smiled. 'No!'

Everyone seemed to just accept Santiago, and to treat him as though he was part of the club. With one exception – Hughie Magowan.

Hughie made no secret of his dislike for Santiago, with snide comments and jibes every time he was in earshot. By the end of the first week, the constant barrage of criticism and insults was beginning to get to the young Mexican.

The reserve squad were playing another training game when the bubbling situation finally came to the boil.

Mal Braithwaite was looking in on the reserves' progress and was trying out different playing formations. He'd put Santiago up front, playing in the lone striker's role.

Santiago wasn't particularly happy about it. As always, he would have preferred his favoured attacking midfield position, but he was getting on with the job, even though he was seeing far less of the ball than he would have liked.

He'd already taken a couple of hefty knocks from big Hughie, and with the frustration of playing out of position and only a few weeks to impress, he could feel his Latin temper starting to rise.

Then, from a high clearance from the opposing keeper, one of Santiago's team-mates headed the ball back. It was a chance. As Santiago controlled the ball and turned towards the goal, Hughie came charging in. The two-footed sliding tackle was high and brutal, and Santiago was sent sprawling onto the hard ground.

Even some of Hughie's own team winced and shouted their disapproval.

'Hughie!'

'Not necessary, mate!'

Magowan got up, looking the picture of innocence as Santiago leaped to his feet and went eyeball to eyeball with the big defender. 'What's your problem!'

Hughie was well used to situations like this. He stood still, arms at his side, waiting and willing the youngster to take a swing at him. He grinned. 'Problem? What problem?'

Mal Braithwaite shouted from the touchline, 'OK, break it up! Walk away!'

The last thing Santiago wanted to do was walk away. He wanted to smash the grinning, taunting face just centimetres from his. But he didn't. He took a deep breath and turned away. As Hughie jogged back into position Jamie Drew walked up to Santiago. 'Forget it, he's not worth it.'

Santiago nodded and rubbed his bruised leg. But the incident soured the rest of the game and he didn't perform well.

He was still seething after he'd showered and changed and was standing in the canteen, queuing for lunch with Jamie.

'Look, forget about it,' said Jamie, seeing Santiago's still clouded face. 'There are plenty of Hughie Magowans around.'

'Yeah, I guess you're right.'

'I know I am. And you don't have time for carrying grudges.'

'You're definitely right about that,' said Santiago as he began helping himself to food.

'How long did they give you?'

'A month.'

'A month! At least I got six. I was at Notts County before this. They signed me from school.'

'And how's it going?'

Jamie shrugged. 'Early days.'

They found an empty table and, as they began to eat, some of the first-team players came in and joined the queue. Gavin Harris was amongst them, but he seemed a lot more interested in the phone conversation he was having on his mobile than in anything on offer at the buffet.

'Gavin Harris,' said Jamie, nodding towards the new arrival. 'They paid more than eight million for him.'

'Yeah, I know, and he plays in my position. He'd better watch his back, huh?'

Jamie smiled, but his face changed as he saw Hughie Magowan walking towards their table with his own lunch tray. He stopped and looked down at the pasta Santiago had chosen and raised his eyebrows. 'No burritos on the menu today? I'll speak to the manager, see if they can get some in special.' Before Santiago could reply, Hughie went on, 'No thanks, I won't join you. You enjoy your meal, you won't be having many more here, will you?'

Magowan walked on and found a table of his own.

'After the tackle he made on you today, he's the one who shouldn't be here,' said Jamie.

Santiago put his fork down by the side of his plate. He had suddenly lost his appetite. 'But he could be right. I don't have long to convince them that I'm worth keeping on.'

Jamie shrugged and dug into his own bowl of pasta. 'Then you'd better have a good look at Newcastle while you've still got a chance.'

'What?'

'I could show you the town tonight. Go clubbing, if you like.'

Santiago thought for a moment. Since his arrival in England he'd spent every night with Glen, and much as he liked him, he realized he could do with a night out with people of his own age. 'Sure. Do I need ID?'

'ID? What for?'

'How old do you have to be here to get a drink?'

Jamie smiled through a mouthful of pasta. 'Eleven.'

Santiago found it hard to shake off the memory of Hughie Magowan's ferocious tackle, and even harder to forget his comment in the canteen.

Training was over for the day, so Santiago went back to the house. Glen was already there, having finished work early. He was in the kitchen making himself a cup of tea when he heard the door open. Santiago came in, dropped his bag on the floor and slumped into an armchair.

'How was it?' called Glen.

Santiago didn't answer.

'Not good?'

'I have a problem with one guy.'

The kettle boiled and Glen poured the boiling water into the teapot. He walked through to the living room. 'Don't tell me: Hughie Magowan?'

'You know him?'

'Oh, I know him, all right, but fortunately we never met in action.'

'He doesn't like me.'

'Yeah, well I can understand that.'

'What? But why? I haven't done anything to him.'

Glen sat in the chair facing Santiago. 'Hughie Magowan is thirty-three; all he's got left is his reputation, and unless every other centre back breaks their leg, he'll never play for the first team again.'

'That's not my problem.'

'No. But you're young, you've got it all in front of you. And on top of that, you've got something Hughie never had. Flair.'

Santiago looked puzzled. 'I don't know this word.'

'It's something most mortals don't have. Most

players, myself included, they play within themselves, to their strengths, they don't expose their weaknesses. But the great players, the ones with true flair, they take risks, because they don't believe they are risks. They control the ball; the ball doesn't control them.'

'And you think I have this . . . this flair?'

'I know you do, lad. So don't let the Hughie Magowans of this world grind it out of you.' He stood up. 'Now, d'you fancy a nice cuppa tea?'

Thirteen

Santiago had thought Newcastle quayside looked great in the daylight, but at night, as the lights bounced off the Tyne, it was stunning.

From the Tyne Bridge down to the new Gateshead Millennium Bridge, arcing across the river to the Baltic Gallery, the quayside was ablaze with light and buzzing with activity as hundreds of young people moved noisily towards bars and restaurants or spilled out onto the walkways with drinks in their hands.

The cold night didn't appear to have the slightest effect on the dress code of most of the revellers: blokes were parading in jeans and T-shirts and young women were strutting along in high heels, minuscule skirts and halter tops.

Santiago was wearing a jacket, done up. He might have acclimatized himself to the cold of the daytime, but the nights were something else.

He watched two girls in tiny mini skirts with bare legs click their way along the pavement towards a bar and shook his head. 'They don't feel cold? It's impossible not to feel cold dressed like that.'

'They don't seem to notice it up here,' said Jamie. 'Must be down to all that Newcastle Brown they drink.'

A Range Rover slid past them and came to a halt outside the Club Tabu, where two burly, dark-suited bouncers stood guarding the entrance.

All four doors of the Range Rover sprang open and Gavin Harris emerged from one of the rear doors with two girls. Two blokes climbed out of the front. They didn't look like footballers. One was a good few kilos overweight and the other was as thin as a stick insect. But they acted and sounded as though they were Gavin's best mates as the bouncers welcomed them all to the Club Tabu, especially the footballer. Celebrities were always welcomed; they were good for business, even if they brought with them a bunch of celebrity hangers-on.

Jamie nudged Santiago. 'Come on, we might get in here.' He ran towards the club. 'Gavin! Hey, Gavin!'

But Gavin and the two girls had already disappeared through the doorway. The larger of Gavin's mates had heard Jamie shout. He turned round. 'Write to the club if you want an autograph. Tell 'em Bluto told you to write in.'

'You cheeky sod!' said Jamie. 'I'm with the club, too!'

Bluto smiled to his friend. 'They all say that, don't they, Des?'

'There's always one who tries it on,' said Des to the bouncers. 'Come on, Bluto, we're missing the action.'

As Gavin's mates made their way into the Club Tabu, one of the bouncers replaced the twisted velvet rope across the entrance door, barring the way to Jamie and Santiago.

'I *am* with the club,' said Jamie to the two stony-faced bouncers.

'We both are,' added Santiago.

'I've never seen you at St James',' said one of the bouncers.

'We haven't played there yet. We're with the reserves.'

The bouncers exchanged a look, uncertain as to whether or not reserves counted as celebrities, even minor celebrities. These guys were paid not only to keep the wrong people out, but also to allow the right people in, and the management didn't look kindly on mistakes.

'What d'you reckon?' said one of the heavies to his mate.

They appeared to be hovering on the side of letting Santiago and Jamie in, when Santiago saw a face he recognized on the other side of the road. 'Hey, Nurse Harmison!'

Roz Harmison was on a night out with her friend Lorraine. She stopped and stared, quickly recognizing Santiago. 'Oh, hello.'

'You want to come in this club with us?'

'No way, that place is full of posers.'

'So where are you going?'

Roz hesitated, but her friend Lorraine was a

lot more forthcoming. 'We're going to the Spyglass. You can come with us if you want!'

'*Lorraine!*' said Roz. 'This was meant to be a girls' night out.'

Her friend smiled. 'Don't worry, they look harmless enough.' She turned back to Santiago and Jamie. 'Well, are you coming or not?'

The Spyglass was a pub more than a club. But it was tastefully decorated, with comfortable chairs and big wooden tables. Best of all, from Santiago's point of view, it had a fire. The logs may have been imitation, but the heat thrown out was real enough.

They found a table close by and sat down with glasses of wine. Eventually Santiago felt warm enough to undo his jacket.

Roz smiled. 'Still getting used to our weather?'

'It's not quite like LA.'

Lorraine was sipping her Rioja wine. 'LA? You're a long way from home.'

'Me too,' said Jamie. 'I'm from Liverpool.'

'Los Angeles and Liverpool. What are you two doing here, then?'

'We play for Newcastle.'

Lorraine didn't hide her surprise as she turned to Roz. 'I thought you'd put players off limits.'

Roz took a sip of her drink. 'They're only trainees.'

'Oh, you're in with a chance, then,' said Lorraine to Santiago. 'Just as long as you don't become a superstar.'

Santiago was totally baffled. 'I'm sorry, I don't know what this means.'

'It means, don't change,' said Roz. 'Don't become something you're not.'

'Oh, I see. At least, I think I see.'

Roz laughed. 'I remember you now,' she said to Jamie. 'How's your toe?'

Jamie's eyes widened in horror. He didn't want to go where Roz was going.

'Your big toe,' she continued. 'Right foot. You had fungus behind the nail.'

As Lorraine grimaced and almost choked on her Rioja, a highly embarrassed Jamie smiled a sickly smile at Roz. 'Thanks. She's bound to fancy me now, isn't she?'

Fourteen

It was raining. Hard. Santiago looked out
through the windows of the reception area at the
training ground and saw many of the first-team
squad arrive for the day's training in their
Ferraris and Porsches; the sort of cars he
had only got close to in LA when he was
cutting the lawn or clearing the drive for their
owners.

He was thinking about what Roz had said in
the pub. *Don't change. Don't become something
you're not.*

Why would he change? All he wanted to do
was to play football. To make his living doing
something he truly loved. The only way that

would change him would be to make him completely happy and fulfilled.

Santiago was already in his training gear. As he turned away from the window, he saw an Aston Martin come hurtling into the car park and skid to a halt on the slippery tarmac. Gavin Harris leaped from the driver's seat and ran for the shelter of the building. He was late. Again.

The coaching staff had decided that training would be indoors today. Santiago sat around for a while, waiting for the day to be rescheduled. Eventually Bobby Redfern told him to get down to the indoor pitch.

He'd never seen the Astroturf pitch until now, and as he walked through the double doors he was amazed at the size of the place. It was enormous, like a hangar for jumbo jets.

Players were already out there, some warming up with easy stretches or slow jogs back and forth across the width of the pitch, others raining shots at the goalkeeper at the far end. Santiago stared again; the goalkeeper at the far end was Shay Given. And as Santiago's eyes scanned the indoor arena he saw that most of the first-team squad were out there.

Mal Braithwaite was standing on the sideline. He saw Santiago's enquiring look directed at him. 'The first team need a good workout before the Bolton game. Play with the reds. Midfield. Get yourself a bib and do your best.'

Santiago grabbed a red bib from the pile and ran onto the pitch, too nervous to join in any of the warm-ups going on around him.

As Mal prepared to whistle for the start of the game, the double doors opened and Erik Dornhelm walked in.

The first few minutes passed Santiago by as though he wasn't there. Even in a training match, the big boys played at a different pace and Santiago was anxiously trying to adjust to the speed and the unfamiliar playing surface.

Mal jogged by him, his eyes on the game. 'C'mon, son, put yourself about.'

It was the wake-up call Santiago needed. He went hunting for the ball, and after a few neat touches, he felt his confidence begin to grow.

Gavin Harris received a pass out wide in his own half. He was looking to offload the ball without too much effort when Santiago nipped in and took it off his toes. Gavin didn't like it, not one bit, and as Santiago moved away, he gave chase, edging Santiago towards the touchline.

The young Mexican stopped dead and Harris hestitated, waiting for that spilt second to make his challenge. But before he could move, Santiago feinted to the left and then did a Ronaldo-like shuffle and went round his right side. He was away.

On the touchline, Erik Dornhelm caught his chief coach's eye and raised his eyebrows in appreciation.

Santiago was moving at real pace. His strikers were lurking, calling for the ball, perfectly positioned for the well-timed pass. But Santiago had Glen's words at the front of his mind. Risk. Flair.

He had those qualities: Glen had told him so. An opposing midfielder attempted a tackle but Santiago beat him easily. With a defender closing in, Santiago looked up. Risk. Flair.

He let fly with a scorching, rising shot. Shay Given flung himself, full stretch, to his left, and just managed to push the ball round the upright.

Santiago frowned. Close, so close, but not quite close enough. As he jogged back into position he saw Gavin Harris glaring at him.

The electrifying run was Santiago's best moment of the game, but by the time Mal whistled for the end he thought he'd given a reasonable enough account of himself.

As the two teams started to pull off their bibs and make for the doors, Erik Dornhelm picked up a football and walked along the halfway line. 'Muñez!'

Santiago ran over to the manager and the other players slowed their departure, curious to see what would happen next.

'When I say "Go", I want you to run as fast as you can to the goal.'

Some of the older players smiled in anticipation of what was to come.

'Go!'

Santiago turned and sprinted. After a few paces, Dornhelm dropped the ball and volleyed it hard. It flew over Santiago's head, and as he ran he saw it bounce a couple of times and go into the empty net.

'Bring it back to me!' shouted Dornhelm, his voice echoing off the high walls.

The young player scooped the football from the back of the net and jogged back to the manager.

Dornhelm took the ball and volleyed it again.

'Bring it back to me!'

This time Santiago ran a lot slower as he watched the ball go into the net again. He picked it up and jogged back.

'What did you learn?' said Dornhelm.

'That you can score from halfway?'

Dornhelm was unimpressed by Santiago's reply. 'That the ball can travel faster than you can. In my teams, we pass the ball. We play as a unit. I'm not interested in one-man shows.'

Gavin Harris was standing nearby and he didn't fail to notice the quick look in his direction as Dornhelm completed his rebuke. 'The badge on the front of the shirt is more important than the one on the back.'

The words were stinging, humiliating, and as

Santiago showered and changed he felt as though the other players were laughing at him. He avoided eye contact with anyone and as he buttoned his shirt he felt the tension in his chest.

There were voices coming from the treatment room and more from the showers, but as he quickly glanced around, he saw that at that moment he was alone.

He reached into his bag, pulled out his asthma inhaler and took a quick hit.

He didn't see Hughie Magowan walk in from the showers and watch him do it.

Fifteen

There was always a huge sense of anticipation at St James' Park on match days, no matter how the team was performing. If the lads were going well, their devoted followers turned up expecting another victory. If they were in a bad run, the fans arrived convinced that this was the match in which their heroes' fortunes would change.

From every direction, black-and-white-clad supporters streamed through the city towards the mighty stadium.

As the terraces filled, most of chatter focused on one topic: that tantalizing finish in the top four of the Premiership which would mean

Champions League football next season. It was still a possibility, but only just.

The team's recent performances had been stuttering, at best, and with Sam Allardyce's well-drilled, highly experienced outfit for today's opponents, everyone knew the match would be no walkover.

Erik Dornhelm was under pressure, and he knew it. A fresh crop of niggling injuries amongst the first-team squad wasn't helping, and today a couple of unfamiliar names had been added to the line-up, including Carl Francis, the young midfielder who had been impressing in the reserves.

Santiago and Glen had something many followers of Newcastle could wait for years to get: tickets for a Premiership match. St James' was all season ticket, apart from some Cup games. But while he was on the playing staff, for however brief a period that might be, Santiago got the opportunity to at least sample the unique atmosphere of St James', to see the pitch he dreamed of running onto and to cheer on his team like any other supporter. Not only that, he'd managed to wangle a club ticket for Glen, too.

As they emerged from one of the access tunnels into the stadium, Santiago stopped and gasped. Nothing he had seen so far in his short time at the club compared with this. The training ground, the indoor facilities, even the exterior of the stadium were amazing, but this . . . this was overwhelming, breathtaking. Huge stands climbed skywards, filled with a sea of black and white.

'Come on, lad, don't just stand there,' said a voice behind Santiago, and he quickly moved on to catch up with Glen.

They found their seats and were flicking through the match programme when a voice came over the public address system to give the final line-ups. Every one of the home team names was cheered, but at different volume levels, depending on the popularity of each player. The name Alan Shearer, as always, received the loudest cheers.

High up in one of the private boxes, the fact that the name Gavin Harris had received fewer cheers than most didn't go unnoticed by the player's agent, Barry Rankin, or by Gavin's long-time and long-suffering girlfriend Christina, who had travelled up from London with Barry for the match.

The glass-fronted room was filled to capacity with guests of the star players, all enjoying complimentary pre-match drinks and smoked salmon sandwiches. Wolfing down more than most were Gavin's two mates from London, Bluto and Des, who were making the very most of their extended stay on Tyneside.

Barry took Bluto by the arm and spoke quietly so that his question went unheard by most in the box. 'So, is our boy behaving himself?'

'Good as gold,' said Bluto through a mouthful of smoked salmon. He saw Christina's doubting look. 'Honest!'

There was a roar from the capacity crowd as the players ran onto the pitch.

'Better take our seats,' said Barry, and he ushered Christina out through the open glass doors into the cauldron of St James' Park.

Erik Dornhelm's face was expressionless as he

sat on one of the luxury, heated, airline-type seats in the Newcastle dugout. Beside him, Mal Braithwaite fidgeted nervously and chewed on his nails as Newcastle struggled to gain ascendancy during the first quarter of the match.

A few metres to their left, Sam Allardyce and his Bolton crew were perched on far less comfortable, bog standard plastic seating in the visitors' dugout. Big Sam didn't appear to care about or even notice the difference in the Home and Away bench seating arrangements. He was up on his feet every few minutes, bawling instructions to his hard-working team.

The crowd was strangely subdued, perfectly aware that the Newcastle team was not gelling and was far from performing like the unit their manager wanted and demanded. They had enjoyed most of the possession, but it had resulted in not one clear-cut chance on goal.

From his position to the left of and above the dugouts, Santiago could see Mal Braithwaite fretting and could almost sense the unease on the bench. Immediately behind the dugouts, the rows of newspaper and radio journalists were busy with phones and microphones, already putting into words for their readers and listeners what everyone inside the stadium knew was a less than dynamic display by the home team.

And behind the journalists, the chairman, the directors and their guests shifted uncomfortably in their perfectly comfortable executive chairs.

The first half ended goal-less, and as Dornhelm and his players disappeared down the players' tunnel, they left with more than a few jeers from the faithful.

In the stands, Glen was less than impressed. 'They're all over the place and Harris isn't in the game.'

Santiago was reluctant to criticize his club mates. 'Carl Francis is playing well.'

'Aye, he looks useful. At least he's trying.'

The second half picked up in exactly the same way as the first had ended. Plenty of Newcastle possession, but no end result. Then suddenly there was a chance. Kieron Dyer played a tight through ball into space for Gavin Harris to run on to. But Harris was off the pace and didn't even connect with the ball as he lunged for it.

The crowd groaned and Erik Dornhelm immediately directed two of the Newcastle subs to start warming up.

The Bolton team seemed to take heart from the miss and began enjoying a period of pressure and dominance. Carl Francis intercepted one attack out wide, but as he looked to turn defence into attack he was brought down by a scything tackle.

Francis rolled on the ground, clutching his knee, and as the crowd roared their disapproval, the referee had no hesitation in pulling out the yellow card.

The injury was bad; everyone could tell that by the number of players from both sides who gathered round. Francis was stretchered off to sympathetic applause from the whole crowd and Erik Dornhelm decided then to make not one, but two substitutions.

Up in the executive box, Bluto could hardly believe it. 'That cretin is pulling Gavin off! It's ridiculous – he's the only one who's done anything all day!'

Barry Rankin and Christina wisely said nothing.

Close to the end, and against the run of play, Newcastle somehow managed to scramble the ball over the line to take the lead. And in the dying minutes they held on against sustained Bolton pressure for a very fortunate win.

As the final whistle blew, Sam Allardyce turned to his opposite number, offered his hand and nodded a 'Well played', saving his full thoughts on the opposition's performance for the post-match Press conference and the *Match of the Day* interview.

It had been a poor game, but as the supporters streamed away from the stadium, they did at least have the consolation of three more precious points.

Gavin Harris didn't hang around in the changing room. He was showered and dressed before the final whistle sounded and soon after he met up with Barry and Christina, along with hangers-on Bluto and Des, who continued to bask in the reflected glory of their famous friend.

Except that their famous friend wasn't feeling particularly glorious. He wasn't happy at being substituted and made sure his agent knew about it as they travelled down one of the escalators leading to ground level from the upper hospitality areas.

'If he's gonna pull me off like that, why did he bother paying more than eight million for me?'

Barry Rankin was always loyal to his clients, and he usually pandered to their inflated egos, but he wasn't beyond putting in a cautionary word when it was needed. 'A little bit more effort might not go amiss, Gavin.'

Christina was standing at Gavin's side. 'And maybe a few early nights.'

Her boyfriend ignored the caustic comment as, a little further down the escalator, Bluto and Des burst into a very bad and very out-of-tune rendition of *Fog on the Tyne*.

Gavin smiled but Christina sighed wearily. 'I come all the way from London and I'm stuck with those morons.'

'They're not morons,' said Gavin. 'They're my mates.'

Christina shook her head, amazed that her

boyfriend couldn't see the truth. 'Gavin, believe me, they are *not* your mates.'

They reached the ground floor and walked out onto the service road passing beneath the main entrances to the stadium.

As they went towards the car park, Barry spotted Glen emerging from another exit with Santiago.

Gavin and his entourage continued on, but Barry stopped and spoke to Glen. 'Hello, mate. I suppose you've still got the needle about LA?'

Glen shrugged. 'You were "working", Barry. I could hear the party in the background.'

'Fair enough,' said the agent, holding up both his hands. 'I was partying. What can I say?'

'You can say hello to my friend here,' said Glen, nodding towards Santiago. 'He's the one you missed.'

Barry stared. 'Yeah? Well . . . what's he doing here in Newcastle?'

Glen smiled. 'Santiago's on the books. See you, Barry.'

They walked away, leaving Barry still staring.

Sixteen

Santiago never tired of football, or of training. He put everything he could into the next couple of weeks, knowing only too well that his time on trial was quickly passing. He felt he was doing well, but whether or not it was well enough was impossible to know. Praise didn't come easily from any of the coaching team.

Some days, when official training was over, he would work on alone. He would heave a huge string bag, bulging with twenty or more footballs, out onto one of the practice pitches and line them up twenty-five or thirty yards outside the penalty box.

Then he would practise his free kicks, and he

would go on practising until every one of the balls was in the back of the net. And then, usually, he would start again.

One damp, gloomy afternoon, he was alone on the pitch. Dark, heavy clouds loomed overhead as he slotted one ball into the net and then walked back to line up for the next attempt.

Over in the reception area, Erik Dornhelm walked from the main building and stopped as he saw the distant figure preparing for the shot. He watched as Santiago took three short strides and curled the ball into a top corner.

Dornhelm's face remained expressionless. He simply walked on to his car, got in and drove away.

Santiago had arranged to meet Roz for a drink later that evening. And that was something else that was worrying him. They were getting on well, very well, and he wasn't looking forward to having to say goodbye if his trial was not extended. All he could do was continue to do his best. And hope.

He walked out of the dressing room and stopped at the large cork noticeboard, covered with various notices and team lists. His eyes scanned the board and rested on the team selection for the next reserve match, looking to see which of his training partners had made the squad. Hughie Magowan was inevitably there, and so was Jamie. And then . . . He read the name once and then again to be absolutely certain.

It was there. In black and white. It was there: S MUÑEZ.

Roz was still on duty at the hospital when Santiago arrived. She was pushing a wheelchair containing a young boy with his leg in plaster along the corridor when she saw the beaming Santiago hurrying towards her.

'What are you doing here? Are you hurt?' She answered her own questions. 'No, you can't be, you're smiling too much.'

'I have some great news. I made the reserve squad.'

'Yeah? That's brilliant.'

'If the boss sees me do well, maybe he'll keep me on.'

'I'm sure he will, Santi.'

'So we celebrate tonight?'

'I finish in half an hour.'

The boy in the wheelchair had been watching the conversation bounce back and forth as though he were at a tennis match. As it finally stopped, he took his chance. 'Do you play for Newcastle then?' he said to Santiago.

Santiago was almost embarrassed to reply. 'Yes.'

The boy tapped on his plastered leg. 'Sign your name on that.'

Santiago hestitated. 'You mean it?'

'Course he means it,' said Roz, pulling a pen from her pocket.

When Roz finished her shift they went down to the quayside and walked across the Millennium Bridge to the Gateshead side of the river. It was still early; most of the bars hadn't even opened. But they were content to just walk.

'I phoned my grandmother while I was waiting for you. She was happy for me.'

They were walking past the huge, glass-walled Sage Centre, as a group of young teenagers, talking football, passed by in the opposite direction.

'They'll all be asking for your autograph soon,' said Roz.

Santiago still remembered what Roz had said in the pub on their first night out together. 'Would it bother you? You never told me, what is your problem with footballers?'

'It's not footballers as such; it's the whole "fame" thing. It's my dad's fault. When I was a kid, he was in a rock band. They had their five minutes of fame.'

'Would I know this band?'

'I doubt it. The point is, some of the players remind me of him. One minute they're nice uncomplicated guys and the next, they're stupid rich idiots who walk out on their families.'

They continued in silence for a few moments, both deep in their own thoughts and memories. Santiago stopped and leaned on the railings, looking across the river, and Roz stood close by him.

'It was my mother who left us,' said Santiago at last.

'She did? Why?'

Santiago shrugged. 'My father never talks about it, but I remember his anger and his drinking. That's why I needed football so much, to get away from it, even as a kid. I always wanted it to be my life.'

'So why did you have to come all this way to make it happen?'

Santiago turned and looked at Roz. 'For that you have to ask the saints. Or maybe what the saints had in mind was for me to meet you.'

Roz laughed. 'Does that cheesy line work for you back home?'

'It sounds much better in Spanish.'

Roz laughed again, but then they didn't say any more. Instead, they kissed, for the first time.

Mercedes was waiting for the right moment. Herman had eaten his evening meal and was sitting in front of the television, as relaxed as he ever was.

Julio looked at his grandmother, silently urging her to get on with it.

She took a deep breath. 'I had a call from Santiago. He sounds very happy.'

Herman said nothing; his eyes were still fixed on the soap playing out on screen. Fantasy worlds were a lot easier to deal with than reality.

'Tell him about the game,' said Julio.

Mercedes tried again. 'He's playing tomorrow night, for the reserve team. After only three weeks! Fantastic, no?'

Herman still didn't look away from the screen and his voice sounded completely indifferent as he replied. 'He left like a thief in the night without saying goodbye. Why should I care?'

Seventeen

The reserves match was being played under lights at Kingston Park, the stadium the team shared with the Newcastle Falcons rugby club.

In the dressing room, the veterans went through the same routines they'd gone through a thousand times before while the young players changed quickly and chatted nervously, knowing that both Mal Braithwaite *and* Erik Dornhelm would be out there watching.

Santiago was changing next to Jamie. 'I wish Glen could be here tonight.'

'Where is he?'

'In London. His son is getting married very

soon. Glen has gone to meet the girlfriend's parents.'

The reserves' coach, Bobby Redfern, came into the changing room and clapped his hands to get everyone's attention. 'Howay, lads, pay attention, now. Claudio's hamstring is holding up all right, so I'll give him a run for at least a half. Santiago, I want you on the right flank – but keep tracking their number eight: he's as slippery as a bag of ferrets.'

Santiago looked bewildered but Jamie smiled. 'I'll translate for you when we get out there.'

'Shut up, Jamie, and listen,' said Bobby. 'I want you to slot in behind the two strikers. And both keepers will get a half each. Right, let's get at it, then.'

The players hung back, waiting for Bobby's all-too-familiar parting shot. 'Oh, aye, and don't let them panic you into playing football!'

It was answered with a barrage of forced laughs and derision.

The tension and nerves of the moment made Santiago feel he needed a hit from his asthma inhaler. He waited as the others began to troop out and reached into his bag. As he took out his shin pads, the inhaler came out with them and bounced onto the floor. Quickly Santiago fell to his knees to retrieve it, but before his fingers reached the small blue cylinder, a size eleven boot came down and crushed it underfoot.

Santiago looked up to see Hughie Magowan smiling down at him. 'Sorry, pal. Was that important?'

There was nothing Santiago could do, but as he walked into the glare of the floodlights his chest suddenly felt tighter – much tighter than it had before.

Less than a thousand spectators huddled together in small groups on the terraces; a few were diehard supporters who never missed a match, but most were men, some with young sons, who just happened to live nearby and had nothing better to do.

Santiago struggled from the kick-off. The damp night air didn't help and soon he was gasping and wheezing like a twenty-cigarettes-a-day smoker. When he glanced towards the touchline he saw that Mal Braithwaite and Erik Dornhelm were already looking less than impressed.

Twenty minutes into the half, Hughie Magowan brought down one of the opposing forwards with his usual style and panache. The referee blew for a free kick and warned the big central defender that the next one would mean a yellow card.

Santiago was pulled back into the defensive wall. Magowan was standing next to him. He grinned. 'What's happened to Speedy Gonzalez tonight? Lost the use of your legs?'

Santiago didn't have the breath to reply.

The free kick was poorly struck and cannoned off the wall. It was the perfect opportunity for a quick counter-attack. Jamie played the ball cleanly into Santiago's path but he had no pace; his legs wouldn't do what his brain was telling them. The speedy number eight Bobby had warned him about quickly overtook him and hooked the ball away for a throw-in as Santiago fell to his knees.

Jamie Drew came running up. 'You OK?'

Santiago nodded and struggled to his feet.

Before half time, the coaches and manager had seen more than enough. The number eight was running rings around Santiago, and even lumbering central defenders were; it was embarrassing.

As the ball went out of play for a throw-in, Santiago looked across and saw a sub stripped off and ready to come on. Bobby Redfern signalled to the referee and then beckoned to Santiago.

Slowly, looking as devastated as he felt, he walked off the field; he couldn't run. He touched hands with the sub and, as he went past Redfern, head bowed, the coach patted him on the back. 'Get yourself an early bath, son.'

Alone in the dressing room, Santiago slumped down on the bench, on the verge of tears. His big chance, probably his only chance, and he'd blown it.

He sat staring across the room, seeing nothing but reliving the nightmarish performance he had given out on the park. Mal Braithwaite walked in and immediately saw the despair etched on Santiago's face.

'What was that all about? Are you hurt?'

'No, coach.'

'What is it, then? Been out on the town?'

Santiago shook his head.

Mal hesitated for a moment. 'Is there something else you want to tell me?'

Of course Santiago wanted to tell him. He was desperate to tell him. But he couldn't; it was too late now.

'No, coach.'

Mal sighed; he never relished this part of the job. 'I don't know, Santi. You've got the skill, and I've seen the pace, but maybe you just don't have the stamina for the English game. Maybe you're best off playing back at home. I'm sorry, son, I have to let you go.'

Santiago had to see Roz. To tell her. To let her know that he'd failed, that he'd let everyone down, that he'd been dumped. And that he was leaving.

He felt ashamed, humiliated, and he slunk away from Kingston Park while the match was still on. No one noticed him go, no one cared.

After a performance like that, why should they? By tomorrow, he'd be forgotten; it would be as though he'd never even been in Newcastle.

Roz lived in one of the high suburbs clustered around and looking down towards the city centre and the Tyne. When Santiago got out of the taxi, walked up to the door and rang the doorbell, he expected Roz to open the door. She didn't.

The door swung back and Santiago was confronted with an attractive woman who was probably in her late forties but was doing her best to look a fair bit younger. The skirt was a little too short and the blouse was a bit too tight; Carol Harmison still saw herself as the rock-chick of twenty years earlier.

Her smile was genuine and welcoming. 'Yes?'

'This . . . this is the home of Roz Harmison?'

'Roz! It's for you,' called Carol, still looking at Santiago. 'You must be the young man from LA. I've heard all about you.'

'Santiago, yes.'

'Well, come in,' said Carol, stepping aside.

Santiago nodded his thanks and stepped into the house. Carol closed the door. 'I went there years ago, when my husband's band was on tour. We stayed at the Hyatt House on Sunset. They called it the Riot House in those days; you wouldn't believe the things we got up to. One time there was this—'

'Mum!' said Roz as she appeared on the stairs. 'Aren't you meant to be meeting your mates at the Wheatsheaf?'

Roz had heard Carol's rock reminiscences before, many times before. They could be entertaining and amusing, but were not for the fainthearted and most definitely not for a first-time visitor to the house.

'There's no mad rush,' said Carol, casting an admiring, appreciative and experienced eye over Santiago. Then she saw the look her daughter was casting in her direction. Words were unnecessary: the look said, *Get lost, Mum.*

Carol sighed. 'But then again, I suppose they are waiting.' She beamed at Santiago. 'Really nice to meet you. You must come round again. I'd love to hear if LA's the same as it was in the good old days.' She grabbed a coat from a stand in the hallway and Roz ushered Santiago through to the living room.

'Great name!' called Carol as she checked her face in a mirror. 'Santiago. So . . . evocative. Bye, then!'

'Bye, Mum.'

The front door slammed, and for a moment Santiago stood looking at a display of framed gold albums and photographs of Carol with various rock bands. They made him think of Glen, someone else with their history on the wall.

'So what happened?' said Roz. 'How did it go? I didn't expect you.'

Santiago turned away from the photographs. 'I was cut.'

'Cut? Where? Show me.'

'No, I was let go. Dumped. They fired me. I came to say goodbye.'

'You're . . . you're leaving?'

'I don't belong here if I'm not in the team.'

'But why? What went wrong?'

'I couldn't tell them. I couldn't say why I

played so bad. I couldn't go to the boss and argue my case.'

Roz took Santiago's hand and sat with him on the big old sofa that took up one side of the room. 'Santi, I don't understand. What couldn't you tell them?'

'That I lied at my physical. To you. I have asthma.'

'Why didn't you say so?'

'Because if I had, I wouldn't even have got a trial.'

Roz was still holding Santiago's hand. She squeezed it gently. 'Look, these things happen to young players all the time. You'll find another team.'

'But not here. I was crazy to think I could make it work. And I've let people down. My grandmother. Glen. I'm going home, Roz. Tomorrow.'

Gavin was pacing anxiously as the taxi drew up. He wrenched open the nearside rear door and immediately recognized Santiago.

'What's going on? You late for training, too?'

'No! I have to get to the station.'

'Why?'

'I screwed up.'

Gavin jumped into the taxi and slammed the door. 'You can tell me about it on the way.' He turned to the driver. 'Come on, Jenson Button. Get us to the training ground.'

Gordon the driver pulled away, not exactly Formula One, but burning rubber as best he could, and as the vehicle sped towards the training ground Santiago told Gavin the full story of the previous night's match, his asthma and the crushed inhaler.

'So who was it who stood on the inhaler then?'

'Hughie Magowan, but it was probably an accident.'

The taxi driver laughed. 'I doubt it. Hughie Magowan's always been a nasty piece of work.'

'D'you mind,' said Gavin. 'This is a private conversation.'

'I feel sorry for the lad, that's all.'

The pulled into the training-ground car park and Gavin grabbed Santiago's bag. 'Let's get this sorted.'

'But—'

'I'll talk to the boss.'

He fished in his pockets for some cash as Gordon turned round. 'So you're *the* Gavin Harris.'

'Guilty.'

'I have to tell you, you're—'

'Yeah, I know, I'm shite. I met your mother earlier and she told me.'

'Well, the truth is, bonny lad, you're not worth eight million.'

'Actually, it was eight point four million.' He handed over a lot more cash than the ride had cost. 'Keep the change.'

The look that Erik Dornhelm gave Gavin and Santiago as he sat behind his desk and they stood on the other side like a couple of naughty schoolboys up before the headmaster gave absolutely nothing away.

But at least he was listening.

'The thing is, and with all due respect, gaffer . . . I mean, Mr Dornhelm, sir,' said Gavin, keeping the subject firmly on Santiago's situation rather than his own, 'the club would be making a big mistake if they let this lad go.'

'Oh, you think so?'

'I've played alongside him, and against him, and I can see he's got it. And so can the other lads. I mean technically, he's—'

'You mean he's better than you?'

Gavin hesitated. 'Well . . . he's in that league. Or he could be. Last night he lost his inhaler. He's got asthma, see. That's why he was staggering around like Puff the Magic Dragon.'

Dornhelm's eyes flicked from Gavin to Santiago. 'This is true?'

'Yes, sir. I tried to hide it.'

Dornhelm clicked his tongue with irritation. 'Lying is a problem; asthma doesn't need to be. You can get treatment. Medication. Didn't your doctor back home explain this to you?'

'I didn't have a doctor back home, just the free clinic in east LA.'

Dornhelm paused, considering, and Santiago and Gavin exchanged a glance.

'People keep pleading your case, Muñez.'

'All I want is the chance to prove them right.'

'You think you deserve it?'

'I know I do.'

Dornhelm almost smiled. But he didn't. Glen Foy, Mal Braithwaite, Bobby Redfern, and now even Gavin Harris had – one after another – told him that this kid had something special, something that needed nurturing and developing.

'See the doctor. Tell him about your condition. And then report for training.'

Santiago couldn't hide his joy. He reached across the desk, grabbed Dornhelm's right hand and shook it vigorously. 'Thank you, sir! *Gracias!* Thank you.' He turned to Gavin and shook his hand, too. 'And thank you, Gavin. *Muchas, muchas gracias!*'

'No problemo, mate,' said Gavin, guiding Santiago towards the door.

'Gavin!'

'Boss?'

'You stay!'

Santiago departed, all smiles, and Dornhelm waited until the door was firmly closed. 'This is a decent thing you did.'

'Yeah, well, he's a good kid, and—'

'But now please explain why you are dressed for a discotheque and are . . .' he checked his watch '. . . forty-seven minutes late for training.'

Nineteen

Glen never got to read the letter; Santiago tore it up before his friend got home that evening. But he did tell Glen what had happened, and about his asthma, and about Gavin Harris's role in influencing Dornhelm's decision to keep him at the club.

Glen took the news philosophically. 'You work hard and show Dornhelm what you can do and I reckon he'll see you all right now,' he said.

He did. Santiago put everything he could into the next few days' training, and an impressive reserve-team performance was rewarded with an extended trial of a further month.

He celebrated with Roz. His fortunes were

changing, and with the time pressure temporarily lifted, his confidence grew and he began to blossom. He became a regular in the reserves starting line-up and got his name on the score sheet for the first time in a match against QPR Reserves.

And there was an added bonus. Santiago was giving the QPR defenders such a miserable time that it became all too much for one of them. His frustration boiled over and he hacked the young player down with a tackle from behind.

As Newcastle players crowded around, the referee pulled out the yellow card and stepped quickly between the defender and Hughie Magowan, who was giving the offender a real ear-bashing.

Soon after, the same central defender had the ball in space. He wasn't blessed with any great distribution skills; he was an old-fashioned stopper, like Hughie, and when he had possession of the ball, his natural instinct was to get rid of it. He didn't get the chance. Hughie came steaming in and flattened him.

The ref whistled and reached for his yellow

card for a second time. 'That was late, Magowan.'

Hughie shrugged and held his hands up. 'I got there as soon as I could.'

The QPR trainer came running on to attend to his prostrate defender and Hughie strolled over to Santiago and winked. 'He'll think twice about nobbling you again.'

'But I thought you didn't like me.'

'I don't, but you see that lass over there?' He pointed to a group of girls in the stand and one of them waved. 'That's my kid sister, and she wouldn't like to see you hurt. She fancies you, says you remind her of Antonio Banderas, whoever he is.'

Santiago laughed. 'Does that mean you and me are OK?'

'What it means, Santiago, is that if you so much as touch her, I'll murder you!'

Santiago and Jamie Drew were forming a dynamic midfield partnership. In the game against Middlesbrough Reserves, Dornhelm and Mal Braithwaite watched and made notes as the two youngsters played an immaculate one-two and Santiago ran on to side-foot the ball past the keeper for his second goal of the match.

His growing fan club began to chant, and in the stand Glen smiled broadly. 'Good lad,' he whispered. 'I knew I was right, I knew it.'

Dornhelm seemed convinced, too. He almost smiled as he watched Santiago run back for the restart. 'Good. Very good,' he whispered.

The following day, Glen's prediction was proved absolutely correct when the trial period was scrapped and Santiago was given a contract until the end of the season.

The key turned in the lock and Santiago pushed the door open just a few centimetres. 'Now you have to wait,' he said to Roz.

'What?'

'I want it to be a surprise.'

'You're crazy.'

Santiago stood behind Roz and put his hands over her eyes. He pushed open the door with one foot, and then slowly led her through the open doorway and into the centre of the room. 'OK,' he said, removing his hands, 'now you can look.'

The spacious apartment was stunning, and so were the views from the picture windows of the bridges across the Tyne.

'Can you believe this?' said Santiago, standing close to Roz and gazing out towards the river. 'A few weeks ago I said goodbye to the city and to you, and now I have a real contract and I move into this apartment.'

'But . . . but how can you afford it?'

As Santiago started to answer, one of the doors leading from the main room opened and Gavin Harris emerged, wearing nothing but a towel around his waist.

'Gavin, say hello to my friend Roz,' said Santiago.

Gavin feigned surprise at the sight of a female in the apartment. 'I didn't say anything about you bringing women here!' He grinned. 'Just kidding. Nice to meet you, love. You're welcome, any time.'

He went back towards the bedroom but stopped at the door and turned back. 'Oh, and see if you can do something about his clothes, will you, love? The beach bum look might be OK in LA but I can't have him lowering the tone of the place now he lives here.' He laughed and disappeared into the bedroom.

'So that's how you can afford it,' said Roz.

'He's a good guy. If it wasn't for Gavin, I'd be back in LA.'

'And he's earned himself quite a reputation since he arrived in Newcastle.'

Santiago would hear nothing against his new friend. 'He's a good guy, Roz. We're professionals, football is our life.'

Roz went back to the window and stared out towards the Tyne Bridge. The sky was darkening and the lights were already beginning to illuminate the quayside. She was thinking of their first drink together at the Spyglass pub. And of her words of warning.

There was no problem in getting into the Club Tabu the second time Santiago arrived at the door. Not when he was with Gavin Harris.

The chief bouncer freed the velvet rope from its brass fitting and stood back. 'Nice to see you, Gavin. How are you, gentlemen?'

'We're good, mate,' said Bluto as he and Des followed them through the entrance door.

The VIP treatment was all new to Santiago. 'Fine. Thank you very much.'

The club was hot and heaving; music pumped from the sound system and the dance floor was jam packed with gyrating, sweating bodies. Gavin led his entourage straight through to the VIP section.

A second velvet rope was released by another bouncer and Gavin walked through to a long, blue-velvet banquette where Barry Rankin sat flanked by two young and very blonde girls. A bottle of champagne was cooling in an ice bucket.

Barry, inevitably, was on his mobile. 'No, Colin, it would be a bad move, a very bad move.' He waved at Gavin and the others as they sat down and then continued his conversation. 'Look, Col, I wasn't gonna mention this but Valencia have been tracking you . . . Yes, for real. Sun, sangria and señoritas. So patience, eh, Colin? You know I'm in your corner twenty-four-seven. Look, gotta go. Laters.'

He flipped the phone shut. 'Gavin! Dude!'

'This is my mate, Santi,' said Gavin over the pounding music.

Barry indicated to one of the blondes to pour champagne and simultaneously waved to a waitress for another bottle. 'How you doing, Santi? I hear it's going well.'

'Yes, very good. Thank you.'

'He notched a pair for the reserves the other day,' said Gavin, like a proud big brother.

More mini-skirted Toon teens began to cluster round the banquette, encouraged by the free-loading Bluto and Des.

As the waitress brought more champagne and fresh glasses, Barry leaned closer to Santiago. 'You've got a contract to the end of the season, right? Who handled that for you then?'

'Glen. He handles everything for me.'

Barry didn't hide his surprise, which was tinged with the slightest hint of disdain. 'Glen Foy? Really? I mean, nice bloke, and I'm told a great player in his day, but what does he know about endorsements? And marketability?'

'I'm sorry?'

'Look, son, you make the first team and I can get you a Gap ad.'

Santiago shook his head. 'It's hot – I think I need some air.'

He went outside. This *was* all new. All different. So different. As he stood looking towards the dark river and the bright lights, he suddenly felt homesick. He pulled out his mobile phone and punched in a number. It was answered on the fourth ring.

'Hello.'

'Julio,' said Santiago in Spanish. 'It's me.'

'Hey! Bro! What's going on?'

Santiago smiled; it was good to hear his brother's voice. They chatted for a few minutes and then Santiago said, 'Is Papa there?'

Herman *was* there, watching television while doing his best not to listen in to the telephone conversation.

Julio put his hand over the phone receiver and spoke to his father. 'It's Santiago, he wants to speak to you.'

Herman looked up from the television screen and for a moment Julio thought that he was going to get up and come to the phone. But then he shook his head and went back to the TV. 'Tell him I'm in the shower.'

'Papa . . . ?'

'Tell him!'

There was no point in arguing. Julio lifted the telephone. 'He can't talk now, Santi, OK?'

Twenty

The season was drawing to an exciting and nailbiting conclusion. From the dizzy heights of the Premiership to the basement regions of Division Three, the final shakedown was beginning to become clear.

In the lower leagues, the first certain promotion places were claimed while some of the teams destined for the dreaded drop already knew their fate. Other clubs were battling for places in the play-offs.

In the Premiership, Newcastle continued to grind out results, with the prize of a Champions League place still tantalizingly close. But with injuries and suspensions playing their part and only two matches to go, that place was by no means certain and several clubs were still in with a shout.

Santiago had settled into the life of a professional footballer and everything that went with it. On the field, he had become a reserve-team regular and had turned in a number of eye-catching performances. Off the field, life was never boring; it couldn't be now that he was sharing an apartment with Gavin Harris.

Gavin seemed to look on Santiago as a particular friend. Perhaps it was because he could see that the young Latin American's friendship was genuine: there were no strings attached. He liked him being around, and if Santiago wasn't always quite comfortable with his friend's lifestyle, he didn't let it show. He was grateful to Gavin, he always would be, so he went along with it all and slipped into the Gavin Harris jetstream and found himself, at times, adopting his jetset ways.

Many of the first-team squad appeared to have at least two mobile phones with them at all times – they seemed to be as essential to the modern footballers as their football boots. They were always using them: talking to agents, arranging endorsements, discussing ghostwritten newspaper articles.

Santiago had even imagined players out on the pitch with their mobiles clamped to their ears; wingers hurtling down the flanks as they discussed a new sponsorship deal, defenders going up for a high ball whilst arranging a photo shoot, keepers saving with one hand whilst clinging onto that precious mobile with the other.

So far, Santiago had just one mobile, but carrying it around at all times was already becoming almost second nature.

He had changed for training and then gone to look at the noticeboard in the corridor to see the line-up for the next reserve-team match. His name wasn't on it; he wasn't even in the squad. He'd been dropped!

He couldn't believe it; he'd been playing so well and training so hard. He flipped open his mobile, intending to call Glen, and realized that it had been switched off since last night. He powered it up and his voicemail informed him that he had messages.

He listened to the first.

'It's Glen. Haven't heard from you for a while. Hope it's going well. Give me a bell if you get a chance.'

Santiago immediately felt guilty. He hadn't called for a few days. Was it a few days? Maybe it was a little longer.

The second message was from Roz.

'Hi. Just finished night school. It's ten past eleven, you're probably asleep. Call me tomorrow.'

At ten past eleven the previous night, Santiago hadn't been asleep – far from it. He'd been out with Gavin, with his mobile switched off.

Santiago made his mind up to call Roz as soon as training was over. He went to go back into the changing room to leave the phone in his locker, but saw Bobby Redfern approaching along the corridor.

'What did I do wrong?'

'What?'

'I'm not on the team; I didn't even make the

bench. I don't get it. I play where you tell me, how you tell me, I score goals, I give a hundred per cent and I get dropped.'

Bobby Redfern smiled. 'I didn't drop you, son. You're not available for selection.'

'What? Of course I am.'

'No lad, you're not. You're going to Fulham on Saturday, with the first team.'

Santiago's mouth dropped open; his breath caught in his chest. He leaned back against the wall and took a deep breath.

'You all right?' said Bobby.

Santiago nodded. 'Yes. Yes, I'm OK. But I must call my grandmother.'

'But it's the middle of the night in California.'

'My grandmother won't mind.'

Twenty-one

The flight in the chartered jet took no time at all. One minute Santiago was settling into his seat fixing his seatbelt and the next he was unbuckling the belt and preparing to get off. The plane just seemed to have climbed to its cruising height and then begun its descent – like a goalkeeper's clearance that goes directly from one penalty box to the other.

The directors, manager, coaches and playing squad moved quickly from jet plane to luxury coach for the second part of the journey to Fulham, the part which would take the longest.

It was just routine for everyone else, but for

Santiago it was another example of how his life had changed so much, and so quickly.

The travelling Toon Army of Newcastle faithfuls had travelled less stylishly but with equal hope, making early-morning starts in crowded cars decked out with black and white. It was another crucial game in the push for that Champions League place, and fixtures were running out fast.

Those who didn't have a ticket, or couldn't get away, waited anxiously back in Newcastle as kick-off time approached.

Roz was at work: she had been unable to swap her shift; everyone wanted to see the match. And Roz would still see it, or at least part of it. She was the favourite nurse of a patient in a private room, an old boy called Mr Ives, and he was already settled comfortably in his chair in dressing gown and slippers, eyes glued to the television set.

Roz put her head round the door. 'Have they mentioned him yet?'

The old boy smiled. 'Not yet, pet, it's just the warm-up. I'll keep you posted.'

Glen was also preparing to watch the match on TV, settled on the sofa in his living room with a sandwich and a can of beer. As he took a bite from his sandwich he heard the first mention of his protégé as the match commentator and summarizer discussed the Newcastle squad.

'There's a makeshift look to the squad today, with all the injury problems,' said the commentator. 'One of the subs, Santiago Muñez, is a completely unknown quantity.'

The summarizer had been doing his home-work. 'Apparently he was discovered playing in a park in Los Angeles by Glen Foy, who was in the Newcastle team when they last won a major honour.'

'Glen Foy!' said the commentator. 'Now there's a name from the past.'

In his living room, Glen took a swig from his can of beer. 'Cheers, mate.'

In the tunnel beneath the stand, the two teams and the subs emerged from their dressing rooms to take the field. There were the usual nods between those players who knew each other well from previous clubs or from international squads. There were a few jokes, a few good-hearted jibes, but it merely masked the tension that all the players felt.

Santiago was one of the last out, awed to be up close to all these Premiership players. Fulham's Steed Malbranque was standing opposite him and seemed to sense the youngster's tension. He smiled encouragingly and Santiago smiled back. And then they were walking out into the arena.

As Erik Dornhelm and Chris Coleman led their teams out onto the pitch, the stadium erupted into a barrage of noise.

The match was being bounced by satellite to scores of countries around the world.

In Santa Monica, USA, it was early morning; palm trees were blowing in a stiff breeze as the second-hand truck Herman had bought pulled to a standstill in the parking lot of an English-style pub called the King's Head.

Herman climbed out of the vehicle and heard voices shouting as he looked at the pub. He walked towards the building and pushed open the door. The place was crowded with ex-pats, most of them wearing Newcastle or Fulham shirts. Many were eating fried breakfasts, which were being washed down with either tea or beer, even though it was just seven a.m.

Herman handed over ten dollars to the guy at the door and found himself a stool at the bar. He had never been in a place like this before, or heard so many hard-to-understand accents.

Three separate screens strategically placed around the bar were showing the game live from London.

The noise level in the bar dropped for a few moments and then erupted again as the referee blew for the kick off.

Santiago was sitting at the back of the visitors' dugout with the other tracksuited subs. He was watching the match, but at times he had to just look around the stadium, hear the noise, feel the tension, to convince himself that he actually was there, and part of it all.

Newcastle didn't start well. Fulham pushed hard for an early breakthrough and the defenders in black and white saw a lot more action than their team-mates up front.

At the hospital, Roz went back to Mr Ives's room. 'What have I missed?'

'Not a lot.'

Roz sat on the edge of his bed. 'How's your leg, Mr Ives?' she said, her eyes fixed on the screen.

'It'll feel a lot better if we come away from here with three points, that's for sure.'

Glen was watching with mixed feelings. He wanted the team to do well, a lot better than they were doing so far, but he wanted Santiago to get his chance as well. He got up from the sofa to fetch himself another beer.

Beer was flowing freely at the King's Head in Santa Monica. Rival fans exchanged good-natured banter as Herman watched, bewildered, wondering if he would get to see his son. By the time the referee blew for half time, the Newcastle supporters knew that their team was fortunate to still be in the match.

In his living room, Glen listened to the half-time analysis as the match commentator sought the views of his summarizer, a former player. 'Newcastle have been on the back foot for most of the first half, Paul, so what do you think Erik Dornhelm is telling them?'

'Keep it tight at the back, and see if they can nick one on the break.'

Familiar football clichés, not rocket science, but accurate all the same. The way Newcastle were playing, the best they could hope for was a breakaway goal.

Glen got up from his chair. 'Just one more beer.'

Fulham were unlucky not to take the lead during the first part of the second period. Twice they went agonizingly close, as Shay Given performed heroics between the posts.

Dornhelm knew he had to change things and ordered two of his subs to get ready to go on.

The ball went out of play and the television camera zoomed in on the Newcastle bench, and Herman got the first glimpse of his son.

But he wasn't coming on; he was still at the back of the dugout as two other subs replaced team-mates who trudged off with that dis-believing look of 'Why me?'

Herman was as disappointed as Glen and Roz

and even old Mr Ives. 'Thought we might get to see your boyfriend. They need someone to shake 'em up.'

The double change did improve things. Newcastle began to see more of the ball and their first clear-cut chance came when a header ricocheted off the woodwork and back into open play.

Newcastle still had the ball, and as it was swung over from out wide, a whole clutch of players went up for the header. There was an accidental but nasty clash of heads and a Newcastle forward went down in a heap.

Blood was flowing from the head wound and both Dornhelm and Braithwaite knew that there was no way their player could carry on.

'Muñez!' shouted Eric Dornhelm.

Santiago didn't respond, he was watching the injured player being led from the pitch.

'Muñez! Warm up!'

Santiago stared: he was going on!

Twenty-two

Herman leaped to his feet as he saw Santiago cross himself and run onto the pitch.

'That's my son!'

Every face in the bar turned towards the proud dad.

'Are you serious?' said one Geordie with a half-finished pint of Newcastle Brown in one hand.

'Yes! That is my son, Santiago Muñez. I am his father, Herman Muñez!'

'Well if he scores, Herman, I'll buy you a pint.'

As Glen finished his third can of beer, he was feeling just as proud as Herman was all those thousands of miles away.

'Quite a day for this young man,' said the

television commentator. 'His first game in the Premiership and his team is desperate for points. Talk about a baptism of fire.'

In the hospital, Roz could barely watch. Her hands were gripping the bedclothes so tightly that they were almost sliding off the bed.

'Hey, I've got to get back in that bed later on,' said Mr Ives, seeing the scrunched-up bedding.

'Sorry,' said Roz. 'Come on, Santi, show them what you can do.'

But showing what he could so was not going to be easy. Santiago was tightly marked and the few touches he got had to be played diagonally or back to his own defenders.

The clock was ticking and on the bench Erik Dornhelm checked his watch. A single point wouldn't be enough.

In the middle of the park, Santiago suddenly robbed a Fulham midfielder. The beaten player made a grab for Santiago's shirt, but was shaken off. Santiago was away out wide. He beat a defender and then cut back inside, closing on the penalty area. His strikers were calling, pointing to where they wanted the ball delivered.

The whole crowd stood up, almost as one.

In Santa Monica, Herman stood up.

In his living room, Glen stood up.

In the hospital, Roz stood up, and so did Mr Ives, against doctor's orders.

Santiago feinted to pass, but then went on, the ball seemingly glued to his feet. He went into the box and the goal beckoned; he pulled back his right foot to shoot and then . . . a crunching tackle sent him crashing to the ground.

There was a moment of stunned silence, and as the Newcastle players turned to protest and the Fulham team looked on in horror, the referee's whistle sounded loud and piercing as he pointed to the penalty spot.

'Yes!' yelled Glen.

'Penalty!' yelled Roz.

'He's not bad, that boyfriend of yours,' said Mr Ives.

In Santa Monica, Herman just stared as the Newcastle supporters in the pub cheered and the Fulham faithful bawled, 'Never a penalty! Never.'

But it was. On the pitch, three Newcastle

players pulled Santiago to his feet, patting his back and ruffling his hair as Gavin Harris collected the ball and placed it on the penalty spot.

'Oh, no,' said Mr Ives to Roz. 'I can't watch if that playboy's taking it.'

But with Alan Shearer nursing a slight thigh strain, Gavin had no intention of letting anyone else near the ball.

Both sets of outfield players gathered at the edge of the box, and the crowd fell silent.

Gavin eyed the ball and then the keeper and then the ball again. He took three short strides, sent the keeper the wrong way and neatly tucked the ball into the opposite corner of the net.

All his previous failings were forgotten, if only temporarily, as he was mobbed by his team-mates and the Newcastle supporters chanted his name.

In the King's Head in Santa Monica, more than half the customers were jubilant, while the others stared into their beer and moaned about injustice.

The big Geordie who had spoken to Herman

earlier got up from his seat and went over to the bar. He wrapped one arm around the beaming Herman. 'You can have that drink, now.'

'It's a little early for me.'

The Geordie squeezed his new mate, almost forcing the breath from him. 'Not in Newcastle it isn't.'

The late goal had taken the sting from Fulham's play. They pressed but seemed to realize that for all their effort, today was just not going to be their day.

It wasn't. The final whistle sounded and the Geordie fans erupted.

Santiago clenched both fists with joy and Gavin ran over and slapped him on the back. 'Well played, mate.'

Santiago didn't want to leave the pitch, it felt so good, but reluctantly he joined the twenty-one others as they trooped off, shaking hands and exchanging a few words with team-mates and opponents.

Dornhelm was on the pitch. He went to Santiago as he approached, put an arm around his shoulder and they turned and walked towards the tunnel together. Santiago felt un-believably proud. Praise from his manager at last.

Dornhelm put his head close and spoke quietly. 'What did you notice when you lined up that shot?'

'I noticed the goal,' Santiago replied, confused.

'You should have noticed the two players who were in better positions than you. But you don't pass, you go for glory all the time.'

He walked on, leaving Santiago crestfallen. What did he have to do to please this man?

The lounge was crowded with players from both teams as they enjoyed a post-match drink with girlfriends, celebrity guests and the usual batch of hangers on.

But Santiago no longer felt like celebrating. He was still smarting from Dornhelm's rebuke, even though Gavin was doing his best to console him.

'Just forget about it, man. The gaffer does that to everyone. You did great, everyone saw that. I'll get us a drink.'

He moved off towards the bar, leaving Santiago to his thoughts, which were mixed. The day had been magical, unbelievable, until his manager had ruined it with those few short, stinging words.

As Santiago decided he had to shake it off, just as Gavin said, he felt a tap on one shoulder.

He turned round, and came face to face with David Beckham.

The world's most famous footballer looked as cool and stylish as ever. He was smiling. 'Santiago,' he said.

Santiago's jaw dropped. He tried to speak but the words wouldn't come so he just managed a 'Hey'. Beckham must have been used to the effect his mere presence could have and he went on to save Santiago's blushes. 'Congratulations, you were amazing today.'

Santiago nodded nervously. 'Oh, thanks!' he said at last. 'My whole family are mad Real Madrid fans. My grandma, she loves you.'

'Well, carry on playing like that, you'll be there one day,' Beckham replied.

Santiago smiled, and then Beckham offered his hand and they shook.

'See you around,' Beckham said as he turned to go.

'Nice to meet you,' Santiago responded, still awe-struck.

Beckham went over to where two other immaculately dressed men were waiting. Santiago's eyes widened as he realized they were Beckham's Real Madrid team-mates, Zidane and Raúl.

Gavin returned with the drinks.

'You see who that was?' said Santiago still staring. 'And who he's with?'

'Yeah, they're over here shooting a commercial. *Mucho dinero*, Santi.' He handed Santiago a glass. 'Come on, drink up and we'll get out of here.'

'Where are we going?'

Gavin smiled. 'This is my town, son.'

Twenty-three

The private party was in the vast presidential suite of a hotel in the heart of London. Huge glass doors led to a balcony with panoramic views of the city.

Santiago was finding it all a bit overwhelming, an unreal end to an unreal day. He was tired; all he wanted to do was go back to Newcastle and to Roz. But Gavin was his friend, and Gavin wanted to party. So they were partying, big time.

A lavish buffet, which had remained virtually untouched, was spread across several tables, champagne appeared to have been delivered by the crateload, music was blaring out and most of the females present looked as though they belonged on the catwalk.

Christina was there, but had shared no more than a few words with her boyfriend. Gavin, as always, was in demand. Gavin was everyone's best friend. Gavin was *numero uno*.

Three girls who looked like models and a couple of guys in expensive suits were hanging on his every word as he outlined how the pressure of penalty-taking 'just never got to him'. Santiago hovered uncomfortably nearby, and then chief hanger-on Bluto called from across the room. 'Gavin, over here! You too, Santi!'

Gavin was always happy to indulge his mates, and with Santiago in tow, he followed Bluto into an adjoining bedroom. A huge, oyster-shaped bed, covered with a pink satin quilt, dominated the garishly decorated boudoir.

'Park yourselves on there,' said Bluto.

'What for?'

'I wanna get your photo, a memento of today,' said Bluto, pulling out a digital camera.

Gavin obligingly sat on the bed and Santiago sat next to him. From out of nowhere three girls wearing nothing but underwear – expensive underwear – suddenly appeared and draped themselves over the two footballers.

One perched on Santiago's knees, the second on Gavin's and the third leaped onto the bed and poured champagne over the two players' heads.

The camera flashed, and as Santiago struggled to free himself from the unwanted attentions of the girl on his lap, he saw Christina appear in the doorway. She shook her head, sighed and walked away.

Ten minutes later, Santiago emerged from the bathroom, having towelled himself off as best as he could.

The music was pumping out even more loudly and Gavin, completely unconcerned by the fact that he was still dripping with champagne, was dancing with Bluto. It wasn't a pretty sight, especially when, urged on by his mate Des and other revellers, Bluto started to do a striptease.

Slowly he unbuttoned his shirt, each button getting a louder cheer. By the time the shirt was pulled out from his trousers and his pale, flabby belly flopped into full view, Santiago had seen more than enough. He walked over to the glass doors and stepped out onto the balcony.

Christina was there, staring out towards the lights of the West End. 'Not your kind of party?'

'I never know what to say.'

Christina smiled. 'You don't need to say much to most of the girls in there.'

'But I have a girlfriend. Well, I think I have. I met someone I like a lot.'

'She's a lucky girl.'

The cheers from inside were getting louder; Bluto's performance was obviously going down well.

'And you and Gavin?' said Santiago. 'How did you meet?'

'A party, pretty much like this one. Same sort of people: musos, models, footballers. He's gone a bit crazy since it all happened for him, now he's a superstar.'

The words hit home, and Santiago thought of Roz and the things she had said to him. But he wanted to stick up for his friend. 'Look, he's a good guy. If it wasn't for Gavin I wouldn't be here.'

'I know,' said Christina. 'Basically he's a great guy. I just wish I'd met him when he'd grown up.'

There was a huge round of applause and raucous cheers from inside the suite, suggesting that the Bluto show had reached its inevitable, gruesome conclusion.

Christina leaned forward and kissed Santiago on the cheek. 'I'm leaving. Don't tell him I've gone – not that he'd notice, anyway.'

Twenty-four

The headline screamed: A NIGHT ON THE TOON!

It was splashed across the front page of the *Sun*, plastered above an accompanying photograph: Santiago, drenched in champagne, a girl on his knee, sitting next to another man, whose face was obscured by the girl draped over him.

The brief but graphic report named Santiago, Newcastle United's new wonder kid, but teasingly omitted the other player's name, referring to him only as a famous first-teamer.

Santiago was standing in Erik Dornhelm's office at the training ground and the newspaper was lying on the manager's desk.

'You want to explain this?' said Dornhelm.

'There's nothing to explain. It was just people fooling around at a party and—'

'When you travel with this club you are an ambassador for the club!' said Dornhelm, more loudly than Santiago had ever heard him speak before.

'Mr Dornhelm, it's not my fault someone took a picture.'

It wasn't difficult to work out what had happened. Bluto, Gavin's so-called mate and Saturday night dancing partner, had sold the photograph. He no doubt realized that the good times with Gavin couldn't last for ever and had decided to make a killing while he could.

'It *is* your fault you exposed yourself to this kind of situation,' said Dornhelm. He picked up the newspaper. 'Who's the other player?'

'Excuse me?'

Dornhelm brandished the newspaper under Santiago's nose. 'It says here there are two Newcastle players. Who is the other one?'

Santiago took a deep breath. 'I'm sorry, Mr Dornhelm, I cannot tell you that.'

'You mean you won't tell me.'

Santiago said nothing and Dornhelm hesitated for a moment, then threw the paper onto his desk. 'Get out of here.'

Facing up to Dornhelm had been bad enough, but Santiago was even more worried about what Roz would have to say.

He hurried to the hospital and found her pushing Mr Ives down the corridor in a wheelchair. The cold stare Roz gave Santiago as he approached was not encouraging.

'Roz, I have to explain about that picture.'

'What picture?'

'The one in the *Sun*.'

'I don't read that rag.'

'Then you didn't see it?'

Roz glared at him. 'I've seen it!'

Mr Ives was enjoying the exchange, waiting for his chance to join in. 'I showed her it. I always have the *Sun*.'

'It wasn't how it looked!' said Santiago to Roz. 'What they say, it's not true.'

'Santiago, I don't want to talk about it. I've

got more serious things to worry about. Like your friend Jamie.'

'Jamie? What about Jamie?'

Roz's face changed from a look of anger to one of concern. 'He was injured on Saturday. Badly injured. While you were posing for team line-ups, he was in here.'

Jamie was in a treatment room. There were electrodes wired to his right knee and he looked pale and anxious as Santiago walked in. But his face brightened immediately when he saw his friend. 'Great game on Saturday, mate.'

'Never mind that – what happened?'

'Bad tackle. And I twisted it as I went down. They sent me here for an M.R.I.'

'What does that mean?'

'Magnetic Resonance Imaging,' said Jamie carefully. 'Although players reckon it stands for "Maybe Really Injured".'

Jamie didn't laugh at the joke, and neither did Santiago.

'You'll be fine. They can fix anything these days.'

Jamie looked at the electrodes fixed to his

knee. 'It felt bad when it happened. I could tell.' He forced a smile. 'Might have to give those salsa lessons a miss for a while.'

Santiago stayed with Jamie until he was ordered to leave and then went searching for Roz again. Her shift was almost over.

'What does the doctor say about Jamie?' said Santiago.

'His meniscus is shattered. And there's a tear in the lateral cruciate ligament.'

Santiago frowned. 'Just tell me, Roz. Will he play again?'

'Not if he wants to walk again.'

When Santiago returned to the apartment he found Gavin engrossed in a PlayStation game connected to the plasma TV. Both his hands were wrapped around the controls and his eyes were fixed on the screen.

Santiago's mind was still full of what he had seen and heard at the hospital. He went through to the kitchen to make a drink.

Gavin called to him, without looking away from the TV. 'Thanks for covering for me, mate!'

'What?'

'The photo. Thanks for not telling the boss it was me.'

'So, we're even! I don't owe you no more favours.'

'Nope! No one owes no one any favours.'

Suddenly Santiago was angry. Jamie's career-ending injury; the way Roz had looked at him when he blurted out his excuses for the photograph. The whole sad Gavin Harris lifestyle was put into perspective. Santiago went back into the other room. 'You don't get it, do you? You're screwing up your life. You lost Christina and you sit there playing a stupid game.'

'She'll be back.'

'No she won't! She can't stand what you're doing, or the guys you hang around with. How d'you think that picture got in the paper? Bluto sold it!'

If Gavin was bothered by Santiago's revelation he didn't let it show. He just kept pressing the PlayStation controls and, on screen, his Ferrari took the lead in the Monaco Grand Prix.

Santiago went to the TV and wrenched out the

connecting leads and the TV screen went fuzzy. Gavin stared at him for a moment, but said nothing. Then he threw the game control onto the floor, got up and went into the kitchen.

As Santiago followed, Gavin pulled back the fridge door and found a fresh carton of milk. Santiago watched as he struggled to open the carton.

'You think I'm some beaner who doesn't know stuff? I'm from LA! I know things! I've seen things! Things you've only seen in movies!'

'Why do they make these things so difficult to open?' said Gavin without looking at him.

'Listen to me! These are the best years of our lives, and how many we got, ten if we're lucky? Less, if we get hurt, like Jamie. Don't throw it away, Gavin!'

Gavin finally prised apart the top of the carton, spilling much of the contents onto the worktop in the process. But instead of drinking, he stood and stared directly ahead, as though he was considering everything he had heard. He nodded and then turned to face Santiago. 'You know what? Why don't you piss off?'

He took a long drink and when he looked at Santiago again, a thin stream of milk ran from one corner of his mouth to his chin. 'Go on. Get out.'

Santiago turned and walked away. The front door slammed and Gavin took another drink of milk. He swallowed it slowly but he didn't look happy. There was a sour taste in his mouth.

Twenty-five

Julio had started helping his dad out at weekends and on some nights after school. He didn't like gardening any more than his big brother had, but he liked the few dollars the work brought in.

They didn't talk much when they worked, but then Herman had never been much of a talker. He just got on with the job and expected those around him to do the same.

Julio had been clearing leaves with the blower. It was the job he liked least. You cleared a patch, you collected the leaves, you turned round and there was a whole new crop of leaves. He knew it would happen, but it wound him up every time it did.

Now the day was almost over and the fresh leaves on the driveway were partly hidden by the lengthening shadows cast by the garden trees.

'You can stay,' whispered Julio as he glared at a leaf fluttering from lawn to driveway. He switched off the leaf blower, carried it over to the truck and placed it carefully into the cargo hold. Any damage might be knocked off his wages. 'Hey, Dad, come on! Grandma's gonna have dinner fixed by now!'

Herman had been working across the garden behind a stand of high bushes, finishing off his day by watering the expensive, specially imported plants the house owners particularly cherished. Herman may not have loved his work, but he was good at it, and conscientious.

As Julio stood back from the truck he was surprised to see a steady trickle of water flowing between the driveway and the lawn. Herman didn't like to waste precious water.

'Dad!'

There was still no reply. Julio walked across the lawn to the thick, concealing stand of bushes. He moved to one end and then through to a second, smaller lawn, surrounded by flowerbeds.

The hose was lying on the grass; the water spurting from it had formed a sodden pool. Beyond the hose, with his head and upper body crushing the precious flowers, lay Herman. Perfectly still.

It was a gentle training day. The season had been long and hard, players were feeling the strain and coaches knew from experience when to relax the routines. Particularly with the final match of the season just days away.

A few first-teamers and some of the reserves were playing a loosening game on one of the practice pitches. Even Hughie Magowan was taking it gently, although it went against his nature.

For once, Santiago hadn't joined in, mainly because Gavin was playing and things between them were still strained.

Santiago was alone, jogging around the perimeter track. He didn't feel great. Not only was he hardly speaking to Gavin, but he also still hadn't made it up with Roz. As he turned towards the main building he saw a figure he recognized. Glen.

Santiago increased his pace. At last, a smiling face.

Glen wasn't smiling when Santiago reached him.

'Hey, Glen. I meant to come over and explain about that thing in the paper.'

Glen shook his head, and Santiago sensed that he was here for a very different reason. 'What is it?'

'Santi, I had a call from LA. You need to talk to your grandmother.'

On the practice pitch, the game stopped as the players saw Glen wrap an arm around Santiago's shoulders and lead him off towards the main building.

'Something up?' said Hughie to Gavin.

Gavin shrugged. 'Dunno.'

The game restarted, but after a couple of minutes Gavin stopped running with the ball at his feet. 'I'm gonna find out.'

He hadn't been feeling particularly proud of himself since his outburst in the kitchen. But apologies didn't come easily with an ego like Gavin's. He walked off the pitch and Hughie followed.

'I thought you didn't like him,' said Gavin.

'I've got used to him.'

Glen was standing in the corridor, outside one of the offices. Through the glass window he could see Santiago speaking on the phone. And he could see the tears in his eyes. He looked away as he heard studded boots on the tiled floor and saw Hughie and Gavin approaching.

'What's happened?' said Hughie.

'It's his father. Heart attack apparently.'

'Is he gonna be all right?' said Gavin.

Glen sighed. 'He's dead.'

Maybe it was the news from America, maybe it was his conscience, maybe he felt that somehow and in some way he'd feel better for getting it off his chest, but something made Gavin go up to Erik Dornhelm as he stepped from his BMW.

'Can I have a word, guv?'

Dornhelm closed the car door and waited for Gavin to continue.

'I was the other bloke in the picture.'

He knew he was telling Dornhelm nothing he didn't already know, or at least strongly suspected, and the manager's straight-faced reply confirmed that. 'I'm shocked.'

'And it was me who dragged Santi to the party. He didn't want to go, it's not his scene. He's got a good head on his shoulders.'

'Why are you telling me this now?'

Gavin still wasn't quite sure. 'I . . . I just wanted to set things straight.'

Dornhelm looked over to a distant training pitch where a group of youth players and apprentices were playing. 'These things happen. Girls, fights, parties. Every time I tell myself, they are boys. Boys with big bank accounts, but still boys. But this is not an excuse for you any more. How old are you?'

Like a Hughie Magowan tackle, the reply was a little late in arriving. 'Twenty-eight.'

Dornhelm raised his eyebrows. 'Twenty-nine, I think.'

'Yeah, well, around there somewhere.'

Over on the practice pitch, someone had

scored, and Dornhelm could see the same sort of exaggerated goal celebrations that kids see on their television screen every time they sit down to watch a match. 'The young players should be looking to you for an example, off the field as well as on it.'

'I hear what you're saying, boss. And you're not the first person to say it.'

Dornhelm nodded, apparently pleased that Gavin had shown enough bottle to make his confession and maybe even think about changing his ways. He was about to walk off when Gavin came up with his parting shot.

'By the way, we were stitched up – that whole photo thing was staged. People like me are always being victimized. It's diabolical, and if I—'

Dornhelm sighed, shook his head and walked away.

'What?' said Gavin.

Twenty-six

There wasn't time for a long goodbye, and neither of them could think of the appropriate words anyway.

The club had arranged the flight tickets quickly and without fuss, and Glen drove Santiago to Newcastle airport.

They parked the car and Glen waited while Santiago checked in. Then they walked to the departures lounge.

'This is it then,' said Glen, knowing that his words sounded hollow and superfluous.

'Yes,' said Santiago quietly. He'd felt numbed since the news of his father's death. Numbed, and helpless, and guilty, and angry, and overwhelmingly sad. For his father, for his grandmother and brother, and for himself.

Of all the ways it could have ended for him in England, it was ending like this. All he could do now was go home.

'Say hello to your . . . I mean, give my best to . . .' Glen was still struggling for words. 'Just tell them I'm thinking of them.'

'Thank you, Glen. For everything,' said Santiago and he threw his arms around the man who had shown more interest and belief in his dreams than his own father ever had.

They embraced for a long moment and then Santiago turned and walked through to departures without looking back.

Glen watched until Santiago had disappeared from view. Only then did he wipe away the tears that were running down both cheeks.

Santiago sat in the departures lounge, unaware of everything that was going on around him, thinking of his father. The put-downs, the rebukes, the stubborn refusal to believe that his son could ever amount to anything more than a hired gardener.

It had always been that way, for as long as he could remember.

His thoughts went back to that long ago night when they had fled Mexico. He saw the blazing searchlights again, cutting through the night. He saw his family, and the others, running from the border guards, up the incline towards the gaping hole in the high border fence.

He saw himself reaching the fence, bending to go through the gap, and the moment his precious, precious football slipped from his hands and went bouncing away downhill. He saw himself turning to chase after it and his father grabbing one arm.

'Forget it, it's only a stupid ball.'

'Only a stupid ball,' whispered Santiago. 'Only a stupid ball.'

'Sir? Sir, we're boarding now?'

Santiago looked up and saw a uniformed flight attendant staring at him. He had missed the flight announcement and the lounge area around his departure gate was empty.

'You need to hurry, sir.'

Santiago grabbed his bag and stood up. He

handed the attendant his boarding pass and started walking. Not towards the departure gate, but away from it.

Alan Shearer and Nicky Butt must have taken thousands of free kicks during their professional careers, but they still practised them. Looking to bend the ball, power it, curl it, using instep or outside of the foot. There was always something to practise, develop, refine.

They were working together, watching each other, offering advice and comments. Nearby, Dornhelm and Mal Braithwaite were working with other members of the first-team squad, running through set-piece moves.

Dornhelm saw Santiago first; he just happened to turn in the direction of the changing rooms. He was jogging towards them, kitted out in full training gear.

Dornhelm watched and waited until Santiago came to a standstill in front of him, like a raw recruit reporting for duty.

'What are you doing here?'

There was a new sense of purpose about the

young Mexican's reply. 'I was sitting in the airport, OK? And I think to myself, now I got an excuse, a reason to give my buddies why things didn't work out. "Hey, my dad died, I had to come home to take care of business."'

The set plays had stopped, Shearer and Butt had stopped, and everyone was listening.

Santiago stared hard at Dornhelm. 'You know why I needed an excuse?'

'No, I don't know,' said Dornhelm.

'Because that's the way my father made me think. He wanted to take away my self-belief, make it impossible for me to have . . . *aspiraciónes* . . . you understand that?'

Dornhelm nodded. 'I understand.'

'But I don't need an excuse! The only person who can tell me I'm not good enough is you! And then I might not believe you! *¿Entiende?*'

'Oh, yes,' said Dornhelm. 'I understand.'

'I wish I could talk to him like that,' said Gavin to his smiling team-mates.

They watched as Santiago walked past them and over to where Shearer and Butt were standing with half a dozen footballs. Without waiting to be invited, Santiago broke into a run and curled the first sweetly into one corner of the net.

He walked back and hit the second into the opposite corner. Then the third, the fourth, and the fifth were dispatched with equal panache. No one said a word; they just watched. Finally, Santiago lined up for the sixth ball and struck it as hard as he had ever hit a ball into the roof of the net.

He turned around, his eyes ablaze, challenging Braithwaite or Dornhelm to complain. When they didn't, he stared from Butt to Shearer.

'Very good,' said Shearer with a smile. 'Now fetch 'em back, will you?'

'You do understand, Grandmother?' said Santiago in Spanish into the telephone.

'Of course I understand, Santi, there is no point in coming back,' Mercedes replied. 'What's done is done; it's God's will. Your father was too stubborn to say it, but I know he was proud of you. We all are.'

Santiago wasn't going to argue with his

grandmother about the pride his father had felt for his footballing son. He had his views, she had hers, and it was best left at that. 'I love you, Grandmother,' he said.

'I love you, Santi.'

Santiago put down the phone. He was back at Glen's house. He was happy to be there and Glen was happy to have him there.

He had tactfully gone outside while Santiago made the difficult phone call to Mercedes. But it had not been half as difficult as Santiago had imagined. She was completely understanding of her grandson's reasoning and decision, just as she always had been.

Santiago wanted to tell Glen about the conversation and thought he was coming back in as he heard the door open. It was Roz.

'Glen let me in,' she said.

'Where is he?'

'Gone for a little walk. Can I stay? I'll go if you want.'

'No. No, please stay.'

Roz smiled and stepped further into the room. She spotted the alcove with Glen's footballing memorabilia and photographs. 'Reminds me of my place.'

It was Santiago's turn to smile. 'That's what I thought when I came to your house.'

They fell into an awkward silence for a few moments, and Santiago gestured for Roz to sit on the sofa. He sat next to her.

'I thought you were mad with me. About the photograph in the paper.'

'It doesn't seem important now.' She looked at him. 'How are you feeling?'

'OK. I think. The worse thing is, I never made my peace with my father.'

'He never made his peace with you, Santi.'

Santiago thought about his father, seeing him as he had seen him so many times for so many years. Working, toiling in gardens, at roadsides, on scrub ground. Digging, raking, shifting leaves, cutting grass.

'I walked out on him; he never forgave me.'

'You don't know that. All those pictures you sent home. Maybe he had one in his wallet.'

The sky outside was darkening. Cold winds, heavy grey clouds, biting cold and piercing rain were no longer strange or unfamiliar to Santiago. 'Home,' he said. 'I'm not sure where my home is any more.'

'I do,' said Roz. 'It's green, and it has goal-posts at each end.'

Twenty-seven

The end of the season was in sight. One game remained. One game, which would determine the following season, and perhaps many seasons to come for Newcastle United. Champions League football wasn't just important, it was vital.

In the media room at the training ground, Dornhelm was talking tactics with the first-team squad as they watched videos of earlier games on a large plasma television screen.

Dornhelm froze the picture and pressed the REWIND button on the remote control. He froze the action again on a moment from the Fulham game and pointed to the screen.

'What were we thinking here? Who is picking

up Malbranque? And who is covering Boa Morte, there?' He turned and nodded at two of his defenders. 'You two, you're too close; you're not married, you know.'

Some of the squad chuckled while the two defenders squirmed in their chairs.

Dornhelm switched off the video and the TV. 'We've had some good results, but everything rests on this last game.'

'And it's only Liverpool,' said a voice from the back.

'That's right, Liverpool. And if you leave them this amount of space you may as well pack your vacation bags now. Go and play golf in Marbella; don't bother turning up for the match.'

Everyone knew he was right. They had shown only glimpses of the football they knew they were capable of for much of the season. But the season wasn't over until the final whistle blew.

'Question, boss?' said Alan Shearer.

'Alan?'

'Where's Santiago?'

'He lost a father. You saw how emotional he was. He needs time to heal.'

'He'd heal a lot quicker if he was in the squad.'

'That's right,' said Gavin Harris. 'And we could use some of his salsa moves if we're gonna crack Liverpool.'

The players were not the only ones clamouring for Santiago's inclusion in the squad.

Since his performance in the Fulham match he had been the talk of Tyneside. In pubs and clubs, cafés and bars, the name Muñez was mentioned time and time again. He even had a record dedicated to him on local radio.

Newspaper opinions were mixed. Some columnists urged Dornhelm to pick the new whiz kid, while others were in favour of a more cautious approach, fearing that Muñez might be a one-match wonder. With so much riding on the outcome, they wrote, throwing the boy into the St James' Park cauldron would be too much of a risk.

Everyone had an opinion, particularly at St James' Park. From cleaner to car park attendant, from doormen to directors, everyone was convinced that they knew the secret to success on Saturday.

Dornhelm heard the voices, read the newspapers and wisely kept his own counsel. Only one person would be selecting the squad for the last match of the season. That person was Erik Dornhelm.

Three days before the match he was working in his office at the stadium when he got a call from the head groundsman. His presence was required – urgently.

He walked from his office, took one of the escalators down to ground level and went through a service tunnel leading into the footballing arena.

Far away to his right, a lone figure was on the pitch, practising free kicks, sending ball after ball into the net. Dornhelm shook his head and stepped onto the turf.

Santiago stopped practising and waited as Dornhelm walked up to him. 'How you doing?'

'OK, boss.'

Dornhelm waited for a moment before

continuing. 'It's a tough thing to lose a father. I remember when I lost mine.'

'Thank you, boss.'

'You shouldn't be here,' said Dornhelm, looking at the scuff marks in the grass. 'The groundsman is having a fit. His turf is sacred.'

'I'm sorry. I just wanted to see what it felt like to be on this pitch.'

Dornhelm stepped over to the ball Santiago had placed for his next free kick and picked it up. 'It's better when there are fifty-two thousand people watching. You'll see what I mean on Saturday.'

Santiago nodded, and then he realized exactly what Dornhelm was saying.

'We're counting on you,' said Dornhelm. 'Now, get off the grass!'

At Foy Motors, work always slowed down as match day drew near. There was so much to talk over. Team selection. Tactics. Formations. They all had to be discussed and debated and decisions had to be made.

Glen could hardly complain; he encouraged it.

And he was as fair in football as he was in everything else. He never claimed that he knew best, that he'd been in football for most of his life, that *he* was the professional. He listened, argued, reasoned, just like one of the lads. Because at heart, he *was* one of the lads. Maybe that was why he'd never made it to the top in football management. Or maybe it was just bad luck.

Foy Motors workforce and management had enjoyed their extended lunchtime discussion and had reluctantly, and not at Glen's prompting, returned to work. Glen was in his office and the others had their heads beneath the bonnets of various vehicles when Santiago arrived. No one noticed, but Santiago was prepared for that. He went to an oil drum, lifted his arms and pounded out a bongo-like beat with both hands.

Somewhere, someone switched off the radio. Glen emerged from the office and Foghorn, Phil and Walter appeared, as if by magic, wiping their hands on bits of oily rag.

'What's going on?' said Glen as he saw Santiago.

Santiago grinned. 'I wanted you to be the first to know.'

'Know what?'

'I'm in the squad for the Liverpool game!'

Glen clenched both his fists. 'Yes!' He rushed over to Santiago and threw his arms around him.

'I told you!' boomed Foghorn, looking at Phil. 'Didn't I tell you?' He turned back to Santiago. 'First day we saw you, I said to Phil, that lad's got it. Didn't I, Phil?'

'No.'

'I bloody did! Didn't I, Walter?'

'No.'

'I bloody did!'

'You said he had no chance.' Walter winked at Santiago. 'Mind, he's always wrong. Good on you, lad.'

Glen could hardly contain his joy; he hadn't felt this good since he had been pulling on the black-and-white shirt himself. 'This calls for a celebration. Clubs, birds, booze!'

'What?' said Santiago and Foghorn together.

Glen laughed. 'I'm joking! It's Blockbuster,

shepherd's pie and an early night for you, lad,' he said to Santiago.

Glen's reputation as a chef was well known. 'If I were you, Santiago, I'd skip the shepherd's pie,' said Foghorn.

Twenty-eight

Match day. Newcastle. The city a sea of black and white. From early morning, the tension and excitement grows. Banners hang over pub doorways, advertising the second-best alternative for those many thousands without season tickets: THE MATCH. HERE. LIVE.

There's no need to say which match; there *is* only one match for the Newcastle faithful.

The streets are clogged with traffic and pedestrians, all heading in one direction, to St James' Park.

Santiago arrived early, to drink in the atmosphere. This time, when he walked through the underground tunnel beneath the stadium, he could legitimately step through the double glass doors reserved for players and officials only.

The doorman held back a door and smiled. 'All the best, Santi.'

Santiago nodded his thanks and walked on through another set of doors. This was it, the surprisingly small area of the vast stadium reserved exclusively for the actual business of preparing for the game.

Everywhere else there were offices, hospitality suites, media rooms, function rooms, corporate rooms, lifts and escalators – long, seemingly endless corridors that snaked from one side of the stadium to the other.

But this part was different; this was the players' domain. Directly ahead of Santiago was the white-tiled tunnel leading out to the pitch. Halfway along the Astroturf-floored tunnel, some steps dropped down, and on the wall above were the words: HOWAY THE LADS.

To Santiago's immediate right was the match officials' dressing room, and further to his right, the visitors' dressing room.

Santiago turned to his left, into the home team's dressing room. It was clinically clean. White tiles from floor to ceiling, light wooden pegs for hanging clothes, and benches of the same light wood. On the benches, perfectly spaced, was each player's kit. Shorts, socks, neatly folded shirts. Santiago saw his own shirt. He couldn't touch it. Not yet.

A single treatment table was in the centre of the changing area, and at one end a flip chart sat on a stand, waiting for the manager to turn any half-time tactical thoughts into artwork.

Through an archway were the showers and individual baths. Santiago smiled, thinking of the old photos he'd seen of footballers splashing about in huge communal baths.

The dressing-room door opened and Mal Braithwaite walked in.

'Blimey, lad, you're early.'

But the time moved swiftly. Supporters bought their programmes and squeezed through turnstiles. Those hovering outside jeered good-naturedly as they watched the Liverpool team coach bus, with its smoked windows, glide into the stadium access road.

Guests were arriving in the private boxes and hospitality suites.

In one of the boxes, Barry Rankin was enjoying a drink with a couple of local businessmen and their wives when the door opened and Glen walked in with Roz and her mum, Carol.

Barry feigned surprise. 'Private box, Glen? You must know one of the players.'

Glen just ignored the remark. Carol had dressed for the occasion, this was just like old times. She was wearing a fake fur coat, which she took off to reveal a figure-hugging top and a leopard-print mini skirt.

She helped herself to a glass of wine and smiled at Glen. 'This is the life. Reminds me of when Roz's dad was famous. They played stadiums like this. I'd be backstage with a Jack Daniels and a—'

'Mum!' said Roz quickly. 'No stories, eh? Not today.'

Carol shrugged and turned back to Glen. 'So, Glen, you're single then?

Glen reached for a drink of his own. 'Aye, lass, and with every intention of staying that way. Got a son, though, and a daughter.'

Glen's daughter, Val, was at that moment walking into the King's Head pub in Santa Monica with Santiago's grandmother, Mercedes, and his brother, Julio.

The pub was if anything even more crowded than it had been for the previous Newcastle match, but this time, the place was more evenly divided between those wearing black and white and those in the red of Liverpool.

It was noisy, hot and heaving with unfamiliar-sounding voices exchanging jibes and predictions.

Val edged Mercedes towards one of the televisions, and as they moved closer Julio tugged at his grandmother's arm and nodded up at the screen. Santiago's name was there, listed amongst the Newcastle substitutes.

'Substitutes?' said Mercedes. 'But he must play.'

Julio grinned. 'Of course he'll play.'

But there were no guarantees. Erik Dornhelm

had given his final pre-match pep talk and his players were about to take to the pitch. They were standing in the tunnel, nervous and edgy, ready to go out. Santiago was at the back, still tracksuited. There was little banter, few words were exchanged; everyone knew what was at stake.

Suddenly they were moving forward, and as they passed beneath the *HOWAY THE LADS* legend, several of the Newcastle players reached up and touched the special words. Santiago did, too. He had to; there might never be another chance.

The sound of fifty-two thousand cheering voices was almost overwhelming as they moved onto the field.

Santiago took his place in one of the airline-style heated seats at the back of the dugout and saw Jamie Drew, Hughie Magowan, Bobby Redfern and most of the reserve-team players sitting a few rows back. Jamie grinned and gave his friend the thumbs-up sign.

Up in the private box, Carol had reluctantly abandoned her wine glass and put on her coat and followed the other invited guests out through the doors to their comfortable seats.

As she settled herself between Glen and Roz she looked down at the two teams lining up far below. 'Oh, I'm a great football fan,' she said to Glen. 'Who is it we're playing?'

And then the whistle blew, and the match began.

Twenty-nine

Gordon, the taxi driver, was racing his cab through the almost deserted city streets. He had to get somewhere fast.

As he neared his destination, the taxi radio crackled into action. 'Gordon, got an airport pick-up for you.'

Gordon flicked a switch. 'Can't, Tommy, no way. I'm running an old lady to the artificial limb centre. She's having a new leg fitted, so I might have to wait quite a while.'

He flicked the switch and pulled the cab to a standstill. Then he jumped from his empty vehicle, locked the door and ran across the road into the pub.

It was packed, but Gordon had a seat and a pint waiting for him close to the TV screen. Gordon was good mates with both Foghorn and Phil of Foy Motors. He edged his way through the tightly crammed bodies and the clouds of blue cigarette smoke and threw himself down on his chair.

He picked up his pint. 'How's it going?'

'We've made all the early running,' said Phil.

Gordon took his first sip. 'How long we been playing?'

'A minute,' said Foghorn.

The early exchanges were hard fought and fiercely contested. For all the overseas players in both teams' ranks, this was an old-fashioned English-style, blood-and-thunder battle, like a one-off cup tie.

It was end-to-end stuff. Crunching tackles were going in on both sides, and before too long the referee reached for his yellow card and the first name went into the book.

Kieron Dyer was the unfortunate player. It could have been any one of a number of others, but the ref was making it clear that he would stand no nonsense.

Newcastle were pressing and Gavin Harris seemed to have lifted his game and was putting in his best performance in a Newcastle shirt. But as a move broke down up front, Liverpool counterattacked with their typical speed and precision.

The ball dropped for Harry Kewell on the edge of the box. He whipped in a shot which Shay Given did well to push out. As the crowd breathed a collective sigh of relief, Steven Gerrard came steaming in for an easy tap-in.

The stadium went deathly quiet, save for a small section high up away to the left of the dugouts, where Liverpool's travelling band of Kopites were as delirious as their idols down on the pitch.

Up in the private box, Glen put his head in his hands, Barry chatted on his mobile and Carol looked forward to another glass of wine at half time.

In the King's Head, Santa Monica, half the customers were up on their feet celebrating while the other half exchanged anxious looks with each other as they sipped their Newcastle Brown.

Mercedes turned to Julio. 'They need Santiago. Why doesn't he bring him on?'

In the pub in Newcastle, Foghorn's voice boomed out louder than anyone's. 'He should put Glen's lad on. I've always said he's good, haven't I, Phil?'

'Shut up, Foghorn,' said Phil, finishing his beer. 'And it's your round.'

The remainder of the first half was played out at the same frenetic pace, and as the referee brought proceedings to a conclusion, Foghorn finally stood up to get the round in.

The television commentators and experts were ready with their first-half analysis.

'Most of the real chances have been made by Liverpool, but Gerrard's goal is the one that separates the two teams at half time.'

'Talk about stating the bloody obvious,' said Foghorn as he moved off with three empty pint glasses.

In the Newcastle dressing room, the atmosphere was subdued as the players and subs listened to their manager calmly and coolly explaining what he wanted and expected from them in the second half.

'You did a lot of things right, and I don't want to see any heads dropping.'

He turned to their right back, Stephen Carr. 'You're giving Kewell too much room on the flank, and we have to cut their flow off in the middle of the park.'

Carr nodded and Dornhelm switched his attention to Kieron Dyer.

'Kieron, I can't risk you getting another card.' He looked at Santiago. 'Santiago, you're on.'

Thirty

'He's put him on!' yelled Glen, grabbing Roz's arm, as the teams came running out for the second half. 'He's put him on!'

In Santa Monica the substitution came as no surprise to Mercedes. 'At last!' she said, jumping to her feet. 'At last the manager shows some sense. Now we'll see a different team.'

And in the Newcastle city centre pub, Foghorn was just returning from the bar with two fresh pints and an orange juice for Gordon the taxi driver.

'Yeah, we know,' said Phil before Foghorn had a chance to speak. 'You told us.'

'Well, I did,' said Foghorn, settling down into his chair.

On the pitch, Santiago was adjusting to the incredible volume of sound sweeping down from the Toon Army banked around the towering stadium. Fulham had been one thing, but this was different – totally, incredibly different. Santiago's legs felt weak; his heart was pumping as he looked across to his left and saw Gavin Harris giving him a thumbs up and a smile of encouragement.

Santiago knew he would feel better once the whistle sounded and he could just play, do what he had always dreamed of doing in the type of arena he had dreamed of playing in. But the seconds passed agonizingly slowly as the referee checked his watch and looked across to his two assistants to ensure that they were ready to resume.

In those few brief seconds, Santiago relived his amazing journey of the past years and months. The boy juggling a football outside the Mexican tenement, the young man shoving cardboard shin pads into his socks and dominating

Americanitos games, Glen Foy waiting to speak to him by the battered old bus, his grandmother spilling his travel tickets onto the table top, and now this. Now this.

The whistle sounded and the crowd roared.

Santiago was not out of place, not for a moment. This was where he was born to be, where he truly came alive. He quickly found the pace of the game and adjusted to the tempo, and in his early touches, speed and agility caused problems for the Liverpool defence.

He was unknown to them; they had never played against him before, unlike the other Newcastle players whose particular special tricks and feints they could at least attempt to read or anticipate.

From one run out wide, Newcastle won a corner. Santiago ran into the box and jostled for position as Stephen Carr set up the ball for the kick.

A curling in-swinger came over at pace and Alan Shearer rose majestically at the far post to head it back into the heart of the crowded box. Gavin Harris volleyed the ball from six yards, giving the keeper and defender on the line no chance.

The net bulged and the crowd went berserk. Liverpool players went hurtling towards the ref, screaming that they had been pushed or kicked. But the ref turned away and pointed to the centre spot.

One–all.

Santiago was just one of the players mobbing the ecstatic Gavin Harris.

In the private box they were on their feet, in the city centre pub they were on their feet, and in the King's Head, Santa Monica, half the customers were on their feet. The remainder were making exactly the same protests as the Liverpool players had made to the ref a few seconds earlier.

'You see,' said Mercedes to Julio in Santa Monica. 'I said we would be better now.'

'*We*, Grandmother?' said Julio.

'Of course, *we*! We are Newcastle now.'

But the joy of the newly enlarged Toon Army was short lived. The *Blaydon Races* was still ringing around St James' when Liverpool retook the lead. The rows of journalists and radio reporters massed behind the dugouts were working overtime as they scribbled in notepads or yelled out the details to their listeners. This was developing into a classic end-of-season encounter, one that would be talked about for years to come.

Two–one to Liverpool. And now Liverpool, urged on by the hugely competitive Steven Gerrard, looking to put the game beyond Newcastle's reach, began dominating all phases of the play.

Santiago was forced to track back and help out in defence. He slid in a well-timed tackle but conceded a corner in the process.

By the dugout, Erik Dornhelm paced nervously, only retaking his seat when the corner was cleared. But it was still all Liverpool. Pushing, probing, going close with shots and headers.

Santiago was seeing more and more of the ball, though as an emergency defender more than as a creative midfielder. But the more he had the ball, the more his confidence grew. Suddenly he intercepted a Liverpool pass and, for once, found himself in a little space.

This was his chance to break. He set off like a greyhound, going past two defenders before sending a glorious cross-field pass to Nicky Butt on the other side of the pitch.

The crowd roared its approval before the move broke down with a timely defensive back header. As the Liverpool keeper gathered the ball and the Newcastle players trotted back to face up, Alan Shearer mouthed a 'Great ball' to Santiago.

It made him feel even better than he already did. Win or lose, this had to be the game of his life.

As the clock ticked on, the momentum of the match gradually swung in Newcastle's favour. They were playing the ball, capturing the midfield, thanks largely to Gavin Harris and Santiago.

Santiago was everywhere, looking for the ball, winning it, wanting it, demanding like he always had with the *Americanitos*. And he was getting it.

With fifteen minutes to go, the Liverpool defenders were panicked into conceding a free kick ten yards outside the box.

Nicky Butt gathered the ball and placed it a little in front of where the offence had taken place. The referee immediately nudged the ball back to the spot from where he wanted the free kick taken and then paced out the ten yards. The Liverpool players argued, but began forming their wall.

Alan Shearer and Nicky Butt waited, quietly discussing which of them would take the shot.

But on the touchline, Erik Dornhelm beckoned to one of his defenders and exchanged a few quick words. The defender nodded and then jogged over towards the penalty box. As the Liverpool wall settled, jostling the two Newcastle players who had joined their ranks, Santiago joined the cluster around the ball.

The keeper was ready, the wall was ready and the referee was ready. He lifted his whistle to his lips and blew.

Shearer feinted to move but then stopped as Butt closed on the ball and tapped it sideways, into the path of the already moving Santiago.

He took six steps, hit the ball with his right foot and sent it spiralling over the wall. Heads turned as the ball curved to the left; the keeper was already diving, his arm outstretched. But he was beaten and the ball flew into the top left-hand corner of the net.

As noise exploded in his eardrums, Santiago ran towards the goal line. The vision of *The Angel of the North* flashed into his mind and instinctively he flung his arms out on each side and stopped running to receive the applause, the cheers and the adulation. A second angel of the north had announced his arrival.

Thirty-one

'GOOOOAALLLLL!!!!!!' screamed Julio in the King's Head, Santa Monica, doing his own more than passable impersonation of the commentator Andres Cantor and bringing the other Newcastle celebrations to a halt as the Geordie ex-pats turned to look.

'That is my grandson!' yelled Mercedes, pointing at the screen. 'His brother!'

Even the Liverpool supporters were staring now.

'It's true,' shouted Glen's daughter, Val. 'And he's from here!'

'Then you shouldn't be back there,' said one of the Geordies. 'Come up here to the front.'

Chairs were moved aside and bodies shifted as Mercedes, Julio and Val were ushered through to the front row and given the very best seats.

'I met the lad's dad,' said the big Geordie Mercedes found herself sitting next to.

'What? How could you?'

'He was here. In this place, for the Fulham game. He was over the moon about his lad's performance. I bought him a drink.'

Mercedes turned to Julio and Val. 'You hear this?'

'Yes,' said Julio.

'I'm so glad,' said Val.

Mercedes looked up at the television screen. She could hardly see the picture; her eyes were too full of tears.

As Santiago jogged over the halfway line he heard the chant coming from the Gallowgate end. It was his name; they were chanting *his name*.

On the touchline, the fourth official appeared and held up the electronic board. The number 3 was glowing. Three minutes; they had just three minutes to claim a place in the Champions League.

'Come on, lads!' shouted Alan Shearer, turning to his team-mates and clapping his hands. 'Come on!'

Liverpool were not going to give it away. A point at St James' in a crucial match such as this would be a massive achievement. And they might still just nick it. A single point for the draw was of no use to Newcastle – they needed the full three points for a win – and in their efforts to find the winner, they could be vulnerable to a swift counter-attack.

That was exactly what happened. As the Newcastle team pushed up, the ball was lost and Liverpool swept forward. A probing ball arced into the Newcastle half, and as the Toon Army held their collective breath, only an interception by the quick-thinking Stephen Carr averted disaster.

Defence instantly switched to attack and Gavin Harris collected the ball in space. He moved forward, drawing two players towards him, then sent a perfectly weighted pass across the field into Santiago's path.

Santiago took the pass in his stride, and a

sudden burst of acceleration took him past and away from first one, and as he cut inside, two Liverpool players.

The route to goal was opening up. Gavin Harris was steaming towards the box on one side of the pitch as Santiago ran on and on. But the defenders were chasing back, too.

Erik Dornhelm leaped to his feet as he watched Santiago close on the goal. 'Pass,' he said grimly, as memories of the Fulham game and training sessions came flooding back.

Santiago reached the right-hand side of the box and the keeper raced out to narrow the angle and smother any attempted shot on goal.

'Pass,' growled Dornhelm, louder than before. 'Pass!'

Santiago drew back his right foot, looking as though he was going for the shot. But then he sent a perfectly placed ball across to the far post for Gavin to complete the simplest of tap-ins on the run.

And Gavin didn't stop running. Not until he reached the corner flag, where he turned and was instantly smothered by every one of the

Newcastle players, including the jubilant Santiago.

Cheers and screams and yells of delight rang and echoed around the stadium.

On the touchline, Mal Braithwaite was hugging Dornhelm. 'He passed,' muttered Dornhelm happily. 'He passed.'

In the Newcastle city centre pub, Foghorn was hugging everyone he could get his hands on.

In Santa Monica, Mercedes was hugging her younger grandson, as half the pub shouted, 'GOOOOAALLLLL!!!!!!' Amid the yells and celebrations, Val reached into her handbag, pulled out her mobile phone and began punching out a number.

In the private box, Roz was hugging her mother and Glen. And when Glen finally emerged from the scrum, Barry Rankin was leaning across to speak to him. 'We should talk about that lad.'

'Talk about what?'

'Representation. He's got to be careful, Glen, there's a lot of sharks out there.'

Glen smiled. 'Oh, I know that, Barry. That's why Santiago's signed with me.'

'What?'

'That's right, with me. You should remember that, next time you're in a Malibu hot tub.'

Barry Rankin was upstaged even further when, for once, someone else's mobile rather than his own began to ring.

Glen took his phone from his pocket and clamped it to his ear, struggling to hear as cheers continued to rock the stadium. 'Hello? . . . Val? . . . What?'

The game wasn't over yet, though. Manager, head coach, supporters: everyone was counting down the seconds as the final moments of the incredible drama were played out.

'Hold! Hold!' shouted Dornhelm to his players.

'Tight!' screamed Braithwaite. 'Concentrate!'

The final minute seemed to last an hour. Liverpool threw every player forward as Newcastle dragged everyone back into their own half.

But then the referee checked with his two assistants and raised the whistle to his lips.

The traditional two short and one long blasts

on the whistle signalled the end of the match, the end of the season and the longed-for prize of Champions League qualification.

Every Newcastle player on the pitch raised both arms in triumph as management and subs ran onto the pitch.

Santiago heard his own name being chanted as he stared, dazed, at the waving, moving ocean of black and white.

Steven Gerrard and then Sami Hyypia came across to shake his hand and offer their sporting congratulations. Gavin Harris ran over, lifted him off his feet and bear-hugged away most of what little breath remained.

And when he was back on the ground and Gavin had run off to receive the congratulations of his manager, Santiago raised his arms again. He waved. As thousands of voices chanted his name, he turned to every side of the stadium, one after another. And waved.

Thirty-two

Glen had raced from the private box, dashed down an escalator, out of the stadium and back in through the players' and officials' entrance.

The doorman didn't attempt to stop him. No one tried to stop him; no one cared.

He went through the second set of doors into the players' tunnel and squeezed his way through the Liverpool players as they headed for their dressing room.

'Played, lads,' he said as he moved in the opposite direction. And he meant it. It had been an awesome game.

He burst out of the tunnel and saw Santiago

just a few metres away. He was still waving to the crowd. 'Santi!' shouted Glen. 'Santi!'

Santiago heard the voice and turned. 'Glen!' He ran over, ready to embrace the man who had turned his seemingly impossible dreams into reality.

But before Santiago could throw his arms around his friend, Glen thrust his mobile phone towards him. 'Someone needs to speak to you!'

'What?'

'Take the phone, Santi!'

Santiago grasped the phone in his trembling hand and pushed it to his ear. 'Hello?'

The King's Head in Santa Monica was rocking as the Newcastle Brown flowed, but Mercedes shouted to make certain her grandson heard what she had to say. 'Santiago! We saw the game! Julio and me. Glen's daughter brought us. You were fantastic. And I must tell you something else. About your father.'

'My father?'

As the celebrations went on in St James' and in Santa Monica, Santiago listened to the story his grandmother had to tell. He just nodded as he listened, his heart thumping and tears coming to his eyes. When he tried to speak, his voice caught in his throat. Finally he managed to blurt out, 'Thank you, Grandmother. Goodbye.'

He shut down the phone and handed it back to Glen.

'When I played in the Fulham game, my father saw me. He went to watch me play,' he said softly.

Glen nodded. 'Aye, lad. And I reckon he is probably watching you right now.'

He threw his arms around the young player and then turned him towards the private box high up in the stand and pointed.

Roz was waving. When she saw that Santiago had spotted her, she blew him a kiss.

Fifty thousand Geordie voices were now shouting and singing their praises.

Santiago looked up at the stands and the massed ranks of black and white, and then his eyes turned back to the green of the pitch and the goalposts at either end.

Roz was right.

This was home.

He punched the air in triumph.

**IT BEGAN WITH A DREAM –
NOW THE JOURNEY CONTINUES . . .**

milkshakefilms

GOAL Ⅱ

**OFFICIAL TIE-IN NOVELIZATION
BY ROBERT RIGBY**

CORGI BOOKS

ACKNOWLEDGEMENTS
GOAL II: LIVING THE DREAM

Goal II: Original story by Mike Jefferies & Adrian Butchart

Goal II: Screenplay by Mike Jefferies, Adrian Butchart and
Terry Loane

Producers Mike Jefferies, Matt Barrelle & Mark Huffam

Executive Producers Lawrence Bender, Jeff Abberley,
Julia Blackman & Stuart Ford

Co-Producers Danny Stepper, Jo Burn, Raquel De Los Reyes &
Henning Molfenter

Associate Producers Allen Hopkins, Stevie Hargitay,
Nicolas Gaultier, Steve McManaman & Jonathan Harris

Special Thanks to
FIFA
adidas
Real Madrid
UEFA Champions League
La Liga

One

Santiago effortlessly avoided a lunging tackle and closed on the goal.

The Newcastle faithful, a sea of black and white on all four sides of St James' Park, roared their approval as Santiago brushed off a second challenge.

His eyes lifted for a split second and his brain made the instinctive and instant, computer-like calculation: range, trajectory, power.

And then, with hardly a break in stride, Santiago struck a perfectly weighted and flighted ball past the despairing dive of the keeper into the top corner of the net.

The crowd erupted, joyously celebrating what

was to be voted the Premiership goal of the season as Santiago raised both arms to the sky in acknowledgement of their adulation.

The Geordie roars thundered around the stadium, into the city streets and down to the River Tyne.

And as Santiago stood, arms raised, the echoes of those cheers could be heard across Europe in a darkened room at the very heart of Spain.

A group of men, all expensively suited, were staring intently at Santiago's frozen image on a huge plasma screen.

They spoke softly, almost conspiratorially, in Spanish, as if they were afraid that unwanted listeners might overhear their words.

The electronic shutters on the windows slowly began to open and daylight spilled into the screening room, revealing a desktop cluttered with photographs, sheets of statistics, video cassettes, biographical notes; everything dedicated to the life and football career of one young man: Santiago Muñez.

The man at the centre of the group turned to

one of his colleagues. 'Harris and Muñez played well together at Newcastle – maybe they would be good together here.'

'But they play in the same position now,' came the instant reply.

He nodded towards the plasma screen and within seconds the Muñez show reel was rolling again, cutting to a different match and a bustling run by Santiago which ended in another spectacular goal.

'Exactly,' said the first man.

Santiago had grown to love Newcastle and its people who had adopted him as an honorary Geordie.

It was a long way from his Mexican roots and just as distant from the run-down district of Los Angeles in California where he had grown up and developed his natural skills as a footballer.

He would, almost certainly, have still been playing local league soccer, as they called it back home, had it not been for a chance encounter with Glen Foy.

Glen, an ex-Newcastle player himself and a

one-time scout for the club, was on holiday in LA when he saw Santiago playing in a park match. He knew instantly he was watching someone special, someone blessed with footballing gifts granted to very few.

Against all the odds, Glen arranged a trial with Newcastle for Santiago, and what followed had since become part of the folklore of the famous Tyneside club.

Sometimes, even after a season and a half, it still seemed like a dream to Santiago – a dream come true.

He missed the sunshine of LA and he missed his grandmother, Mercedes, and his younger brother, Julio, but life in Newcastle had incredible compensations: the designer clothes, the top-of-the-range BMW, the beautiful new home.

And then, of course, there was Roz.

Roz was a nurse; they had met soon after Santiago arrived in Newcastle, and little more than a year later, they were planning their wedding.

Life was wonderful. It could hardly get better. Santiago had moved swiftly from park player to St James' Park hero.

The Toon Army knew he was a great, natural goal-scorer, and many of the faithful predicted that some day he would challenge the scoring feats of even the legends, Jackie Milburn and Alan Shearer.

But, of course, that depended on the club being able to hang on to a player now regarded as one of the hottest properties in football.

Two

The BMW drew to a halt in the wide driveway of the new house and Santiago switched off the engine and stepped from the vehicle.

He'd been for a run after training and had enjoyed every minute of it. Pre-season was a time of mixed emotions, the huge anticipation of the campaign that was soon to begin and the frustration of counting off the days until the first Premiership match.

Santiago went into the house, pulled off his sweatshirt, walked past boxes still waiting to be unpacked and decided he would get himself a drink before taking a shower.

As he entered the living room, heading for the

kitchen, he saw Roz sitting on one of the expensive sofas they had recently bought. She was deep in conversation with a smartly dressed young man.

The young man was pointing out something of particular interest in a colour brochure, and on the sofa and the nearby coffee table were various fabric swatches and colour charts.

'Hi,' said Santi as the young man looked up and smiled. Santiago didn't see Roz's frown as he continued on to the kitchen and went to the fridge.

A few minutes later, as Santi downed another mouthful of orange juice, he heard the front door close.

Roz walked into the kitchen and she wasn't looking happy. 'It's ten to five, Santi. The meeting with the wedding planner was at four.'

Santiago's eyes widened as he realized exactly why he was in big trouble. 'Roz, I'm sorry, I lost track of time . . .'

'We're supposed to decide on this stuff together.'

Santiago smiled and shrugged his shoulders,

going for the charm offensive, which usually worked. 'What do I know about the colour of the flowers and the menus? You decide; you're good at that. As long as you show up at the wedding I'll be happy, even if you're only wearing your nurse's uniform.'

Roz shook her head and forced back a smile. She was used to Santiago's tactics. She lifted a hand and went to give him a playful slap but Santi grabbed her wrist and pulled her close.

'You Latin boys are so cheeky,' said Roz, trying to push him away.

But Santiago wasn't giving up. He moved in for a kiss and then stepped back with a look of mock horror. 'You wouldn't leave me at the altar, would you? You are going to turn up?'

'I might,' said Roz, feigning complete in-difference. 'If you're lucky.'

Santiago wrapped both his arms around Roz and drew her closer. But before he could kiss her again, she put both hands on his chest and shoved him away.

'Go and have a shower. You stink.'

Santiago laughed, but instead of going to the

shower, he decided to check out the latest sports news on Sky. He picked up the remote and switched on the TV, where a report on Real Madrid's arrival in Tokyo for their annual pre-season tour had just begun.

The entire first-team squad were making their way through the airport, as fans screamed and cameras flashed. They were all there: Beckham, Ronaldo, Roberto Carlos, Zidane, Casillas, Guti, all the superstars. And in the thick of it all, smiling, waving, loving every moment, was Gavin Harris.

'Look!' yelled Santiago to Roz. 'It's Gavino!'

Roz raised her eyes to the heavens and didn't bother to even glance towards the TV.

But Santiago's eyes were glued to the screen. Gavin Harris was his friend, his buddy, and for a brief while, he had been his team-mate at Newcastle.

Then Real had surprised the football world by swooping for Gavin. It was a major shock; Gavin was a terrific player – there was no doubt about that – but he wasn't getting any younger and he had a well-deserved reputation for enjoying a good time, which many pundits predicted could only shorten his career.

But Gavin had begun well and had scored his fair quota of goals. Then the goals started to dry up. And for a striker, goals were what counted.

Santiago and Roz were seated at the table in the Indian restaurant with Jamie Drew and his girlfriend, Lorraine, and Roz's mum, Carol.

Jamie was Santi's other good mate from his earliest days at Newcastle United. They had played in the reserves together as two hopefuls, but while Santiago's career had soared to dazzling heights, Jamie's had gone in completely the opposite direction.

One bad tackle in a reserve-team match had resulted in a shattered meniscus and a torn cruciate ligament in his right leg. It meant that he would never play professional football again.

But Jamie was a Liverpudlian and a born optimist; he usually managed to look on the bright side of life, and if there was ever a twinge of jealousy at Santiago's success, he never let it show.

Jamie was genuinely delighted that his friend had made it to the big time, and besides, he and Lorraine had their own reasons to be cheerful. Lorraine was eight months pregnant, and as the others studied the restaurant menu, she proudly pulled the latest ultra-sound photograph of the baby from her handbag.

She passed the photograph to Roz, who looked at it and smiled.

Carol was more interested in the wine than in blurry images of unborn babies. 'Time for a toast, I think.' She raised her glass and looked at Santiago and Roz. 'To your new home.'

They drank the toast and then Lorraine turned to Santiago. 'Will your granny be coming over for the wedding?'

'I wouldn't like to be the one who tries to stop her,' smiled Santiago. 'But she's going to need subtitles for Jamie's Best Man speech.'

Jamie ignored the laughter and concentrated on the menu. 'You going for the extra-hot vindaloo again, Santi?'

Santi nodded. 'Sound good to me.'

'Oh, have a bit of consideration, Jamie,' said

Roz. 'I'm the one who has to share a bed with him.'

Santiago and Jamie were still laughing when they saw Glen Foy approaching the table.

'Hey, Glen,' said Roz, indicating a spare chair. 'Good timing, we're just ordering.'

Glen didn't sit down. 'No thanks, I had a late lunch.' He looked at Santiago. 'Can I have a word?'

'Sure, of course. Grab a chair.'

Glen shook his head. 'No, in private.'

The restaurant kitchen was hardly private. Cooks were busy at sizzling pans and steaming pots, and waiters were gliding in and out shouting orders and collecting dishes.

They were all far too busy to pay any attention to Glen and Santiago, who was standing like a rabbit frozen in a car's headlights, his eyes wide with amazement as he tried to take in what Glen had just told him.

'You *are* joking?'

'I wouldn't joke about this, Santi. I've been on the phone for hours.'

Glen had never planned on being a footballers' agent. He ran a garage, specializing in doing up vintage cars, but when Santiago was offered his contract with Newcastle there was no one else he wanted as his representative. So Glen had taken the job, a little reluctantly. He wasn't a natural in the role; most agents were pushy, brash, outgoing, but he wanted the best for his young protégé, so he was giving it his best shot.

'They want to meet, Santi,' he said. 'But we have to keep this quiet, OK?'

Santiago nodded, still dazed at what Glen had told him.

The evening passed in a blur; Santiago hardly tasted the vindaloo. He sat at the table, only half-hearing the conversation about babies and weddings and new homes, wanting to shout out what Glen had told him, but he knew he couldn't say a word.

He broke the news to Roz when they got back to the house. Roz tried to stay calm. She nodded, asked a few questions and then decided that she too needed a few minutes to take in all the implications.

Santiago was sitting on the bed, still in a daze, when Roz emerged from the en-suite bathroom, still brushing her teeth.

'But you're happy here,' she said through a mouthful of toothpaste.

'I couldn't be happier,' answered Santiago.

'And you've got two more years on your contract. You're not leaving Newcastle, the fans will go mad. You're the best player they've got.'

'I haven't been offered anything; it's just a meeting. No commitments.'

Roz shrugged her shoulders. 'OK. So when are they coming to us?'

Santiago smiled broadly. 'They're not.'

Three

Real Madrid: the biggest, the richest, the most glamorous, the most successful football club on the planet.

Nine times European champions, twenty-nine Spanish League titles, twelve Spanish Cups, the UEFA cup twice, the Spanish Super Cup seven times, the Intercontinental Cup three times. The glory list goes on and on.

The club and the players are constantly in the spotlight and constantly in demand all over the world. They were playing Jubilo Iwata in Tokyo in a pre-season friendly as Santiago and Glen took their first breathtaking looks at the Ginza district of the city.

Rain was falling steadily, but the dazzling neon lights illuminated the night, highlighting the chic clubs, the futuristic architecture and the swarming, heaving mass of humanity.

Santiago and Glen were in the back of a limousine which had collected them from the airport and was easing its way through lines of traffic towards the luxury Park Hyatt Hotel. A towering billboard, featuring an immaculately groomed David Beckham shaving with a Gillette razor, stood out amongst the mass of advertisements.

Glen saw Santiago looking nervously up at the billboard and smiled.

'Who knows?' he said.

The limo slid to a standstill outside the hotel where more than a hundred Madrid fans were waiting, beneath umbrellas and with cameras at the ready, for the return of their heroes from the Jubilo match. Most of them had been there for hours and would happily wait for many more just to catch a close-up glimpse of one of *los galácticos*.

As Santi and Glen emerged from the limo,

many of the waiting crowd turned to look, but only a few bothered to snatch a quick photograph.

Santiago and Glen hurried through the rain to the hotel entrance where a smiling, expensively dressed man was waiting. 'Welcome, Mr Muñez, and Mr Foy. My name is Leo Vegaz, player liaison.' He looked up at the teeming rain. 'I personally arranged the weather so you would feel at home.'

They were swiftly checked in to the hotel and shown up to their suites. It had been a long, tiring flight, but Santiago was wide-awake and alive with nervous energy. This was all happening so quickly and suddenly.

He grabbed a quick shower and emerged, wrapped in just a towel. On the huge plasma TV, the highlights of the Real match were being shown. Santiago smiled at the skills being displayed by the *galácticos* as he moved over to a tray of sushi, sitting on a tabletop. It looked good, and Santi realized that he was hungry, but before he could pick up one of the delicate mouthfuls, the room telephone rang.

Santiago hurried across to the phone and picked up the receiver.

It was Glen, and he didn't waste his words. 'They want to see us.'

Santiago could see himself in one of the room's mirrors, naked apart from the towel wrapped around his waist. 'What, *now*?' he said.

Santiago's suite was cool but the presidential suite was something else. The décor and furnishings were black, ultra-modern and minimalist, and the two-metre floor-to-ceiling windows gave a panoramic view of Tokyo.

Leo Vegaz had escorted Santiago and Glen into the suite where one man was standing by the windows, looking out over the city. He turned as he heard the door to the room open and walked towards Santi with his hand outstretched. 'Rudi Van Der Merwe,' he said. 'I'm the club coach.'

'Yes, I know,' said Santi as they shook. 'Pleased to meet you.'

Glen held out his own right hand to the Madrid coach. 'Mr Van Der Merwe, it's a pleasure. I'm honoured to shake your hand, sir.'

Van Der Merwe nodded modestly and then looked at Santi. 'You've come a long way at short notice. Do you think you're ready for Real Madrid, Muñez?'

Santiago had no chance to reply. The door opened and two men entered. One was instantly recognizable to almost anyone in the world of football. It was Florentino Pérez, the President of the world's most famous club.

Leo Vegaz was ready to make the introductions. 'Gentlemen,' he said to Santi and Glen, 'may I introduce our President, Señor Pérez, and the club's director of football, Señor Burruchaga.'

'Thank you for coming,' said Pérez, looking directly at Santi.

Glen was determined to make all the right noises and to extend the correct courtesies. 'We're very happy to be here. Thanks for bring-ing us over.'

Pérez nodded to Glen, but he was very obviously focused on the player. 'How was your trip over, Santiago?' he asked in Spanish.

'Fine, thanks,' replied Santi, also in Spanish. 'It's great to be here.'

Leo Vegaz gestured to the comfortable-looking sofas grouped around a low coffee table and all six men sat down.

The introductions were over and Burruchaga was ready to get down to business. 'We've been watching you play,' he said to Santi. 'You had an impressive last season.'

Santiago shrugged. 'I'm just part of a great team.'

Señor Pérez nodded, identifying immediately with Santiago's words about being part of a great team. 'Real Madrid is unique in the word of football. We demand total dedication. We pride ourselves on being the ultimate exponents of the beautiful game. We want to offer our followers the ultimate football experience.'

Santiago listened intently to every word. He knew full well that Señor Pérez would have said the same words many times when talking about his beloved club, but that didn't make the sentiments any less impressive.

The six men were weighing each other up, making assessments, particularly Van Der Merwe, but Burruchaga was the one wanting to push the meeting on; as far as he was concerned, discussions over football philosophy could come later.

'With the World Cup next year, many players are on the move,' he said, looking at Santi. 'And we want you, Santiago. We're confident that we can make this work.'

Santiago turned to Glen; it was moving on even faster than he had imagined and there were still so many questions to be answered.

Of course he wanted to play for Real Madrid; who in their right mind wouldn't? But Santiago wanted to *play* football, and the way Michael Owen had spent much of the previous season warming the substitutes' bench had entered his thoughts many times since he had heard of Real's interest.

Owen was one of the best strikers in world football, so where might that leave him? But Santi knew that however good a player, sometimes a transfer just didn't work out. The Real delegation obviously believed he could fit into their system and he had to keep believing in his own ability to play at the highest level. And a day can be a long time in football, and in the destiny of its star players, as Santiago would soon discover.

'We have to act quickly,' said Burruchaga. 'The transfer window closes at midnight tomorrow.'

The nine-hour time difference between Newcastle and Tokyo was doing nothing to help Santiago communicate with Roz. And not only that, Roz's duties as a nurse meant that she couldn't just leave her mobile switched on to take calls whenever she wanted.

Santi had left texts and voicemail messages but, so far, there had been no response. And he had to make a decision. Almost immediately.

He walked back into the bar of the Park Hyatt Hotel where Glen was sitting staring at two ice-cold beers. Santi shook his head as he sat on the stool. 'I left another message.'

As they reached for their beers, a familiar, friendly voice boomed into their ears and Gavin Harris wrapped one arm around them both. 'All right, ladies?'

Santiago laughed; Gavin almost always made him laugh.

'Gavino!' he said, standing up to hug his old friend.

Gavin turned to Glen and they shook hands and then Gavin gestured to the barman for another beer. 'You'll hate Madrid,' he said to Santi. 'No snow, no rain, no mud. And they all speak Spanish!'

Glen spoke urgently but quietly; all this was meant to be a secret. 'We haven't said yes yet!'

'What are you, mental?' said Gavin, eyeballing Glen's modest suit and speaking loudly enough for almost everyone in the bar to hear. 'With your ten per cent you could splash out a bit. Get yourself a new suit, maybe even a full make-over.'

Glen was used to Gavin's sense of humour. 'Just what I've always dreamed of.'

Santiago took a sip of his beer. 'It's a big decision, Gavino. Roz and I just got this great new house, and—'

'*House!*' said Gavin, interrupting. 'Are you trying to tell me you came halfway round the world for a night of karaoke? No one says "no" to Real Madrid.'

Santiago knew that Gavin was right; even with the fears that he could find himself spending matches on the bench like Owen, it would be crazy to turn down an opportunity like this, an opportunity that would probably never come again. If he rejected Real Madrid now, the club would be unlikely to come knocking at his door for a second time.

He was thinking over Gavin's words as Van Der Merwe and Burruchaga entered the bar and walked over to them.

Van Der Merwe smiled at Santi and Glen and then checked his watch before giving Gavin a look that was loaded with meaning.

'I'm just trying to put him off, boss,' said Gavin, grinning guiltily. 'We've got enough kids on the squad.'

'It is a big decision,' said Van Der Merwe to Santi. 'Very tempting. All that money.'

'I just wish I had more time.'

'Ah, the transfer deadline,' said Burruchaga. 'It helps to focus the mind. In these matters, I have one foolproof tactic. Listen to your heart, then listen to your head. And when you have listened to your heart and your head, do exactly as your wife tells you.'

The old joke raised a few polite laughs, even from Gavin; after all, Burruchaga was Real Madrid's director of football.

But Santiago hardly managed a smile. He still had a life-changing decision to make – and he hadn't yet spoken to Roz.

Four

The newspaper back pages were screaming the headline:

OWEN JOINS NEWCASTLE

Over weeks of speculation, rumour and denials, there had been talk of his moving back to Liverpool, or to Chelsea, or Arsenal, or even to one of the Italian giants, but finally the deal was done and the news was out; after just one season with Real Madrid, Michael Owen was returning to the Premiership with Newcastle United.

It was no great surprise that Owen should

choose to leave Real; a player of his international standing could never be content to spend so much time warming the bench, waiting to make cameo appearances.

And even though his 'goals per minutes on the pitch' ratio had been higher than any striker in *La Liga*, everyone knew that it was only a matter of time before he moved on. But Newcastle was a shock choice, and now the rumour mill was spinning again as the Press, pundits, supporters, and even players wondered what it meant for the other strikers at the club.

The sports journalists and fans were out in force at Newcastle Airport when Santiago and Glen finally made it back from Tokyo. Questions were fired in like bullets as they moved through the crowd towards a waiting car.

'Is it true, Santi?'

'Are you leaving Newcastle?'

'Have you signed for Real?'

Santiago just smiled and stayed silent while Glen did his best to give non-committal answers, trying to say nothing, but in fact, saying everything.

Santiago knew that Roz was back at the house, waiting, and he was anxious to get there so that they could talk things over.

When he stepped from the car and walked towards the house, he was welcomed by two Sky-digital engineers, working from the basket of the hoist on the top of their white van. They were adjusting the satellite dish on the wall of the house as the radio in the van blared out more on the debate over Santi's future now that Michael Owen had arrived.

'Hey, Santi,' shouted one of them as Santiago approached. 'You're not leaving us, are you?'

Santiago said nothing, but as he went into the house and on into the sitting room, he saw immediately that the TV was switched on: yet more coverage on the Michael Owen signing and his 'unveiling' at St James' Park.

The TV pictures showed Owen looking a little bewildered but smiling broadly as he shook hands with manager and club chairman and then proudly held up the famous black and white shirt which already bore his name. And the coverage finally confirmed one of football's worst kept secrets: Santiago was moving in the opposite direction, to Real, on a two-year contract.

The story was everywhere; there was no escaping it.

And there was no escaping Roz's anger as she emerged from the kitchen and gave Santiago no chance to speak. 'How could you do this without talking to me?'

'I had to make a decision,' said Santi. 'I couldn't get through to you.'

Outside, the two satellite dish engineers could hear Roz's raised voice and were hoping that maybe they might learn, first-hand, exactly what happened in Tokyo. One of them lowered the basket a little so that they could peer through the window as Santiago continued with his excuses.

'I tried to call. On your cellphone, here at the house.'

'You could have waited! Asked for more time! I'm your fiancée, for God's sake!'

Roz grabbed her coat. She was due to leave for work and as far as she was concerned there was nothing more to say. She stormed out of the house, slamming the front door and glaring at the two men in the basket as she stomped towards her car.

They smiled sheepishly and watched as Roz drove away.

'That could have gone better,' said one of them as he began to raise the basket again.

Santiago waited until the evening before going to see Roz at the hospital. She was on the late shift and Santi reckoned that if he left arriving at the ward until late, they might be able to talk because most of the patients would have been settled down for the night.

He was right. He entered the ward and saw the other duty nurse, who recognized Santi instantly and nodded to a small side ward. 'She's in there.'

Santiago gently pushed open the door and looked through. Roz was checking the pulse of an elderly patient called Mr Ives. He was a regular in the ward, with a long-term medical condition that needed frequent monitoring. And he knew Santiago well.

'Oh, here he is,' he said as Santiago stepped nervously into the room. 'The git who's stealing my beautiful Rosalind away from me. You're in the bad books today, son.'

Santiago didn't need telling that, and Roz wasn't making it any easier for him as she kept her eyes on her patient. 'You save your breath, Mr Ives.'

Mr Ives looked at Santiago, waiting for him to continue, mischievously enjoying his obvious discomfort.

'You might think that this is easy for me,' said Santiago.

Roz still wasn't looking at Santi, but Mr Ives was watching him flounder as he searched for the words.

'I love you, Roz, and I want to marry you. None of that changes. But right now, before we have kids, responsibilities, we can go places, do things, just you and me.'

Roz saw Mr Ives's eyes switch to her as he waited for her response. She spoke without turning back to Santi. 'I don't understand what you're asking. Are you saying you want me to come and live with you in Spain? I'm not sure I want to live in Spain, Santi. I love Newcastle.'

'I love it, too. This town has been good to me. If I hadn't come here, I wouldn't have found the most important thing in my life . . . *you*.'

Mr Ives smiled and nodded at Roz. 'He's got a point there, love.'

'But what about our house?' said Roz, almost as if she was asking the question of Mr Ives. 'And the wedding? And my mum, and my job? I've got my exams at Easter.'

'You can come and see me on your days off. I'll fly back when I can. Roz, I can't walk away from this chance. This is my life, and I want you there with me.'

Slowly, Roz turned to look at Santiago. 'But I can't even speak Spanish.'

'I'll teach you,' said Santi with a smile.

Roz was melting. She smiled as Santiago moved closer but was still determined to have the final word. 'I'm not eating paella.'

Santiago laughed out loud and then wrapped his arms around Roz and kissed her.

Mr Ives was smiling, too. As Santiago glanced

in his direction, he beckoned him over to his bedside.

The young footballer let go of his fiancée and went to Mr Ives. 'Do us a favour, lad,' he said almost in a whisper, making Santi lean closer so that he could hear. 'If you see that Gavin Harris fella, tell him he's *shite*!'

Five

A new signing for Real Madrid always sparked more than just interest in the city. It ignited the love, the passion and the obsession for football and for the club felt by the majority of Madrid's people.

The Press conference hastily arranged to mark Santiago's signing was being avidly watched on television screens throughout Spain – but almost everywhere in Madrid.

In hotels and bars, in hospitals and residential homes, in garages and fire stations, even in the city prison, people clustered around TVs to get their first look at the new boy.

Santi had just been presented with his team

shirt and was smiling for the regulation photographs.

'Now that I'm here, I just want to play football,' he said in answer to a reporter's question.

The reporter came straight back. 'Do you think you'll get much first-team action?'

Before Santi could answer, his new coach, Rudi Van Der Merwe, was quick to reply. 'As you all know, at Real we have the best strikers in the world. The competition is fierce. No player wants to sit on the bench and Santiago is no different.'

Roz was sitting at the back of the room and her smile was almost as broad and as proud as Santiago's as he became a Real Madrid player.

But Real is not the only famous football club in Spain's capital city: there is also Atlético de Madrid. And while Atlético has never reached the dazzling heights of its more illustrious neighbour, it still also has its own history, its tradition and its fanatical followers.

In a run-down bar in one of the poorer quarters of the city, where old Atlético pennants and faded match posters decorated the tobacco-stained walls, the Real conference was being watched on an ancient TV set by the few customers nursing their beers.

The regulars watched with a mixture of disdain and envy; Real could afford the players their own club could only ever dream of signing.

There was a close-up shot of Santiago as he expressed his genuine joy at the move. 'I couldn't be happier. Since I was a kid I always dreamed of playing for Real.'

In the bar room, an attractive woman in her mid-forties, who was standing behind the bar, stared at the TV screen as though she had seen a ghost.

One of the customers drained his glass and placed it on the bar top. 'Another beer, please, Rosa.'

The woman did not move, she did not even hear him, she just keep staring at the face on the television screen.

The elderly customer turned away from the bar and looked over to where a man was perched on a stepladder, as he replaced a fluorescent light strip. 'Hey, Miguel,' called the customer, 'your wife is eyeing up the young men again.'

'Rosa-Maria,' snapped the man on the stepladder. 'Another beer for José, please.'

The startled woman reacted as though she had been woken from a dream. But she quickly regained her composure and reached for the empty beer glass, forcing herself not to snatch another look at the television screen.

In one corner of the room, a group of scruffy young teenagers were clustered around a table-football machine, shouting noisily each time a goal was scored.

'Enrique,' called Miguel from his stepladder. 'You done your homework?'

A wiry and unkempt-looking thirteen-year-old glanced up from one end of the table. 'I'll do it later.'

'You'll do it *now*!' said Miguel. The new fluorescent strip was fixed and Miguel stepped down onto the floor. 'And you lot,' he shouted to the other kids. 'Get out! Go home!'

The kids knew better than to argue and they departed with mutters and surly looks as Enrique glared at his father and headed off to begin his homework.

Madrid was going to take a lot of getting used to, for both Santiago and Roz.

The following morning they kissed goodbye on the steps of their hotel on the *Calle de Zurbano* before setting off on their own journeys of discovery.

For Santiago, it was day one of training, his first visit to the incredible new training complex on the edge of the city, and his first meeting with the rest of the squad.

For Roz it was day one of getting to know the city, the place which – if all went to plan – would be her home before too long.

By the time Santiago arrived at the space age training ground, his nervousness had grown to acute anxiety. He stepped from the car and felt a familiar tightness in his chest, which usually meant he needed a hit from his asthma inhaler.

He took the inhaler from his pocket, breathed the chemicals deep into his lungs and immediately felt better. As he slipped the inhaler back into his jacket pocket, he heard the expensive purr of a powerful engine and stopped to watch as a silver Bentley pulled into the parking area.

Gavin Harris was at the wheel, all smiles, all style, radiating success. He got out of the car, took off his sunglasses and grinned at Santiago. Words were not necessary; this really was a different world.

They walked towards the changing rooms together, past a group of young kids who stood peering through the barrier fence. A few of them called out to Gavin and he waved an acknowledgement. Among the watchers was Enrique, the thirteen-year-old from the run-down bar.

Gavin enjoyed describing some of the delights of Spanish living that awaited his friend as they changed for training. But Santiago was hardly listening; he was focused on making a good impression on the coaching staff and his new team-mates once the session got under way.

The sun was beating down as they walked towards the training pitches. Players were beginning gentle warm-ups under the watchful eyes of the coaching staff, including former Liverpool and Real star, Steve McManaman.

Macca, as he was known throughout football, had been a great favourite with the Real supporters, the Madridistas, during his time at the Bernabéu, playing a leading part in two successful European campaigns. When he retired from playing, coach Van Der Merwe had been quick to snap him up as an assistant trainer, deciding that his experience would be invaluable for the present squad.

The *galácticos* were in a group together. Some of the most famous names in football – Raúl, Zidane, Roberto Carlos, Ronaldo and David Beckham – were easing their way into the session, chatting, laughing, supremely confident.

Santiago had briefly met Beckham once before, in a London bar after his Newcastle debut against Fulham. The world's most famous footballer had watched the match during a brief visit to the UK to shoot a commercial, and afterwards he had sought out Santiago to offer his congratulations.

When Santi told him that he was a Real Madrid fan, Beckham had said to him, 'Carry on playing that way and you'll be there one day.'

And now he was. He was a Real Madrid player. It was still hard to believe, but it was true.

He stood back self-consciously, watching Gavin high-five the other players and wondering if Beckham would remember their brief encounter.

Then the England captain turned towards him, smiled his famous smile and held out his hand in welcome. He remembered Santiago perfectly well.

Roz had enjoyed her day. She window-shopped at famous name designer stores, she watched Madrid's beautiful people promenade along wide, tree-lined boulevards in the heart of the city and she even took in some culture with a visit to the Prado Museum where she gazed, awestruck, at paintings she had only ever seen on posters or in the pages of magazines.

But sightseeing is best shared, and by mid-afternoon, feeling a little lonely, she was back in the suite at the Santo Mauro Hotel, flicking through the TV channels, searching for something in English she could watch.

She flicked on to a channel where a documentary on bullfighting was being shown. Roz's eyes widened as a preening matador closed in for the kill on a bloodied bull, which snorted and raked the ground with one hoof as it eyed its approaching assassin. The matador raised his sword and Roz quickly pressed the remote.

She found a shopping channel. They were the same the world over; a beaming, glamorous presenter held up a thin gold necklace as she enthusiastically told her viewers what an absolute bargain it was. Roz couldn't understand a word but she knew exactly what the presenter was saying.

Roz sighed and pressed the remote again. This time it was a cartoon channel, dubbed in Spanish. She was ready to give up when the door opened and Santiago entered carrying a bulging carrier bag.

'Were you training or shopping?' she asked him.

Santiago didn't reply. He took the bag and emptied the contents onto the king-size bed. It was like Christmas had arrived early. Roz gazed at the pile of mobile phones, iPods, designer sunglasses and other assorted items that Santiago had been presented with at the end of his first day at work.

'Why do you need four phones?' asked Roz as she picked up one of the mobiles. 'Can I have one?'

Santiago nodded and then opened a glossy Audi car brochure dedicated to the top-of-the-range model. 'Pick a colour,' he said. 'Any colour.'

Roz raised her eyebrows. 'Santi, you're going to have to score a lot of goals.'

Six

In England, football supporters *go* to football matches. In cities and towns all over the country, they stream from every direction into the stadiums, like lines of ants returning to the nest.

At Real Madrid, the supporters *gather*. For hours before kick-off, the streets and squares around the Santiago Bernabéu stadium gradually fill as fanatical Madridistas congregate to talk, to eat, to drink, to sing, to worship their heroes, to celebrate the spectacle they are waiting to witness.

Almost all the matches are played in the evening. As the night cools, the bars spill their customers onto the streets, souvenir and food sellers do brisk business, music pounds from mobile discos, the air is full of shouts and chants and songs, which grow louder and more passionate as kick-off approaches.

The magnificent Bernabéu towers over the city. The Bernabéu *is* football history. Its museum is one of the most visited in all of Spain. Cabinet upon cabinet line its galleries, displaying the original or the replica of the numerous trophies won by Real. From the twenty-eight regional titles of the earliest days to the European and inter-continental trophies – they are all there, a treasure trove of honour, proudly earned and displayed for the world to see.

There are photographs and TV monitors showing grainy film of the great moments and the great players in the Real story – Di Stéfano, Puskas, Gento and many, many more. The ghosts of the past are a constant reminder to even the *galácticos* of today of what is demanded by the club and by its supporters.

On match nights, the Bernabéu sits, like a modern-day Colosseum, and awaits the arrival of the eighty-five thousand spectators.

Slowly, the heaving mass of humanity moves into the magnificent stadium and the banked tiers fill. On cold nights, massive heaters burn down from the canopy to keep off the winter chill. Floodlights turn the immaculate playing surface a dazzling emerald green. Supporters chat and chant and study the giveaway match programmes as they listen for news of the team line-ups and the arrival of the modern-day gladiators.

But the gladiators of ancient Rome knew nothing of the luxury that is enjoyed by today's superstars as they prepare to enter the arena.

The dressing rooms are magnificent. Marble floors, blue and white tiled walls, individual power showers, spa baths, separate treatment areas, even the gold-finished washbasins look as though they have been specially imported from a millionaire's mansion.

In the 'home' dressing room, the players' personal lockers each have a huge action photograph of the superstar set into the door.

Santiago was struggling to take all this in as he sat next to Ronaldo. The chosen eleven and the substitutes were changed and ready for the coach's pre-match briefing. And although the good-natured banter was flying around the dressing room, just as it does in every dressing room before every match, there was an air of tension. Even the world's greatest players can take nothing for granted; when the whistle blows, they still have to perform.

Santiago had been named as one of the subs; there was no guarantee that he would even get onto the pitch, but he was more nervous than he had ever been in his life. His mobile beeped and he saw that a text message had arrived.

He opened the text and read the words: *Good luck, from Julio and Grandma.*

Santiago smiled. He'd known they wouldn't forget and he knew that they would be watching the match back in LA on the brand-new, wide-screen TV he had bought for them.

As the players around him joked and laughed, Santiago thought of his father, Herman, who for so long had been opposed to his son pursuing a career in football. They had argued fiercely many times, but unknown to Santi, when he made his debut for Newcastle, Herman had been proudly watching on a television at a bar in LA.

Santiago learned about it much later, from his grandmother, but he never got the chance to talk it through with his father. Herman died from a heart attack soon after; father and son were never reconciled.

Rudi Van Der Merwe entered the dressing room and the banter immediately ceased. Van Der Merwe waited for a moment before speaking. 'You only ever lose the battles you don't fight. Make me proud. Play with honour. Play with grace. And heart. But above all, play with dignity.'

That was it. The talking was over. The players stood up, ready for battle to commence. In the Champions League.

Seven

The Champions League; the world's premier club competition. For some clubs, those from the smaller footballing nations, just qualifying for the group stages is a major achievement.

The chance of home and away ties with the likes of Real Madrid, AC Milan or Manchester United is the dream of the footballing minnows from every far-flung corner of the continent.

But for Europe's big guns, qualifying from the group stages is an absolute necessity. Tricky encounters with little-known teams who look on the match as their own European Final are always a potential banana skin waiting to be slipped on. A win is nothing more than is expected; a defeat, and coaches and managers begin to hear the sounds of knives being sharpened.

Santiago was at the rear of the line of players making their way down the granite steps of the players' tunnel and on through the blue protective covering leading to the pitch, but he heard the ear-splitting roar of the crowd long before he stepped into the open.

Thousands of cameras flashed and the white plastic flags which bear the Madrid logo and are freely distributed to supporters before the match were being waved in welcome, making it appear as though the Bernabéu itself was on the move.

High up in the stadium, Roz and Glen were taking their seats in one of the stunning executive boxes. There were four rows of tiered seats for the guests, and television monitors strategically placed for close-up views of the action.

Roz noticed the inquisitive and slightly critical looks cast in her direction by a couple of expensively dressed young women who were presumably the wives or girlfriends of other players. But Roz was too nervous for Santiago to worry, for the moment, about how she measured up.

She turned to Glen. 'Santi'll be bricking it by now.'

Glen nodded. 'He's not the only one.'

In LA, Santiago's grandmother, Mercedes, who was as knowledgeable as anyone on the finer points of football, had invited the neighbours in to watch the match. And not just the next-door neighbours; half the neighbourhood was crammed into the tiny living room of the house, which sat on a hillside, almost in the shadow of the Dodgers' Stadium.

Mercedes and Julio had invited in all their friends, but had made sure they had the best seats in the house.

A graphic showing the teams and subs appeared on the TV, and Julio yelled in delight as he saw the final name in the Real list. 'Look, Grandma. Santiago is one of the subs!'

Mercedes nodded but said nothing; she was only happy when her grandson was *on* the pitch.

In the stadium, Santiago was making his way to the substitutes bench. Before he took his seat he glanced up to the bank of seats reserved for club officials and VIPs. There was even a seat that was always reserved for the King of Spain.

Santiago's eyes settled on the club president, Señor Pérez, and on Burruchaga, the director of football. Everyone was expecting so much from him, if he got his chance.

Away to the left, the infamous group of supporters known as the *Ultra Sur* were well into their familiar chants, drums were beating and white flags and scarves were urging the referee to get the match underway.

And then it was. Real were facing Olympiakos of Greece in their first group match, and from the outset the Madrid team slipped into its silky, stylish rhythm.

Zidane beguiled the opposition with a series of deft touches, Beckham supplied an array of raking cross-field passes, Ronaldo made bustling, probing runs and Gavin Harris, who hadn't scored for fourteen matches, was unfortunate with a couple of half-chances.

Santiago watched every moment, marvelling at the many flashes of brilliance. But for all the dazzling skills, there were no goals in the first half, and the teams left the pitch to regroup and reconsider tactics.

In the dressing room, Santiago sat with the others, listening intently as the coach talked of subtle changes in tactics and urged his players on to greater effort.

The minutes passed swiftly and soon Santi was back on the bench as the second half settled into a similar pattern as the first. Near misses, moments of magic, half-chances.

The clock ticked around to the eightieth minute and the sense of frustration was as acute for the Madrid players as it was for their supporters.

Van Der Merwe looked along the bench and gestured for Santiago to warm up.

Santi felt his heart begin to pound. As he got to his feet he realized that he could hardly stand up, let alone warm up. He forced himself to move and began to jog towards the *Ultra Sur*, keeping his eyes on the action.

From a ball out wide, Gavin Harris had a glorious opportunity to snatch a goal. But with only the keeper to beat from five yards out, he pushed his shot wide of an upright.

The crowd bayed its displeasure and as Santi jogged back towards the bench, the nod from his coach was all that was necessary to tell him to get ready to go on. He stripped off his tracksuit, feeling, almost hearing, his heart thudding in his chest.

Gavin was the man to make way for Santiago. As they met on the touchline, he embraced his friend and Santi ran on to take up his position, to the welcoming roars of the Bernabéu.

There was no more time for nerves; he had to make his mark.

Up in the executive box and out in LA, Santiago's loved ones were praying that the few remaining minutes of the match would be enough for him to at least give a glimpse of his skills.

But at first, nothing happened for him. He made a couple of runs, but the other members of the team were not yet familiar with his style of play.

He was close to the halfway line when he heard his coach shout his name.

Santiago looked over to Van Der Merwe and saw him gesturing for him to drop into the space on the left, just outside the box. Santi nodded and jogged into position.

Real pressed again, desperately searching for a late winner, and from a deflected shot from Ronaldo, they won a corner.

David Beckham hurried to the corner flag and curved in a great ball, but an Olympiakos defender just managed to rise highest to head it away from the danger area.

Santiago was lurking at the edge of the box. He watched the ball as it dropped towards him. There wasn't time to think about passes, or to look for team-mates in better positions; the ball was just asking – crying out – for a first-time volley.

Which was exactly what it got.

Santiago timed his shot perfectly and the ball hurtled at ferocious speed across the box and into the top corner of the net.

The entire stadium seemed to erupt. On the

touchline Van Der Merwe, Steve McManaman, Gavin Harris and the other Madrid substitutes leaped to their feet and punched the air in triumph. Up in their executive box Glen and Roz were hugging each other as the other guests watched. In LA the screams of joy were echoing down the street. And on the pitch Santiago was engulfed by his fellow Madrid players.

When he finally emerged from the scrum, he looked up to the heavens and silently dedicated his goal to his father.

The last few minutes passed agonizingly slowly for Real as Olympiakos pressed for an equalizer, but then the referee's whistle sounded for the last time and Santiago heard his name ringing around the Bernabéu.

Eight

Rosa-Maria found it difficult to hide her emotions as she watched Santiago's post match interview on the TV in the bar.

The regulars were following the interview closely; nodding sagely as Santiago attempted to describe his feelings at the moment he saw the ball crash into the net.

Young Enrique was standing at the back of the bar, watching the watchers. When he was certain that everyone else was focused on the TV, he struck.

A wallet was invitingly perched on one of the tables, temporarily ignored by its owner. Swiftly and skilfully, Enrique snatched it away and then slipped quickly through the rear door of the bar.

Only one person saw what had happened.

Out in the dark alley behind the bar, an older teenager called Tito was waiting for Enrique. He held out his hands as the younger boy approached and snatched the wallet away, pulling out the few notes and then checking to see if there were any credit cards.

Before either of them could speak the back door of the bar swung open again. The older boy glared at his young partner in crime, threw the wallet to the ground and then turned and ran with the cash.

Enrique had no time to follow. Before he could move he was roughly grabbed. He winced as he heard his mother's furious voice. 'Have you lost your mind?'

The teenager tried to struggle free but there was no escaping. Rosa held him firmly by the shoulders, her eyes ablaze. 'You want me to visit you in jail? You make the wrong choice now and there's no going back.'

Enrique stopped struggling and just stared at the ground as his mother spoke more calmly, trying to make him see sense. 'Enrique, don't you realize, this is wrong?'

'Like I have choices,' snapped Enrique.

'But of course you do. That new Real player, Muñez, he had nothing, just like you. And look at him now.'

'Yeah, look at him now,' sneered Enrique. 'He *was* poor and I'm gonna *stay* poor. We got so much in common, right?'

He wrenched himself free and went to walk away.

'Enrique, wait!' shouted Rosa-Maria.

The teenager stopped and looked back. His mother was staring at him, but her eyes were suddenly fearful and uncertain.

'What?' said Enrique. 'What is it?'

Rosa-Maria glanced at the door to the bar, as if she were afraid that someone might come out and overhear what she was about to say. 'Enrique, you must promise not to tell your father,' she said, almost in a whisper, 'but I have a secret that I left in Mexico.'

Paparazzi. A word common to every language;

the gangs of freelance photographers are known the world over. They lurk outside nightclubs or fashionable restaurants, they haunt the homes of the superstars, they wait on beaches, outside hotels and at airports in the hope of snatching a one-off picture that will earn them big money from the tabloid newspapers or glossy magazines.

Sometimes they hunt in packs, on other occasions they operate singly, but the aim is always the same: snatch a celebrity photo that will sell, the more compromising or embarrassing for the victim the better.

The paparazzi were out in force as Gavin, Santi, Glen and Roz stepped from the vehicle outside one of Madrid's most fashionable restaurants. Cameras flashed as their owners jostled for position and shouted for attention.

Roz stayed close to Santiago, blinking at the flashlights and the unwanted, intimidating attention.

A voice nearby shouted out in English. 'Oi, darling, show us a bit of leg!'

Roz turned angrily in the direction of the voice and as she did so, one of her heels caught on the pavement. She tripped and stumbled forward, falling to the ground. It was a perfect paparazzi moment; the night was flooded with white light and the synchronized sound of clicking cameras.

Santi and Glen rushed to help Roz to her feet while Gavin stood back and smiled for the photographers, making sure they got him from his best angle.

Roz was still shaken as they made their way into the restaurant where a beaming maître d' was waiting for them. Gavin reached into a jacket packet and handed over some notes to the maître d' who smiled and gestured for them to follow.

He wasn't leading them to a table. They went straight through the restaurant into the kitchens, past cooks and waiters who nodded their thanks as Gavin handed out more euros, and then out through a door at the back into a narrow, dimly lit passageway.

On the other side was the entrance to another restaurant, smaller, a lot more discreet and totally paparazzi-free. Gavin ushered them in and the restaurant owner welcomed him like an old friend.

The atmosphere was much quieter and a lot more relaxed, but before they could finally enjoy their meal in peace, they had to endure one more photo as the owner added to his collection of pictures of the rich and famous visitors to his establishment.

Glen turned to Gavin. 'Is it like this all the time?'

'It is actually,' answered Gavin. 'They're all mad. Total lunatics.'

'You love it though, don't you?' said Roz as she tried to fix the broken heel of her shoe. 'All this attention.'

'At the end of the day, I'd much rather be out with my friends,' said Gavin with a shrug. 'Having a nice meal, with some good conversation. There's more to life than just football.'

Roz thought back to the time when Gavin and Santiago had shared an apartment in Newcastle. She smiled. 'What, you mean like X-box games?'

Gavin grinned. 'Don't get me wrong, I do love it and it pays the bills. But I've got other interests now.' He reached for a bottle of red wine and poured some into a glass for Roz. 'Like this.'

'Like what?' said Roz as Gavin poured wine for the others.

'Wine. I've made an investment in a tasty little vineyard in France. Could be my future.'

Roz lifted the glass to her mouth and took a sip. She swallowed the wine and then screwed up her nose and grimaced. 'It's corked!'

Gavin's eyes widened. 'Is it?' He grabbed the bottle, took a sniff at the wine and shrugged as if to say, 'Smells all right to me.' He was checking the label when a couple of familiar figures approached. One was Barry Rankin, Gavin's agent, and the other was the Real Madrid and former Everton midfielder, Thomas Gravesen.

Gravesen nodded a 'hello' and headed for their table, but Rankin stopped. 'How's the fettuccini?' He saw the bottle in Gavin's hand. 'Try the '95, Gavin, it's got a lovely nose on it.'

'You know everyone, right?' said Gavin, wisely deciding that maybe it wasn't the moment to demonstrate any more of his newly found expertise on wine.

Rankin nodded. Before Santiago had signed up with Glen, he had made a couple of attempts to get in first. He reached for Roz's right hand and kissed it. 'Charmed.'

Roz snatched her hand back as Rankin turned to Glen. 'Mr Foy; lovely to see you.'

'Barry,' said Glen, looking as though the feeling was far from mutual.

But disdainful looks and rejection meant nothing to Barry Rankin; it was all part of the job as far as he was concerned. He reached across the table to shake Santiago's hand. 'Let's do coffee sometime, Santi.'

He smiled once more and then continued on to his table as Roz looked at the hand he had kissed. 'I hope I didn't catch anything,' she said.

Glen and Roz were booked on to an early flight the following morning; there was just time for Santiago to go with them to the airport before being driven on to training.

The car journey passed in virtual silence. Glen was in the front with the driver and Roz and

Santi were in the back, neither of them looking forward to the moment of parting.

They reached the airport and as Glen tactfully hovered a couple of metres away and the driver stood waiting with a rear door open, Santi and Roz hugged and then kissed goodbye.

'Come on,' said Roz quietly to Santiago. 'Jump on the plane with us. No one will know.'

Santiago smiled. 'I think my new coach might notice.'

'But the house is so empty without you, Santi.'

'You'll be fine. It's only a couple of weeks, it'll be like you never left.'

'I love you,' said Roz, not caring if Glen, or the driver, or the whole world heard her words.

Santi was a little more reserved. 'Me too.'

They kissed again and then Roz wrapped both her arms around Santiago, reluctant to let him go. As Santi looked over Roz's shoulder, he saw the driver tap his watch and gesture that it was time to leave.

Glen had seen it, too. 'Right, then,' he said loudly, 'time to go, Roz. We'll miss the plane.'

Roz sighed and picked up her suitcase and

Glen went to Santiago and shook his hand firmly. 'Call me if you need me, son.'

And then, they were gone, and Santiago was heading towards the training ground, suddenly feeling very alone.

Nine

The days passed swiftly and Santiago quickly settled into the new training routine and found himself more at ease with his new team-mates. He continued to marvel at the skills of not only the *galácticos* but also of the new younger generation of Real players like Robinho and Sergio Ramos.

And the other members of the squad recognized that Santiago had the talent, pace and instinctive, predatory touch of a natural goal-scorer to become a worthy wearer of the famous white shirt of Real.

Santiago loved scoring goals, in practice matches almost as much as in the real thing.

From the sitter to the spectacular, each one gave him a buzz, but especially the spectacular, which had become something of a Muñez trademark. And that could only be a good thing at Real Madrid, where the fans had been brought up on the spectacular.

The Real coach, Rudi Van Der Merwe, was not the flamboyant type. He went about his business in his own particular way. He was totally effective and thorough, a motivator. He had his players' respect and no one messed with him.

And Van De Merwe never seemed to miss a thing. During training he seemed to have the ability to talk on his mobile phone, check lists of stats or notes prepared by his assistants and still be aware of everything that was going on around him.

He was talking on his mobile when his eyes settled on Gavin Harris, twenty metres away on the pitch.

Van Der Merwe finished the phone conversation and then beckoned to his chief physio. 'Harris's calcaneus deltoid is playing up,' he said as soon as the physio joined him. 'Keep an eye on it.'

The physio stared at his boss and then turned to watch Gavin as he ran for a ball. Only a highly trained and skilled eye would have noticed the slight hesitation in stride. The physio turned back to Van Der Merwe and nodded.

On the training pitch Santiago had just scored with a shot from just inside the box when Van Der Merwe spotted the club's director of football, Señor Burruchaga, walking towards him.

Burruchaga had made no secret of his admiration for Real's new signing and had already hinted that he believed Santiago should be in the starting line-up.

Both the coach and the director of football were fully aware of their responsibilities at Real. The coaching and team selection was down to Van Der Merwe, while other footballing matters, such as identifying and pursuing transfer targets, were Burruchaga's domain. It was the common European system, and one increasingly adopted by British clubs.

But Burruchaga didn't always appreciate where his job ended and Van Der Merwe's began. He joined Van Der Merwe on the touchline and glanced over at Santiago as he jogged back towards the centre circle.

'You think Muñez is ready for a full game?' said Burruchaga without looking at Van Der Merwe.

The coach shook his head. 'No. Not yet. I think he needs to settle for a while.'

But Burruchaga obviously had different ideas. He turned and looked deliberately at the coach. 'Maybe you should think again.'

He walked away, giving Van Der Merwe no chance to reply.

There were always young fans hanging around the training ground entrance as the players made their way to and from the complex. They clustered around their heroes in the hope of a word or an autograph.

Santiago always had time for the fans. He knew where they were coming from, particularly the obviously poorer kids. He'd been there for most of his life, and now that life was so much better, he didn't forget. So when a group of youngsters came hurtling towards him as he left training that day, he stopped and took the pens, photographs, programmes and scraps of paper that were thrust towards him.

He thought he had signed them all before heading to his car, but at the back of the noisy gaggle of youngsters, one smaller kid stood clutching a football he had wanted autographed.

It was Enrique and he had missed his chance. He turned away looking hugely disappointed and began the long walk home.

He was deep in thought as he wandered down the central divide of one of the motorways that ring the city. Vehicles hurtled by in both directions, but Enrique seemed oblivious to the roar of engines and the hot blasts of air as huge lorries thundered past just a few metres away.

He reached a dusty expanse of waste ground and meandered on towards the outskirts of the city. When he arrived at the metro he did what he always did; he jumped over the turnstile. Enrique didn't think about paying for the ride, and anyway, he couldn't, he had no cash.

Eventually he came to the all-too-familiar surroundings of his home. The ageing, crumbling blocks of flats, the narrow, neglected streets. This was the other side of Madrid, the side that Roz had not even glimpsed during her day of sightseeing.

Enrique walked along a narrow back alley and emerged to see a gang of his friends playing football on a bone-dry scrap of land. It wasn't the Bernabéu, but for the kids tearing from one end to another as they battled and shouted for the ball, it could have been.

Enrique dropped his own football and rushed to join them and soon he was in the thick of the action. He took a pass from one of his friends and skipped away, easily avoiding a couple of clumsy tackles as the dust swirled around him.

He lifted his head and prepared to shoot for goal, or for the couple of ragged sweatshirts dumped on the ground that represented goalposts.

Before the youngster could bring his foot through to make the shot he was thumped from behind and found himself sprawled on the ground, eating a mouthful of dust.

He looked up and saw his bullying friend, Tito, grinning down at him. The ball was long gone.

Ten

Real's early season form was good, but it could have been better. The team was beginning to gel in most areas, from defence through to attack, with one notable and very obvious exception – Gavin Harris.

Coach Van Der Merwe was giving his misfiring striker every opportunity to rediscover his shooting boots but it was proving a painful process.

Santiago was becoming accustomed to spending each match on the bench, with only brief cameo appearances to his name. He knew he had been impressing in training but Van Der Merwe seemed set on making his newest signing wait for a full ninety-minute appearance.

It was difficult for both Santi and Gavin. They were the best of friends, but they were professionals and they knew that they were rivals for the one coveted place in the starting line-up.

Santi got his chance to show the boss exactly what he could offer in a *La Liga* game. He was occupying his ususal seat on the bench, watching with growing frustration as his team-mates battled to overcome stubborn and determined opposition.

Gavin was trying his heart out but he was always slightly off the pace, which didn't help when he fluffed the best chance of the game from close in.

The crowd groaned as one and Gavin shook his head and turned away from the goal, avoiding making eye-contact with his team-mates.

On the bench, Van Der Merwe turned to Santiago and gestured for him to go on. Gavin's number was already being held up on the substitution board. He was coming off.

He met Santiago on the touchline and smiled as they touched hands. Santi ran on, kissing his necklace for luck, but Gavin's smile turned to a scowl as he went to the bench, glaring at the coach.

'I could've gone the whole game, boss,' he said, taking his seat alongside the subs.

Van Der Merwe was watching Santiago run towards the penalty box. He didn't look at Gavin as he replied. 'We need young blood, Harris.'

There were not many minutes left; Santiago, once again, had little time to try to find the rhythm and pace of the game.

Roz was sitting alone up in the stands. She was wearing a Real scarf, gripping it tightly, willing Santiago to make another telling contribution to the match.

An opposing player went down after a tackle and rolled on the turf in apparent agony. The challenge had looked innocuous enough, and the Madridistas whistled their displeasure at the apparent timewasting tactics as the ref allowed the player to receive treatment.

Sometimes, a sudden change of personnel in the opposition can unsettle and temporarily confuse even the most experienced of defenders. And that was exactly what happened.

Soon after the restart, the Real keeper, Casillas, gathered the ball and threw it out to

Salgado. He moved swiftly away on the right flank before passing to Guti, who played the ball quickly on to Raúl, who instantly back-heeled it to Beckham and then ran on to collect a clever one-two.

The opposing defenders were being dragged out of position as they tried to figure out and counter Santi's pace and positioning.

They didn't have time. After a jinking run from Ronaldo, and a swift interchange of passes between Guti and Gravesen, the ball went out to Beckham on the right. He sent a looping cross into the box, and from close to the penalty spot Santiago leaped into the air and executed a spectacular scissor kick, which beat the keeper low down to his left.

Santiago had come off the bench again to grab a winner close to the end, and as the cheers rang around the Bernabéu, every one of his Real teammates rushed to congratulate the super sub.

Gavin was face down on a physio bed, receiving treatment after the match. His thigh was hurting badly, even though the physio was an expert at his job, applying exactly the right amount of pressure in exactly the right places.

Gavin grimaced, trying to hide the pain, as Santiago entered the treatment room, already showered and dressed and doing his best not to show too much delight at scoring the winning goal.

'Hey, come on, Gavin,' he called. 'How much longer are you gonna lie there?'

His friend turned and smiled. 'I can't turn down a free Swedish massage, can I? Pedro here is very sensitive. I wouldn't want to hurt his feelings.'

The physio had heard it all before. He just smiled and gave the player a slap on the thigh.

As Gavin feigned mock agony he saw Van Der Merwe walk into the room. He sat up quickly and grinned at the coach, not wanting him to think that there was anything seriously amiss. 'All right, boss?'

'How's the thigh?' asked Van Der Merwe.

'Good as new, boss.'

Van Der Merwe was not easily convinced; he could see straight through Gavin's bravado. 'The human body is a biological wonder. It can achieve miracles, but it is not indestructible.' He was staring straight into Gavin's eyes. 'Football. The running, the falls, the tackles. We all have a shelf life. Remember that.'

For once, Gavin seemed lost for words, but Santiago was ready to leap to his friend's defence. He looked at Van Der Merwe. 'Even you, boss?'

Gavin's eyes flicked from Santiago to Van Der Merwe. He was expecting some sort of reprimand, but the coach just smiled, silently appreciating Santiago's fighting spirit.

For a few moments no one said a word until Santiago decided that perhaps he had gone a little too far with the few words he had directed at his new boss. He knew how much playing football meant to Gavin, despite all his talk about new business ventures and vineyards. Surely Van Der Merwe could understand that.

Santiago looked at the coach. 'Don't you miss playing?'

Van Der Merwe considered for a moment before replying. 'A lot of people would give anything in the world to be in your position, Muñez. I'm not one of them.'

He turned and started to leave as Gavin eased himself from the treatment table. 'Hey, boss?' he called.

Van Der Merwe stopped by the doorway and looked back.

Gavin was back to his usual, irrepressible self. 'Aren't you gonna wish me a happy birthday?'

Eleven

Gavin was famous not just for his football, but also for his parties, and he had decided that his birthday bash was going to be one of his most memorable.

As Santiago and Roz walked into Gavin's rented villa in the hills above Madrid their eyes widened in disbelief. The place must have been worth a fortune, and not a small fortune.

It sprawled over a huge area on different levels. The main room was like the most exclusive nightclub in the world, with designer furniture and modern artwork that looked as if it had been loaned by one of Madrid's major galleries. Through sliding smoked-glass doors, they glimpsed an indoor pool lit as dramatically as the rest of the house.

Music was thumping and everywhere there were people. Most of the team had been invited, with their wives or girlfriends. They were mingling with Madrid's beautiful people. Smiling, laughing, chatting. There appeared to be at least three girls to every guy. But that wasn't a surprise; it was Gavin's party.

Santi was beginning to feel part of it all. He was wearing a perfectly cut black suit and feeling as cool as he looked. As they edged their way through the room, looking for Gavin, everyone was smiling or nodding their appreciation and admiration for the new kid on the block, the new goal-scoring sensation.

Gavin appeared, squeezing his way through a clutch of beautiful women. He grabbed a bottle of champagne and some glasses from a passing waitress and beamed at Santiago and Roz. 'Welcome to the Pleasuredome!'

'Happy birthday, Gavin,' said Roz, kissing him on the cheek. 'Twenty-nine again?'

Gavin just grinned. 'So what do you think of

all this? Leased it from some friend of Madonna's.'

'Yeah, it's beautiful,' said Roz. 'But does the Pleasuredome have a loo. I'm desperate.'

The birthday boy pointed across the room and Roz headed off while Santiago took a glass of champagne Gavin pressed into his hand.

Santi was still gazing in awe around the luxurious villa. 'This must have set you back a few bucks.'

Gavin shrugged. 'Barry sorts it all out. I just sit back and enjoy the ride.'

As if on cue, Barry Rankin came wandering over, a fat cigar held between two fingers of his right hand and each arm wrapped around a beautiful girl. 'All right, my son,' he said, as the girls detached themselves and planted birthday kisses on Gavin's cheeks.

Rankin obviously enjoyed having his arms around someone, so he draped one across Santi's shoulders and pulled him close. 'Santi – cracking goal tonight. Respect. But what are you thinking bringing Roz here, man? This is what you could call a *singles* party, *amigo*.'

He guided Santi across the crowded room and out through doors at the rear of the house. On a five-a-side pitch a couple of Madrid players were showing off their skills to a group of girls and close to the house, more bikini-clad girls were posing, rather than swimming, in the outdoor pool.

Rankin looked at the girls and then at Santiago and raised his eyebrows.

'Roz is my fiancée,' said Santiago.

'Yeah,' said Rankin as he stared at the girls in the pool. 'And soon she'll be back in Newcastle defrosting her ravioli meal-for-one while you're out here surrounded by . . .' He looked at the girls in the pool again. '. . . all this. Think I fancy a swim.'

Rankin strolled away and Santiago went back into the villa to find Roz. He found Gavin first and they were speaking together when a tall, glamorous woman with long, gleaming, dark hair and a smile that could have graced a toothpaste ad eased her way up to them.

'Good evening, Gavin,' she said in excellent English. 'Aren't you going to introduce me to your friend?'

'Of course,' answered Gavin, suddenly not quite his usual, brash self. 'Jordana García, meet Santiago Muñez.'

As Jordana fixed her eyes on Santiago, Gavin reached up and gently stroked her cheek. 'She can't resist me.'

Jordana didn't look away from Santiago. 'I'll try.' She offered her right hand to Santiago and they shook.

'*Hola*, Santiago.'

'*Hola*.'

'Nice suit. Dolce?'

Santiago nodded.

'Not a bad goal tonight. You must be exhausted after, what was it, seven whole minutes on the pitch.'

She was still holding his hand.

'Hands off, Jordana,' said Gavin. 'He's spoken for.'

Jordana released Santi's hand and then glanced at Gavin with a look that said, 'So what?' She smiled at Santi again.

Roz was battling her way through the partying hordes feeling completely out of place. There were so many tanned, beautiful women around, every one of them with the looks and figure of a supermodel. It was all a long way from Newcastle.

Finally, she found Santi at the bar with the most glamorous, sophisticated-looking woman of the lot.

'Roz,' said Santi quickly. 'This is Jordana, she's in television over here.'

The two women smiled, weighing each other up.

'Hi,' said Jordana. 'Santi was just telling me about your wedding plans. You're a lucky woman.'

'Not half as lucky as he is,' countered Roz.

Jordana turned back to Santiago and spoke in Spanish. 'I'll have to get you on my show sometime, before every station in Europe snaps you up.'

Santiago could see Roz's irritation at being excluded from the conversation. He pointedly replied in English. 'Thanks, but I'm not into all that stuff.'

Roz's look of irritation was turning to one of

anger. She'd understood nothing of Jordana's comment and Santiago's reply left her wondering exactly what the television presenter had suggested.

And it didn't get any better as Jordana raised her eyebrows with a look of mock shock and said to Santi, 'Excuse me, but did you just say "no" to me?'

Santi laughed and so did Jordana. But Roz just smiled politely. She didn't get the joke, and she didn't want to.

It was a long, long night, even by Madrid standards; almost time to get up by the time Santi and Roz prepared for bed back at the suite at the Hotel Mauro.

Roz had been burning to ask Santi a question ever since her encounter with Jordana, and she couldn't wait any longer. 'What did you think of that TV woman?'

'Who?' answered Santiago innocently.

'You know exactly who I mean. Miss "Did you just say 'no' to me?" Did you like her?'

Santiago shrugged. 'She's OK. I think Gavin has a thing for her.'

'Well, she definitely likes you.'

Roz was watching Santi closely, waiting to see how he responded, and Santi could sense his fiancée's feeling of insecurity. But instead of being instantly reassuring he decided to tease her a little. 'Well, I am pretty irresistible.'

'Yeah, and big-headed, too,' snapped Roz.

Santiago laughed as he grabbed Roz and pulled her close. He kissed her gently and then looked into her eyes. 'I love *you*, Roz. Remember?'

Twelve

The car drew up outside an imposing, futuristic-looking mansion with huge windows and towering square columns supporting the massive roof.

Roz stared from the car window. 'Santi, why are we here?'

Santiago was already out of the vehicle. As Roz followed, gazing up at the impressive but imposing façade, he gestured proudly. 'This is our house.'

Roz's eyes widened. 'You've . . . you've bought it?'

Santiago nodded enthusiastically. 'Yeah, I did.'

'Oh. Oh, you haven't?'

'Yeah. What do you think?'

Before Roz could answer, Santiago, with a smile that was almost as wide as the mansion, was dragging her towards the front door. 'Wait till you see inside.'

The interior was just as impressive and just as overwhelming. Roz followed Santiago around, almost in a daze. Huge rooms, some on split levels, most of them painted a dazzling white. Enormous canvases of bewildering modern art, cascades of flowers in massive glass vases. So much, almost too much, to take in.

'This is nice,' said Roz as she followed Santi into the state-of-the-art kitchen.

Santi pulled a bottle of champagne from a fridge big enough to hold a side of beef. 'I wanted to surprise you; I knew you'd love it. It belonged to some very famous designer. It's got seven bedrooms, each with en-suite bathrooms.'

He was starting to sound like an estate agent. Roz wandered back into the main sitting room as Santiago wrestled with the cork on the champagne bottle.

The place *was* beautiful, but in a cold, almost

clinical way, and to Roz, at least, it didn't feel like a home.

She stood gazing up at an ugly modern painting, trying to work out what it meant, or even if it had been hung the right way up, as Santiago came in with two glasses of foaming champagne.

'A lot of the things inside the house and the furniture were designed by the guy who owned it.' He looked around their new home. 'Do you like it?'

'Er . . . I don't know what to say,' said Roz as she took the glass Santiago offered. He hadn't picked up the irony in her voice; he was buzzing with excitement and almost exploding with pride.

Roz lifted her glass and joined Santi in the toast to their new home, trying desperately to like it as much as he did.

Santi took one quick sip of the champagne and then checked his watch. 'I have to go. See you after training. There's a set of keys for you in the kitchen, so make yourself . . . at home.' He kissed her quickly and then hurried away. Roz sighed and sipped her champagne. She looked up at the modern painting again and decided that, whatever it was meant to be, it was watching her. And she didn't like it.

The place was so quiet, more like a museum than a house. Roz went upstairs to take a closer look at the *Palacio de Muñez*. In the master bedroom she switched on the TV before continuing with her tour. The sound of other voices was comforting, even television voices speaking in Spanish.

When Roz had checked out the six other bedrooms with their six en-suite bathrooms she found her way back by following the sound of the television voices. A daytime magazine programme was in full swing but Roz didn't even glance at the screen as she went to look at the largest and most lavish en-suite bathroom of the lot.

It was only as she emerged and heard the name Santiago Muñez that she looked at the TV. Two presenters were discussing the previous night's match and Roz glared as she realized that one of the presenters was – Jordana.

Roz picked up the TV remote and stabbed violently at the OFF button.

* * *

It was another brief visit. Roz had juggled her shifts with other nurses to make the trip possible and on the day before her return to Newcastle, she left the new house in an attempt to make herself more familiar with Madrid.

She wasn't adapting very well to this new way of living. It was fine for Santi; he had his football, his friends, his team-mates. Roz had only Santiago; her work, her friends, everything she knew and liked were in another country.

But she left the house determined to find her way around and learn more about the city. Two hours later she was lost in a run-down district far from the usual tourist attractions and feeling slightly scared by some of the hostile looks she was getting from the locals.

She was relieved when her mobile rang. It was her mum, Carol, calling from a hairdressing salon back in Newcastle.

Carol loved the fame by association she was getting these days and after a quick 'hello' she made sure all the other clients at the hairdresser's knew exactly what she was talking about. 'I'm reading a magazine, pet. It's full of pictures of Gavin's party. There's one of you and Santi opposite a pic of the Beckhams. Did you get talking to Victoria?'

'No, Mum.'

'Oh, really?' said Carol, making it sound as if Roz and Victoria were the best of friends. 'Her David's looking fine. Are those new shoes you're wearing?'

'Yes, Mum.'

'They go lovely with that handbag.'

'Thanks, Mum.'

In the salon, Carol was studying all the photographs closely. She spoke more quietly. 'One thing, Roz, love.'

'Yes, Mum?'

'You could do with a bit of spray tan, pet.'

When she ended the call, Roz was feeling even more depressed. She headed back towards the city centre and came to a busy road where she had to wait to cross at traffic lights.

As she turned to look in the direction of the oncoming traffic, a moped flashed by and the young rider quickly reached out and snatched

Roz's handbag away, almost knocking her to the ground.

Before she could even shout, the moped had disappeared. Roz turned and looked at the other pedestrians waiting to cross. No one said a word.

Santiago was watching television. Bored. He'd had a good day at training, Van Der Merwe had praised his commitment and work rate and he'd arrived home feeling good and that soon he'd get his chance in the starting line-up.

As he drew up in the Audi, he'd seen Roz sitting outside the locked house, unable to get in because her keys had been in the stolen handbag.

Since then, they'd spent a difficult few hours and now Roz was sitting at the long dining table, surrounded by medical textbooks and files full of notes as she studied for her exams which were approaching fast.

Santi flicked off the TV and walked over to Roz, still with the remote in one hand. He stood behind her and rested the remote on the table, looking down at the vivid photographs of infected wounds and open sores in the textbooks.

He grimaced – they weren't exactly the sort of pictures to encourage a romantic evening – but he leaned forward and kissed Roz's neck.

Roz continued with her notes. 'I've got to study, Santi. This is my chance to do some specialist, theatre nursing. I don't want to stay on the wards for ever.'

Santiago reached over to the book and closed it. 'You can study on the plane tomorrow.'

'I need to do it now,' said Roz, opening the book again. 'And I'm tired.'

'Yeah, me too,' said Santi. 'But I'm not gonna see you for another two weeks.'

Roz took a deep breath, picked up the TV remote from the table, and pressed the ON button. She looked up at Santiago and handed him the remote.

Roz worked until late – her trips to Madrid were causing her to fall behind on the work she had to do for her exams. When she woke up the following morning, she turned over in the bed to see that Santiago was not there.

She pulled on a dressing gown and went down

to the kitchen to get some orange juice from the fridge.

On the fridge door was a note, held in place by a Real Madrid logo fridge magnet.

The note read:

Gone to training. A driver will pick you up at noon. Have a safe flight, will call you later. S xx

Roz sighed and pulled open the fridge door.

Thirteen

At Real Madrid everything is based on meticulous preparation. Even when they are playing at the Bernabéu, the squad gathers at a luxury hotel in the city on the evening before the match and spends the night there.

The following day is devoted to a gradual build-up to the match. Light meals, tactical discussion with the coaching team, and plenty of relaxation before the entire squad is ferried by coach the short distance to the Bernabéu for the match itself.

It's similar to how an English team might approach an FA Cup final. The difference is that Real do it for every game.

Santiago was relaxing in the jacuzzi in the hotel spa with his team-mates Casillas, Gravesen and Guti. Gavin had just climbed from the pool and slipped into a white towelling robe.

As the others chatted and joked, he reached into the pocket of his robe and pulled out one of his mobile phones. He punched in a number and the call was answered quickly.

'Hello?'

'Hey, Jordana. You busy?'

The television presenter instantly recognized the English accent. 'Gavin. You know I always have time for you.'

Gavin glanced back at the players lounging in the jacuzzi. 'I'm going crazy in here. It's like a five-star prison full of blokes. D'you fancy joining me? It's a shame to waste such a nice cell.'

Jordana laughed. 'I'd love to, Gavin, but I have no time. And you should rest, you need to score tonight.'

This time Gavin laughed. 'That's why I phoned you.'

Jordana's put-down was razor sharp. 'Gavin,

darling, scoring *off* the pitch is not your problem.'

Gavin winced; he'd walked into that and he was as aware as everyone that he desperately needed to get a goal or two – and soon.

Someone in the jacuzzi cracked a joke and the others hooted with laughter.

'Is Muñez with you?' said Jordana into her phone.

'Yeah.'

'Put him on.'

Jordana certainly had some nerve; Gavin almost laughed at the cheek of it. He looked over at Santi and held up the mobile. 'Someone wants a word.'

Gavin threw the phone, taking Santi by surprise. He grabbed at it and missed and the mobile was only centimetres from the bubbling jacuzzi when Casillas's lightning reflexes saved it from a watery end.

The Spanish goalkeeper put the phone to his ear and adopted the worst American accent any of them had ever heard as he spoke. 'Hey, baby, Santi here. What's happenin', sugar?'

The others thought it was hilarious and even Gavin smiled, but Santiago snatched the mobile away. 'Hello?'

'Hi, Santi, it's Jordana, from Gavin's party.'

Santiago was hardly likely to have forgotten their first encounter. 'Yeah, hi.'

'My producers are very keen to get you on the show. I told them you'd do it as a favour. I knew you wouldn't mind.'

The other players were watching and listening intently, as interested as Jordana was in Santiago's reply.

By the time they climbed from the jacuzzi, Santi had suffered ten minutes of good-natured ribbing. They went to the showers where Ronaldo was already standing beneath a stream of hot water. The brilliant Brazilian listened with a smile as the phone call story was recounted once again.

Gavin, Santi and Gravesen were wearing just towels around their waists and hotel slippers on their feet as they got into the elevator together to return to their rooms.

Santiago didn't notice the look that Gavin and

Gravesen exchanged as Gavin pressed the lift button.

The elevator moved and then stopped with the familiar ping as the doors slid open. Santiago's eyes widened; they'd stopped at the hotel lobby.

The next second he felt the towel around his waist being yanked away and both Gavin and Gravesen shoved him out of the elevator as Gavin hit the lift button again.

The doors were almost closed as Santiago looked back and saw his grinning team-mates waving at him.

'*Adios, amigo!*' smiled Gavin just before the doors met and the elevator began to rise.

The hotel lobby came to a standstill as receptionists and guests stared at the stark naked young man desperately trying to hide his embarrassment with one hand at the front and one at the back. He wanted to run but there was nowhere to run to; he wanted to hide but there was nowhere to hide; so he just stood there, frozen like a statue with a manic grin on his face.

It got even worse when the Real coach Van

Der Merwe entered the lobby from the street. He saw Santiago instantly – he could hardly miss him – and he turned to face the young player.

Van Der Merwe had seen the old 'shove him naked out of the elevator' gag played many times before. 'Looks like you forgot something, Muñez.'

Santiago swallowed hard. 'Yes, boss.'

Santiago was desperate to cover his embarrassment as he began punching at the elevator buttons.

The coach watched him, completely straight-faced. 'And, Muñez?'

'Yes, boss?'

'What is it I tell you that matters most?'

Santiago thought for a moment before replying. 'Dignity, boss. Dignity.'

Van Der Merwe nodded and then walked away. Santiago didn't see the slight smile on his face.

Every striker goes through spells when the goals just won't come. A lean period, a drought. It happens to the very best and when it does all the player can do is get his head down and keep going.

But sometimes even that doesn't work. A striker's game is based on instinct, on naturally sensing the moment to make the run, to hit the shot, to leap for the header. When everything goes well it can almost be easy, or at least, it can look easy to the supporters.

But when it goes wrong, when the goals dry up, when the striker has to *try* too hard, then it can be embarrassingly painful to watch, and the star front man suddenly looks like an awkward novice.

Managers and team-mates try to make it better, talking about the striker being a 'team player helping others to score goals', and about his 'overall contribution to the game', but it doesn't really help the player. He knows. He's there to score goals. That's all that matters. Goals.

Gavin was in the darkest depths of a barren goal-scoring run. He'd been unlucky; he'd seen the ball hit the crossbar, or ricochet from the uprights or crash into the side netting. Goalkeepers had made spectacular saves; defenders had made dramatic goal-line clearances, leaving Gavin desperate and, at times, wondering if he would ever put the ball into the net again. But he had to. He didn't care how, from his feet, from his head, his knee, his chest, anywhere would do. A lucky goal, a flukey goal, he'd even take someone else's deflected shot, as long as the goal was credited to him.

But that goal wouldn't come. He knew full well he was trying too hard, he knew his play was deteriorating, that it was becoming almost embarrassing. But one goal – just one – could change all that.

The Champions League match was against the Norwegian side, Rosenberg. They were no pushovers but just before the interval, after Gavin was brought down outside the box, David Beckham scored with a trademark bending free kick.

The visitors replied soon after the break and from then on both teams had their chances, and several of Real's fell to Gavin. They were no more than half-chances, really, but on a good day he would have grabbed one of them. But his hesitant attempts barely troubled the Rosenberg keeper.

His misery was being compounded by the jeers that had begun to sound from some sections of the Bernabéu whenever he had the ball.

Then another chance came, the best of the lot. Gavin was temporarily unmarked inside the box as he received a through ball from Guti. He just had to swivel and shoot, hard and low. He'd done the same thing thousands of times before it was easy.

He swivelled, he shot, hard and low, and then he watched the ball miss the target by at least a metre.

The crowd groaned, the whistles echoed around the stadium and when the substitution board was held up displaying his number, Gavin was not even slightly surprised. As he took his seat on the bench, there was no angry look cast in the direction of Van Der Merwe. Gavin knew the coach was right; he'd deserved to be taken off.

Santiago's elation was equal to Gavin's despair. He was on, with longer than usual to contribute to the game. There was time to settle, to find the rhythm, to be more than just a ten-minute wonder.

He was feeling confident, maybe a little over confident. He collected the ball close to the halfway line as Real turned defence into attack. There were three of his team-mates in excellent positions but instead of making any of the simple passes, he decided to run at the defender, closing in on him.

It was a bad decision. The nimble defender easily robbed Santiago and sent a long, hopeful ball towards the Real box.

The Real defence was caught flat-footed as Rosenberg counter-attacked and only a stunning save from Casillas prevented the visitors from going ahead.

On the bench, Van Der Merwe shouted his fury. 'Muñez! Open your eyes! Pass the ball!'

For the first time, Santiago experienced the Madridistas' displeasure as the dreaded whistles came from the terraces. His captain, Raúl, ran over as he walked, head bowed, back to the centre circle, and explained, in a few short, sharp sentences, exactly what was expected of him.

The game restarted and Santiago reminded himself that he was part of a team. Gradually he slipped more comfortably into the pattern of play. He made a couple of good passes and started to link with Ronaldo, but the crowd was growing impatient for the winning goal.

It came with only seconds remaining.

Santiago was the most forward Real player when he collected a probing ball from David Beckham.

This time, he had no option; he had to go for goal. He wrong-footed one defender and then skipped neatly between two more. There was only the keeper to beat and as he advanced quickly, Santiago calmly curled the ball into the net.

On the bench, Van Der Merwe smiled his approval. 'Sometimes you don't need to pass.'

Santi had done it again – he'd come on as a substitute and scored the winner – and as his name was chanted over and over by the faithful, he joined Ronaldo and Robinho in a samba of celebration.

Back in the dressing room after the final whistle, Van Der Merwe's post-match summary was not quite so celebratory.

The players sat by their lockers and listened in silence as the coach made his point to them all. 'You were taking stupid risks; you could have thrown it away. I told you to control the game, close it down when necessary, but instead you gave me a mountain of unforced errors.'

He paused for a moment as the players considered his words. 'We were lucky tonight, but if we play second-rate football against Milan, or Liverpool, or Chelsea, they'll bury us.'

A few of the squad exchanged looks; they'd won the match, surely they deserved a few words of praise.

Van Der Merwe was quick to sense the mood. 'That said, it was a good result, with good goals. And for that, well done.'

But the dressing down wasn't over, for one player, at least. Van Der Merwe's eyes rested on Gavin. 'Except for you, Harris. What's going on with you? Are you ever going to score for me again?'

Gavin felt his cheeks redden as his team-mates looked away in embarrassment. But he was man enough to admit his failing. He looked back at Van Der Merwe and spoke quietly. 'Right now, it doesn't feel like it, boss. Right now, I'm a very bad player.'

The coach nodded his head, surprised at Gavin's unexpected frankness. 'Well, I admire your honesty, but I wish you'd told me this before I signed you.'

Even Santiago could find no words of comfort for his friend. And besides, he had his own performance and his own place in the Real pecking order to think about.

Footballers can be selfish – in a way, they have to be – and opportunities have to be grabbed when they come along. As Santiago left the dressing room and walked towards the players' exit, he met Van Der Merwe coming in the opposite direction. The coach nodded and walked by, but Santiago had something to say.

'Coach?'

Van Der Merwe stopped and turned back. 'Muñez?'

Santiago was nervous but determined to make his point. 'I'm fitter than I've ever been. I'm scoring, I'm feeling great.'

The coach said nothing – he wasn't making it easy – so Santiago had to continue. He took a deep breath. 'I think I'm ready to start a full game.'

He'd said it; he'd stated his case, and Van Der Merwe looked at him closely.

'When you're ready to start, Muñez,' he said slowly and deliberately, 'I promise you, you'll be the first to know.'

* * *

MUÑEZ – SUPER SUB

Santiago wasn't the first player to be given that title in the newspaper headlines and he wouldn't be the last, but the Madrid Press seemed very happy to make him the latest recipient of the honour.

Enrique was sitting in the bar with the back

page of the newspaper on the table top in front of him as he and a few of the regulars watched a replay of the previous night's wonder-goal.

The teenager was meant to be working, clearing up, doing the jobs that he was routinely meant to do. His father, Miguel, walked in from the room at the back of the bar and scowled as he saw his son staring at the TV set.

'Enrique,' he shouted, 'go clean out the ashtrays.'

Enrique didn't even look away from the TV as he replied. 'I'm watching the game.'

It was the wrong response. Miguel came storming over and switched off the set. He glared at Enrique. 'And when they pay you for watching TV, you'll have a great career. Until then, you roll your sleeves up and get your hands dirty.'

He stormed away, leaving Enrique embarrassed and the regulars wondering whether there was time to go to another bar to catch the replays of the post-match interviews.

Fourteen

Roz was at work; it hadn't been the best of days.

She was on her break, deep in thought as she sat on the stairs of the fire escape close to her ward and sipped a comforting cup of tea.

Her mobile rang and she saw that it was Santiago. She flicked open the phone and answered the call, trying to sound brighter than she felt. 'Hi, Santi.'

She could hear the roar of an engine as well as Santiago's voice. 'You're not going to believe what I just bought us.'

Roz couldn't stop herself from sighing. 'Go on.'

'Guess.'

'I don't know, Santi.'

Santi wasn't picking up the vibes coming across on the phone.

'Come on, Roz.'

'I'm not in the mood for games, Santi.'

Santiago obviously was: he was buzzing. 'A Lamborghini.'

Roz said nothing.

'It's white. A convertible. *So* cool.'

There was still no response. Roz took a sip of her tea, as Santiago, at the wheel of his new toy, waited to hear her excited response. It didn't come.

'Roz?'

'Mr Ives died this morning,' said Roz softly.

There was a slight pause before Santiago spoke. 'You should have said something.'

'You never asked.'

'Look, I'm sorry, Roz, really. About Mr Ives. I know you . . . he was a nice guy. I just wanted to share my news; thought it might brighten your day.'

Roz shook her head as she replied. 'My day is about as dark as they come, right now. I was going to phone you, just to have someone to talk to. But I didn't want to bring you down, too.'

'I'm sorry.'

The swing doors to the corridor opened and one of Roz's colleagues poked her head through and gestured that she was needed back on the ward.

Roz nodded. 'I've got to go,' she said into the phone, and hung up.

The day didn't get better. It was a long, hard shift, and by the time Roz got back to the house that evening she was feeling even more down. And slightly guilty. What did she have to complain about? There was this lovely house in Newcastle, and there was an imposing mansion out in Madrid. She should feel great. Lucky. Privileged. Even grateful.

But she didn't. It was all too strange and unreal, and neither of the houses actually felt like home. She decided to snap herself out of her depression by doing something positive; a bit of DIY therapy might help. She'd had the paint she'd chosen for the sitting room for ages. Now was the chance to get it onto the walls.

When her mum, Carol, arrived a couple of hours later, Roz had covered the furniture and carpet with dustsheets and was well stuck into painting the first wall.

Carol didn't offer to help. She'd had her hair done again and was wearing a brand-new pair of snakeskin boots.

She perched on the edge of a dustsheet-covered sofa and watched her daughter painting the wall. 'You could pay someone to do that, you know. A professional.'

Roz continued rhythmically moving the paint roller up and down. 'I like doing it; makes the place feel more like home.'

Carol sighed. She relished her new status of glamorous mother-in-law-to-be of a famous foot-baller and she didn't want it threatened. And besides, she loved her daughter and she liked Santiago enormously, famous or not. Carol didn't want their relationship to founder but she knew that things were not going well.

'Roz, love,' she said gently, 'Santi's head is going to be full of a million different things now he's out there in Madrid. You should be one of them, the most important one.'

'But I need to be here,' said Roz, working faster with the roller. 'They need me down at the hospital, and all my friends are here. And even if I was out in Madrid, I wouldn't be allowed to see him. He's in hotels with the team for half the week.'

'Not much use having this classy house if it's just you in it, is it though, pet.' Carol stood up and walked across the room. She took the paint roller from Roz's hand and turned her daughter round so that she could look into her eyes. 'I'm serious, love. It's only a few hundred miles to Madrid, but if you let it, it could become a world away.'

She smiled and Roz smiled back, feeling glad that her mum was around to talk to.

Then Carol felt a cold, wet sensation on her right hand. She glanced at the roller; paint was running down the handle and then falling in steady drips. She looked down and saw the splodge of paint on her brand-new snakeskin boots and recoiled in horror.

Fifteen

Desperate situations need desperate remedies and Gavin had decided that his situation was desperate. Training had never been the favourite part of his life as a professional footballer but now he was training harder than ever before.

And not just in the club sessions. In the evenings, he was working out like crazy in the gym at his villa. Pumping iron, doing sit-ups, pounding out the miles on the running machine, riding the static bike.

But even at home, as he pedalled the bike and watched a football magazine programme on the gym TV, he couldn't escape the pundits' damning verdict as they replayed and discussed his many missed scoring opportunities.

Gavin frowned and pedalled more furiously.

The following day, at official training, he played a practice match as though it were a cup final. Chasing every ball, diving into the tackle with the enthusiasm of a schoolboy.

He was almost enjoying it, remembering what it was like when he first started to play, until he received a crunching tackle himself and fell heavily. As he lay on the ground, the memory of a thousand similar crunching tackles came flooding back.

Strikers get used to taking more hard knocks than players in the other areas of the pitch; it goes with the territory. It doesn't mean that the tackles hurt any less, and slowly, but remorselessly, all those tackles take their toll.

But Gavin wasn't going to let it show, not yet anyway. He just grinned as Santiago walked over. He held out his arm so that the young player could haul him to his feet.

After training, Gavin had another massage on his left thigh. It was aching like mad but he tried to ignore the pain by leafing through a magazine as the physio worked on his tortured muscles.

Gavin turned a page and saw the photographs and the strap line:

Readers' Phone Poll:
MUÑEZ or HARRIS – who should START?
YOU DECIDE!

Gavin angrily hurled the magazine towards the bin in the corner of the room.

It missed the target.

Santiago was already on the way out of the training complex. The Lamborghini was purring like a contented cat as he eased it towards the main road. He slowed to almost a standstill as he prepared to slip into the line of traffic when suddenly he saw a flash of movement at the off-side of the vehicle and felt a thump as something struck the car.

Santiago yelled out in shock. He'd hit someone. He felt his heart pound and then sighed with relief as he saw a scruffy young kid get to his feet and walk round to his side of the vehicle. He had no idea that the 'accident' had been deliberate as the teenager stuck his head in through the open window.

'Are you OK?' said Santiago.

'My name is Enrique,' said the teenager in Spanish. 'I'm your brother.'

'What!' said Santiago, completely baffled. 'What are you talking about?'

'My mother was married to your father, Herman Muñez. In Mexico City.'

Santiago froze, his mouth gaping open, his mind racing.

'I have proof,' said the boy.

He pulled an old photograph from his pocket, pushed it through the window and, when Santiago didn't take it, dropped it onto his lap.

It was too much for Santiago to absorb and he felt the panic beginning to rise. He shoved the Lamborghini into gear, saw the gap in the traffic and roared away, leaving the boy watching the vehicle as it disappeared in a cloud of dust.

Santiago drove fast. Too fast. He was sweating, breathing hard, feeling the tightness in his chest. He reached for his inhaler and took a hit. Roz. He had to talk to Roz; she would tell him what to do, how to react.

He grabbed his mobile and hit the SPEED DIAL button for the Newcastle house. The phone rang a couple of times and then Santiago heard Roz's voice.

'Sorry, we're out at the moment. Leave us a message and we'll—'

Santiago hit the END CALL button and dropped the phone. He fumbled for the photograph that was still on his lap.

It was a woman. Dark hair. Dark eyes. But could it really, possibly be . . . his mother? Now. After all these years.

He threw the photograph onto the seat next to him, dropped a gear, and gunned the car down the dual carriageway.

When Santiago pulled the Lamborghini into the car park of the location of his first TV commercial he was still feeling confused, scared, threatened and downright angry. The car skidded to a halt and as Santi opened the door and got out, the commercial's producer came strolling over from a catering truck.

'Santiago,' he smiled. 'I'm glad you made it. We're ready to start.'

The young footballer's usual easygoing and friendly attitude had gone. 'How long will this take?' he snapped.

The producer raised his eyebrows and indicated the way, still smiling but thinking to himself that here was yet another young player who was swiftly growing far too big for his footballing boots.

And it all took far longer than Santiago had imagined. Maybe it was down to his attitude; he was surly and uncooperative from the start, but it was all different and completely new to him.

The setting and costume didn't help. Santi was in a mock-up of a Japanese panelled room with trees and mountains in the background. He was dressed in an orange kimono and was wearing a headband. Sweltering under the glare of the harsh TV lights, he felt like a complete idiot. He was supposed to look and sound as if he absolutely adored the taste of 'Total Tofu', but after twenty-six takes he looked as though he would rather die than taste one more mouthful of the stuff.

Santiago's mind was full of the images of the boy at the car window and the photograph, which still lay on the passenger seat. He heard someone shout, 'Rolling,' and a young guy with a clapper board stood close to his face, snapped the board and said, 'Take twenty-seven,' before walking out of shot.

The set went completely silent and then the director, standing behind the camera, looked towards Santi and said, 'And ... action, Santiago.'

Santiago was holding chopsticks, and on the table was a plateful of 'Total Tofu'. Santi lifted a small amount to his mouth, chewed it for a couple of seconds, put down the chopsticks and smiled a cheesy grin straight to camera.

Then he spoke the words that, after twenty-six takes, were imprinted on his brain. 'And that's why I go for Total Tofu, every time. Total Tofu, the super-food for the Super-Sub!'

He held the cheesy grin for what seemed like

agonizing hours until he heard the director shout, 'Aaaaaaaand . . . Cut! Lovely. Great.'

Santiago spat the rest of the half-eaten tofu into a bucket just out of shot, thinking that at last it was over.

Then the director shouted again, 'Let's go for one more.'

It was more than Santi could take. He got up from the table, glared at the director and stormed off in the direction of the make-up room.

The producer turned to the director and sighed. 'What's that old saying? Never work with children or animals – or footballers!'

Santiago was staring at his troubled reflection as he held his mobile to his ear and waited for the call to be answered. 'Come on, pick up. Pick up.'

At his workshop in Newcastle, Glen had heard his mobile ringing and was wiping his hands on an oily rag as he saw Santiago's name displayed on the phone. He answered the call. 'Santiago!'

'This is *not* on, Glen!' yelled Santi into his phone. 'These people are making a fool out of me.'

'Who, son?' said Glen, taken aback.

'This commercial. David Beckham gets Gillette, and I get freaking tofu!'

Glen was his usual, philosophical self. 'It's good money, Santi. And we've got to start somewhere.'

'But it's disgusting. Look, why don't you try eating it for five hours straight. I mean, gimme a break, here.'

'Santi, I'll have a word with—'

'I'm better than this, Glen!' shouted Santiago and then hung up.

Glen stared at his phone, bewildered. Something was wrong. Seriously wrong.

Sixteen

The Lamborghini skidded to a halt outside the house; at this rate it would need a new set of tyres before there were a thousand miles on the clock.

Santiago got out and went to the front door, his breath shallow and his chest tight. He went inside, taking another hit from his asthma inhaler; he'd used it a lot over the past few hours.

He was about to flick on the lights as he walked into the dining area when he saw the candles on the dinner table. And not just candles; the table was set for dinner, for two.

He stopped and stared, and then he heard a

voice coming from the kitchen. 'I hope you're hungry.'

Roz appeared from the kitchen, holding a spatula and smiling. 'I made your favourite.'

It was another surprise. A shock. He'd had no idea that Roz was planning to visit, but this time Santiago couldn't have been happier. He rushed over and hugged her. 'You don't know how glad I am to see you.'

Quickly, the story spilled out: the boy at the car, the photograph, and the feeling of panic that Santi been fighting ever since. Roz listened to every word and looked briefly at the photograph, and then she suggested that maybe they should eat so that Santi could calm himself down before they decided what to do next.

Santi nodded his agreement.

'Good,' smiled Roz. 'I came a long way to cook this meal.'

It was a good suggestion. The food was great, and a couple of glasses of wine helped, too. As they ate, Santi described the agonies of making his first television commercial.

And as he relaxed, he was even able to

see the funny side of it all.

'This is so good,' he said, finishing the last of the chicken Roz had prepared.

'Yeah, I'm sorry it was chicken, but they were all out of tofu down at the shops.'

Santiago reacted with mock horror and then his eyes rested on the photograph that sat on the table between them.

Roz picked it up and studied it more closely. 'Did the boy say anything else?'

'I dunno. When he threw that at me, I was so freaked I drove off. I couldn't breathe.'

'But you always talked about wanting to find her.'

'I know, but I can't deal with it now. In my head she was gone for ever.'

Roz nodded and put the photograph back onto the tabletop. 'She does really look like you.'

Maybe, thought Santiago, as he looked down at the dark eyes that seemed to be staring back at him. But there was a way of finding out for certain.

* * *

In the house in LA, Santiago's grandmother, Mercedes, stared at the printout of the photograph her grandson had emailed to her. She had dreaded this moment for so long.

She picked up the telephone and dialled the number.

Roz was in bed, sleeping, but Santiago was still downstairs, gazing aimlessly at the television. He couldn't sleep until this was sorted.

He grabbed the telephone at the first ring. '*Si?*' he said quietly.

'Santiago, where did you get this photo graph?'

'Is it her, Grandma?'

There was a silence for a few moments, but the silence only confirmed what Santi had come to believe during the long day and evening.

His grandmother spoke at last. 'From the day you went to Spain, I feared this moment would come.'

'You *knew*! You knew she was here?'

'I couldn't tell you, Santiago. I did not want to cause you pain.'

Santi was pacing around the room, not

wanting to wake Roz, but his voice hissed with anger. 'But she's my mother, and you didn't tell me. My God, Grandma, what gave you the right—?'

'The *right*!' said Mercedes, equally angry now. 'That woman left us, Santiago. She just walked away and left your father in pieces. I never saw my Herman smile again; he was empty inside. She broke his heart, Santi, and I swore, the day she left, that I would never let her hurt one of my boys again as long as I lived.'

Santiago sat back on one of the sofas and tried to speak more calmly. 'But this is my choice, Grandma. She's my mother.'

'She abandoned you, Santiago. What kind of woman does that? What right has she now to be back in our lives?'

Santiago sat there for a long time. Thinking. Wondering. Imagining. Trying to drag back into his memory moments from his childhood. Eventually, he fell asleep, but his dreams were troubled and disturbing.

Seventeen

Valencia: traditionally one of the strongest outfits in *La Liga* and, with a more than useful campaign underway, a severe examination for Real, even at the Bernabéu.

And in the build-up to the match, Real coach Rudi Van Der Merwe had come under more pressure to give Santiago a place in the starting line-up.

But as Van Der Merwe pondered his decision, he had no idea that, after weeks of being desperate for a chance of a full ninety minutes in the team, there was suddenly something, or someone, even more important than football at the forefront of Santi's mind: his mother.

During training he'd gone through the motions, putting in the work but with none of the joy he'd felt during his first couple of months at the club.

And when the squad took up its residency at the hotel on the day before the match, he avoided his team-mates and took no part in the usual banter and laughter.

As Santiago boarded the bus leaving the hotel for the Bernabéu he felt strangely detached from it all. The supporters were thronging the streets on the approach to the stadium. Chanting. Singing. Santiago heard none of it.

The bus pulled into the shelter of the Bernabéu and as the squad got off and headed quickly towards the double glass and stainless steel doors, which proudly bear the badge of Real Madrid, Santiago suddenly heard his name called from somewhere in the crowd of supporters pressing for a close-up view of their heroes.

'Hey, Santi! Bro! It's me!'

Santiago stopped. His eyes scanned the sea of shouting, laughing, calling faces. And then he saw him. Enrique. The teenager was peering out from the crush of fans, doing his best to wave.

'I need to talk with that kid,' said Santiago to one of the security guards, pointing into the crowd.

But it was impossible. The security guard knew his job: he was there to protect the club's multi-million euro investments, not to fish kids out of the crowd. And besides, he could hardly hear what Santiago was saying. He ushered him forward and Santiago found himself being carried along through the doors and into the relative quiet of the stadium.

Most players find themselves adopting some form of pre-match ritual, whether consciously or subconsciously. Some do it for good luck; others do it because they have always done it. The way they undress, or put on their kit; right sock first, or left. The way they tie their boots; their own, particular stretching exercises; the gentle pat of the club badge on their shirt, or the kiss of the necklace. The silent prayer. Every team is made up of individuals, each with their own particular ways.

The Real players were changed and ready. They were watching one of Van Der Merwe's assistants write the names of the starting line-up onto a board.

No one, with the possible exception of goal-keeper Casillas, was a guaranteed certainty to start, and even the *galácticos* breathed a little more easily as they saw their names appear.

The assistant had almost finished; Harris was the next name due to appear. Instead, he wrote: *Muñez*.

Only one player reacted; Gavin put on his tracksuit top and walked away. The others remained silent – even the best of them had been there themselves.

Santiago gave no indication of delight, and his team-mates probably thought he was being sensitive to Gavin's feelings. But it wasn't that.

Van Der Merwe came into the room and went straight to Santiago. 'You're starting tonight, up front with Ronnie.'

Santi nodded blankly, almost as though he was in a dream, and Van Der Merwe stared at him for a few seconds, trying to read his thoughts and hoping that the experience of walking out to face Valencia would not prove too overwhelming for the young striker.

During the pre-match warm-up, as the stadium filled, Santiago went through his stretching routine. He ran and practised shots, and even exchanged a few words with other players. But he did it all as though he was on autopilot, as though he would rather be somewhere else. On this, the biggest night of his life.

The team and substitutes went back to the dressing room for Van Der Merwe's final briefing, and then, as kick-off time drew ever nearer, the captain, Raúl, began his own pre-match ritual. He slipped on the captain's armband and then, one by one, he kissed each player on the head.

When he reached Santiago he planted the kiss on his head and then whispered quietly, 'This is your moment.'

Santiago nodded again. He was somewhere else, somewhere a long way away. Ronaldo was sitting next to him, and even a hug of good luck from the smiling Brazilian received no response.

And then they were on their way; through the dressing-room doors to the granite steps where the referee and his assistants were waiting. The Valencia players emerged from their own dressing room, and some nodded an acknowledgement to their rivals as they formed their own line on the steps.

The two lines of players began to move, their studs sounding loudly on the stone steps. There were few words now. They walked on through the blue covering and out into the glare of the floodlights and the welcoming, ear-blasting roar of eighty-five thousand voices.

The thousands of waving white flags, the ringing cheers and chants, the pounding thump of the drums; they were barely registering for Santiago as he took his place in the line-ups across the centre circle.

The two teams stood and waved to every side of the stadium, acknowledging the adoration, and then they broke away and jogged into position.

Santiago shook his head. He had to

concentrate – he had to focus his mind and give everything for the full ninety minutes.

The referee checked with his two assistants and as he brought his whistle to his lips a sudden hush fell over the Bernabéu. And then the whistle sounded.

Both teams started cautiously, and then, from a Valencia clearance, Santiago collected the ball thirty-five yards out. He was slow bringing it under control and was easily robbed by a Valencia midfielder.

Santi turned to give chase. As with most strikers, tackling was hardly one of the strongest areas of his game, but the tackle he put in from behind was late, high and dangerous.

The Valencia player went down in a heap and the shrill sound of the referee's whistle cut through the night air. Everyone in the stadium knew that Santiago was about to receive a card; the only question in some minds was which colour it would be.

It was red. The referee had no choice; it was a clear decision. Santiago was being sent off after just five minutes. He stood rooted to the spot, unable to believe it had happened. But it had. The Real protests and the whistles from around the ground were pointless.

The Real captain, Raúl, came over to Santiago, sympathetically put an arm on his shoulders and nodded to him to leave the pitch.

He forced himself to move, jogging head bowed to the touchline, where he pulled off his shirt and avoided looking towards the bench as he went straight down into the tunnel.

On the bench, Van Der Merwe could hardly contain his fury, but he had to: decisions needed to be made. He nodded towards coach Steve McManaman and then along the bench to his substitutes.

Real needed to replace the firepower they had lost up front and, in the irony of ironies, Gavin Harris was coming on, so soon after losing his place.

The man to give way was French midfield maestro, Zidane. Gavin was getting another chance.

Santi showered and changed alone, feeling shame, remorse, regret; a tumble of mixed emotions as he relived his moment of madness. He'd let everyone down: the club, his coach, his team-mates – and himself. He just wanted to get away from the Bernabéu and the scene of his humiliation as quickly as he could.

He jumped into the Lamborghini, edged into the dark Madrid streets and flicked on the vehicle's TV monitor. The match was being broadcast live, and ten-man Real were defending manfully against determined opposition.

It seemed almost unbelievable to Santi, as his eyes flicked from the road to the screen, that he was watching the spectacle that he had been part of for those few fateful minutes.

Gavin was playing like a man possessed, going close on goal and helping out in defence as Valencia pushed and harried and strove for a – so far – elusive goal.

Valencia's Uruguayan playmaker, Regueiro, was causing huge problems down the flanks and sending in teasing, wicked crosses, which his team-mates had failed to convert, thanks largely to the brilliance of Casillas in the Real goal.

Santiago's dismissal had set the tone for a

hard, bruising encounter, but somehow Real were holding on.

It looked as though the match would end goalless, but then, from an increasingly rare Real attack, the ball came into the Valencia box from out wide at no more than waist height.

Gavin was just outside the six-yard box. He flung himself forward, timing his diving header perfectly, and the ball rocketed into the net.

In the car, Santiago smiled for the first time that evening as the match commentator went into raptures over what he called a 'great goal'.

On the pitch, Gavin was still flat out. He rolled over onto his back, heard the roars of the Madridistas and smiled up at the night sky.

Team-mates came diving in on him, first Robinho, then Raúl, then Gravesen, forcing out the last breath from Gavin's almost bursting lungs.

But Gavin just laughed. He was back; the goal had come at last.

Eighteen

The Buddha Bar is one of Madrid's top nightspots, and a favourite with many of the Real players.

It sits in a less than glamorous location by the side of a ring road on the outskirts of the city. But the customers don't go to admire the scenery outside the Buddha; they go for the action.

In the darkened interior, numerous Buddha statues, large and small, stare down with unseeing eyes from every available space. They perch behind the bar, they hover above doorways and they hide in secluded alcoves, reflecting an aura of tranquillity that contrasts completely with the energy generated by the revellers at the club.

The place throbs with movement and electricity. In the well of the dance floor, beneath the searching, darting glare of strobe lights, hundreds sway to the thudding beat. On the gallery above, groups cluster around low tables, vainly trying to be heard above the pounding music, checking out the fashions worn by others and casting envious eyes towards the small roped-off VIP area, where burly security men permit only the chosen few.

All around, waiters and waitresses perform miracles, dodging and weaving between tightly packed bodies, waving arms and outstretched legs as they balance trays full of glasses and bottles on one raised hand with the dexterity of circus conjurors.

Santiago had not bothered going through to the VIP area. He was sitting at the bar, nursing a beer, having watched Gavin's goal replayed on one of the giant TV screens. The commentator had been right – it was a great goal, and the sense of elation on Gavin's face as the camera zoomed in for a close-up was even greater.

Santi was pleased for Gavin but desperately

disappointed for himself. And *in* himself.

As he sipped at his beer he saw the glamorous Jordana García gliding towards him.

'Hey,' she said. 'Hello, hothead.'

'Hello, Jordana.'

The TV presenter kissed him on both cheeks and then got straight to the point. 'It's crunch time, Santi. I want to interview you on my show while you're still playing for the club.'

Santiago almost laughed. 'You're not going to give up, are you?'

'At last,' smiled Jordana. 'You realized.'

They sat talking together for some time and as they left, the paparazzi were clustered at the exit, cameras poised and ready.

'Can I give you a ride?' asked Santiago as he waited for his car to be brought round from the VIP car park.

The white Lamborghini slid to a standstill, and as the car valet got out and held open the driver's door Santiago looked at Jordana, expecting her to be impressed.

'No thanks, I'm cool,' she smiled. She kissed him on the both cheeks and the paparazzi cameras flashed, and then she got in behind the wheel of the Lamborghini, just as an identical vehicle pulled up immediately behind the first.

Santiago stared and then smiled as he closed the door of Jordana's vehicle. She looked in her driver's mirror and saw the second vehicle.

'But you do have great taste,' she said through the open window before shoving the vehicle into gear and roaring away into the night.

Nineteen

Sleep didn't come easily to Santiago for the next couple of nights.

The sending off troubled him deeply, but not as much as the photograph of his mother. It was a constant reminder that she was there, in Madrid; so close, and yet as far away as she had been for most of his life.

Santi would prowl around the huge house late into the night, trying to picture his mother's life, wondering if he would ever get to meet her. Eventually, he would fall, exhausted, onto one of the sofas and slide into dream-filled sleep.

Roz had managed to get an extra few days in Madrid by swapping shifts with one of her colleagues. She needn't have bothered. Santi was remote and distant, even though Roz was doing her very best to be supportive.

Santi was sleeping soundly on the sofa when she walked in and saw, immediately, the unhappiness etched into his usually sunny features.

'Santi . . .' she said softly, but he didn't stir. Roz knew that he was emotionally drained. She decided to let him sleep for a little longer.

Later, she made coffee and prepared fresh orange juice and croissants. She arranged them on a tray, walked into the living room and set the tray down on the coffee table.

Santiago was still sleeping and Roz went and kissed him lightly on the forehead. 'Santi . . .'

He didn't move.

'Santiago, come on, it's late.'

He opened his eyes, for a moment not really seeing Roz, or knowing where he was, or quite what was happening. His head was still in his dreams.

And then Roz came into focus and her words registered. 'It's late,' she'd said. 'Any news from your gran?'

But suddenly Santiago wasn't thinking about his grandmother, or his mother, or anything but the time.

He sat up and turned to stare at the clock on the wall. It read 12.50 pm.

'*No!*' breathed Santi, leaping from the sofa.

'What?' said Roz.

'Why didn't you wake me?'

'I tried but you were—'

'I'm gonna miss the team plane,' yelled Santiago, hurtling up the stairs.

He was back in less than a minute, with a bag in one hand and his Real Madrid blazer in the other. He grabbed his car keys and ran to the door without a word or even a look at Roz.

The front door slammed and a few seconds later Roz heard the roar of the Lamborghini's engine. And then *she* was angry, furious; she didn't deserve to be treated this way. She picked up the tray she had lovingly prepared, hurled it onto the floor and stomped towards the stairs. So much for her surprise visit – she was going home.

* * *

He called to apologize and make his excuses, but there were no excuses. Players just didn't miss the official team plane. Ever.

By the time Santiago had battled his way through the heavy traffic, negotiated temporary road works and found somewhere to park at Barajas airport, the team flight to Trondheim for the return Champions League match with Rosenberg had long since departed.

The player liaison director, Leo Vegaz, had tersely given Santiago instructions on what he was to do about making his own way to Trondheim when they'd spoken on the phone. Van Der Merwe had been too incensed to even speak to Santiago.

Panting and dishevelled, Santi arrived at the ticket counter and slapped down his Platinum AmEx card.

'Trondheim, please,' he said in Spanish. 'First class.'

The desk clerk raised his eyebrows, as if to say, 'You'll be lucky, mate,' before replying. 'One moment, *señor*, I'll check what's available.'

It was easy to become accustomed to first-class air travel. The wide seats, the extra legroom, the obliging flight attendants serving champagne and canapés.

Santiago enjoyed none of that. He was way back down the plane, close to the toilets, wedged between a huge American tourist wearing a Hawaiian shirt and a sombrero that he wasn't taking off for anyone, and a puzzled-looking Spanish kid who couldn't quite believe he was sitting next to a real-life Real Madrid player.

The blazer was right and the face was right – he'd seen it enough times on television lately. But what would a superstar be doing stuck back here in economy?

Finally, the kid decided to go for it. He pulled out a pen and took the sick bag from the pocket in the seat in front of him and handed them both, without a word, to Santiago.

Santiago smiled weakly and signed his autograph. He gave the sick bag and the pen back to the boy and then felt the large American nudge him in the side.

'Hey,' said the American, as Santi turned to look. 'Are you famous?'

Santi smiled again and shook his head.

Leo Vegaz was waiting for Santiago as he emerged from Arrivals at Trondheim airport into a bitterly cold day.

'Big trouble,' he said to Santiago, ushering him towards a waiting car. 'No player has ever missed the team plane before.'

'I know,' sighed Santi. 'I know.'

Rosenberg had taken huge encouragement from their performance at the Bernabéu. They had come tantalizingly close to a famous draw and now, on their home pitch and in conditions they were used to, they were pressing hard for an even more famous victory.

Snow was falling in big flakes, which were picked out in the glare of the floodlights like millions of swirling moths. It was bitingly cold. Up in the stands, Glen, wearing a scarf and his warmest coat, couldn't stop his teeth from chattering.

On the bench, Santiago sat with the other subs, wrapped in layers of Adidas gear. Many of his team-mates out on the pitch were wearing gloves, struggling against the temperature and a team determined to make a little history.

It was hard for the Real players, particularly the Brazilian contingent, accustomed to playing their football in a totally different climate, to find their normal rhythm and pace in the icy night air. Gavin Harris was giving his all, hunting down the ball, covering more ground than anyone as he searched for that elusive goal.

The first forty-five minutes had been goalless. Gavin had one fine attempt well saved by the Rosenberg keeper, and in the Real goal, Casillas had pulled off a couple of minor miracles to keep out the opposing strikers.

During the half-time talk, Van Der Merwe hadn't even glanced in Santiago's direction as he encouraged the team to greater effort.

And they were trying hard as the second half progressed, but it was far from easy.

Then, as the Rosenberg defence moved out, Guti played a neat ball through to Gavin. He ran on quickly, like his old self, and sent his shot cleanly and powerfully into the net.

It was there. He'd done it; he'd scored again. He raised his arms, he danced for joy, he punched the air.

And then he glimpsed the Rosenberg fans pointing towards the far touchline. He looked back and saw the referee's assistant, still with his flag raised, and he realized that the goal had been disallowed for offside.

It had been a marginal decision, and television replays would show that it was correct, but Gavin couldn't believe his bad luck. It was almost as though he was cursed.

But at least he'd put the ball in the net. He'd done it, he would do it again, and next time the goal would stand.

For the next few minutes, Gavin seemed to almost redouble his efforts, and then, perhaps unsurprisingly, he pulled up sharply as he chased a loose ball.

It was cramp. Old-fashioned cramp. And it was bad. After a couple of minutes of treatment, the trainer indicated to the coach that it wasn't going to ease quickly and Van Der Merwe had no option but to take off the night's most committed player.

As Gavin hobbled towards the touchline, Van Der Merwe locked eyes with Santiago for a moment and then nodded to one of the other subs to go on.

He looked at Santi again. Words were not necessary.

The match petered out into a goalless draw, and even the Rosenberg players appeared to be pleased to get off the pitch and back to the warmth of the dressing room and a hot shower. No one was thinking about exchanging shirts as they hurried towards the tunnel.

When Glen went into the dressing room he found Santiago sitting alone on the bench beneath the lockers.

'*Buenos días*, son,' he said, getting little more than a nod of acknowledgement in return.

He sat down next to Santiago. 'I got a call. There's going to be repercussions, they're talking about a hefty fine.' Glen sighed. 'Not a day for the memoirs, eh?'

It was as though Santiago hadn't heard. 'Nil–nil and he had me sitting on my freezing backside for ninety minutes.'

'He's the coach; it's his call. He's sending you a message, Santi, and you need to listen.'

Santiago turned and glared at his agent, his friend, the man responsible for giving him the opportunity to turn his lifelong dream of becoming a professional footballer into reality. But all that was far from his mind as he spoke. 'Don't patronize me, Glen. I'm doing commercials for tofu while you're fixing cars in Newcastle.'

'I'm only a flight away, son,' said Glen. He'd never seen Santiago like this before. 'And I came as soon as they called.'

'Yeah, well I need someone full-time, Glen. In Madrid, to support me off the pitch.'

Glen could see the direction the conversation was taking. 'Perhaps this is where I get off, then.'

Santiago didn't reply; he just stared at the floor.

The argument wasn't about tofu commercials, or opportunities that needed to be seized. Glen knew that perfectly well. There was something more troubling Santiago – something unspoken that was hurting him deeply, something that was forcing him to take out his anger and frustration on his closest friend and staunchest supporter.

Glen held out his hand. 'It's been a great ride, Santi. A privilege.'

Santiago took Glen's hand and shook it. But he didn't look at him. He couldn't: they both knew that it was the end.

The disappointment and hurt showed clearly on Glen's face as he turned away and walked to the door. Then he stopped and looked back. 'You know, your plate's getting so full so fast, son. You should watch what falls off the edge.'

He turned away and walked through the door, leaving Santi still staring at the floor.

Twenty

Santiago had arrived back from Trondheim to
find the house horribly empty. Roz had pinned
the briefest of notes to the fridge door before
leaving.

Since then Santiago hadn't spoken to her by
phone. Or to Glen. He didn't know what to say
to either of them.

Each day he'd arrived at training hoping to see
the young kid, Enrique, again. There was so
much more he needed to know now.

But if Enrique was there, Santiago didn't spot
him.

And so he'd spent the evenings moping

around the house, watching television alone, thinking about calling Roz or Glen and then deciding against it, and staring at the photograph. Of his mother.

Gavin had had a terrific night, but as far as he was concerned, the night was still young.

He drove back to his villa with two girls from the Buddha Bar. They got out of the car, giggling, and stumbled up to the front door.

Gavin slid his key into the lock, whispering to the girls in appalling Spanish, and found that the key wouldn't turn. He frowned, pulled out the key and gave it an accusing stare, and then tried again. It still wouldn't turn.

The girls were becoming impatient; it was cold at that hour of the morning and their flimsy outfits were not exactly suited to a late-night wander around the garden.

Gavin trampled over the nearest flowerbed and went to the large picture window which spread across most of the living room. He cupped his hands to the glass and peered inside. For a moment he thought he'd been burgled, but *everything* had gone. All he could see was a few black garbage bags, stuffed full with clothes – his clothes.

'Oh, no!'

One of the Spanish girls tapped him on the shoulder. She was holding an envelope she had found pinned to the bottom of the door. Gavin ripped open the envelope and, peering closely in the darkness, read the letter that was inside.

'What!'

The girls stared at him; this wasn't the way they were expecting the night to continue.

'We have to go. Where do you live? I'll have to take you home.'

Their English was no better than Gavin's Spanish: they were totally confused. Gesturing with both hands, Gavin ushered them back to the car and they got in. He started up the engine and drove quickly away, listening to the girls speaking loudly to each other as they tried to figure out what was going on.

'I've been evicted,' he said when the opportunity to get a word in eventually came. 'Evicted! You understand? How do you say evicted?'

The girls didn't understand, but one of them answered Gavin with a few quick words, making him mistakenly think that she knew what he was saying.

'Yeah, that's it, right. They've repossessed the property, thrown me out. I owe money.' He could see them looking at him blankly, so he attempted a mixture of Spanish and English. '*Denaro!* I have no *mas denaro*! *Nada!*'

The girls' look of confusion turned to one of fury, and one of them began to yell in Spanish. This time, she had jumped to the wrong conclusion. 'You think we want *money* to go back to your house! What the hell do you think we are?'

Gavin didn't understand a word, so he just blustered on. 'My agent. Barry scumbag Rankin. He had me invest in some bogus vineyard in France for my pension. *Si? Comprende?* I have nothing left! Nothing!'

'*Stop!*' screamed the girl, who still thought Gavin was talking about paying them for the pleasure of their company.

'What? Stop? Here? Why?'

'*Yes!*'

The car screeched to a standstill and the two girls got out, screaming at Gavin and slamming the door so hard that it made him shudder.

As he drove away he could still hear their yells.

It was almost dawn when Santiago was woken from a troubled sleep by the sound of the door buzzer. He got out of bed, and wearing just his boxer shorts, he padded over to the videophone and pressed a button.

Gavin's grinning face came into view on the small black and white monitor.

'Any room at the inn?' he said.

Santiago knew that after the Trondheim incident and his shameful actions in his fleeting appearance in the Valencia match he would have to work doubly hard to regain Van Der Merwe's confidence. And before he could even be considered for team selection he had to serve a suspension.

But his head wasn't right. As Roz wouldn't return his calls and he'd split with Glen, there was only his new houseguest, Gavin, to talk to. And although Gavin was great for a laugh, Santiago wasn't in the mood for laughs.

He would rather have been alone, but he couldn't refuse his friend. After all, Gavin had taken him in when they were both at Newcastle.

Santiago was hoping that it would be a short-term arrangement, but he wasn't encouraged when he asked Gavin how long he thought he would be staying.

Gavin just shrugged and said, 'Quite a while, I reckon.'

When he went on to explain the extent of his financial problems, thanks to the expert advice of Barry Rankin, Santiago realized that he really was in for the long haul. And Gavin wasn't the easiest houseguest; he was more like a big kid who needed a lot of looking after. But at least he was never boring and eventually Santiago decided that he just had to get on with things.

But the thought that his mother and half-brother were out there somewhere in Madrid was with him all the time.

He stayed low-key at training, putting in the work and sticking to the rules. There were plenty of stories in football of players who'd upset the boss and then spent the remainder of the season out in the wilderness, omitted from the first-team squad before being shipped out of the club during the next transfer window. It was the nightmare scenario, but even at Real Madrid, no player was bigger than the club.

In the following league game, Gavin scored again in an impressive Real performance. Despite his financial woes, he appeared to be back to his irrepressible best, even off the pitch.

One evening, he was down in the huge basement parking area at Santi's house, playing 'keepy-uppy' with a football.

Santiago walked down the stairs; he'd been trying to get through to Roz on the phone. 'She won't speak to me. I don't know why she's so angry.'

Gavin flicked the ball up onto his thigh and then knocked it over to Santi.

'Well, I can understand. She's there all alone,' grinned Gavin as Santi juggled the ball on his instep a few times before sending in back down the hallway. 'While you're out with dark-haired Spanish beauties.'

'But I'm not out with dark-haired Spanish beauties,' said Santiago as the ball came back.

Gavin watched as Santi demonstrated a few of the skills he'd learned from the Brazilians at Real, juggling the ball between instep, thigh, heel and shoulder.

'Yeah, very good, but you've still got some serious grovelling to do, my son.'

The ball was returned faster and Gavin took it on one thigh. He let it drop to his instep and then flicked it up so that he could head it back towards Santi. Gavin wasn't famed for his heading ability and the ball went high to Santi's left.

He instinctively moved back to stop it. He didn't see the bicycle lying on the cement floor. His left foot twisted in the spokes of one of the wheels and Santi went down with a yell.

Gavin stared as Santi lay sprawled across the bicycle, flinching in pain as he reached down to his injured leg.

'Come on, stop messing about,' said Gavin, walking over to Santi. 'You Latinos are always diving.'

Santi looked up at him. 'This is serious man. It really hurts.'

They say that bad things come in threes. Valencia had been bad, Trondheim had been even worse and the broken bone in his foot completed the most unwelcome hat trick of Santiago's brief career.

Van Der Merwe went ballistic. The injury meant that Santi would be out of action for at least ten weeks. He would miss a vital chunk of the season; important league games, the remaining Champions League group matches and well into the knockout phase.

The furious coach banned his player from going anywhere but the training ground or his home. And when Santiago told him that he had been planning to return to England for Christmas, the coach replied with just two words. 'Forget it!'

Santiago's one consolation was that when

Roz heard about the injury – from Gavin – she did at least agree to speak to him on the phone.

The conversation began well enough. Roz was sympathetic; being a nurse she'd seen and dealt with far more serious injuries, but she did her best to sound concerned and understanding.

Santiago was at home, lying on the sofa, with his leg up and his foot in a bright blue orthopaedic boot. A pair of crutches rested against one of the chairs.

They had been chatting for about five minutes when Santiago took a deep breath and finally told Roz that Van Der Merwe had banned him from travelling home for Christmas.

There was a moment of stunned silence. 'But he can't do that,' said Roz at last. 'I've got everything planned. Jamie and Lorraine are coming round with little Keanu. My mum's doing the turkey.'

'I know. And all I want is to be is with you, now, at home. I feel like I'm under house arrest.'

'But I don't understand. What's the point in them keeping you over there? You can't even do any training.'

Santiago shifted uncomfortably on the sofa as he felt a painful twinge in his foot. 'They pay me, Roz; they call the shots. I'm sorry, I can't change that.'

Roz couldn't hold back her anger. 'I can't believe this. You promised. It's not fair and it's not that much to ask. All the times I've been over to Madrid and you've not come home once, Santi, you've not even set foot in Newcastle. You *said* we'd have Christmas together.'

'Roz, it's out of my hands. I—'

'*No*,' said Roz, interrupting. 'It's just another excuse. If you hadn't sacked Glen he could have sorted it out. Well, I'm getting sick of it, Santi. *Sick* of it!'

She hung up and Santiago flinched as another stab of pain jarred through his foot.

Twenty-one

Real Madrid safely, if unspectacularly, negotiated the group stages of the Champions League, but even before Christmas it looked unlikely that the club would add to its tally of twenty-nine league titles.

Barcelona already looked well set to retain the title, although outsiders Osasuna were putting up a spirited challenge.

Gavin was training furiously and playing well in a team that wasn't quite firing on all cylinders, while Santiago could do nothing but sit and watch and wait impatiently for his injury to heal.

He spoke to Roz several times and appealed to Van Der Merwe to change his mind about letting him return to England. But there was no shifting the coach; he wanted his troublesome striker where he could see him, believing that he could still play a significant part in the closing weeks of the season – if he could regain his fitness and if he could stay out of trouble.

Santiago was dreading Christmas Day, and when it arrived it was as gloomy and depressing as he had feared.

He called his grandmother and brother in LA and then he called Roz, who chatted brightly as she described the Christmas Day she was spending with her mum and their friends, Jamie and Lorraine, with their new baby.

She told him about the presents, the decorated tree, the Christmas lunch with crackers and paper hats. 'Little Keanu loves the lights on the Christmas tree. He's such a beautiful baby, pity he looks like Jamie.'

She was doing her best to sound cheerful, but Santiago knew that behind the jokes and laughter, Roz was feeling just as lonely as he was.

Later, as he and Gavin shared a Christmas dinner of take-away Chinese food straight from the boxes, Santi found himself wondering about his other family, his mother and his half-brother. How, he wondered, were they spending their Christmas Day? Were they thinking of him, too?

They were, although neither of them mentioned it to the other. Enrique's father, Miguel, had surprised his son by giving him a Christmas present of a brand-new football. It was an uncharacteristic gesture of kindness from Miguel, who had even gone to the trouble of wrapping the ball in paper.

Rosa-Maria sat with her husband and watched Enrique unwrap the present. His eyes widened in delight as he saw the football and he smiled his thanks to his father. Then he looked at his mother.

He knew then that as she watched him holding the football, she was thinking of Santiago, just as she knew that he was thinking of Santiago.

But Miguel knew nothing of their thoughts. Rosa had never told him about the existence of her sons, Santiago and Julio; she had been afraid of his response. And now, when she wanted too tell him, she feared that it was far to late.

At Santiago's house, Gavin finished the last of his steamed chicken with noodles and licked his lips.

He glanced over at the glum-faced Santiago and sighed. Santi needed cheering up.

'Right, then,' said Gavin. 'Fancy a game of charades?'

When New Year's Eve arrived, Madrid was covered in a blanket of snow. It made Santiago even more depressed.

Gavin had moved on from charades and party games to organizing the sort of party he preferred. He'd arranged for a few of the Real players and their wives or girlfriends, along with some other close friends, to come over to the house to see in the New Year. And like all Gavin's get-togethers, he'd invited a few extra girls, just so that he didn't get lonely.

As the party got into full swing downstairs, Santi went up to his room, to leave a message on Roz's phone.

He knew that Roz was working, and as she'd be midway through a late shift on a busy ward, there would be no way she could take a call as midnight approached in Madrid. So Santi's only option was to leave a message.

'Hey, Roz. I can't believe we're not together on New Year's Eve. I'll make it up to you, I promise.' He paused for a moment. There was a lot more he wanted to say but it wasn't the moment; it would have to wait until the next time he saw her. 'I love you, Roz. Happy New Year.'

He ended the call and eased himself up, grabbing the two crutches that had become like two friends who had long outstayed their welcome, and moved cautiously over to the window. Snow was covering the parked cars and Santi stood staring into the darkness until the sound of the party downstairs broke into his thoughts.

Midnight was getting near and Santi realized that as the party was at his house, he should at least be downstairs with his guests to see in the New Year. But crutches and an orthopaedic boot hardly helped with the party mood.

He hobbled down the stairs to be met by one of the late arrivals – Jordana. She greeted him at the foot of the stairs with a bottle of opened champagne in each hand.

'Why the long face, Santi?' she smiled. 'It's party time!'

Carefully, she led him to where the partygoers were dancing before raising one of the champagne bottles to his mouth so that he could take a drink.

'Come on, let's dance.'

It wasn't exactly dancing, but Santiago did clump around on his crutches as best he could as his dancing partner gave him more champagne.

As the last seconds of the old year ticked away, Gavin, unsurprisingly accompanied by two girls, led the countdown to midnight.

'TEN . . . NINE . . . EIGHT . . . SEVEN . . .'

More voices joined in the countdown chorus as Jordana moved closer to Santiago.

'SIX . . . FIVE . . . FOUR . . .'

Santi knew exactly what Jordana had in mind; it was the New Year and a kiss was the tradition.

'THREE . . . TWO . . . ONE . . . *FELIZ AÑO NUEVO! HAPPY NEW YEAR!*'

The yells and cheers rang around the room, along with the usual hugs and kisses.

And Jordana kissed Santiago, gently at first. Then she stood back for a moment and stared deeply into his eyes. She moved back and kissed him again. But this time the kiss was long and passionate.

Santiago woke up late the following morning. He lay on his bed, his head thumping, and slowly the events of the previous night came back into his mind. Or some of them.

He stared at the ceiling for a few long minutes before gradually easing himself into a sitting position, putting his head into his hands to try to stop the pounding in his brain.

Without thinking, Santi threw his leg off the bed to get up and was instantly rewarded with a jolting reminder of his broken foot as pain seared up through his leg. He gasped and fell back on the bed, deciding that further movement wasn't a good idea for the next few minutes.

Gavin was sitting at the kitchen table eating from a bowl packed with cereal, yoghurt and carrots when Santi finally hobbled in on his crutches. He watched, but said nothing as Santi went to the fridge and opened the door.

Santi took a long drink and stared out through the window at the snow. When he turned back he saw that Gavin was watching him.

'What?'

Gavin shook his head and went back to his breakfast.

'What?' said Santi again.

'I didn't say anything,' said Gavin through a mouthful of cereal.

'But you were looking at me, with a . . . *look*.'

'No, I wasn't.'

They stared at each other, Gavin silently challenging his friend to make his confession. But Santi decided that it was probably wisest to say no more. He shrugged irritably and then hobbled back to the kitchen door.

'Nothing happened,' he called as he went out.

Gavin smiled but didn't reply.

A few seconds later Santiago came back into the room. '*Nothing* happened!'

Twenty-two

It was falling apart. His career. His life. Santiago felt that everything was spiralling downwards, out of control. And the only way he could stop the downward spiral and start rebuilding his future was to discover the truth about his past.

He'd talked it over with Gavin, who'd been a surprisingly good listener after all. Santi showed him the photograph of his mother and told him of his meetings with his half-brother, and Gavin had agreed that the only way to deal with the situation was by confronting it.

But that wasn't easy. Santiago had no idea where his mother was living, and he hadn't seen Enrique again.

Even though he was still wearing the plastic boot, Santiago was attending training every day. He did light gym work to maintain his upper body strength and received expert treatment and physiotherapy to his injured foot.

He could even drive, with care.

Each time he arrived and left the training facility he looked out for Enrique, and finally, as he drove off at the end of a session, he saw him at the edge of the crowd.

Santiago pulled the vehicle to a halt and pressed the button to open the passenger side window. 'You want a lift?'

Enrique raised his eyebrows and then turned and smiled at the crowd gathered around the exit, looking as though catching a ride with a Real Madrid player was something that happened to him all the time.

He got in and Santiago drove away.

They didn't speak for while. Santiago was unsure of what to say and Enrique was too fascinated and enthralled by the ultra-cool vehicle.

He pushed every button there was on the

satellite navigation system and grinned with delight at the graphics.

'Hey,' he said at last. 'If I had one of these, I'd get respect. I'd drive to the ocean, man, and never come back.'

He explored the glove box and then checked out the CDs, frowning at Santiago's taste in music.

'Take this left,' he said as they approached one of the run-down areas of the city. Santiago did as he was instructed, thinking that perhaps Enrique was taking him to his home. And their mother.

The teenager grabbed Santi's phone and the spare pair of sunglasses he kept in the glove box. 'How d'you work the camera on this phone?'

He didn't wait for an answer; the camera on the phone was easy enough to operate. He slipped on the shades and snapped a photograph of himself and then grinned at the results.

'Next right.'

The vehicle slid smoothly into a district unknown to Santiago, with narrow streets and shabby, neglected buildings. The few people out on the streets stared in surprise as the

Lamborghini slid by and Enrique beamed at them through the tinted windows.

He started flicking through the speed dial list on Santi's mobile and then hit a number. 'Hey, Mr Van Der Merwe, you wanna give me a trial? I'm much better than my big brother.'

Santiago snatched the phone away, horrified. He cut the call, relieved to see that it had gone unanswered.

'Just stop it, will you?' he said to Enrique.

Enrique eased himself back in the seat, wondering what he could do next.

'Tell me about your mother,' said Santiago.

The youngster shrugged. 'What's there to tell? She gives me a hard time, so I stay away as much as I can.'

It wasn't the answer Santi had been expecting and he was still trying to work out his next question when Enrique pulled Santi's sports bag from the rear seat and began rifling through it.

'This is really cool,' he said, exploring the Adidas gear in the bag.

Santiago stopped the car as a traffic light turned to red and then watched as one of his sweatshirts dropped from the bag onto the floor of the car.

'Look, will you sit still! What's your problem, man?'

Enrique turned on him angrily. 'You want to know my problem? I'll tell you. I live in a dump, my mum works herself into the ground, and you're driving around in this like some sort of movie star. That's my problem!'

Before Santiago could reply, his half-brother threw open the passenger side door, leaped from the vehicle and ran off down the street, with Santiago's sports bag in one hand.

'*Hey!*' yelled Santi, struggling to get out of the car. There was no way he could give chase – he couldn't risk damaging his injured foot any further, and the plastic boot wasn't going to give him any help even if he tried.

He saw Enrique disappear down an alleyway and then heard the sound of a car horn as the traffic light turned to green.

He looked back and glared at the driver of the vehicle waiting behind his. The driver raised both hands and gestured for Santi to get his car moving.

'*All right!*' shouted Santiago. 'I'm going!'

Enrique's new football sat on his bed. He was hurriedly stuffing the sports gear he'd stolen from Santiago beneath the bed when his mother came into the bedroom. She didn't knock; she'd seen him run quickly across the bar with the bag.

'What did I tell you about stealing?' she said furiously as Enrique turned towards her.

'I didn't steal it. Santi gave it to me.'

Rosa's eyes widened. She closed the bedroom door quietly and grabbed her son by the shoulders. 'Santiago? Are you insane? I told you we can never be part of his life.'

'But he's my brother!' snapped Enrique, trying to pull himself free. 'Why is this something I have to hide?'

'Because . . .' They both knew why, but Rosa-Maria couldn't bear to say the words. Instead, she slapped her son across the face. 'In this house, you do what you are told!'

Before Enrique could argue back, the door opened and his father came in.

'What the hell is going on?'

Rosa-Maria released her grip on Enrique. She stared at him, her eyes making a silent appeal to keep their secret.

Enrique looked at his mother with contempt. Then he snatched his football from his bed, brushed quickly past his mother and father and ran down the stairs.

'Well?' said Miguel to Rosa-Maria.

'He's . . . he's . . .'

She stooped down and pulled the sports bag from beneath the bed. 'He's been stealing again.'

Enrique hadn't gone far – he'd headed for the bare patch of ground where he and his friends usually played their pick-up games of football. But Tito was the only one there. He was throwing stones at a huge billboard when he saw Enrique approaching with his new football.

He grinned. 'Nice ball.'

Enrique nodded proudly and handed over the ball when Tito held out both hands.

The older boy inspected the ball carefully and bounced it on the ground a couple of times. Then, before Enrique could stop him, he drew back his right foot, dropped the ball and volleyed it as hard as he could.

Enrique gazed in horror as the football sailed away through the air and over a high wall that bordered the makeshift football pitch. The ball was gone. For ever.

Enrique's eyes blazed with fury and he leaped at the smirking Tito, throwing wild punches into his body and at his face. But the bullying Tito was not only older and bigger than Enrique, he was also a lot stronger.

He grabbed the smaller boy's flailing arms and in one swift, brutal move, he lifted him off the ground and slammed him down in the dirt. He laughed once and then strolled away, oblivious to the tears in Enrique's eyes.

Twenty-three

El clásico – the classic. It isn't a local derby because the two teams are from completely different regions of Spain. But it is the big one, for both Real Madrid and Barcelona, and for their supporters.

The two clubs are traditionally Spain's biggest and bitterest of rivals. Their encounters spark hundreds of column inches of speculation and comment in the Press and hour upon hour of coverage on television and radio. The build-up begins weeks before the match and always leads to fierce debate.

There are plenty of British matches which annually ignite old rivalries: Glasgow's Old Firm battle between Rangers and Celtic, the clash of the Lancashire giants, Manchester United and Liverpool, the north London derby between Tottenham and Arsenal, but even these do not quite compare. In Italy, there is Milan's Inter versus AC. All over Europe and throughout the footballing world there are certain matches that fire the imagination and the passion of players and supporters alike.

But something, somehow, sets Real Madrid versus Barcelona apart. It is *the* one. The ultimate encounter. It is simply, *el clásico*.

The *galácticos* of Madrid were matched by the superstars of Barcelona: Deco, Messi, Eto'o, and of course, the man voted as the very best player in the world, the sublimely skilled Brazilian, Ronaldinho.

The Barcelona maestro gives names to the best of his magical tricks with a football. He calls one 'The Chewing Gum' because the ball appears to be stuck to his feet.

As the match progressed, the lithe Brazilian displayed his full repertoire of brilliance, beguiling the Real defenders and bringing grudging appreciation from even the partisan Madridistas.

Ronaldinho, ably assisted by the young Argentinian, Messi, was creating havoc in the Real defence.

But then close to the end, and against the run of play, there was a moment of joy for Real, and for one player in particular, who was demonstrating exactly why so many clubs had paid so much money for his skills during his long career.

Gavin was having a blinder, and enjoying every second of it. And the much-travelled and much-maligned striker's joy was complete midway through the second half when, from a pass across the face of goal from outside the area, he was there to skilfully side-foot the ball into the net.

All the missed chances, the fluffed kicks, the bad matches, were instantly forgotten by the wildly celebrating Madridistas. Gavin had scored in *el clásico*.

He was a hero again.

Santiago and Jordana sat opposite each other in comfortable chairs on the classy set of her TV show.

The television crew bustled around, making their final preparations for the show, which was broadcast live every day. They ignored Santi and Jordana; everyone had a job to do and the added pressure of a live broadcast meant split-second timing, which left no room for errors.

It was the first time Santi had seen Jordana since their encounter on New Year's Eve, and while she was her usual smooth, sophisticated self, he was feeling edgy and a little embarrassed.

Jordana was partly amused at her guest's nervousness, but she was in work mode; the show and the interview were what mattered most.

She spoke softly in her native Spanish, seeking to put Santiago more at ease in the unfamiliar surroundings of the studio. 'You must be dying to play again.'

Santiago shrugged self-consciously, for the moment avoiding eye contact with the super-confident presenter. 'Yeah, it won't be too long now,' he replied, slipping easily into Spanish himself.

'I'm glad you're finally here, giving me the exclusive.'

'Sure, no problem,' said Santi, half-heartedly.

It was hardly the dynamic attitude that Jordana was looking for.

'Listen,' she said firmly. 'I hope you're going to give me a juicy interview.'

Santiago lifted his eyes and glanced around the studio. No one was paying them the slightest attention. 'Yeah, I'm OK with you torturing me in front of the world on TV, as long as what happened between us stays between us.'

Jordana smiled. 'You're only keeping your promise. And let me give you the benefit of my experience, Santi. Nothing in life is free. The sooner you learn that, the better it will be for you.'

'What happened between us was a mistake,' said Santi, quietly but urgently. 'I was drunk, and very lonely. I'm not like that.'

Jordana knew exactly how to push Santi into the mood she wanted for the show. 'Look, Santiago, if you don't want to be treated like a child, behave like a man. What happened, happened.'

Santi's eyes flashed. 'That's right. And I'm here to make sure things are clear. It'll never happen again.'

She'd done it, sparked up her guest into a fiery mood, exactly how she wanted him and at exactly the right time. 'Very good. Priorities right, eyes on the ball. Now, Santi, just give me a great interview!'

The studio floor manager got the thumbs up from the control gallery and began the count-down to the show, both verbally and by using the fingers of his right hand to count off the final five seconds. They were about to go live.

'Three . . . two . . . one . . .' He pointed at Jordana; they were on the air.

She beamed into camera. 'Hello and welcome. Today I have the honour of having here as my very special guest Real Madrid's new star player, Santiago Muñez.'

Twenty-four

Eminem was pumping from the Lamborghini's sound system as Santiago pulled into the driveway at the Buddha Club.

He got out and nodded to the car valet waiting to take the vehicle round to the parking area. A few of the paparazzi were lurking by the entrance, as usual, on the hunt for that big moneymaking photograph.

'Oi, Muñez,' called one, in English. 'You gonna show us that fiery Mexican temper of yours again?'

The comment was designed to provoke Santi into an outburst of anger, but it didn't succeed. So the photographer tried again. 'Hope you liked the photo-spread in *Heat* magazine!'

Santi glanced at the smirking Englishman but continued on into the club and the disappointed photographer turned to one of his colleagues and shrugged his shoulders. 'Worth a try.'

Several of the Real players were already in the club. A huddle of defenders – Salgado, Helguera and Jonathan Woodgate – were clustered around a table along with Gavin. When Santi finally made it through to his team-mates, Salgado stood up and held out his mobile phone. 'Hey, Santi, what's going on? This is the third time you've called me.'

Santiago frowned. He hadn't called Salgado once, let alone three times. He checked through his pockets and quickly realized that he must have left his phone in the car.

His car!

He grabbed Salgado's mobile, put it to his ear and immediately heard the Eminem CD he had been playing when he arrived.

Someone was in his car!

He shoved Salgado's phone back into his hands and turned back towards the entrance, pushing his way through the hordes of startled clubbers.

The paparazzi were still keeping their vigil as Santi emerged from the club and ran up to the parking valet.

'Where's my car?' he said urgently.

'In the car park, sir. Round at the back.'

'Show me!'

Before they had taken more than a few steps, the Lamborghini came skidding around the side of the club and Santiago saw with horror that Enrique was behind the wheel. The teenager gave his half-brother the single finger gesture as the car flashed by and onto the road.

Santi tore out in pursuit. A taxi was approaching the club, the driver looking for the early departures from the Buddha. He wasn't expecting to see a young man standing directly in his path in the middle of the road, frantically waving both hands to flag him down.

As the cab skidded to a halt, the English photographer fumbled for his own keys and ran back to the car park.

The elderly taxi driver stuck his head out of

the window and yelled at Santiago. 'You lunatic! You got some kind of death wish?'

There was no time to argue. Santi wrenched open the passenger door and leaped into the beaten-up old Skoda, pointing towards the tail-lights of the Lamborghini.

'That's my car! Don't let it out of your sight!'

The cab driver's eyes narrowed and his neck craned forward as he stared into the darkness; he could just see the back of the high-performance car weaving from side to side along the long stretch of road.

'You want me to . . . ?'

'The white Lamborghini, yes!'

'A *Lamborghini*! In *this*?'

'*Yes! Follow that car!*'

The old cab driver grinned an almost toothless grin. For years he'd been waiting to hear those words. He crossed himself, pulled his bifocal glasses down from the top of his head, jammed them into place and then shoved the Skoda into gear.

The tyres screeched as it pulled away and the cab driver's smile was even wider as he burned rubber for the first time in his life.

A few seconds later, the English photographer emerged from the car park perched on a Lambretta scooter, which whined like an out-of-control lawnmower as the paparazzi man also gave chase.

Twenty-five

Enrique was no Michael Schumacher, but then the Lamborghini was hardly designed for a driver of his size. Even with the seat moved fully forward, his feet barely reached the pedals, and as he drove he constantly had to raise himself up to see over the steering wheel.

Going in a straight line was not too difficult, as long as he didn't try to go too fast, but rounding a corner was a completely different matter.

Once he got off the ring road, the real problems began. He rounded a corner too quickly and almost lost control as he saw the roadworks up ahead. Late. Too late.

Warning cones scattered like bowling pins in

every direction as he ploughed through them, and at the next bend an oncoming car had to swerve violently to avoid the Lamborghini.

Enrique saw the flashing headlights and heard the blaring horn, but only glimpsed the vehicle as it swept by. Then he heard the crash as the other car hit a bottle bank by the roadside. But Enrique didn't slow down.

The old taxi driver did, but only long enough to check that the driver of the crashed car was unhurt. As soon as Santiago saw him emerge from his battered vehicle, he urged the driver on.

'Stay with him, but don't spook him.'

'But I can catch him,' said the driver, enjoying every second of the drama. 'Just give me a chance.'

'No. Follow him. That's all.'

The taxi driver squinted through his bifocals; maybe it was more like the movies just to follow. But that didn't mean he couldn't edge a little nearer.

They were travelling into the city centre and the traffic was getting heavier, making Enrique's struggle to keep the Lamborghini under control even more difficult. The slightest pressure on the accelerator sent it rocketing forward.

He reached a junction and cut directly across the path of a line of cars, causing the driver of the first to brake violently. The two following vehicles had no chance to stop and Santi and the taxi driver passed seconds later and saw the tangle of smashed headlights and bent fenders.

As the old Skoda drew closer to the Lamborghini, the taxi driver craned forward again and squinted through his glasses.

'There's no one driving it!'

Just then, Enrique's hand emerged from the window again and he gave another single finger gesture.

The taxi driver shrugged. 'It's a little guy.'

Enrique was beginning to panic; he hadn't expected his joyride to turn into a chase. He had sneaked into the car park and had been amazed to find the vehicle unlocked with the keys still in the ignition. He slipped into the car and fooled around with Santi's mobile for a while, loving the way he could pretend for a few minutes that the Real Madrid stars on the speed dial were *his* friends. And then, impulsively, he decided on a quick joyride; now he had to get away while he could. He hit the brakes and wrenched the wheel hard to his right, swerving into a side street. But the pursuing taxi stayed with him.

The teenager put his foot down, going too fast for the narrow road. He took another corner and the back end of the vehicle fishtailed, taking out wing mirrors and denting the paintwork of a couple of parked vehicles.

Enrique was losing control, but in his panic he kept his foot hard down on the accelerator pedal. He clipped a parked motorbike on his nearside and then saw the bend ahead as he wrestled with the wheel, jerking it right to left and back again.

He had no chance of making the turn. As the car slewed round, Enrique saw the newspaper vending kiosk; he was going to hit it. He closed his eyes, tightly, instinctively. He heard the terrifying noise at the moment of impact.

And then darkness closed in and he felt or heard nothing more.

The taxi rounded the corner and screeched to a standstill. Santi leaped from the vehicle and tore over to the wreckage of the Lamborghini, crunching over broken glass and breathing brick dust as he wrenched open the buckled driver's door.

Enrique was slumped forward over the steering wheel, his head cut and bleeding badly.

'Enrique!'

There was no response. Gently, Santiago eased his half-brother back in the seat. His eyes were closed and his face was deathly pale.

'Enrique!'

Santiago saw that his hands were still shaking as he gripped the plastic cup of steaming vending-machine coffee.

He was sitting in the hospital waiting room, and the questions being fired at him from the two police officers as they adopted the 'good cop, bad cop' routine were not helping one bit.

'And you say you just lost control?' said Bad Cop.

'I told you, I was distracted, my cellphone rang. I know I should have ignored it.'

'And the boy with you?'

'A friend's son. I already told you that, too.'

The officers exchanged a look; the story didn't ring true to either of them.

The old taxi driver had been a hero, forcing his ancient Skoda into a lightning drive, through back streets and short cuts to the hospital.

Santiago ran into the casualty unit with the bleeding Enrique in his arms and the expert staff moved swiftly and efficiently into action.

The last Santiago had seen of his brother was when a doctor hurried into the treatment cubicle as nurses checked for pulse and blood pressure. Santiago was ushered away to the waiting room, where he had prepared his story for the police.

It had seemed the best thing to do, for Enrique's sake, but the story wasn't going down well.

'The boy is knocked about pretty bad,' said Bad Cop.

'He didn't have his seatbelt on.'

Good Cop took the softer approach. 'How much alcohol did you say you had, sir?'

'I didn't, I'm not drunk. I just lost control of

the car. It happens. Right now, all I care about is the kid. I want to speak to him.'

'Maybe after *we've* finished talking,' said Bad Cop.

Then a camera flashed, startling Santiago and causing him to drop the plastic cup.

The English photographer had worked hard to get the photo, trailing halfway around Madrid on his Lambretta before finally tracking down his victim.

Santiago snapped. 'You scumbag!'

He leaped to his feet and launched himself at the photographer, landing one heavy punch to his face before being dragged back by both police officers.

'Señor Muñez, I am placing you under arrest,' said Good Cop as he pulled the handcuffs from his belt.

The photographer hauled himself off the floor, wiping blood from his mouth as he checked that his precious camera was undamaged. It was fine, and the photographer wasn't thinking of retaliatory punches – his retaliation would be a million times better and a lot more lucrative.

The camera flashed repeatedly as Santiago was bundled down the corridor.

'See you in court, Santi!' grinned the delighted and suddenly much wealthier photographer, licking away the blood on his lips.

The police officers pulled Santi to a standstill for a moment while they secured the handcuffs.

And in that moment, he saw her.

His mother. For the first time in many years.

As Santi was about to be dragged away, the lift doors opened and she was there, looking scared and bewildered.

She saw Santiago and their eyes met and Rosa-Maria froze, feeling an icy chill flood through her body as they stared at each other.

Santiago almost burst into tears. Now. After all this time. He was so close to her now, at last. And he was about to be led away in shame.

He wanted to call out to her, but no words would come. And then he was bundled away, lost from his mother's sight. Again.

Rosa-Maria closed her eyes tightly as the tears welled up against her eyelids.

Twenty-six

The nightmare wasn't over. Not by a long way.

Santiago was driven to a police station where the formalities of being charged were completed.

He watched as his possessions were listed and placed in a bag, he obeyed every instruction as his fingerprints were taken, and he stared passively as his mug-shot photographs were captured, front and profile. It felt even worse than being photographed by the leering English paparazzi cameraman.

Just before Santiago was led away to spend the remainder of the night in the cells, he was given the opportunity to make a single phone call.

Suddenly, he felt completely alone. He didn't know who to call. Here he was, a famous footballer known throughout Spain and Europe, and there was no one he could instantly turn to.

Gavin would still be out celebrating and in no condition to come to his aid. He couldn't put Roz or his family through any more torment. There was no one at the club who would react with sympathy to his latest misdemeanour.

He finally realized there was only one person he could call. He picked up the telephone, punched in the number and listened to the ringing tone.

'Come on, pick up. Please, pick up.'

Eventually, the call was answered. The voice was quiet, and the Geordie accent was unmistakable.

'Hello?'

'Glen, it's me. I'm sorry for calling so late, but I couldn't think of anyone else.'

In the darkness of his bedroom in Newcastle, Glen glanced at the clock at his bedside. It was after three a.m., and Glen was not in the mood for an early-morning catch-up call, especially from someone who had so recently fired him.

'I'm flattered,' he said with more than a hint of sarcasm.

'I need your help, man. I've really messed up this time and I'm in a lot of trouble.'

'What is it, now?'

'My car's a wreck, Glen, and I hit a photographer; he was goading me. I've been arrested. The Press are gonna have a field day over this, trashing my life.'

Glen sighed. 'Sounds to me like you're well able to do that for yourself without needing any help from the papers.'

'Everything I touch has gone wrong, Glen.'

'I'm not your agent any more, Santiago, remember?'

'I know I . . . I don't deserve this, Glen. I really don't. I'm sorry.'

'Don't apologize to me,' said Glen, interrupting. 'Save it for those who need it.'

Glen was angry. And hurt. But he wasn't going to let Santiago know about the hurt he was feeling; he had too much pride in himself for that.

He let his words sink in for a moment before continuing.

'You're not a kid any more, you're a grown man. You've earned a lot of praise on the pitch; it's time to earn some respect in the real world. Where it matters.'

Glen couldn't see the tears running down Santi's face, but even if he had, he would have ended the conversation in the same way.

'Until you've done that, son, you're on your own. Goodnight.'

It felt as though he had slept for little more than a few minutes, huddled uncomfortably on a small hard bed in the dark, cramped cell.

Santiago felt himself being shaken, none too gently, by the shoulder. He opened his eyes to see the Real player liaison director, Leo Vegaz, staring down at him.

He handed Santi a pair of sunglasses. 'You're going to need these.'

They emerged from the police station into a

rainy Madrid morning and a hail of flashing cameras as the paparazzi continued with Santi's total humiliation.

'Say nothing,' said Leo as journalists crowded around and fired off questions. He hurried Santi into the back of a waiting vehicle and as they drove away, he handed him the bag containing his possessions.

And then he gave him just one of the many newspapers lying on the seat between them.

Santi was front-page news. The mangled wreckage of his car was pictured in full colour and the accompanying article didn't make good reading.

And it wasn't over when he got home. The paparazzi camped out by the front gates of the house throughout that day, and the next, making Santiago feel like a caged animal.

All the while, Glen's stinging words came back to haunt him. *'You're not a kid any more. It's time to earn some respect.'*

He was right. Santiago knew things had to change. But nothing *could* change until he had finally come to terms with the situation that had invaded almost every waking moment and most of his dreams for the past few months.

He knew he had to confront Rosa-Maria. Face to face.

But things were about to get even worse for Santi.

High-profile Premiership players who move to Spain are always a target for the paparazzi, and even an innocent moment can look totally different by the time the photographs make it to the tabloids or the glossy magazines.

Maybe Santiago should have remembered that when Jordana kissed him as they stood by her white Lamborghini outside the Buddha Club. Even though that had been weeks earlier, long before Christmas, the photographs had only just appeared in the pages of *Heat* magazine.

That moment had been innocent, even though the events of New Year's Eve hadn't. But it was the kiss outside the Buddha that was finally to prove too much for Roz when she saw the photos.

The headline didn't help either:

SUPER-SUB SCORES AWAY FROM HOME!

One of Roz's friends at work had given her the magazine, but not out of malice; she just wanted Roz to know before the gossip started spreading around the hospital.

Santiago was delighted when he looked at his mobile and saw that the incoming call was from Roz. But the delight didn't last for long.

'How *could* you! You didn't even have the sense to do it in private; you had to flaunt it in front of the whole world!'

'What?' said Santi into his phone. 'What are you talking about, Roz?'

'About *you*! And *her*! You're in all the magazines, Santi, with that . . . *woman*!'

'Magazine? What woman?'

'Oh! So how many have there been? Is she the real reason you couldn't come home at Christmas? How long has this been going on?'

Santiago realized that Roz had to be talking about the kiss outside the Buddha; he remembered the cameras flashing. 'Baby, you're getting it all wrong. The Press twists all that stuff.'

'I can *see* it here in front of me, Santiago; I can *see* what you've been doing. Stop lying.'

'But I'm not!'

Roz wasn't going to be convinced. 'If that's the type of girl you want, then fine, Santi, you can have her.'

'Look, I'm sorry, Roz,' said Santiago desperately. 'Things are all messed up, right now.'

'You've made a fool of me, and I don't deserve it!' shouted Roz. 'I *knew* this would happen.'

And then she hung up.

Twenty-seven

Gavin knew full well that very few footballers could do a Teddy Sheringham and play on at the highest level until the age of forty.

For most players, when they reach thirty, they discover that the clock seems to be ticking more loudly and that the football seasons pass more swiftly. Gavin had passed that milestone, and with it had come the realization that he wanted to prolong his career for as long as possible.

So he continued to work furiously in training, and it was paying off. And it wasn't just the training; he was also moderating his wild lifestyle – not completely, but significantly. There were fewer late nights out clubbing, he cut back on the booze, and he paid serious attention to his diet.

As Real moved on to the semi-final of the Champions League, he was the outstanding player and the goals came often.

'Goals are like buses,' he told Santiago. 'You wait for ages for one to come along . . .'

'And then three or four arrive together,' smiled Santiago, finishing off the old cliché.

Santiago was also making good progress, and Gavin was there to support and encourage him as the plaster cast on his leg was removed and he took his first, tentative steps back to full fitness.

There were long sessions just walking on the treadmill and hours in the aqua-therapy pool and with the physio. But slowly and steadily the strength came back and at last he was able to join the rest of the squad in training.

The season was proving a difficult one for Real, despite their progress in getting to the Champions League semi-final.

In a move that shocked the entire football world, club president Florentino Pérez announced his resignation and was replaced by

Fernando Martin. The new man hinted that the era of the *galácticos* might be coming to an end.

He warned all the players that he expected hard work and effort in training and on the pitch, urging them to make him, the club and the supporters proud.

No one took the words more to heart than Gavin, and as Santiago regained match fitness, he too set out to prove to the new president, and to his coach, that Real's investment had, after all, been a wise one.

Van Der Merwe and his assistant, Steve McManaman, watched him closely during training, and when Santiago scored a fine goal in a practice match, the head coach was satisfied enough to consider him for selection.

But he had to be eased back in slowly; this time Van Der Merwe was not going to be rushed into another wrong decision.

Santi made a couple of brief but encouraging appearances from the bench in league fixtures but he sat out the first leg of the Champions League semi-final.

The surprise opponents were Olympique Lyon

from France – not one of the biggest names in European football. But under ex-Liverpool boss, Gérard Houllier, they were storming away with the French league and had waged an impressive Champions League campaign.

In the first leg in France, Real held out for a nil–nil draw. It meant they only needed to snatch a single goal and then defend in numbers at the Bernabéu to make the final.

But safety-first football was not the way Van Der Merwe operated. And neither did his players.

Twenty-eight

Rudi Van Der Merwe wanted any team he selected to play attacking football, to play the beautiful game as it should be played.

And as the whistle sounded for the kick-off to the second leg, that's exactly what he was expecting.

Santiago's impressive cameo appearances in the league matches had earned him a place on the bench. Van Der Merwe had not considered including him in the starting line-up: he was not yet fit enough for a full ninety minutes, and besides, Gavin's form fully justified his selection.

Van Der Merwe was starting with his strongest line-up, including the English centre back, Jonathan Woodgate, who had suffered a cruel run of injuries since his move to Real.

The first minutes confirmed Van Der Merwe's belief in the positive, with his side playing attractive, attacking football, particularly up front, where Gavin, Raúl and Ronaldo were involved in some dazzling exchanges leading to a couple of outstanding saves by the Lyon keeper.

But there were no goals when Lyon won a free kick in a dangerous position just outside the box.

Gavin took his place in the wall as the former Arsenal striker, Sylvain Wiltord, prepared to take the kick.

He struck it well and the ball flashed inches wide of the upright, temporarily silencing the Bernabéu faithful.

Real stuck to their attacking guns, forcing a series of spectacular saves from the Lyon keeper, who was having the game of his life.

Gavin was the unluckiest of all the Real forwards; by the time the match reached the hour mark he had been denied what had looked certain goals three times by the inspired keeper.

On the Real bench, Van Der Merwe was

considering changes when, after a foul outside the Lyon box, Real were awarded a free kick. Passions and tempers were running high and players from both sides rushed in to join the debate over the decision.

Gérard Houllier stood glum-faced on the touchline: the free kick was in perfect David Beckham territory and the Frenchman was fully aware of the damage the Englishman could inflict from that range and territory.

Beckham placed the ball deliberately. He was just to the left and seven or eight yards outside the penalty area. A three-man wall shifted from side to side, following the shouted orders of the Lyon keeper.

And then Beckham struck the free kick. Virtually everyone in the stadium was expecting a curling shot, but the ball bent out wide, across the face of goal.

Three Real players made their runs as the Lyon defence back-pedalled furiously and the keeper moved anxiously across his goal line.

Gavin had timed his run to perfection. The speeding ball dropped and bounced once and he struck it viciously with his left foot. It was a sweet goal, the type players and coaches practise time after time on the training ground. And all that practice had made it work perfectly.

Gavin had done it again; the man who didn't score for seventeen matches was now scoring at a rate of almost a goal a game.

There were no complaints when the substitution board went up a couple of minutes later and Gavin saw that he was being taken off and Santiago was coming on. Gavin had done his job; he deserved a rest.

As Lyon pressed for an equalizer, Santi was swiftly up with the pace of the game. He had to be: after his long lay-off he was desperate to be part of the big-time action again.

He collected a sweet pass from Roberto Carlos and, with a dazzling display of trickery, left two Lyon defenders for dead, before firing a shot across goal that was just wide of the upright.

The Madridistas roared their approval, acknowledging with their whistles and cheers what they had been missing during the long months of Santi's absence.

Soon after, from the deftest of back-heels from Ronaldo, Santi, with his back to goal, wrong-footed the entire Lyon back line with a sweet touch and turn.

He had a sight of goal; he'd made the chance for himself and he was going to take it.

As two Lyon defenders turned to give chase, Santi took two strides, lifted his head and then struck the ball venomously. The diving keeper had no chance as the ball flashed by and the net bulged.

As the Bernabéu erupted with joy, Santi went hurtling towards the crowd, arms raised. Every one of his team-mates ran in ecstatic pursuit and on the touchline, Van Der Merwe, Macca and the entire Real bench were punching the air in delight.

Real were two up: they were almost in the final of the Champions League.

Lyon threw everyone forward in the final few minutes, but the Real defence, marshalled superbly by Woodgate, hung on until, after 120 long seconds of added time, the whistle sounded for the end of the match.

Real had done it! They were there. In the final of the Champions League, where they would meet the English Premiership club, Arsenal.

The post-match television interviews were well underway, and Gavin stood patiently in the corridor leading from the dressing room, giving the routine answers to the routine questions footballers receive after a big match victory.

'It was touch and go out there,' said the British television interviewer, stating the obvious before thrusting the microphone towards Gavin's face.

Gavin was all smiles; elated at the way his season had turned around. He couldn't resist answering with every footballing cliché he could remember: 'Yeah, well, they had us pinned down for the first forty-five minutes, but those Lyon boys will be sick as parrots 'cos it's a game of two halves and it ain't over till the fat lady sings. That's football.'

The interviewer's next question wiped the smile off Gavin's face.

'D'you think you'll play in the final or do you think the coach will choose Santiago instead?'

Before Gavin could think of the words to answer, the massed microphones and cameras swung across to Santiago.

'Santiago, you got Real Madrid into the final, can you tell us how you feel?'

Santi was ready with the diplomatic, team-first answers. 'I'm just glad we made it through to the final. It was a great team effort.'

Another interviewer fired in a question:

'Everyone knows that you and Gavin are buddies; this must be putting a lot of pressure on your friendship.'

Santiago glanced over at his friend before answering. 'Look, we're part of a team. But first, we're friends.'

Twenty-nine

Santi stood at an upstairs window of his huge mansion and peered down at the massed hordes of paparazzi camped outside the front gate.

Real's progress to the Champions League final had only increased the media obsession with the lives of the star players, and particularly of Santiago Muñez.

He had been big news on and off the pitch ever since his arrival in Madrid, and with the final fast approaching, the so-called 'gentlemen of the Press' knew that big money was there to be made if the slightest indiscretion or the merest hint of further scandal could be captured on camera.

Santi was still desperate to track down his mother, Rosa-Maria, but apart from training sessions he had been a virtual prisoner in his own home. At this rate, he would never find her.

He glanced down into the garden and saw one of the men he'd employed to tend the grounds that he never went in for fear of a cameraman popping his head over the wall.

And then Santi smiled. He had an idea.

The lurking paparazzi had no idea that Santiago had even left the house when he was driven away from the rear gate, sitting between two gardeners in the back of a truck.

Santiago almost laughed at the irony of it. For years he had done exactly this every day as he scratched out a living as a gardener to the rich of LA with his father, Herman. He had stared enviously at the mansion homes and the manicured gardens as he raked leaves and trimmed lawns.

Now he was rich – he had it all – but at this moment it felt as though he had nothing.

The search had to begin somewhere, so he

went back to the area where Enrique had jumped from the car and gone running off with his sports bag at the end of their first meeting.

Santiago carried Rosa-Maria's photograph with him. He went into cafés and stopped people on the street, showing the photograph, asking if anyone knew her or where she might be. He got nothing in return but shrugs and shakes of the head.

Madrid was a big city. She could be anywhere.

He tried again the following day, moving from street to street, district to district. Eventually he met a couple of hard-looking young guys on the corner of a street. They were obviously not football fans, as neither of them recognized Santi as he took out the photograph and asked them if they knew the woman.

They were weighing up Santiago warily, looking at him more than at the photograph.

'You don't look like police,' said one of them at last.

'I'm not,' said Santi quickly. 'I just need to find her.'

Reassured, they looked at the photo again.

'I might know where she works,' said the second guy.

'Really?' said Santi, feeling his heart start to pound. 'Where?'

The young guy shrugged his shoulders; there was still some bargaining to be done and Santiago was wearing an expensive Rolex on his wrist.

The young guy nodded down at the Rolex. 'That's a nice watch.'

It was early evening when Santi stepped from the taxi and stared across at the small bar on the far side of the road. He didn't know the exact time; he no longer had a watch.

Nervously he walked across the road, pushed open the door and went inside. It was busy, and noisy, but the chatter stopped completely almost as soon the first person recognized Santiago.

Within seconds everyone had stopped drinking and speaking and was staring in disbelief at the sight of the famous Real Madrid player who had appeared in their midst from nowhere.

Rosa-Maria was behind the bar, concentrating on the drink she was pouring. She suddenly became aware of the silence and looked up to see Santiago standing perfectly still, halfway across the room.

Her eyes widened, her mouth fell open and everyone in the room watched as she whispered one word. 'Santiago.'

Miguel was also behind the bar, as confused as his customers as mother and son stared at each other but said nothing.

Slowly, Rosa-Maria walked from behind the bar and went to her son. She stopped in front of him, her eyes fixed on his as if she were searching to discover everything she had never known about the long years of his life she had missed.

She raised her right hand, going to touch his cheek, but then snatched it away as if she were afraid that if she touched him he might disappear.

But Santiago caught her hand in his. He held it firmly, scared now to let go.

And then, without either of them knowing how it happened, they were hugging, holding each other so tightly, tears filling both their eyes.

The customers in the bar stared at one another, bewildered and slightly embarrassed at the very private and intensely personal scene they were witnessing.

Miguel was the first one to speak, not quite certain why he decided to empty the bar, but knowing that somehow it was the right thing to do. 'Right, closing time, drink up everyone.' There were a few, half-hearted mutterings of complaint, but Miguel had made up his mind. 'Early night tonight, we'll see you all tomorrow.'

Thirty

There was so much to say, so much to learn, but now that the moment had finally come they were both struggling to find the words. They were sitting at a table in one corner of the bar, speaking hesitantly and haltingly.

Miguel was behind the bar, cleaning glasses and occasionally darting quick looks in their direction. He had asked his wife little and his mind was tumbling with the few words of explanation she had offered. They, too, had much to discuss, but it could wait. For now.

Santi had to ask the questions that had been burning him up for so long. 'Why did you go? Why did you leave us?'

Rosa-Maria looked nervously at her son, knowing that her confession had to be made.

'It's . . . it's hard to explain. It had nothing to do with you?'

'It had everything to do with us,' said Santiago almost angrily.

Rosa-Maria nodded. Her story was difficult to tell, but she knew that if she and Santi were going to attempt to build a relationship, it had to be told.

'I abandoned you. I . . . I was walking home one night and . . . and two men attacked me. One of them was . . . he was your uncle. I managed to get home, but I knew that I could never tell your father what happened.'

Santi could see the pain in his mother's eyes as the memories returned.

'And I panicked, and I ran away.'

Santi's mind was churning. 'But never even a call? Nothing?'

'Santiago,' said Rosa-Maria defiantly, 'I came back three weeks later, and you were all gone. And no one could tell me where my family had disappeared to. And those who could, wouldn't.

Then I found out it was too late: you had left Mexico.'

She glanced across at her husband, Miguel, and then looked back at Santiago.

'When I saw you on the television I wanted to get in touch with you so much, but I was sure that you wished me dead.'

Santi reached out and took his mother's hand again. 'How could you think that? I was angry. My dad was angry. He died full of anger. At you, at everything, at the world.'

His words were almost as difficult for Rosa to take as her own story had been to tell.

'He loved you very much,' said Santi.

Tears filled Rosa-Maria's eyes again. 'I'm . . . I'm . . .' She leaned forward and kissed Santi's hands. 'Forgive me.'

Santi nodded. 'Everything's going to be OK,' he said softly. 'You'll see.'

The sun had set over the towering billboards – one showing Real Madrid's new star Santiago Muñez – but the kids were determined to continue with their football match until it was too dark to see.

Enrique wasn't letting the cast on his arm or the cuts and bruises on his face stop him from throwing everything into the game, especially as the bullying Tito was on the opposing side.

A small girl was running up and down at the edge of the makeshift pitch, hardly involved in the action, particularly when the larger boys came thundering in her direction.

She stopped running when she saw the two figures approaching. And then she stared.

'Enrique!'

Enrique had the ball – he didn't want to lose it – but the girl shouted again urgently.

'*Enrique!*'

The ball rolled away as Enrique looked up and everyone's eyes followed the girl's pointing finger.

Rosa-Maria was walking towards them – with Santiago.

'Hey, bro,' he said as he reached Enrique. 'You want a game?'

Enrique beamed and nodded, for once lost for words. But his joy was made complete a few minutes later as Santiago effortlessly avoided a lunging tackle from Tito and casually knocked the bully to the ground, leaving him sprawled face down, eating dirt.

Santiago's other brother, Julio, was at home in LA, playing a game on his computer, when a new window opened on his screen to inform him that he had an email.

He went to his mailbox, saw that the email was from Santi and read the few brief lines of explanation. Quickly, he began to download the attachment.

'Grandma,' he called. 'Mail from Santi.'

Mercedes came in from the kitchen. She stood behind Julio and together they watched a photograph gradually appear on the screen.

It was Santi, with Enrique and Rosa-Maria. They were smiling, self-consciously but happily, and Mercedes could see for herself the pride and delight in her older grandson's face. She had been so afraid that if he found his mother there would be more pain and heartache.

But the photograph told the story. Santiago looked so happy.

Mercedes sighed as she thought of her own

son, Herman. He had never forgiven Rosa-Maria for deserting them, and neither had she. But nothing could change what had happened in the past and as she stared at the photograph, Mercedes realized that what mattered most now was the future. It was time to move on.

She squeezed Julio's shoulders and smiled as he turned and looked up at her.

'Your mother,' she said. 'Now we must do something about you meeting her, too.'

Roz was sitting in the darkness. She was perched on the bottom stair of the house in Newcastle, struggling to hold back the tears as she played Santiago's phone message for a second time.

'It's good you're out. This way I can say what I need to say. Everything has turned inside out since I came here. The money, the fame, without you it's nothing, Roz.'

Roz could hear that Santi was struggling to get the words right as he hesitated.

'I finally met my mother. Not knowing was tearing me apart. It's still hard to take in, but I think things might be OK. It's going to take time.'

He paused again and Roz pictured him in Madrid as he made the call.

'I'm not going to make any more excuses for what I've done. All I can say is I'm just so sorry for treating you the way I have, for pushing you away. I've been a total jerk.'

Roz smiled. He was right about that. He'd been stupid, irresponsible, selfish, and just like he said, a total jerk.

But there were things that Roz wanted to say to Santiago, too. Things that she'd never had the chance to discuss with him before their world had so completely and dramatically fallen apart.

She looked down at her stomach and marvelled again at the swelling that seemed to increase slightly almost every day. She was almost six months pregnant. Santiago didn't even know that he was going to become a father.

'I want to make things right,' he said, nearing the end of his message. 'Please call me. Let me know if you'll give me a second chance. I love you, Roz.'

Thirty-one

The build-up to the Champions League final sparked unprecedented levels of debate and speculation in the Press and media: Harris or Muñez, who was it to be?

Gavin had been playing well and was scoring again. But Santiago was a proven match-winner, and despite his off-the-field antics, what mattered most to everyone was that Real won the match.

Van Der Merwe was on the telephone in his office when Santiago came in looking as though he was spoiling for a fight.

'I'll have to call you back,' said Van Der Merwe into the phone before hanging up.

'What is it?' he said, looking up at Santi.

'Are you going to start me?' demanded Santiago firmly. 'In the final?'

Van Der Merwe sighed with irritation. 'I seem to remember us doing this dance once before. Don't you?'

Santiago stared hard at the coach. 'Play Gavin.'

'What?' said Van Der Merwe, taken aback. 'Is this some kind of game, Muñez?'

'No, boss,' said Santiago. 'I just want to ask you to keep me on the bench. Start Gavino. If he plays well in the final he could still make the England World Cup squad.'

Van Der Merwe shook his head. One minute Muñez was telling him to start him in the team and the next he was asking him to leave him out.

'I love football,' said Santiago before his coach had a chance to speak. 'But without my friends and my family, it's not enough. When I came here I was . . . dazzled by it all; I lost sight of what was important and did my best to throw everything away.'

'Muñez—'

'Let me finish, please, boss,' said Santi urgently. 'Gavin's been with me all the way. He's my *friend*. And while I've been running around like an idiot, he's been working hard and earning his place. But he's running out of time and he can't finish this season on the bench.'

Santiago let out a long breath. 'That's all I'm asking, boss.' He turned to go.

'Muñez?'

'Boss?' said Santi, turning back.

'I pick the team.'

Thirty-two

Miguel slid the key into the lock of the entrance door to the bar, watched by Rosa Maria and Enrique. He turned the heavy old key, pulled it from the lock and then rattled the door handle to check that the door was actually secured as Enrique waited impatiently and his mother just smiled.

Across the street stood a gleaming Audi. An equally well turned out driver was waiting to open the doors for his VIP passengers.

They crossed the road and the driver smiled at them as he pulled open one of the rear doors. On the back seat were flowers for Rosa-Maria and three Real shirts, each bearing the name, Muñez.

Santiago's newly found family were on their way to watch the final of the Champions League.

His other family – grandmother Mercedes, and brother Julio – were ready, with what seemed to have developed into the LA branch of the Real Madrid supporters' club crammed into the living room of their house. Mercedes was, as always, in the seat of honour closest to the television screen, and Julio was at her side.

Roz was at home in Newcastle, with only her mum, Carol, for company. Roz had to see the final, but in her condition the safest place to do so was from the comfort of an armchair. She, too, was staring at the television as pundits made their pre-match forecasts and predicted a close but exciting final.

Glen had chosen to watch the match in a Newcastle pub, along with some of the staff from his garage. If things had worked out differently he would have been there, close to the action, giving Santi support and words of encourage-ment before taking his reserved seat in one of the executive boxes.

But things hadn't worked out differently, and

all Glen could do now was watch from afar, like hundreds of thousands of other football fans all around the globe.

The Bernabéu had been selected as the venue for the Champions League final long before the competition got underway.

It was the luck of the draw as far as Real Madrid was concerned, but Arsenal, too, would feel at home with their fans filling half the stadium.

Arsène Wenger had performed near miracles in getting the side he was patiently rebuilding to the final. Many of his stalwarts had either moved on, as in the case of Patrick Vieira, or were suffering from long-term injuries.

But the Arsenal injury crisis had meant the emergence of several new young stars, including the dynamic and feisty English midfielder, TJ Harper.

The Real players sat nervously on the benches in the dressing room, waiting patiently for Van Der Merwe to begin his pre-match talk.

Van Der Merwe smiled. 'I have taken you as

far as I can, to Base Camp.' He paused for a moment and then nodded towards the door. 'Out there, that's Everest.'

A few of the players nodded their appreciation at his words.

'The legends are watching you: Di Stéfano, Butragueño, Sánchez. Remember them, and remember you deserve to be here. To make history. As a team. You are one step away from the ultimate achievement, the biggest prize in club football.'

He held up his team sheet, knowing by heart every name he had written down without needing to refer to his notes, and began to reveal his starting line-up.

'Casillas. Salgardo. Woodgate. Helguera. Carlos.' He paused. Everyone was staring intently. 'Zidane, Beckham, Guti, Robinho. Ronaldo.'

Real's hugely popular skipper, Rául, had been injured in the build-up to the final and was not fit enough to start the match.

Only one place remained. Van Der Merwe locked eyes with Santiago as he said the final name.

'Harris.'

Gavin's eyes widened in surprise. He looked over at Santiago and saw that he was smiling at him, sharing his joy.

As the players filed from the dressing room, heading for the tunnel, their coach's final words of encouragement were still ringing in their ears.

'You made it. The Champions League final. I don't want you to forget why you're here, but I want you to play as if you have nothing to lose. Forget the money, forget the Press, forget the cameras. Forget everything. Enjoy.'

The Real players came face to face with their opponents at the entrance to the tunnel. Many were old friends, old rivals, or in some cases old sparring partners.

The two teams began the long walk down the tunnel, hearing the tumultuous noise that was building towards its crescendo. As they emerged into the dazzling lights of the Bernabéu, the deafening sound ringing around the stadium rose to a level that few had ever experienced.

They reached the centre circle and formed the line-up for the UEFA anthem and then they began the traditional handshakes, with the Real players moving along the Arsenal ranks, nodding and offering a brief 'Good luck'.

Henry, Bergkamp, Cole, Pirès, Ljungberg. Even without the inspirational Patrick Vieira, Arsenal was still a team packed with potential match-winners. And apart from the established stars, they also had TJ Harper, their new young superstar with the looks and the confidence of a music rapper or movie star.

David Beckham shook his hand and nodded. 'TJ. Good luck.'

Harper smiled broadly and then glanced towards Gavin who was next in line.

'Ain't me who's gonna need the luck, bro,' said Harper to Beckham.

As Gavin took Harper's hand, the Arsenal player leaned in close and whispered something in his ear. The psychological games were beginning.

Gavin stood back and a look of anger flashed across his face. Harper walked away, laughing at drawing first blood in the battle of the minds. David Beckham put a hand on Gavin's shoulder;

he knew all about opponents with wind-up tactics.

'Take no notice,' was all he said. It was enough. Gavin smiled and nodded and then went jogging off to take up his starting position.

On the bench, Santiago exchanged an anxious look with Steve McManaman. They had both seen Gavin's furious look during the handshakes.

The referee checked with his assistants and then raised his whistle to his lips and the piercing shrill penetrated even the roar of eighty-five thousand voices.

The Champions League final was underway.

Thirty-three

The match couldn't have got off to a worse start for Real – or for Gavin Harris.

In the very first minute, as he collected a short pass, he was robbed by the quick-thinking TJ Harper, who set off on a run towards the Real goal.

Gavin turned to give chase and quickly made up ground. Just as Harper reached the box, Gavin made his tackle. It was well timed and clean, but Harper went down dramatically.

The referee came racing in, and as Gavin clambered to his feet, he heard the whistle sound and saw him pointing to the penalty spot.

There were looks and shouts of disbelief from

the Real bench and from the Madridistas, but worse was to come.

The ref reached into his top pocket and for a moment Gavin's heart was in his mouth at the horrifying thought that he was about to suffer the same fate as Santiago had in the match against Valencia.

But the card was yellow. Gavin turned away, feeling relief but dismay, as well as anger towards Harper, who had, at very best, 'earned' the spot kick.

The Arsenal midfielder had already grabbed the ball and placed it on the spot for the penalty. The Real supporters' jeers and whistles of derision were still ringing around the stadium as Harper prepared to take the kick.

It was perfectly placed, low and hard into the left corner, and although Casillas guessed correctly and dived the right way, the ball easily beat his outstretched arm.

Arsenal were a goal up after just one minute. And as Real tried to regroup and counter the early disaster, it quickly began to look as though the Premiership team would go further ahead.

Their moves were quick and incisive, and the Premiership-style pace was close to overwhelming the more measured build-up of Real.

Bergkamp was just wide with a rasping shot and Henry, darting through his favoured left channel, went even closer with a header as Arsenal totally dominated.

The *galacticos* of Madrid were being out-played and out-thought as they struggled to overcome the setback of losing a goal so early on.

On the bench, Santiago was living every move and feeling every tackle, desperately wanting to be part of the action, yet willing Gavin to make a special contribution to the final.

But it was all Arsenal. Freddie Ljungberg was causing havoc on the left flank, twice bringing stunning saves from Casillas, who was undoubtedly Real's player of the first half.

Real were fortunate not to be further behind when the referee brought the first half to a close, and they trooped off the field looking bewildered and bemused. They needed to get back in the dressing room. To regroup. To recover.

As the players entered the tunnel, separated by

the steel grille that divides the stairway, TJ Harper decided to add to Gavin's frustration and fury.

'Oh, dear,' he mocked. 'We do look upset.'

Gavin couldn't stop himself from slamming both hands against the steel. 'You cheating, cocky—!'

Steve McManaman was just behind Gavin. He pulled him away. 'Leave it, Gav! He's not worth it!'

Once the Real players had settled onto the benches in the dressing room, Van Der Merwe began his half-time team talk by kicking out at the tactics board. It clattered to the floor. No one said a word, but Macca decided to do the diplomatic thing by picking up the board. He was rewarded with a glare from the coach.

Van Der Merwe turned to Gavin. 'Harris!'

It was the moment Gavin had dreaded ever since his booking. He was being taken off.

'Harper made you look like an idiot!'

'I know, boss. But please, just give me—'

He didn't get the chance to finish.

'I want you to push forward. I'm bringing on Santi: he'll play in behind.'

Gavin breathed a huge sigh of relief. He'd been reprieved, and Santiago was coming on to add to the Real firepower.

Van Der Merwe spent the remainder of the interval reminding his players how they had allowed Arsenal to dominate and even intimidate them during the first period, and they went back out onto the pitch fired up with new energy and determination. They were one down, but great teams could come back from much greater deficits. And they *were* a great team. They had forty-five minutes to prove just how great they were.

Thirty-four

As Santiago waited on the touchline for the referee's signal that he could join the second half action, Van Der Merwe gave him a few last tactical instructions.

'Find Becks with some one-twos, wide on the left. They won't be expecting that.'

Santi nodded, and as the referee beckoned him onto the pitch he knew that his mother and Enrique would be watching from their seats up in the executive box and that his grandmother and Julio would be glued to their TV set out in LA.

And Santi knew that back in Newcastle, Glen and Roz would be watching, too. He had to play the half of his life, for all of them.

At the pub in Newcastle, the whole bar erupted in cheers and applause as they saw their former favourite sprint onto the field.

One of Glen's mechanics – the aptly nick-named Foghorn, because of his booming voice – shouted his pleasure. 'Here we go, lads, an injection of Geordie skill!'

He turned to Glen. 'Your lad's gonna do the Toon proud, Glen.'

Glen nodded and smiled with pride, but his whispered reply went unheard in the cheers and shouts of the packed bar. 'He's not my lad any more.'

Santiago was quickly up with the pace of the game, and he followed his coach's instructions to the letter. In a sweet move he found Beckham wide on the left and was in the perfect position to receive the returning ball.

Deftly, he back-heeled the ball to Gavin, who was following up at pace. He took the shot on the run from twenty-five yards out and it flashed just wide of an upright.

On the bench, Van Der Merwe nodded his satis-faction to Macca. This was better. Much better.

But Arsène Wenger was also absorbing the change in the Real tactics and was plotting his own changes. It was almost like a game of chess, with the two Grand Masters on opposing benches, deciding on their moves and adapting their tactics as the drama unfolded.

Santi, Gavin and David Beckham, more used to the English style of play than most of their team-mates, were beginning to cause Arsenal problems, and as the second half settled, Real looked as though they might yet be capable of inflicting some serious damage of their own.

But then Thierry Henry struck a demoralizing blow, demonstrating yet again why he is the most feared and most coveted striker in the English Premiership. He collected a pass close to the halfway line, and then set off on a mazy, electrifying run. He left two defenders in his wake and approached the box through the left channel. Casillas came charging out to meet him, but as a third Real defender made a despairing tackle, the Frenchman fired the ball hard and low across the diving keeper.

Henry was already racing away in triumph

as the Arsenal supporters began to celebrate a classic goal.

Real were two down and looking as though they were down and out.

As the minutes ticked by, and Real threw everything into all-out attack, Arsenal came agonizingly close to adding to their tally on more than one occasion.

Both managers made changes, but far from switching to all-out defence, the Gunners continued to press and probe and push for the third goal. Henry was inspirational, outshining even his fellow Frenchman, Zidane, who was doing everything he could to drag Real back into the match.

Real were still playing football, but it was increasingly desperate football.

Thomas Gravesen had come on to add some steel to the Real midfield, but still Arsenal were dominant, and with only seven minutes to go, there seemed to be no possible way back.

Henry collected the ball just outside the box. He jinked one way and then the other, wrong-footing Jonathan Woodgate, and then found

Freddie Ljungberg, who came sprinting into the area.

As he hurtled across the box and shaped to shoot, Roberto Carlos tore across the area, clattering in with a sliding tackle which brought the Swede crashing to the ground.

This time there was no debate, no arguing. It was a definite penalty.

TJ Harper looked to be the coolest person in the stadium as he carefully placed the ball on the spot for his second penalty.

The Bernabéu went silent.

Up in the executive box, Rosa-Maria clasped her son Enrique's hand. In LA, Mercedes was doing exactly the same with her grandson, Julio. In Newcastle, Roz reached out and took her mother, Carol's, hand, and in the city centre pub, Glen clenched his fists. Even Foghorn was silent.

The Real keeper, Casillas, steadied himself, leaving his decision on which way to dive until Harper started his run-up. Whichever way he went, it could only be a calculated guess.

The Arsenal and Real players hovered on the edge of the box, waiting to pounce or try to clear should the ball be saved and bounce back into play.

But Harper had no intention of letting the ball finish up anywhere but in the back of the net.

He began his run-up and Casillas made his decision. Harper hit the ball hard and high towards the top-right corner. Casillas had guessed correctly. He leaped across his goal line, arms at full stretch and he felt the ball thud against his fingers and onto the crossbar.

It span through the air and as it dropped, Santiago was quickest to react, even quicker than Harper, who ran in to challenge. Santi swivelled and hoofed the ball as hard and as high as he could, into the Arsenal half.

It soared away, skywards, leaving many of the players rooted to the spot, just watching.

But Gavin was off and running, tearing up the field as he followed the flight of the ball.

It was one on one: Gavin versus the Arsenal keeper, Lehmann.

They were charging towards each other like express trains, looking as though they were hurtling into an unstoppable, head-on collision.

Gavin watched the ball as it dropped; he could hear Lehmann thundering towards him. But he never took his eyes off the ball.

There wasn't time to let it bounce; he had to hit it on the volley. He unleashed his shot with all the venom he could muster.

Lehmann could do nothing to stop it. The ball passed him like a missile and he could only look back in disbelief as it rocketed into the net.

Gavin didn't stop to celebrate. He followed the ball into the goal, grabbed it and went tearing back towards the centre spot.

There was still a chance. Just.

Thirty-five

There were four minutes remaining. Four minutes for Real to try to force the match into extra time.

Arsenal had given up all thought of attacking football. Now it was their turn for desperate defence. But Real were suddenly a team inspired; suddenly, in the very last moments, playing football worthy at last of the Real of old.

Zidane threaded the ball to Ronaldo, who found David Beckham out wide. He slid a measured pass through to Gavin, who was in position to shoot again. That was what the Arsenal defence were expecting, but Gavin cleverly sent across a long pass, which sat up invitingly for Santiago.

His first-time shot thundered back off the crossbar, and all around the stadium there were groans of despair and frustration.

But the attack was still alive, with Gavin and Beckham urging their team-mates on with clenched fists and snarls of encouragement.

A lunging tackle earned the Gunners a few seconds' respite from the onslaught but, more importantly for Real, it gave them a corner.

Beckham went to the corner flag to place the ball, and on the bench, Van Der Merwe and McManaman checked their watches yet again.

The corner sailed over, deep into the heart of the penalty box, swinging away from the keeper, but he bravely raced from his line and punched it away.

The forty-five minutes were up. Arsène Wenger was on his feet, glaring at the fourth official and pointing towards his watch.

But there were two minutes of additional time. Still two minutes for Real to grab an equalizer.

Lehmann's punched clearance had not got Arsenal out of trouble. After a midfield tussle, Roberto Carlos intercepted the ball as it bounced free. It was all-out attack now. It had to be. He ran at the Arsenal defence, dragging two players with him towards the corner flag.

Before either of them could make the tackle, the Brazilian thumped in a cross.

Santiago was on the edge of the box. He knew for certain that the ball was going to drop for him; he knew for certain that he was going to volley it home.

He did.

Lehmann hardly saw it and had no chance to stop it.

Everyone in the stadium and millions of television viewers around the world could barely believe what they were witnessing. This was a comeback to compare with the great comebacks in footballing history.

The Arsenal players were stunned and staring at each other. How could it have happened? The trophy had been theirs; it had been almost within touching distance, but now the dreaded spectre of extra time hovered over them.

And the momentum was all with Real.

The Madridistas were still screaming their

delight as Arsenal restarted the game. But they were in disarray: they lost possession and the ball was with Real once again.

Guti threaded it through to Gavin and he swept it imperiously on to Santi, who saw another shooting chance. He shaped for the shot but a despairing lunge from TJ Harper brought him down and the referee blew for a free kick.

The two additional minutes were virtually up and the Arsenal players crowded around the ref, urging him to blow for full time.

But David Beckham already had the ball.

He calmly placed it for the free kick and the Arsenal defenders hurriedly took their positions in the wall, following the barked instructions of Lehmann.

The free kick was in exactly the right sort of range for a Beckham speciality dead-ball attempt, and at just the right angle to bend around a wall.

The Bernabéu went silent.

In LA, Santiago's grandmother mouthed a silent prayer and, up in the stands, his mother did the same thing.

Santiago watched; Gavin watched; it seemed as though the whole world was watching as Beckham rocked back on his left foot for a moment before beginning his run-up.

He struck it perfectly, even more perfectly than the legendary free kick he had struck for England against Greece.

The Arsenal defenders leaped high to try to intercept it, but the ball arced over their heads and curled into the top corner, past the outstretched hands of the diving Lehmann.

The Bernabéu erupted as Beckham wheeled away in triumph and the final whistle sounded. Miraculously, almost unbelievably, there would be no need for extra time.

As Beckham turned back, Gavin and Santiago were there. They leaped into each other's arms, screaming their joy and basking in the tumultuous adoration of the Madridistas.

The three goal scorers were together.

Champions of Europe.

NOW THE DREAM CONTINUES . . .

thirsty. He smelled water, fresh water, nearby, but he didn't want to leave this spot in case the Collins family came back for him. So he lay there, a little brown puppy more gangling than chubby, more dog than baby, more awkward than adorable. He lay there with his head on his paws until the sun set and the world around him turned black and he saw no lights anywhere. He'd never been in a world without lights, and that made him shiver, and that made him whimper, and then he let out such a disconsolate howl that he frightened himself and a few other critters nearby.

He began running very fast down the road, toward the scent of human civilization.

Snix sat with his head cocked, watching. Waiting. Expectant. Then, not so expectant, more hopeful. Then, sad. Snix lay down with his head on his paws, his eyes fixed steadily on the dirt road where his family's car had last been – he could still smell the gas fumes, and Cota's light fragrance.

No other cars passed. It was just after Labor Day. Everyone had left the island. Well, not everyone, 'of course – twelve thousand people still lived and worked on the island, but none were strolling that hot day on a secluded sandy track through the moors.

September was much like August on the island of Nantucket. The sun beat down on the crackling brown grass and on Snix. Overhead, small planes zipped back and forth, taking people from the island back to the mainland. From time to time a sparrow would tweet and flutter from one tree to another. Snix watched a spider creep across the dirt road and disappear in the bayberry bushes. That was about it for action that afternoon.

Snix was by no means a stupid dog, but he was naturally loyal and he was young and naïve. He didn't have the experience even to consider the possibility that the sweet-smelling long-haired girl who hugged him and cuddled him and chucked him under his chinny-chin-chin was never coming back for him. So he waited. His stomach growled. He got very

At the beginning of the family's summer vacation, Cota doted on Snix, letting him sleep in her bed, brushing his coarse coat, tickling his fat belly, and taking him for lots of walks up and down Main Street on Nantucket, with Snix tripping fetchingly over his rhinestone leash.

Three months later, Cota was fourteen instead of thirteen. Her hair was two inches longer, her legs were three inches longer, her bosom was three inches fuller, and she didn't need a pet of any kind to get noticed. Meanwhile, Snix had lost his puppy fat and his roly-poly ways. He now wore a mournful and slightly baffled expression, having gone from adored to ignored in three short months.

At the end of the summer, the Collins family did what many vacationers do when they return home from their holiday – they left their adopted pet behind. They drove their black SUV out to the moors in the middle of the island, where dirt roads ranged over low hills and past small ponds, where rabbits, moles, and deer hid in the bushes. They removed Snix's collar, name tag, and leash before Cota opened the door, leaned out, and set the pup on the dry, end-of-summer grass.

'Bye, Snix,' the teenager chirped hastily, slamming the door shut.

The family's large black SUV roared off, leaving a cloud of sandy dust floating in the air.

2

Prologue

This tale begins, as do many Nantucket tails, with a dog. A Norwich terrier, the runt of the litter — which made him very small indeed — a stubby, sturdy, tan, pint-sized pup with a face like a fox's, ears like a panda's, and the dark passionate eyes of Antonio Banderas.

His name was Snix.

Back in his chubby days, he was adopted by the Collins family visiting from Rhode Island. His plump bumbling made Cota, their teenage daughter, squeal that he was *so cute*. Cota named him Snix because she knew no other dog in the world had ever been named Snix. Cota was at the age when she wanted to be noticed for being the kind of special girl who would have a dog named Snix.

Much gratitude goes to the Jane Rotrosen Agency, especially my agent, Meg Ruley, and to Christina Hogrebe and Peggy Gordijn.

Thank you, Wendy Schmidt and Wendy Hudson, for keeping independent bookstores alive on Nantucket.

Thank you, Charley, for everything.

And Merry Christmas to everyone, from Nantucket.

Nancy Thayer

and Del Wynn and their sons Patrick and Riley.
Thanks to Laura Simon, Jim Gross, and Susan Simon.
Thanks to Suze Robinson and Kat Robinson Grieder
and James Grieder and their son, Will. Thanks to
Dionis Gauvin, who I hope will bring her husband,
Mike Mills, one year. Thanks to our son, Josh Thayer,
and his partner David Gillum. Thanks to Jonathan,
Katie, and Elizabeth Hemingway, and to Jonathan's
mother, Nancy Rapaport. Thanks to Leslie Linsley,
Jon Aron, and Gretchen Anderson. Thanks to Mimi
and Dwight Beman and their daughters Allie,
Elizabeth, and Ann, and Ann's husband, Roger Nina
and their daughter, Natalia. Thanks to our daughter
Sam and her husband, Neil Forbes, and their children
Elias, Adeline, and Emmett, who have begun, understandably, having Christmas Eve parties at their house
on the mainland.

Everything changes. New people come and beloved
people go far too soon. The island stays — and a pun
is in that word.

I also want to thank my publishing family at
Ballantine who have provided so much wisdom,
laughter, and support: my radiant editor Linda Marrow,
Gina Centrello, Libby McGuire, and Dana Isaacson.
Thanks to Junessa Viloria, Kim Hovey, Penelope
Haynes, Alison Masciovecchio, Ashley Woodfolk, and
Quinne Rogers.

Acknowledgements

Enormous thanks to my agent and fabulous friend Meg Ruley, who grew up on the island, for suggesting *A Nantucket Christmas*. She knows more than anyone how Nantucket can be a light in the darkness.

For years, my husband, Charley, and I gave a party on Christmas Eve. Our guests were, and are, the light in the darkness to me. Thanks to Charlotte Maison, who over the years became Charlotte Kastner, and her husband, Tom Kastner. Thanks to her son Karl Schoonover and his partner Lloyd Pratt. Thank you to Pam Pindell and her daughters Rebecca Sayre and Casey Sayre, and Casey's husband, Steve Boukus, and their children Torin and Kyra. Thanks to M.J.

FOR MEG RULEY

First published as an Ebook in Great Britain in 2013 by
HEADLINE PUBLISHING GROUP

First published in paperback in Great Britain in 2014 by
HEADLINE PUBLISHING GROUP

1

Cataloguing in Publication Data is available from the British Library

ISBN 978 1 4722 1595 6

Typeset in Bembo by Palimpsest Book Production Limited,
Falkirk, Stirlingshire

Printed and bound in Great Britain by
CPI Group (UK) Ltd, Croydon, CR0 4YY

Headline's policy is to use papers that are natural, renewable and
recyclable products and made from wood grown in sustainable
forests. The logging and manufacturing processes are expected to
conform to the environmental regulations of the country of origin.

HEADLINE PUBLISHING GROUP
An Hachette UK Company
338 Euston Road
London NW1 3BH

www.headline.co.uk
www.hachette.co.uk

Nancy Thayer
A Nantucket Christmas

headline

By Nancy Thayer

Stepping
Three Women at the Water's Edge
Bodies and Souls
Nell
Morning
Spirit Lost
My Dearest Friend
Everlasting
Family Secrets
Belonging
An Act of Love
Between Husbands and Friends
Custody
The Hot Flash Club
The Hot Flash Club Strikes Again
Hot Flash Holidays
The Hot Flash Club Chills Out
Moon Shell Beach
Summer House
Beachcombers *
Heat Wave *
Summer Breeze *
Island Girls *
A Nantucket Christmas *
Nantucket Sisters *

* Available from Headline

Nancy Thayer is a *New York Times* bestselling author who has written twenty-five novels to date, including *Beachcombers*, *Heat Wave*, *Summer Breeze*, and *Island Girls*. Her work has been translated into many languages, and her novels are enjoyed by readers the world over. She lives year-round with her husband on Nantucket Island.

You can find out more about Nancy by visiting her website at www.nancythayer.com.

Praise for Nancy Thayer:

'Nancy Thayer is one of my favorite writers . . . Here is a book to be savored and passed on to the good women in your life'

New York Times bestselling author Susan Wiggs

'Full of emotion . . . this novel is delightful'

Romance Reviews Today

'Nancy Thayer's gift for reaching the emotional core of her characters is captivating'

Houston Chronicle

'Thayer has the knack of creating likeable characters who grapple with problems that will strike a chord with many readers'

Globe

CHAPTER 1

'Robin Hood!'

The tough, weatherbeaten man standing in a clearing in Sherwood Forest waited as his voice echoed through the trees. His name was Gareth, and he looked as if he had spent most of his life out of doors. His clothes were ragged and sweat-stained and he carried a small pack and a staff. There was no answer to his call and, after a moment's hesitation, he walked on.

He reached the top of a hill where he could see more of the forest and, cupping his hands, he once again called 'Robin Hood!' A frown crossed his good-natured face when there was no reply and he sighed, feeling tired and discouraged.

'Who are you?'

The quiet voice, when it came, startled him. He could see no one. Then, as he watched, Robin Hood's band of outlaws appeared from the trees, one by one.

Into view came the slow-witted, gentle Much, and the Saracen Nasir once the slave of the terrible Simon de Belleme – dropped lightly from a tree. The chubby face of Friar Tuck peered over a bush; then, his bow at the ready, Will Scarlet stepped swiftly from the bushes, and after him the giant figure of Little John emerged. The beautiful Marion followed, and last of all came Robin Hood, the leader of them all. What had seemed a deserted part of the forest had almost miraculously been peopled by the outlaw band.

Marion recognized Gareth immediately and, surprised and delighted, came towards him.

'Gareth! Gareth of Leaford!' she said with great warmth.

'Aye, that I was, Lady Marion,' Gareth smiled. 'But I'm Gareth of Uffcombe now.'

'You know him?' asked Robin with surprise.

'Indeed I do!' said Marion. 'He was steward to my father.'

'Aye, I used to be,' said Gareth, looking fondly at her.

'What are you doing in Sherwood, then?' asked Robin.

'Yes, what do you want with us, friend?' echoed Little John, a shade belligerently.

As Gareth paused, seeking the words he needed to explain his mission, Robin gazed intently at him. 'You need help, don't you, Gareth?' he said, with a sudden flash of that strange intuition he possessed. Gareth could only nod in amazement.

The outlaws led Gareth back to their camp, fed him and gave him something to drink before settling down to hear his story.

'When I left Leaford after your father's death, my lady,' Gareth began, 'I took service with Earl Godwin.'

Marion nodded. 'I knew him when I was a child. He's a kind man. He fought with my father in the Holy Land.'

'Aye,' said Gareth. 'But I'm not one for life in a castle bailey, and so after a year of that I got restless. I moved on. That's how I came to be in Uffcombe. They're friendly folk and – well – I liked the place!'

He paused for a moment, looking at the faces of the outlaws, uncertain how to continue his tale. Robin urged him to go on.

'We live in terror – all of us,' said Gareth quietly, looking round to see if he was being believed. 'Night after night they ride. You never know when they are coming. Sometimes it'll be a week – even longer, maybe. And just when you think it's all over, they – they come streaming out of the darkness!'

'Who?' asked Robin.

'I don't know!' said Gareth after a pause. 'Nobody knows. Some say they're from hell!'

'Oh, so it's demons now, is it?' mocked Will.

'Demons!' whispered Much, who was frightened by the tale.

'You haven't seen 'em,' retorted Gareth to Will. 'I – I don't know what they are. But they kill and they burn – and – and drag away whoever they want. They – they fly down into the village.'

'Fly?' said Scarlet, glancing round at the others with a look of scorn.

'I tell you no one's safe from the Hounds of Lucifer,' said Gareth, and Will laughed out loud at him. 'The Hounds of Lucifer?' he roared. 'The man's raving!'

With a gesture at Will that silenced his laughter, Robin asked Gareth quietly if any of the villagers had tried to stop the Hounds. Gareth shook his head. He was ashamed.

'You see,' he said, 'all the way here I tried to think out what I'd say to you – how I'd tell it. I've heard plenty of stories about you – and I hoped so much that they were true. That's what brought me here. Hope!'

There was silence, then Robin got to his feet, his thoughts on that distant village and the nightmare that had befallen it.

'We can't leave Sherwood – that's for certain,' said Will.

'Why not?' sneered Little John. 'Scared of the Hounds of Lucifer, are you?'

'It's nothing to do with us!' countered Will angrily.

Robin asked Gareth how far away Uffcombe was, and was told five days. 'Five days!' moaned Friar Tuck, aghast at the thought of such a journey.

Will Scarlet was still brooding. 'Why go half way across England when we've our own people to fight for?' he demanded.

'Our own people!' Robin exclaimed angrily. 'Who are our own people? The people of Sherwood? Do we only help them?' He drew the magnificent sword he had been given by Herne the Hunter, the mysterious horned god of the forest, and held it up to the sun.

'This is Albion, one of the Seven Swords of Wayland. We swore on this sword to help the poor and oppressed. Not just the people of Sherwood.'

'He's right, Will,' said Tuck.

Little John agreed. 'I say we should go.'

Only Much seemed anxious. 'What about the demons?' he asked.

'There won't be any, Much,' said Robin. 'I promise.'

Will sighed.

'Not much chance, have I?' he said with a wry grin. 'If you've all decided to go to the devil, I'll have to go with you!'

By nightfall, the outlaws were ready to begin the long journey to Uffcombe. They carried packs on their backs and all were armed with swords, longbows and quivers full of arrows. They looked what they were – efficient, deadly, masters of the art of forest warfare. Little John kicked out the fire and they slipped silently through the forest towards the river, following it westwards.

As dawn rose, Robin found himself thinking back to the warning Herne had given him when he went to take his leave.

'Hear me and heed me, for I am Herne, Lord of the Trees. They that seek to shatter the bolts that hold back the Evil One must first take Albion from you. Guard it with your heart's blood!'

Robin's hand tightened on the hilt of his sword as he walked. No one would take Albion from him and live!

Some miles from Uffcombe, and joined to the mainland by a narrow causeway, the ancient Abbey of Ravenscar stood atop a rocky island, surrounded by the restless sea. On a calm day the singing of the nuns could be heard by fishermen mending their nets along the shore. The Abbess was Morgwyn of Ravenscar, venerated by the people of the West Country for her holy and pious life.

Morgwyn, a tall and beautiful woman of great dignity and power, was walking in the cloisters with the local Sheriff. The fussy little man was telling her how Father Thomas – the priest at Uffcombe – had been mortally wounded by a gang of villains who had desecrated a tomb, presumably seeking treasure.

The Abbess was deeply shocked by what she heard. 'And is there no hope for the priest?' she asked the Sheriff.

'No, reverend lady, none,' he replied, shaking his head. 'His wounds have become poisoned. Nothing can save him.'

'It's horrible!' shuddered Morgwyn, raising her hands to her eyes. Then she crossed herself.

'The villains must have thought that there was treasure in Sir John's tomb,' said the Sheriff.

'Murder and sacrilege!' whispered Morgwyn, to which the Sheriff replied that God would surely punish them.

'Indeed! But meanwhile, Sheriff, you must find these men,' ordered the Abbess.

'Oh, I will, honoured lady,' he promised. 'They won't escape, I can promise you!'

The Sheriff looked round at her as they continued their walk. 'I – er – believe that the church lies in your patronage?' he said, slightly nervous.

'Why do you ask?' replied Morgwyn, knowing perfectly well.

'I have a nephew, reverend lady,' he said. 'He is most devout and – er – very accomplished.'

'Perhaps we could discuss the matter after Father Thomas's death,' Morgwyn suggested with a hint of reproach in her voice. 'It is unseemly to consider who is going to be his successor until all hope is gone.'

'Forgive me,' muttered the chastened Sheriff. 'I meant no disrespect.'

They had now reached an archway beyond which the Sheriff's men were waiting for him. Morgwyn stopped and the Sheriff bowed deeply to her. 'May the blessed Trinity protect and strengthen you for the good government of holy religion,' he said piously.

'Amen,' answered Morgwyn, and watched the Sheriff mount his horse and ride away with his men. Then she turned away.

The steward to the Abbey stood nearby, watching the scene. It was none other than Peter Verdelet.

Morgwyn looked after the Sheriff. Her face had changed dramatically. 'Greedy little swine!' she muttered. Then she turned on Verdelet who had hastened to her side. 'And you, Verdelet,' she hissed savagely at him, 'you can't even kill a priest!'

Verdelet shrank away from the Abbess. He knew better than to say anything when Morgwyn was angry. He knew her for what she really was. Her apparent piety and holiness were a mask hiding her true nature, for in reality she was the High Priestess of the Cauldron of Lucifer and the nuns of Ravenscar Abbey were all witches. It was Morgwyn who ordered the Hounds to ride.

She and her followers believed that the Devil, whom they called Lucifer, was the real creator and ruler of the world, and that he had been unjustly banished from heaven. It was their belief that Lucifer would eventually overthrow God and rule in heaven eternally, replacing good with evil.

That night in the great cavern under the Abbey, Morgwyn stood dressed in scarlet robes, with her long dark hair trailing down her back. She moved towards a circular stone altar around which knelt the nuns, now no longer in their habits but in shifts daubed with magical signs. Like Morgwyn, their hair hung loose and their arms and shoulders were bare. A fire burned in the centre of the altar, giving the only light in the cavern, and on the altar were five identical swords, their blades all pointing towards the fire like the spokes of a wheel.

Two places in the circle of swords remained to be filled. Morgwyn lifted the sword Orias gently into its place, then stared ahead as if she were in a trance.

'O Lord Lucifer,' she intoned in little more than a whisper, 'proud Spirit – I bring thee Orias, the Sixth Sword!'

'He that is bound shall be free,' whispered the witches intensely, 'and he that rules shall be overthrown!'

CHAPTER 2

It was early evening when the outlaws finally reached Uff-combe. All of them were weary and footsore, especially fat little Tuck who was most unused to this kind of hard, fast travelling. As they reached the watermill on the outskirts of the village, Gareth pointed out the miller, Adam, who was unloading a cart. It was clear that strangers were not welcome in Uffcombe, and the glance Adam threw at the outlaws was far from friendly, until he recognized Gareth's face among them.

'Gareth,' he started, but Gareth hurried up to him and said, 'It's all right, Adam. They're friends. They've come to help us.'

'No one can help us,' said Adam gloomily. 'Still, I'm glad of your company. Mine's a lonely life.' Then he looked nervously round at the trees. The light was already beginning to fade.

'Come inside,' he said, leading them into his spacious stone mill. It was a square building with ladders and steps leading up to higher levels. Sacks of flour were piled high.

'They're going to fight for us,' said Gareth, but Adam shook his head despairingly and said that people couldn't fight the dead. Gareth asked him if 'they' had ridden again.

Adam sighed deeply. 'How should I know?' he asked gloomily. 'I lock myself in at nightfall.'

Robin was gazing at a white circle on the flagstones when the outlaws joined him. They looked inquiringly at Adam.

'Salt!' he said. 'I don't move out of that circle until sun up. This valley is cursed with demons – cursed, I tell you! Nothing can save it, nothing!'

While he was speaking, Marion walked to where a

strangely shaped root lay on a rough table. It looked something like the shape of a man.

'That's a mandrake,' said Adam.

'Yes,' she said, 'it's for protection, isn't it?'

'Against the Hounds of Lucifer?' asked Robin quickly.

'Do you think that arrows or swords can hold them off?' grunted Adam gloomily.

'A lot better than salt!' said Robin.

Adam stared at him in amazement. 'But they ain't human. Can't you understand?' he asked. 'You might as well shoot at the moon!'

'How do you know they ain't human?' asked Will, but Adam ignored him and instead turned to Gareth: 'You should never have brought 'em here. They are all going to die!'

'Now listen to me,' said Little John. 'You can surround yourself with salt, soot or sausages for all I care, friend, but we've come too far to turn back now. Men or demons, they're going to be dealt with.' And with that Gareth and the outlaws left the mill and headed for Uffcombe.

The village, when they reached it, appeared to be totally deserted. However, it soon became clear that the frightened villagers had seen them coming and had taken refuge inside their homes. Gareth suggested tackling each house in turn, but Robin stopped him with a gesture. Striding into the centre of the village green, Robin cupped his hands round his mouth and called out to the hidden and terrified people he knew were hiding behind every door and shutter.

'Is this the way you welcome people who've been asked to help you?'

There was silence. The outlaws looked round the village, but no one appeared.

'What's the matter with you?' shouted Robin. 'Are you all scared of the dark?'

There was still no sound. Robin started again. 'Look at us! We haven't got a single tail between us! We're not demons – we're men!'

The silence continued. Then, as the outlaws watched, a few villagers began appearing in the doorways of their huts. Soon there were about thirty people standing silently and staring at the outlaws.

Tuck was the first to break the silence. 'Shall I take a collection, Robin?' he asked slyly. Robin laughed, then called to the villagers. 'Come closer, friends. We won't bite!'

Several young men edged forward, followed by a few more, until gradually the villagers began to lose their fear of the newcomers. They came hesitantly from their huts and barns and stood near the outlaws.

'Good!' said Robin. 'Now listen to me. Gareth went a long way to bring us here. We've come to help you. You can't really believe that demons can come from hell to torment you.'

One of the village elders, Philip, came forward angrily and said, 'We've seen them!' There were murmurs of agreement from the rest, except from one man who was watching Robin keenly. His name was Cedric and he was one of Verdelet's spies.

'So you've seen them,' Robin continued. 'What do these flying demons look like? Do they breathe fire?'

'Don't mock us,' shouted Philip. 'Three people have been killed and five carried off, including my son James. Did we imagine that? Trampled crops! Homes burned down! And you laugh at us. We don't want you!'

'All these things of which you have told us can be done by men – and men can stop them,' argued Robin.

'Why should we listen to you, wolf's-head?' Philip shouted furiously. 'That's what they are – outlaws – with a price on their heads!'

'Anyone feel like earning it?' roared Will.

Gareth tried to get the villagers' attention. 'They rob the rich and greedy,' he said, 'not people like us,' but he was howled down. The uproar grew until Marion stepped forward and the villagers fell silent as she began to speak.

'I am Marion of Leaford,' she said simply. 'Gareth once served my father. He was a knight – a Crusader – and if he'd known these men he would have loved them, because they believe in justice. Not the cruel justice of Sheriffs and their lords but justice that protects the helpless and weak and gives them hope – sometimes even courage.'

The crowd was silent now and she went on. 'Give us time to become your friends, and if there's evil then we can join together to defeat it!'

There was a moment's silence and then Philip came and took Robin's hand, apologizing for speaking hastily. 'We both did,' said Robin.

'Let's welcome our new friends,' said Philip, and all of them did so except Cedric, who stood watching the scene grimly.

The next day was bright and sunny. Philip showed Robin where the 'flying' invaders came from. Robin climbed on to the roof of one of the houses at the lowest level, and looked up at the cliffs. 'Get me a horse!' he ordered. Some minutes later he was riding along above the village. The people gasped as he suddenly turned his horse and came leaping down from roof to roof until he reached the ground. 'Flying horses?' he inquired with a smile.

The demonstration put new heart into the villagers and soon Little John was showing them how to use a quarterstaff, while Much taught the children how to sling stones at a target. The whole village was alive with activity and hope. Meanwhile Marion was hearing from Philip's wife Mary that their Sheriff was as frightened as everyone else. Their master Sir William was away in Normandy fighting with King Richard, so there had been no one to help them until the outlaws had come to Uffcombe.

'We're glad you've come!' she said. 'Forgive our harsh words earlier. Fear made us blind!'

'When did they take your son, James?' Marion asked, her heart bleeding for the grieving woman.

'Two months ago,' said Mary sadly, telling the awful story of the night her son was snatched away by the Hounds of Lucifer.

Neither of the women were aware that they were being

closely watched by Cedric, who was hoping to pick up some useful information to take to his master. However, his unusual interest was noticed by Nasir as he sharpened his sword, and he resolved to keep a close eye on Cedric.

As the sun sank behind the cliffs that evening, a lonely rider reached the mill. His arrival struck fear into the heart of the miller, for this was none other than Verdelet himself. Like Cedric, Adam was one of Verdelet's minions, bound by black magic to serve his master's needs though for the moment living as an ordinary villager in Uffcombe. Trembling, Adam told Verdelet of the arrival of the outlaws and the preparations that were being made to meet the next ride of the demons.

'How enterprising!' sneered Verdelet. 'It's time these snivelling villagers were taught a lesson they won't forget. The outlaws must die. The Hounds of Lucifer will ride tonight!'

That night an unearthly mist enveloped Uffcombe village, blotting out the moon and the stars. Robin had gathered all the villagers together in the great barn and encouraged them to make merry. While Will and Little John were entertaining everybody with the story of one of their more amusing encounters with the Sheriff of Nottingham, Robin slipped outside.

The mist curled and slipped darkly between the cottages, seeping into Robin's lungs as he stood and listened to the night sounds. The distant crash of waves against the cliffs was strangely muffled. The horses shifted uneasily in the stables and Philip's old watchdog, Wulf, growled and got stiffly to its feet, its hackles rising. There was a burst of laughter from the barn and, as it died away, a faint thrumming sound came through the mist. Robin began to doubt whether he had really heard it when, with a fresh eddy in the mist, it became stronger and he realized that it must have been there for some time, mingling with the other sounds of the night. But now it was a sound on its own, and it could mean only one thing – the ride of the Hounds of Lucifer!

At Robin's alarm, the villagers sprang into action. Little John raced to light the bonfires they had prepared, while the rest of the outlaws took up their positions.

There was barely time for Robin to look round and check that all was ready before the Hounds were upon them. Determined to terrify the villagers into submission, Verdelet had equipped them with bull-roarers – flat strips of wood tied to string, which made a horrifying sound as the Hounds whirled them above their heads. On they came, riding down the cliff-face, hurling smoke-pots to left and right. For a moment even the outlaws believed they were facing demons. It was enough. The villagers' nerve cracked and panic spread like wildfire among them. It was all the outlaws could do to prevent them from running screaming out of the village.

'That's what they *want* you to do!' Robin shouted. 'Get back to your posts! They're only men! Remember, I want one of them alive!'

His words had the desired effect – and not a moment too soon. The fight would surely have gone against the outlaws without the support the villagers could give.

At a warning cry from Marion, Robin whirled round to see two of the Hounds thundering towards him. There was no time to shoot. He leapt up on to a low wall and caught one rider a bone-shattering blow with Albion as he passed. The other rider dragged his steed round and advanced again, a fantastic light gleaming in his eyes. From his saddle he rained blow after blow on the outlaw and Robin was forced on to the defensive. Sensing victory, the rider began a demonic chant which seemed to sap the very strength from Robin's bones. He slipped and fell awkwardly across the wall, and his opponent was swift to take advantage. Desperately, Robin rolled away and the first thrust missed him by a hair's breadth. Cursing furiously, the rider raised his sword for his final blow, but Robin threw himself forward and Albion slipped beneath the enemy's guard and thrust deep into his heart. With a fearful scream, the rider toppled from his horse and crashed to the ground.

Breathing heavily, Robin leapt to his feet and looked round to see how the rest of the outlaws were faring. In the glow of the bonfires, he saw Little John and Nasir fighting back to back, surrounded by the Hounds on horseback. As he watched, Marion loosed an arrow and one of the riders attacking Little John fell. Will Scarlet, too, was fighting well and more than one of the attackers lay dead at his feet.

Robin set an arrow to his bow and felled another of the Hounds as the next wave rode past and then, suddenly, the enemy were in retreat.

'I want one of them alive!' Robin shouted again. Will heard him, launched himself at the last of the Hounds as he galloped by, and brought him crashing down. Within seconds the captured rider was bound hand and foot, glaring angrily at the outlaws through the slits in his mask.

'Get everyone here!' ordered Robin. 'The whole village!'

Little John banged on the doors of the huts and shouted, 'They've gone. The Hounds have gone!'

With cries of joy, everyone poured out and cheered. 'I told you they were men!' said Robin triumphantly.

Will and Little John grabbed the captive and pulled back his hood. Like all the Hounds he wore a death's-head mask. Little John tore it off. There was a gasp from everyone, a cry of horror from Philip and a scream from his wife Mary. It was their son James!

The rest of the villagers were almost as stunned as the horrified parents. They had thought James dead – dragged off by the Hounds. He shrank back against the hut in terror.

'Don't you know me, James?' asked his mother, steppng towards him. James whipped a knife from his robe. He muttered under his breath and, before anyone could stop him, he raised the knife and stabbed himself to the heart. Cedric gave an evil smile. His secret was safe.

In the main hall of Ravenscar Abbey, Morgwyn, now once again in the dress of an Abbess, sat alone. To her came Verdelet with a terrified Adam at his side. She heard how

Adam had warned Verdelet of the strangers, and when Verdelet explained that he had felt he could handle the situation himself her rage was terrible. Then he told her of the attack, and of how they had been ambushed.

'And killed?' hissed Morgwyn. 'Some of you were killed?'

'Yes, my lady, five of us,' said Adam.

'But not you,' replied Morgwyn maliciously. 'Why was that?'

'I – I was lucky,' he said nervously.

'I wonder if you were,' Morgwyn whispered, then turned to confront both of them.

'You sicken me,' she said. 'You have been chosen to serve the lord of this world and to accomplish his will. This is how worthy you prove yourselves to be!'

She rounded on Verdelet. 'In one night you have undone much of the Cauldron's work.' She spat at him. 'You're *nothing*! Nothing! Servant! Messenger! Acolyte! And sacrifice, if I demand it!'

She paused for a moment, then resumed her chilling attack.

'Do you fear him, Verdelet? Do you fear our master the Lord Lucifer?'

Verdelet said nothing.

'I have no fear of him,' said Morgwyn proudly. 'He comes to me in dreams – shining like the sun – proud and glorious in his evil.' Then she started to write.

Her letter was to the great Earl Godwin. She told him that Uffcombe was in the hands of outlaws and begged him to send soldiers at once to deal with men who feared neither God nor the Holy Church. Then she handed the parchment to Verdelet, who was soon galloping thankfully away.

In Uffcombe, Robin and Marion were trying to comfort the grieving parents. Philip gave Robin a small leather bag he had found round his son's neck. 'Why should he turn against us?' sobbed Mary. 'He was so frightened, too – he didn't seem to know who or where he was.'

The answer to Mary's despairing question wasn't long in coming. Tuck called Robin over to the barn and gave him a small square of parchment. Each of the dead Hounds of Lucifer had carried a similar piece. Slowly, Robin opened the little bag Philip had given him and took out the parchment it contained. The words on each square were written in Latin in heavy black letters and they were all the same. Tuck translated, with growing horror on his face.

'"We have signed a treaty with death and with hell we have made a pact".' His voice faltered. 'By heaven! These beauties gave themselves to the Devil!'

'Or were forced to,' said Robin.

'What's behind all this?' asked Little John.

'Satan, Lucifer, the Evil One – whatever you like to call him,' Tuck replied. 'He's always on the lookout, for bodies as well as souls. He's a spirit, so he's after flesh to – to clothe himself and become Antichrist.'

'You'll believe anything!' Little John sneered.

'No – but it's better than believing nothing,' Tuck reproved him.

Robin knelt by the bodies. The boots of the riders were dusty with flour. After a moment's thought, he rose and hurried from the barn without a word. Much followed and asked Robin what he was going to do. 'I'm going to the mill,' Robin told him. 'But I'm going alone!'

He ran along the track through the woods, his heart beating with excitement. He was sure that somehow Adam was connected to the Hounds of Lucifer. He approached the mill cautiously but there was no one to be seen. So finally he walked up to the door and knocked. There was no answer. Finally, he tried the latch, found it was open and went in. The circle of salt was still on the floor and the place had a frightening atmosphere. Robin started searching, the upper floor as well as the main part of the mill. Finally, in a small bare room where Adam kept his ropes and harness he found what he was after – Adam's Hounds of Lucifer death's-head mask. He examined it closely and then turned to go.

A sound behind him made him whirl round. The miller was coming at him, his face twisted with fear and hatred. He grabbed Robin and knocked him off balance with the speed of his charge. Robin fell heavily into a pile of flails and wooden poles, to be followed swiftly by the hefty body of his opponent, who gripped him by the throat and did his best to throttle him. Robin tore Adam's hands away but the miller attacked him again, lashing out with his enormous fists. It was all Robin could do to block some of the blows until the miller finally landed a massive punch on the outlaw's temple, which sent him sprawling against the pile of waiting sacks in the corner.

Clouds of flour billowed up and covered the two men. Adam grabbed a fallen flail and attacked Robin again. But now Albion was out and Robin was able to hold his own. Adam attacked again and again, a demonic fury blazing in his eyes, and Robin fought back with a grim determination. At last, as the miller, his breathing laboured, raised his weapon for a new assault, Robin feinted with Albion in his right hand and used his left to land a crashing blow on the miller's chin. Adam's legs buckled and he sank to the floor, defeated.

'Get up!' gasped Robin.

He tied the miller to a post and ripped open his shirt. Around his neck hung one of the leather amulets worn by the Hounds of Lucifer. Robin tore it off.

'What are the Hounds of Lucifer, Adam?' The miller stared at him in silence. 'Who tells them to ride?' He paused. 'Is it you?'

Still no answer. Adam stared vacantly past Robin's head, with his lips firmly closed. But when Robin drew the square of parchment from the amulet, Adam's face become contorted with fear. He pleaded with Robin not to tear the parchment.

'What are the Hounds?' Robin asked him again. 'This is your mark.' And, holding up the parchment, he said: 'You've given yourself to Satan. Why? Were you forced to?'

Adam nodded.

'Who by?' asked Robin.

'Don't make me tell!' pleaded Adam and, as Robin started tearing the paper, he began to sob.

'Who tells the Hounds to ride?' asked Robin, continuing to tear up the pact, and Adam blurted out, 'The Lady of the Cauldron.'

'The Cauldron?' repeated Robin.

'The Cauldron of Lucifer, the most powerful coven in England,' moaned Adam. 'Bishops and barons and such. It's said that if the Cauldron wants you dead you'd better hurry and dig your own grave!'

'And who is the Lady?' asked Robin.

'I can't tell you,' moaned Adam. 'She'd know. She knows everything. She'd torture me.'

'Adam – I want to help you,' said Robin, compassionately.

'I *have* to serve them,' Adam cried. 'They came to the mill one night, three of them. Told me I'd been chosen to prepare Lucifer's coming. They told me I'd die in three days if I didn't do as they said. Then they put a spell on me. A curse! Three days later I felt I was being stabbed. They'd made a mommet – a doll. Then they came again and stood round me waiting for me to die. They showed me the doll, stabbed it, and the pain ripped through me. I'd have agreed to anything!'

'So you signed,' said Robin. 'Now . . . who is the lady?'

'I can't tell you!' pleaded Adam, and Robin began to tear little pieces of the parchment once again. The game went on until Adam suddenly shrieked, 'Morgwyn of Ravenscar! I'm lost!'

'Morgwyn of Ravenscar?' repeated Robin.

Adam nodded. 'I'm lost,' he groaned as Robin untied him. 'I'm as good as dead!' He buried his face in his hands.

As Robin hurried back to Uffcombe, he was suddenly surrounded by men-at-arms and he cursed his lack of vigilance. Had he not been so excited by what he had learned at the mill, he would not have fallen into the ambush. When asked, he claimed to have been helping Adam at the mill.

'I've never seen you there before,' said a thin man riding

beside the Captain of the soldiers. 'I'm Peter Verdelet and I know the miller well. You're a stranger to these parts.' The Captain's face hardened with suspicion. 'You say you're a labourer, but you carry a sword and there's blood on your arm.'

'Got that freeing the mill wheel,' said Robin. 'And my father was a soldier. He left me this sword when he died.'

'I don't like peasants with swords,' said the Captain. 'Give it to me!'

But Robin remembered the oath he had made to Herne and, despite the fact he was outnumbered, he drew Albion and attacked the soldiers in a desperate attempt to escape. Verdelet blocked his way and gasped with astonishment when he saw the sword in Robin's hand. It was the Seventh Sword of Wayland!

Finally, the outlaw leader was overwhelmed and Verdelet wrested Albion from him in triumph, only to be forced to give it to the captain who told him coldly that Robin was *his* prisoner.

All this had been seen by Much, who had come looking for Robin. Now he followed the party as they set off to the mill with Robin tied to the Captain's horse.

The mill was empty, then the Captain saw Adam's body floating on the pond. It was pulled out of the water and the Captain came over to Robin. 'Repairing the mill wheel, were you?' he sneered. 'You'll hang, you know.'

'I didn't kill him,' said Robin.

'Drowned himself, did he?' mocked the Captain. 'Take him to the Earl!' Robin was led off under guard.

'Look there!' shouted Verdelet, catching sight of Much, who darted away into the undergrowth. 'To the village! Quickly!' ordered the Captain.

Luckily Much could run like the wind, but there were still only minutes to spare. As soon as the outlaws realized the danger they were in, they grabbed their weapons and vanished into the trees. Philip bravely tried to throw the soldiers off the scent but was thwarted by Cedric, who bowed to Peter

Verdelet and pointed all too accurately at the woods which hid the outlaws.

Outraged at this treachery, Will Scarlet, who had been watching with the rest from the trees, swiftly set an arrow to his bow and sent it winging towards Cedric. With a gasping cry Cedric fell, Will's arrow through his chest. 'Lucifer!' he whispered, and then died.

'Never liked spies,' Will said grimly, satisfied with his work. The next moment, the outlaws were under attack.

'Forward!' ordered the Captain, but seconds later two of his men fell to the ground dead and two were wounded. 'Pull back!' he ordered, much to the fury of Verdelet.

'Why don't you attack?' Verdelet raged.

'And lose the rest of my men?' asked the Captain.

'A brave decision!' sneered Verdelet.

'No, a sensible one,' said the Captain and led his men away.

'They've had enough,' said Much.

'Don't you believe it,' said Will, but Little John agreed with Much. 'It'll be dark soon,' he said.

Marion looked bleakly at the soldiers as they rode away. Friar Tuck took her hand. 'We'll get him back, little flower,' he said.

As he stumbled across the moors behind the soldier's horse, Robin wondered what had become of Marion and the outlaws. And somewhere the voice of Herne intoned words that only he could hear:

'They that seek to shatter the bolts that hold back the Evil One must first take Albion from you. Swear to guard it with your heart's blood ... Your heart's blood ... Your heart's blood ...'

CHAPTER 3

That night the outlaws held a moonlight conference in the forest.

'Where were they taking him?' Marion asked Much.

'To the Earl, they said,' Much told her.

'Earl Godwin,' said Marion, her spirits lifting slightly. 'My father's friend!' Then she asked anxiously, 'Do they know who Robin is?'

Much shook his head. 'They don't,' he answered, 'but they say he killed the miller. He drowned, you see!'

'They'll hunt us,' said Marion, and all agreed.

'If we're caught, they'll kill us all,' said Little John.

'Or take us to Nottingham,' said Will.

'Same thing!' said Tuck.

'I said we should never have left Sherwood,' said Will angrily.

'You still came, though, didn't you?' said Little John sarcastically.

'I had no choice,' Will exploded. 'But if you'd listened –'

'Listened!' erupted Little John. 'Always know best, don't you?'

'I'll thump both of you in a minute,' promised Brother Tuck.

There was a long silence; Will said: 'All right then. What do we do now?'

'Get after Robin,' said Little John.

'Which way?' asked Will wearily.

There was a pause. 'The castle's at Gwydion,' Marion said. 'Let's go!'

Meanwhile, Verdelet had reached Ravenscar Abbey and

had told Morgwyn that the Seventh Sword had been found. Morgwyn listened to his story with disbelief.

'An outlaw, Verdelet? A wolf's-head with the Seventh Sword of Wayland? It's incredible!'

'I'm sure of it, Lady,' he insisted. 'I swear by the Lord Lucifer himself that it was Albion.'

Morgwyn moved past the kneeling steward, deep in thought. Almost to herself she murmured, 'Who is he? Who is this man? Why do I fear him?'

'There is no need to fear him, Lady,' Verdelet assured her. 'Earl Godwin will have him by now.'

Morgwyn looked hard at him. 'Yes,' she said, 'and the sword!'

In the dungeon of Gwydion Castle Robin sat against a pillar, tied hand and foot. The Captain appeared and ordered the two guards on duty to untie the prisoner. Soon, Robin found himself being escorted along a passageway, and he looked around for any possible way of escape.

He was marched into the main hall of the castle and taken to where the Earl stood with a group of his knights. The Earl was a tall, grey-haired man in his late fifties, who looked like a soldier. He was a harsh man but a just one, and had no time for intriguers like the Sheriff of Nottingham.

'You are one of the armed men who have been terrorizing the village of Uffcombe?' he asked Robin sternly, and when Robin answered 'No', he asked, 'Then I suppose you deny killing the miller?' Robin was indeed quick to deny it.

'I'll put him to the ordeal, my lord,' said the Captain grimly, but the Earl shook his head. 'Not yet,' and he turned back to Robin.

'Let's try again, shall we?' suggested the Earl, after staring hard at Robin. 'What's your name?'

'Robin of Sherwood,' Robin replied.

'He told me he was ...' the Captain started to say, but a look from Earl Godwin quelled him. Godwin asked Robin who his master was, but no answer was forthcoming.

'Sherwood is five days' march from here,' he went on, 'so what were you doing in Uffcombe?'

'Defending it!' Robin replied, and it was all the Earl could do not to laugh. 'Were you now?' he said. 'That's original, at least. Against whom were you defending it?'

'The Hounds of Lucifer,' said Robin, upon which the Earl and his knights turned away in contempt. 'It seems you've brought me a madman,' the Earl said.

'Ask the people of Uffcombe, my lord,' said Robin.

'Be silent!' the Captain roared.

Godwin turned back to Robin. 'You expect me to believe that you and your – your companions – tramped across England to defend a village against devils?' he asked incredulously.

Robin said nothing. Godwin picked up Albion from the table. 'This sword,' he said. 'Where did you get it? Quickly!'

Robin said he could not tell him.

'Surely you can do better than that!' exclaimed the Earl. 'I can't believe that such an inventive brain could fail to explain away a mere weapon.'

'The sword is mine by right,' said Robin in ringing tones.

'By right, eh?' said the Earl. 'Right of conquest? Inheritance? Or theft . . . ?'

'It was entrusted to me,' said Robin, but when Godwin asked him by whom, he replied, 'You wouldn't believe me.'

'No, I don't expect I would,' said Godwin angrily. 'I've dealt with villains like you before. Never content with ordinary lies, for that would make them ordinary villains. And they're so stuffed with conceit that they believe themselves beyond ordinary justice. And that, they delude themselves, gives them the right to commit any crime they please!'

'The miller at Uffcombe took his own life after I'd discovered he led the Hounds of Lucifer,' said Robin, which provoked a roar of 'Back to the devils again!' from the Earl.

'Not devils,' said Robin. 'Men wearing masks.'

'Pretending to be devils, eh?' said Godwin. 'I see! And why should the miller kill himself?'

'Because he feared the power of the Lady who had forced them all to sign pacts with the devil,' Robin replied.

Earl Godwin gazed at him. 'Your imagination is boundless,' he said.

'I'll have him whipped!' said the Captain eagerly.

'Who was it?' asked Godwin. 'Who made them sign these pacts with the devil?'

Robin paused for a moment, then said quietly: 'Morgwyn of Ravenscar.'

There was a moment's pause; then the Captain hit Robin hard across the mouth as he shouted, 'You filthy villain!'

The Earl was more restrained, for all his anger. Quietly and with dignity he said, 'You've surpassed yourself.' Then, after a brief pause, he went on harshly: 'Suppose I tell you that it was the Abbess who asked me to help her against you and your ruffians? One of the most holy and venerated women in the kingdom! I was right – you are either mad or possessed. Get him out of my sight!'

As the soldiers dragged him away, Robin shouted: 'I beg you! Not for mercy, but to protect the sword! She will send for it!'

The Earl paid no attention as Robin was dragged from the hall. 'He's a wolf's-head, I'm sure of it,' he repeated to himself, and then ordered the Captain to step forward.

'Send a messenger to Nottingham,' ordered Godwin. 'If he's wanted there, that dreadful little man de Rainault can deal with him. And the others, too. Hunt them all down!'

The Captain bowed and left, while Godwin examined the inscription on Albion. He looked at the door through which Robin had been dragged, a puzzled frown on his face, and then slid the sword back into its scabbard.

Meanwhile, there were visitors on the way to Gwydion Castle. Morgwyn in her guise as Abbess was riding there with Verdelet, two of her nuns and several Abbey guards, one of whom was carrying the banner of Ravenscar Abbey.

The visitors were greeted by the Earl and his retainers, Godwin telling Morgwyn how honoured he was. 'Had I known earlier that you were coming –' he began, but Morgwyn interrupted. 'Perhaps, my lord, it is better that you didn't. A simple greeting is always preferable.'

'Indeed, yes!' said Godwin, leading her to a seat. 'Too much fawning and posturing these days. All this new-fangled chivalry! I'm old-fashioned, I'm glad to say.'

'Then I'll dispense with courtesies and come directly to the reason for my visit,' said Morgwyn with a smile. 'My steward tells me that your men failed to capture all the ruffians who were at Uffcombe.'

'They escaped into the forest, reverend lady,' said the Captain. 'One was captured.'

Morgwyn had gathered as much, she said, and Godwin assured her that he had him safe. 'And the sword?' asked Morgwyn.

The Earl looked at her, recalling Robin's words, and Morgwyn continued. 'He had a sword, I understand. A sword of great quality.'

Godwin confirmed it, and when Morgwyn asked to see it he ordered the Captain to fetch it. He asked the Abbess why she was interested in it.

'It is the reason I'm here,' said the Abbess. 'Verdelet thinks it may be the sword of Sir Geoffrey of Aconbury, a Crusader martyred in the Holy Land.'

'Sir Geoffrey of Aconbury?' queried Godwin. 'I don't recall –'

'After his capture, he was tortured,' Morgwyn explained. 'He refused to renounce Christ and accept the heathen faith. His body was recovered when the Saracens were driven back. His family bequeathed a chapel at Ravenscar where masses could be said for the repose of his soul. His sword was placed on the altar and remained there as a holy relic until it was stolen. It seems possible that the villain in your custody may be the thief.'

The Captain returned with Albion, and Morgwyn's eyes gleamed. Verdelet had been right. She took the sword and piously praised God and his saints. 'It is indeed the sword of the noble martyr Geoffrey of Aconbury,' she said in hushed tones.

They sat and talked for a while and eventually Earl Godwin told the Abbess about the capture of Robin and the accusations he had made.

'It was a wild tale. He was babbling about the Hounds of Lucifer and people who had made pacts with the devil.'

'The wretch must have lost his reason,' said Morgwyn, crossing herself.

'Either that or he's possessed,' mused Godwin, 'because he crowned his lies by laying the blame for all this magic and devilry on you!'

Morgwyn looked suitably appalled, and Godwin went on. 'Unbelievable, isn't it?' he said.

'Quite unbelievable, my lord,' said Verdelet. 'Such an evil tongue needs tearing out!' But the look he got from Godwin made him regret having spoken so brutally.

In the meantime, Marion and the outlaws had reached Gwydion Castle. Most of them remained in hiding, while Marion and Tuck bravely marched up to the gate and demanded an audience with Earl Godwin. Marion's name was her passport and soon she was announced in the Great Hall.

'Marion of Leaford!' Earl Godwin said thoughtfully to the Abbess. 'Her father was with me in Palestine. Brave as a lion. When I think of all the fine men who died on that campaign ... We fought in leather jerkins; now soldiers case themselves in iron from head to toe and call it chivalry!' He looked up as Marion entered.

She knelt at his feet, pale and clearly distressed. He drew her up and said: 'You were a child when I first came to Leaford. Little Marion. You climbed so high to pick that apple for me ... do you remember?'

'I remember,' said Marion, and Godwin went on, 'I was so frightened you would fall.' Marion said she had torn her dress and that her nurse had been angry with her; Godwin stared at her affectionately, muttering, 'Yesterday. It seems like yesterday!'

Suddenly the Earl recalled that others were present and introduced Marion to the Lady Abbess of Ravenscar.

'Why have you come to Gwydion?' Godwin asked Marion.

'To beg for mercy,' she said, 'for Robin of Sherwood.'

Godwin was startled, and a buzz of excited conversation filled the hall. 'Robin of Sherwood?'

'Yes, my lord,' she replied. 'Because I am Marion of Sherwood, his wife!'

There was a moment of stunned silence, then Godwin gasped: 'His wife? But – but the man's a wolf's-head!'

Marion took a deep breath and said very firmly, 'He fights to defend the weak and the helpless.'

'No, Marion!' gasped the astounded Godwin, while Morgwyn whispered sadly, 'Poor child! poor child!'

Marion turned to her. 'Believe me, reverend lady,' she pleaded, 'he could never, never –'

'I shall pray for you, Marion,' Morgwyn cut in. 'May your eyes be opened!'

'You talk as if I don't know him!' Marion cried passionately. Then she turned to Godwin. 'I beg you to let me see him! I beg you, my lord!'

The Earl was moved by Marion's outburst. He looked at the Captain, who led her away with Tuck. When Morgwyn had raised her eyes to heaven and asked that the saints restore Marion to God's mercy, he and all those present fervently added, 'Amen!' Then Morgwyn rose and took her leave.

Down in the dungeon of Gwydion Castle, where Robin was tied to a pillar, a torch gave a flickering light and two guards were seated at a bench. They sprang up as the Captain came down the steps with Marion and Tuck. Marion embraced Robin passionately, clinging to him as she answered his rapid, whispered questions.

'Come closer,' he said. 'There's an Abbess, Morgwyn of Ravenscar –'

'She's here!' Marion interrupted.

'Then she's come for the sword – for Albion!' breathed Robin.

'What are you whispering?' asked the Captain, coming towards them. Robin whispered a warning to Marion that Morgwyn meant to use Albion for evil. 'You've got to stop her,' he said, just as the Captain reached them. 'That's enough,' he ordered.

'Tell the others,' Robin said urgently as the Captain dragged Marion away.

'That's enough, I said!' shouted the Captain.

'Take your hands off me, you oaf!' Marion ordered and, as the shamefaced Captain released his hold, she swept from the dungeon with dignity. Seeing the speaking look she cast at him as the door swung shut behind her, Robin smiled, knowing that some devious little plan for getting him out was already working in her mind.

He was right. No sooner had they reached the Great Hall again than the first part of Marion's plan was set in motion. Bearing a weeping Marion on his arm, Tuck approached Earl Godwin once again.

'My lord,' he said hurriedly, 'now that the Lady Marion is safely here, my task in bringing her to you is over. I commend her to your protection, my lord. How easy it is for the young to fall prey to temptation . . .' He let his voice tail away suggestively and was rewarded by the Earl's promise to shelter Marion. Tuck's task was done; he gave her his blessing and left, only waiting until he was out of sight of the hall before gathering up his long robe and sprinting for the outlaws' hiding place.

Meanwhile Morgwyn, triumphant and relaxed, was riding with her procession through the trees. 'Great Lucifer led us to Albion,' she said to Verdelet.

'Praise his name!' he replied.

Morgwyn's eyes shone with anticipation. 'You will send messengers from Ravenscar tonight to summon the Cauldron. It is time.' She purred with pleasure. 'The Seven Swords of Wayland! The long quest is over!'

Ahead of the procession the outlaws were waiting. As it

drew near they came out from the undergrowth and raised their bows. The procession drew abruptly to a halt.

'Let me pass,' commanded Morgwyn, but Scarlet shouted, 'Nobody moves!'

'This is an outrage,' said Verdelet. 'You scum. Don't you recognize the most Holy Abbess of Ravenscar?'

'That's not what we've heard,' jeered Little John, and Tuck added, 'We've heard a different tale!'

'So you're one of them,' said Verdelet scornfully, 'and still dressed as a friar!'

'I am a friar,' Tuck replied. 'And what are you?'

'I'll see you punished. All of you!' hissed Morgwyn.

'And we'll see you in hell,' shouted Little John. 'Give us the sword!'

Morgwyn stared hard at the outlaws, then dismounted. She walked towards Verdelet and held up her hands for the sword. Verdelet gave it to her as the outlaws waited, silent and tense. She drew Albion partly from its scabbard, baring its inscription; then, holding it horizontally, she came slowly towards Little John, removing the sword completely from the scabbard. Suddenly her eyes blazed.

'*Schemes Amathia!* – Sun be Silent!' she cried.

A blinding flash leapt from the blade. The outlaws were dazzled and Morgwyn seemed bathed in a red light. Far away in the castle dungeon, Robin reacted sharply, seeing the scene in the trees for a single vivid moment.

Morgwyn looked at the blank faces of the outlaws who stood as if bewitched. 'You dogs,' she snarled. 'Now you will bark for me!'

CHAPTER 4

That night, beneath the black, sleeping walls of Ravenscar
Abbey, the devil-worshippers of Lucifer's Cauldron made
ready for the coming of their dark lord. Morgwyn, triumphant in her role as High Priestess, greeted Verdelet at the
bloodstained altar and welcomed the Hounds of Lucifer
ranged behind him. Then she turned to one of her nuns, a
dark-eyed girl dressed in a white shift with her hair flowing
loose down her back, and took Robin's sword, Albion, from
her. She turned towards the altar and raised the sword above
her head.

'Proud Lord!' she exulted. 'Light-bearer! Lucifer!'

'Lucifer!' repeated the nuns.

'Star of the morning! Receive the Seventh Sword!' she
cried.

'Son of the dawn, we call on thee!' the nuns shouted.

'I bring you Albion, charged with the powers of light and
darkness!' Morgwyn slowly laid the great sword on the altar,
where it completed the circle of swords placed there, blades
pointing towards the fire blazing at its centre.

She turned, raised her hands above her head and cried out
to the assembled worshippers.

'It has begun!'

Far away from the noise of the Cauldron, Marion lay
listening to the night sounds of Gwydion Castle. It seemed to
take a long time before the castle finally settled down to sleep,
but eventually she was satisfied that all its occupants slum-
bered. She rose, dressed quietly and crept out into the dark
passage. Pausing for a moment at her door, she began her
long, dangerous journey to the dungeons. Well practised in

the art of moving silently, she made her way down the stairway to the Great Hall, where some sixth sense suddenly made her freeze. She shrank back into the shadow behind a pillar while she tried to work out what had alarmed her. She could hear nothing; she could see nothing out of the ordinary. Then, just as she was about to leave her hiding place, a faint glimmer of light appeared at the far end of the hall. Two guards were coming her way! She held her breath as they passed close by and waited until their steps echoed away into the darkness before moving on. At last, she found the small door which opened on to the spiral stairway leading down to the dungeons. There would be guards below, she knew, and she would have to get past them somehow. As she reached the bottom of the stairs, keeping as close as she could to the shelter of the wall, she took a deep breath and peered cautiously round the door.

Fortune favoured her. The guards were neglecting their duties and were playing an animated game of knucklebones at the table in one corner of the dungeon. The only light came from the rush lamp on their table, which threw deep shadows across the rest of the chamber. Robin was still in the same place as before. She could see that he was awake by the lamplight glittering in his eyes as he watched the game. Suddenly, with uncanny instinct, Robin sensed her presence and turned towards her. She made a warning gesture, and he smiled and looked deliberately away as she edged through the shadows towards him. Then she cut his bonds with the sharp little knife she had carried concealed in the folds of her dress. As the cords parted, one of the guards stood up and stretched, yawning.

'You're too good for me – I'm cleaned out!' He straightened up and glanced over to where Robin sat. Marion froze. The guard ambled over to the door through which Marion had entered and shut it with a bang.

'Could have sworn that door was shut ...' He glanced round the dungeon, his gaze coming to rest on Robin, who was feigning sleep.

–36–

'You'll be saying that the place is haunted next,' laughed the other guard. 'Come! Let's have another game. Winner takes all!'

After another hard stare at Robin's slumped form, the first guard returned to the table and the game began again. Marion slipped the little knife into Robin's hands and they both waited until the guards' attention was fully on their game.

The younger guard was losing and wasn't too pleased about it. His companion took up the knucklebones for the final throw and crowed with triumph as he caught them all on the back of his hand. 'I've won!' he cried, sweeping the little pile of coins towards him.

At that moment, Robin leapt to his feet and threw himself at them.

'No, *you've lost*!' he shouted as his first blow landed.

Within seconds it was all over. The guards, taken totally by surprise, were soon gagged and trussed up with the ropes that had bound Robin. Swiftly, silently, Robin and Marion made their way up the stairs, across the Great Hall and out into the moonlit courtyard. All was quiet. Somewhere a dog barked, the guards on the wall exchanged a murmured word and a horse neighed.

'Horses!'

Keeping to the shadows, they cautiously crept towards the sound. Two great black horses were in the nearest stable. They were inclined to be restive but Marion quietened them with her hands on their soft noses before helping Robin to saddle them up. Once outside, Robin and Marion mounted and urged the horses into a headlong gallop towards the main gate. Again surprise was on their side: the men-at-arms guarding the gate scattered as they rode through, and they found themselves riding out towards the trees in a matter of seconds. A crossbow bolt whined viciously through the air as they rode away, and far behind them they could hear the clanging of the bell as the alarm was given. But they were away ... Marion's plan had worked!

They rode all through the night and by dawn found themselves on a narrow path in the depths of the forest. Suddenly Robin stopped and grabbed Marion's rein; he could feel that there was danger ahead.

'What is it?' Marion asked in a whisper.

'There's someone ahead. It doesn't feel right . . .'

They dismounted as quietly as they could and tethered the horses. Working their way through the undergrowth, using all the woodcraft they possessed, they came to a small clearing. Robin was about to cross it when he saw a tiny movement out of the corner of his eye. He threw himself to the ground, pulling Marion down beside him.

'Up there!' he whispered, pointing towards a rocky outcrop at one end of the clearing.

'It's Little John!' said Marion, as she recognized the tall figure keeping watch. She started getting to her feet, but Robin pulled her back down.

'Keep down!' he ordered. 'There's something wrong!'

Marion stared at him in disbelief.

'But it's John!' she said, getting to her feet again. She waved and called the outlaw's name before Robin could stop her.

As soon as he heard her voice, Little John's head snapped round in her direction. But instead of the friendly wave Marion was expecting, the big outlaw set an arrow to his bow and sent it speeding towards her. Marion was too horrified to move but Robin dived forward and knocked her to the ground just as the arrow whistled past their heads. He dragged her back into cover and then forced her into a run. Behind them they could hear Little John shouting to the other outlaws.

'Nasir! Will! I've spotted them! Circle round and cut them off!'

Robin and Marion snaked through the forest, keeping low, weaving and using every move they knew to throw off pursuit. But this time their enemies were not Gisburne's soft, stupid soldiers – they were the hardened outlaws of Sherwood, who knew all the tricks. Soon Robin was forced to realize that he and Marion were surrounded. They lay panting in the depths of a holly bush while they tried to work out their next move.

'Why are they hunting us?' Marion asked.

'It's Morgwyn! It must be!' Robin said between clenched teeth. 'She's used witchcraft and magic to make them her slaves! It's the only explanation!'

'But what can we do?'

'I don't know. Honestly, I don't know!'

The hunters were closing in on them. They heard Much's birdcall from the left, with Nasir's answering call to the right. Then ahead of them they heard Little John's shout.

'You can't escape us, Robin of Sherwood!' There was a triumphant note in his voice. 'Show yourself!'

Little John had made a mistake. A mistake born of over-confidence. His shout had told Robin exactly where he was. 'I taught him a better strategy than that,' Robin whispered grimly.

They started to crawl off in another direction. Much almost came upon them, but just at the last moment Robin threw a twig to Much's blind side and he spun round to face the noise – away from the fugitives. They crawled on.

'I think we're through,' said Marion at last. 'They're behind us!'

Cautiously they got to their feet. And at that moment, Will jumped down from a tree in front of them, an arrow already on his bowstring. 'Don't even breathe!' he warned them.

The hard, unfriendly look on Will's face stung Robin. 'Will! Will, you know who I am! I'm Robin and this is Marion! You know us. We're friends!'

'I don't know you,' said Will flatly, the tip of his arrow not wavering an inch. 'All I know is that you are the enemy. Both of you!'

Robin tried again. 'Who are you, then? Tell me your name!'

Will looked confused.

'Your name. What is it?' Robin persisted. 'I'll tell you. Your name is Will Scarlet. Once upon a time, you were Will Scathelock. Scathelock. Remember that, Will? Remember why you changed it? Remember why I'm called Robin i' the Hood?'

Will's confusion grew as he struggled to remember. For a moment his eyes left Robin's face and that was the moment Robin had been waiting for. He jumped on his former comrade and threw him to the ground. Will's arrow sped harmlessly into the trees, while the two men grappled. But before Robin could knock any sense into him, Marion screamed. He looked up and saw with a sudden shock that the other outlaws had found them: Little John's sword was but an inch from his face, while Nasir held Marion in an iron grip. Slowly, Robin eased himself to his feet and the point of Little John's sword followed him all the way. Will Scarlet struggled to his feet from beneath Robin, while Tuck and Much kept their bows trained on the prisoners. There was no escape.

'What has she done to you all?' said Robin, gazing intently at each of the menacing faces in turn. But he got no answer. Realizing that there was no point in struggling further, Robin and Marion allowed themselves to be bound and marched off by their erstwhile friends.

It was a long walk and a silent one – so unlike the normal companionable banter the outlaws would have kept up on a long journey like this one. Marion could feel her heart sinking as she speculated on the fate awaiting them when they reached their destination. Morgwyn of Ravenscar was certainly a powerful enchantress if she could so enslave brave and loyal men like these.

Eventually the sad procession reached the sea again as their path took them along the high cliffs to the west of Uffcombe.

Suddenly a ragged man appeared on the path ahead of them, bringing them all to a halt. He wore a necklace of shells and dried seaweed, while the claws and wings of various seabirds hung round his shoulders. His eyes stared wildly and, fixing Robin with his glare, he began to chant in a language the outlaw leader only dimly recognized as Welsh.

'*Diawliaid dirifedi!*' he cried. '*Rhwygant eu cnawd! Chwipiant hwy!*'

He was certainly a terrifying creature; Little John blanched as the wild man came close up to him and peered into his face as though searching for something. He subjected each of the outlaws to this in turn and then continued his chanting, this time with more strength.

'*Cynrhon fydd eu dillad!*' he howled.

'He's mad!' said Will, trembling. 'Let him pass!'

The outlaws parted to let the wild man through but only Marion saw that as he reached Robin he deftly sliced through the outlaw's bonds and slipped a knife into his hands. In a flash the wild man was away, running, uttering bird-like cries, spinning and chanting, watched by everyone except Robin and Marion. Robin took his chance, broke the last threads of the ropes which bound him and leapt for the cliff edge. As he ran the outlaws tried to catch him, but with no success. He paused momentarily at the edge of the cliff and looked down to the sea crashing on the boulders below, but, at Marion's cry of warning, he looked behind him, saw he had but seconds to play with, took a deep breath and jumped, entrusting himself to Herne's care.

Little John was the first to reach the spot from which he had jumped and Nasir was soon behind him. However, they could see nothing moving on the rocks below. There was only the sea and the waves.

'He must be dead!' said Will confidently.

'Aye. A fall like that ... bound to be dead,' Little John agreed.

They looked at Marion but she wasn't giving anything away. The outlaws took a last look over the cliff edge but still could see nothing, and so continued towards their destination.

Morgwyn of Ravenscar was far from pleased to hear that

the outlaws had let Robin slip through their fingers. She raged at them for a while, but this was poor sport since the outlaws merely stared blankly back at her. Eventually she accepted their assurance that Robin was indeed dead and decided to content herself with the one prisoner they had brought with them.

She turned to Marion. 'You should have stayed in Sherwood,' she said silkily. 'But then, I wonder how long it would have taken me to find Albion?' She paused. 'The true lord of this world, Marion, is Lucifer. You must believe me. His power is everywhere – in all of us!'

Marion refused to allow herself to be drawn. She kept her chin high and ignored Morgwyn, looking every inch a Crusader's daughter.

Frustrated even of this little amusement, Morgwyn turned back to the outlaws she had enslaved. She ordered the nuns to tie them up. 'You have served your purpose,' she said coldly. 'I have no further need of you.'

She drew herself up to her full height, took a deep breath and, with her eyes closed, began a muttered incantation. Marion watched anxiously, wondering what new horror was about to be unleashed. After a few minutes, Morgwyn's eyes opened and Marion could see the demon light glowing in them. The enchantress approached the outlaws one by one, snapped her fingers in their faces and muttered some magical word.

At the noise of her fingers the outlaws blinked, screwing up their eyes as though they were blinded by a great light. Then, as the evil enchantment fell away from them, they began to realize what had happened. They struggled impotently against their bonds and cursed.

'Where's Robin?' Much asked tremulously.

'You killed him!' Morgwyn replied triumphantly. 'You captured him for me, but you bungled it and he managed to jump from the cliffs. But no one could survive that fall. He's dead!'

The outlaws stared at her in disbelief and growing anger.

'By heaven, if that's true, you'll pay for his life with your own!' thundered Little John.

Morgwyn sneered at his innocence.

'Not by heaven, I can assure you!'

CHAPTER 5

Robin's body lay in the surf, bruised and motionless, yet he was still alive. His eyes flickered open and by a tremendous effort of willpower he managed to heave himself on to his elbows, then on to his knees. Finally he staggered to his feet – but collapsed after a few tottering steps. 'Marion!' he whispered.

He forced himself up again and made his way painfully over to the cliffs where he began to climb, inching his aching limbs from toehold to toehold. The rock face was dangerously soft and crumbling and at times Robin was sure that he was stuck, unable to move either up or down. Then, just as he was within reach of the top, the tiny ridge under his right hand gave way and it was all he could do to hold on with his other hand. His feet slipped and for one sickening moment he hung there, clinging on by his fingertips, desperately scrabbling at the rock face for another hold and knowing that he was about to fall.

Then a scrawny arm shot over the cliff top and grabbed his hand just as his fingers were giving way. With amazing speed Robin was hauled over the top of the cliff and lay there shaking and panting for a while, before he thought to thank his rescuer. To his astonishment, he had been saved by the wild man who had staged the diversion which had allowed him to escape!

He thanked the man in broken Welsh and was surprised to hear him answer in English. 'That was a close one! It was lucky I came back.'

He led Robin to a small hut among the rocks and gave him some food. As he ate, Robin told him his story.

'Where were they taking you?' the wild man asked.

'Ravenscar Abbey.'

He choked over the broth. 'Easy, boy! You're lucky to be alive!' said his friend. 'Funny thing, luck! Look at me – never had any! An archer I was – one of the best . . . till I got a taste for the King's venison.'

He held up his right arm and Robin saw that he had no hand. He knew it must have been lopped off as a punishment for stealing the King's deer.

There was a magnificent bow and a quiver of arrows hanging against the wall, looking out of place in these strange surroundings. The wild man followed Robin's gaze and sighed.

'She's beautiful, isn't she? Welsh, you see, like me. A longbow like that takes some strength, I can tell you. Or at least, it used to.'

'Why do you keep it?'

'Because I'm a fool,' he said bitterly. 'Don't ever go after venison now.'

Robin stayed the night with the lonely wild man, gathering his strength before setting out for Ravenscar Abbey again.

As evening fell, Morgwyn returned to the caverns beneath the Abbey to make her final preparations.

'Elidor, Beleth, Flaures, Morax, Solas, Orias – and Albion,' she intoned, showing each of the swords in turn to Marion and the outlaws. Verdelet and the Abbey guards stood watching nearby.

'On each of their blades are words of high magic,' whispered Morgwyn, 'words unspoken since they were made. Wayland knew the danger; that was why he scattered them. And for hundreds of years they stayed apart. Two were buried, others lost in battle, and some were so cunningly hidden that no one had knowledge of them. Except the Cauldron of Lucifer! The Cauldron knew their power. The search took many years – many lives!'

'Why? Why do you need them?' asked Marion.

Morgwyn turned slowly towards her. 'Can't you guess?' she

breathed. 'I could make you worship him, but you must give yourself willingly. Bound by a solemn pact, you will live to serve the Lord Lucifer for ever! Power and riches shall be yours. Every wish, every desire satisfied. Come to him!'

She turned to Marion, who shrank back, shuddering.

Outside, the members of the Cauldron of Lucifer, the thirteen leaders of all the people bound to Morgwyn and her hellish pact, were assembling, watched secretly through the trees by Robin, who was working his way closer and closer to the castle. The wild man's beautiful longbow came easily to his hands as he toyed with the idea of picking off the members of the Cauldron one by one. However, he stopped himself in time, realizing that such a move would be bound to raise the alarm and he would be risking the lives of Marion and his other outlaw friends. Instead he waited patiently until the bustle had died down in the courtyard before creeping up to the gates.

There were two of the Hounds of Lucifer on guard and Robin knew that he had to kill them both silently. Through the fading light he took aim and skilfully dropped both men before they knew what was happening. He ran over to them and dragged their bodies into the shadows before stripping one of them.

Moments later, cloaked and hooded, he had made his way into the Abbey and down the long steps into the huge cavern below.

An eerie red light from the fire on the stone altar bathed the assembled members of the Cauldron and the nuns in attendance on them. To one side, Robin saw with delight that all his friends were still alive and apparently unharmed, though imprisoned in a small cage. For the moment, it seemed that everyone's attention was focussed on the altar, as Morgwyn led the devilish incantations which would begin the ceremony to raise their dark lord. The sound of his footsteps hidden in the chanting, Robin edged his way round to the cage.

'O great Lucifer, lord of all rebellious spirits,' Morgwyn

cried. 'I invoke thee by thy many names – by Asmodeus, Creator of Judgement; by Satan the Adversary; by Behemoth the Beast; by Diabolus the Devil, killing both body and soul; by Demon, which signifies Cunning over Blood; by Belial who is masterless; and by Beelzebub, Lord of the Flies.'

As she named the seven names of Lucifer she held each of the Seven Swords of Wayland in turn, as if to consecrate them before returning them to their place on the altar.

Tuck, deeply alarmed, whispered to Marion. 'She's summoning the devil! She's bringing Lucifer into the world!'

'Using the power of the swords,' gasped Marion. '*That* is why she needed them!'

The swords glowed strangely, then, suddenly, light streamed from the points of the blades towards the fire at the centre of the altar. 'Claim thy world!' exulted Morgwyn, and the rest cried '*Agla Aglon Diabolus!*' 'Come to us!' Morgwyn beseeched Lucifer. '*Surgat!*' cried the worshippers.

Light blazed from the altar, forming a column in the air, dazzling the onlookers. Thunder rolled round the cavern and the earth trembled.

Wildly excited, Morgwyn called out, 'The sacrifice, Verdelet!' Verdelet hurried to the cage, calling the guards to follow him as the maddened screeching rose wildly to the roof of the cavern. The noise was terrifying. There were shrieks of '*Agla Aglon Diabolus!*' and above them, the voice of Morgwyn imploring Lucifer to appear.

In the very heart of the light streaming upwards from the altar a vague shape was forming, as shouts of '*Surgat! Surgat! Surgat!*' rent the air.

Meanwhile Verdelet ordered the guards into action. The heavy doors of a huge trapdoor were thrown back to reveal a blazing pit beneath. The cage containing the outlaws was hanging directly above the pit and Robin realized with horror that Verdelet intended to lower the outlaws into it, roasting them alive as some kind of sacrifice. As Verdelet moved towards the winch, Robin attacked.

Taken by surprise, Verdelet crashed back against the cage,

winded, but swiftly recovered. He threw himself at Robin, clutching wildly at the outlaw's throat. With the strength of a madman he forced Robin to the very edge of the pit, knocking his feet from under him. The heat roared up from below, singeing the hair on Robin's head and sucking the air from his lungs. Verdelet's face leered triumphantly above him as his vision blurred and the blood thumped in his head. With one superhuman effort Robin broke Verdelet's stranglehold and kicked up, lifting his enemy high into the air. For an endless moment, Verdelet teetered on the edge of the pit and then, with a despairing cry, fell back into the engulfing flames.

Robin picked himself up quickly, expecting a further attack, and was relieved to discover that the battle with Verdelet had gone unnoticed by all except the outlaws. Everyone's attention was drawn to the awesome shape forming in the light in the altar. The demonic chanting reached a crescendo and throbbed round the echoing chamber.

'Venite! Venite! Lucifer venite!'

The ceremony was clearly reaching its terrible climax and there was no time to lose. Robin threw back the bolts on the cage and the outlaws poured out. With Verdelet's sword in his hand Robin led them towards the altar, brushing aside Morgwyn as he ran.

In the light from the altar a shadowy figure could be seen: a tall shape, with cloven hooves, horns and a baleful glare. For a heartstopping moment Robin looked into the eyes of the Devil, before snatching up Albion, his sword.

A maniacal scream of rage came from the dark lord, drowning every other sound. Then in an instant the evil light was extinguished and Lucifer had gone.

There was a moment of stunned silence in the cavern. Then Morgwyn screamed with rage and pounced on Robin, clawing at his eyes like an animal. He was too quick for her. He grabbed her wrists and spun her round, his sword at her heart. The outlaws each took one of Wayland's swords from the altar and rushed to Robin's side, just as the enraged members of the Cauldron reached him. The battle was fierce and long.

The Cauldron went berserk and the outlaws were hard pressed. In the thick of the nightmarish struggle, Morgwyn broke away from Robin and fled from the chamber.

'Let her go!' Robin shouted. 'We'll catch her later!'

The desertion of the High Priestess was the turning point of the battle. The outlaws, with their forest-hardened strength and aided by the keen edges of Wayland's swords, soon polished off the last of the demon worshippers.

They wiped the blood from their blades and solemnly threw each of the swords into the flaming pit, to prevent them from ever being used for evil again. Only Albion remained, for this was Herne's sword and Robin had sworn to return it to him.

Meanwhile, Morgwyn was running, half stumbling, across the causeway leading from the Abbey, her hair whipping round her in the cold night wind, her robes dishevelled. She was sobbing hysterically. Her eyes looked wildly round at the sea on either side of her. 'I feared him! Why?' she asked herself. 'Why did I fear him? *He was dead. Dead.* But he still came to Ravenscar! *He still came!*'

Behind her, the sound of galloping hooves splashing across the causeway made her turn in fear. If this was the outlaws chasing after her, she was lost. Her heart quickened as she recognized the gleaming masks and blood-red cloaks of the Hounds of Lucifer, and she stood confidently waiting for them. But the Hounds raced on unseeing, galloping closer and closer. Morgwyn screamed as she realized her danger. It was too late. She fell under the hooves of the plunging, screaming horses with the name of her dark lord on her lips and the bitter taste of failure in her mouth. Morgwyn of Ravenscar had paid the price of her evil ways and all her plans had been destroyed by the courage of the Sherwood outlaws.

CHAPTER 6

The wooden plate sped across the ale-house and shattered a large earthenware jug. There was a roar of laughter, and Bertrand de Nivelles, tall, swarthily handsome and dressed in dark leather and chain mail, called: 'Your aim is improving, Guillaume!'

'Thank you, my lord!' grinned the huge Brabançon mercenary, and prepared to hurl another plate at a second jug on the table. While some of the mercenary band stood watching, others were raiding the kitchen. The unhappy wife of the innkeeper vainly tried to stop the Brabançons stealing food until Bertrand, still laughing heartily, strode over to her. He took her by the throat, rammed her head savagely against the wall and knocked her unconscious. Her anguished husband went to her aid and Bertrand, still laughing, backhanded him, knocking him to the floor.

Guillaume was busily smashing chairs and stools, systematically wrecking the place. The unfortunate pot boy crouched in a corner as bottles were hurled at him. Two brave locals were struggling with the terrible men from Brabant, as the ale-house keeper staggered towards his wife. A Brabançon came from the kitchen, holding two rabbits above his head in triumph, and when Bertrand asked him if he'd found any chickens, he roared, 'Plenty! But I'm too drunk to catch 'em!'

One of the Brabançons began using his fists on the unfortunate ale-house keeper, and then two of them held him and poured ale over him while a third used an axe to smash open a barrel. Ale was soon flowing over the floor.

Bertrand de Nivelles was feeling very pleased with himself – and was somewhat the worse for drink. He climbed unsteadily on to his horse as his men came out of the ale-house bearing their loot – sacks of food and grain, bottles and goatskins of mead.

Bertrand looked round at his men and gave his orders. 'To Nottingham! I think we've rather outstayed our welcome here!'

The Brabançons were now all mounted and they moved off with Bertrand at their head. In cheerful mood, Bertrand burst into song.

'Put a sword in my hand,' he sang heartily, and his men joined in loudly and drunkenly.

'Put a sword in my hand and your money in my purse,' they chanted, and Bertrand answered with 'I'll be yours to command!'

'While your enemies curse,' they warbled, some hardly able to stay on their mounts, and Bertrand continued with 'But if they have more silver than you can supply –'

'Then they'll be my masters and you, my lord, will die!' roared his men, as the terrified villagers watched their oppressors vanish from sight . . .

Robin, Will and Friar Tuck came to the crossroads on which the inn stood some while after the Brabançons had left. Broken plates and splintered trestles still littered the ground around the inn door, while the pot boy mopped up the pools of ale on the floor. The innkeeper lay groaning with his head in his wife's lap. On seeing Robin and his companions, he just managed to murmur, 'Brabançons!'

'Why did they do it?' asked Robin.

'It's their idea of a good time,' said Tuck.

'We welcomed them,' said the innkeeper, 'gave them all they asked. They drank too much – went wild – I couldn't stop them. I thought they would kill us all.'

'You were lucky,' Robin replied quietly.

'It's a shambles, Robin,' said Will, emerging from the kitchen. 'They must have used axes.'

'Brabançons! Land pirates – the worst kind of mercenaries,' said Robin grimly.

Will started at Robin's words. He turned away and walked a few paces, his fists clenched. The innkeeper's wife looked questioningly at Robin, who stared at Will's retreating back, then turned and said, 'It was men like these who killed Scarlet's wife.'

Will returned to his friends. He was in a very dangerous mood. 'Which way were they heading?' he asked, and one of the villagers pointed.

'Nottingham,' said Tuck.

Will looked at Robin, waiting for him to give the word, but he remained silent. 'Well?' he asked his leader.

Robin shook his head.

'But why not?' asked Will.

'Because they're mounted and we'd never catch them,' Robin replied, and Tuck added, 'He's right, Will!'

Will could barely contain his rage, but he knew that Robin was right.

Robin came over to him. 'We'll get them,' he said. 'I promise you. We'll get them!'

In St Mary's Abbey, Abbot Hugo was being shaved by a nervous monk, fearful that he might cut the skin of the angry man, who would not sit still.

'So Gisburne thinks he can hold one of my men on his authority, does he? I was afraid when my brother appointed a man such as Gisburne as his deputy sheriff that his ambition would lead him to overstep the mark!' The monk approached again with the razor, but Abbot Hugo waved him away furiously. 'That will do,' he said gruffly, feeling his chin. 'I must have words with Gisburne!'

Sir Guy of Gisburne was lolling in the Sheriff's chair in the Great Hall of Nottingham Castle when the Abbot was announced.

'You are holding one of my servants,' said the Abbot. 'I want him released.'

Gisburne remained seated. 'He's been released.'

'When?' demanded the Abbot.

'After his sentence,' replied Gisburne, sounding bored.

The Abbot stared at him. 'You sentenced him?' he asked in amazement as well as anger.

'Certainly,' replied Gisburne coolly, 'I caught him poaching.'

'You mean to say – you – you –' spluttered the Abbot, and relapsed into silence.

Gisburne stirred himself and nodded. 'His right hand, my lord,' he told the Abbot, as if discussing the weather.

'By God, Gisburne!' the Abbot burst out, but Gisburne broke in. 'I would remind you that as Sheriff I –'

This was too much. '*Sheriff!*' exploded the Abbot. 'You are *not* Sheriff. My brother appointed you his *deputy*! And in my opinion, he was out of his mind to do so!'

'As Sheriff, my lord Abbot,' said Gisburne icily, picking out every word with rapier-like precision, 'I have the right to administer justice as I see fit!'

The two men stared angrily at one another. Abbot Hugo managed to control himself with the utmost difficulty.

'All right, Gisburne,' he said at length. 'It's obvious that the whole thing's gone to your head. You've mutilated my servant and I don't intend to let the matter rest. And when my brother returns from London . . .'

'I shall tell him,' Gisburne spat out. 'Poaching in the royal forests is a serious crime, and the penalty no more than just. My men here have been explaining their failure to stamp it out.' He gestured towards a small group of men dressed in the livery of the castle. The Abbot had failed to notice them in the angry heat of his arrival.

'And this is the reason for my good servant's punishment, is it?' said the Abbot sarcastically. 'No wonder they call you Guy the Gamekeeper!'

In the group of castle servants, the chief forester moved uncomfortably, cap in hand. He was a big countryman and very much in awe of his surroundings.

'I don't rightly know what to say, my lord,' he ventured.

'There's – there's always more poachin' this time of year, on account of the Blessing!'

Gisburne raised his eyebrows: 'The Blessing? What are you talking about?'

'Never heard of it, have you?' mocked the Abbot.

'It's an old festival,' explained the forester. 'The people of Sherwood keep it – a sort of feast, like – to celebrate the coming of summer. Must go back hundreds of years. It – it begins tomorrow night.'

'Does it!' said Gisburne, half angry, half bored.

'Well, my lord,' the forester continued, 'there's feasting in Sherwood, and ... you see ... nothing can be killed during the few days before the Blessing. No blood must be shed.'

'So they shed it beforehand – is that what you're trying to say?' asked Gisburne.

'Yes, my lord,' said the forester.

Gisburne leapt to his feet. 'And you let them!' he shouted savagely.

'No, no, my lord!' said the forester. 'But it's hard to prevent!'

'So you turn a blind eye to it,' sneered Gisburne. 'You know when this orgy's about to take place and you keep out of the way!'

'No, my lord!' cried the forester, and the others muttered agreement.

'Be silent!' thundered Gisburne. 'You say it is tomorrow night?' The foresters nodded.

'I wouldn't do anything foolish, Gisburne,' warned the Abbot. 'Sherwood's no place to be after dark.'

'Do you think I'm afraid of shadows?' Gisburne asked scornfully.

'No,' replied the Abbot, 'but your men are from the villages – they share these superstitions.'

'Soon, my lord Abbot,' replied Gisburne, 'I shall have men who fear nothing.'

The foresters looked blankly at their tormentor, and the

Abbot stared hard at him. What was the wretched man up to now? he wondered.

He was not left in doubt for long. The foresters had been dismissed, and the Abbot and Gisburne were sharing a large meal in hostile silence when the band of Brabançons arrived.

Bertrand de Nivelles swaggered down the Great Hall of Nottingham Castle, followed by his men carrying their swords and crossbows. Heady with power and somewhat the worse for drink, Gisburne was delighted to see Bertrand, shouting his name – and slurring it slightly – at the top of his voice. Abbot Hugo said nothing, but stared angrily at the drunken Brabançons.

Gisburne and Bertrand embraced. 'My old friend!' cried Bertrand. 'It's been a long time! You've been in the wars I see.'

Gisburne sobered up for a moment and fingered his scars ... those marks left from his last encounter with Robin Hood.

'So you've a score to settle?' asked Bertrand.

'Later – we'll talk later,' answered Gisburne.

Bertrand rapped him in the stomach. 'You've put on weight,' he said.

'Not an ounce!' Gisburne assured him.

'You have, you know,' said Bertrand. 'You were a damned sight thinner at Argentan.'

Gisburne pulled a face. 'We starved at Argentan,' he said.

'Maybe,' said Bertrand. 'But we fought like tigers. Back to back, knee deep in blood!' And he drew his sword. Gisburne, his spirits reviving, laughingly drew his and the two fought playfully.

It was soon clear that Bertrand was sharper and faster than Gisburne. With a laugh he disarmed him and roared with delight, turning to acknowledge the cheers of his men. Gisburne picked up his sword, doing his best to conceal his embarrassment.

'And the massacre at Montauban?' said Gisburne, determined to get his own back. 'Remember that? When you were trapped under your horse and I ...'

'Not me,' broke in Bertrand quickly. 'That wasn't me!'

Gisburne insisted, but Bertrand refused to admit it. 'No, Guy,' he said. 'You've mixed me up with someone else. But I've never forgotten when we stormed Chauvigny and you fell off the siege ladder and killed two of my men! I've dined out on that story for years!'

'It *was* you under that horse!' said Gisburne sourly.

'No, Guy, no!' smiled Bertrand. 'Anyway, here we are at your command, ready to serve you – *if* you can afford it! "The daring shall triumph!" That's the motto of the Nivelles!' Then he stared at Hugo, belched loudly and asked who he was.

'Abbot Hugo de Rainault,' said Gisburne, and Bertrand swaggered up to him and gave him a mock bow. Hugo was not amused.

'Your servant, my lord!' said Bertrand. 'I am Bertrand de Nivelles.'

'Yes,' said the Abbot contemptuously, 'I've heard of you!'

'One of the finest soldiers in Europe,' proclaimed Gisburne.

'One of the richest,' answered Abbot Hugo.

'True, my lord,' said Bertrand with a sneer. 'Fighting's nearly as profitable as praying!'

While his men laughed, Abbot Hugo asked Bertrand what he was doing in Nottingham. Bertrand put his arms round Gisburne's shoulders and chuckled. His dear friend Guy had asked him to come and bring his men along.

'Brabançon cut-throats?' inquired Hugo, raising his eyebrows.

Bertrand was not amused. 'Watch your tongue, priest,' he snapped.

'Don't you talk to me like that,' warned the Abbot.

'I'll talk to you how I please!' shouted Bertrand. 'As I talk to any man. Even one in skirts!' This caused another roar of laughter from his men.

Abbot Hugo exploded. 'I'll have you excommunicated!'

'You're too late,' replied Bertrand smoothly, 'It's already been done!'

The Abbot, shaken, turned to Gisburne: 'Are you mad to

invite these brigands here? Send them back immediately, before they have a chance to murder our people!'

Bertrand looked at him in silence for a moment, then said flatly and quietly, 'We're here for a purpose – and we're staying.'

Abbot Hugo, beyond rage now, answered him in the same vein. 'I know your purpose,' he said. 'Rape and pillage!'

Gisburne looked thoughtful as he listened to the two. 'Who's to blame for most of the deer killed in Sherwood?' he asked.

There was a moment's silence, and then Abbot Hugo said simply, 'So that's it.'

'With their help,' said Gisburne, 'I shall kill Robin Hood and everyone who supports him.'

The Abbot stood up. He looked hard at Gisburne, and said with great emphasis, 'You're out of your depth!' Then he swept out. Bertrand called after him. 'And you're out of order, priest!'

Everyone laughed and Bertrand embraced Gisburne once more. But the bear hug was not enough to stop Gisburne feeling a little uneasy.

CHAPTER 7

Early next morning Gisburne and the band of Brabançons rode out of the castle. They were heading for the village of Wickham, which lay on the outskirts of the forest. Gisburne had long suspected the villagers of more than just friendly relations with Robin Hood's men.

The village was decked out for the festival of the Blessing. In the centre there was an altar on which lay a pair of antlers surrounded by wild flowers. Most of the villagers were going about their normal business, little knowing the peril about to threaten them.

Suddenly there was the sound of hooves and into the village galloped Gisburne, Bertrand and the Brabançons, wheeling their horses round as they shouted and swore. Mothers picked up their children and soon everyone was facing the invaders apprehensively.

'I'm looking for venison,' snarled Gisburne, 'and the means of acquiring it. Search the village, Bertrand!'

The Brabançons and their leader dismounted, tied up their horses, and hurried towards the huts.

A tall, powerful-looking blacksmith called Edward came towards Gisburne. He was the head man of his village, a down-to-earth, likeable man. 'You're wasting your time, my lord,' said Edward. 'There's nothing here, I swear it!'

Gisburne looked over to the altar. 'What's that?' he asked, and Edward stated the obvious – that it was an altar. 'An altar?' barked Gisburne. 'With antlers on it? That's proof of poaching!'

Edward chose his words carefully. 'Those antlers are nigh on a hundred years old,' he said. 'If you want the man who killed that stag, you'll have to dig him up!'

Some of the villagers risked a laugh, but stopped when they saw the havoc Bertrand and his men were causing – searching their huts, pulling people outside and hurling their belongings from the doors.

'You call this law?' asked Edward.

'The only law,' Gisburne replied savagely, and was about to strike him when a Brabançon called out urgently, 'Here's something!'

The men gathered around a large ash tree. Flowers were piled against it, and garlands hung from the branches. Gisburne saw the villagers exchanging nervous glances.

'So that's where you hide things you shouldn't have!' said Gisburne with relish.

'No, my lord,' said Edward. 'That tree is sacred.'

Bertrand swung round when he heard the words and roared with laughter. 'A holy tree!' he chortled, and his Brabançons rocked with merriment at the absurdity of such a thing. Gisburne moved towards the tree, but Edward and the villagers were quicker, standing between it and their tormentor. 'My lord,' said Edward, 'this tree is sacred to Herne.'

'Search it!' ordered Gisburne.

As Bertrand and his men moved forward, the villagers retreated and gathered round the tree, linking their arms. The Brabançons started pulling them away, punching and kicking the defenders who could offer no real resistance. One by one, they were knocked out or hurled to the ground; Edward was one of the first to be battered nearly unconscious. In a moment he staggered to his feet, but was set upon again and kicked and punched until he collapsed. And all the while Gisburne watched the scene impassively.

Once the villagers had all been driven from the tree – or carried away by those of their friends who had enough strength left – the Brabançons climbed the ash and searched among the branches. They found nothing.

Gisburne could hardly believe it. 'Nothing?' he asked.

'No bows, no arrows, not even a sniff of venison,' said one of the searchers.

Gisburne turned furiously on the villagers. 'You'll burn in hell, you filthy heathens,' he raged at them. Then he seized an axe from one of the Brabançons – a great battleaxe – and attacked the sacred tree.

There was a roar of anger from the villagers, and Edward tried to quieten them. 'I beg you, my lord!' he pleaded with Gisburne, who turned on him, shouting, 'I'll teach you to worship trees, you blasphemous villain!' He swung the axe wildly, bringing down the sacred offerings and decorations and trampling them underfoot.

'He's cursed!' cried Edward, as Gisburne again swung the axe which bit deeply into the tree. Edward closed his eyes and prayed. 'Herne, Lord of the Trees,' he said, 'let him know your power. Let the terror of darkness hunt him down and hold him in the coldness of death!'

Meanwhile, Bertrand and his men watched Gisburne's futile and furious attack on the tree with amusement. The villagers watched, too, standing hopeless and defeated, some of them sobbing in their anguish.

The scene was too much for Bertrand. As Gisburne's antics became more absurd by the minute, he turned to his men. 'What a hero!' he guffawed.

Deep in the forest, Robin suddenly shivered. With his spoon frozen half way between mouth and wooden bowl, he felt as though an icy hand had run the length of his spine. Edward's prayer to Herne had touched Robin's sixth sense – the forest was in danger. He got up, his every nerve taut, the rest of the outlaws staring at him.

'What is it?' Marion asked.

'Gisburne!' said Robin.

By the time they reached the village on the outskirts of the forest, the sacred tree lay dying on the ground, the festive garlands wrecked and trampled by the Brabançon brigands. A small knot of villagers were gathered around the stump, nursing their bruised and battered limbs.

'Which way did they go?' Robin asked one of them, who pointed the way out of the village.

'Towards Elderford.'

'If we cross the stream at Denley, we'll cut them off,' said Little John.

'Then let's go,' said Robin.

The outlaws prepared to leave as the villagers looked on fearfully. 'We can't go!' said Marion suddenly. 'It's the time of the Blessing!'

There was a startled silence; then Edward explained. 'If you shed blood,' said he, 'then Herne's Blessing will be denied and the harvest will fail.'

Robin exploded. 'But that's ...' He broke off, suddenly aware of the full significance of Edward's words. Marion said quietly, 'You're Herne's son.'

Robin turned away and walked some paces, confused and frustrated. Marion followed him. He looked back at his men.

'No bloodshed!' he said. 'Herne forbids it.'

'*Tell that to the Brabançons!*' roared Will.

Little John kept up the pressure. 'Go to 'em, Robin! Tell 'em it's the time of the Blessing. Tell 'em we can't fight back – that we're powerless until after tonight!'

'They'll raid every village,' said Tuck.

'And you're going to let 'em,' Will said bitterly.

'What about tonight? What if they come into the forest tonight?' exclaimed Little John fiercely.

There was a tense pause as Robin desperately racked his brains for a solution to his nightmarish problem. Suddenly he decided to act. 'We'll capture them. Unharmed!'

The Brabançons' track wasn't hard to follow; burned thatch and trampled crops pointed the way. Much and Marion, scouting, came back to report that Gisburne and the Brabançons were resting by a stream not far ahead. Robin ordered John to follow him while Will, Marion, Nasir, Much and Tuck took up their positions among the trees.

As they neared the stream, Robin and Little John moved silently through the undergrowth. They caught sight of their prey – Robin took an arrow from his quiver and put it on his bow. On the far bank of the stream Bertrand stood talking to Gisburne. Robin took aim.

'There's no point in hanging around here, Guy,' said Bertrand. 'We may as well move on. I'm hungry.' One of his men handed him a bottle. As he took it, Robin released the arrow, shattering the bottle. Everyone dived for cover.

'Gisburne!' called Robin to his old enemy.

Bertrand raised his head, but Gisburne pulled him down again. 'Keep low!' he whispered. 'His aim's deadly!'

After a moment Robin turned to Little John. 'Show yourself,' he ordered.

'You'll get us killed!' muttered the big man. He moved forward, out of cover, with Robin behind him. 'Can you hear me, Gisburne?' Robin called again. 'I don't like the company you keep.'

Bertrand signalled his men to prepare to charge across the stream. 'Come on – take the bait!' muttered Robin; then he shouted, 'Pay 'em off, Gisburne, and you can all leave Sherwood – alive!'

Gisburne was puzzled. Why was his hated foe offering to let them go? It didn't make sense! 'We're sitting ducks,' he called. 'You could have killed all of us. Why didn't you?' Robin waited while the answer began to dawn on Gisburne. 'Because it's the time of the Blessing, isn't it?' called Gisburne.

'Took him long enough!' said Robin in a low voice to Little John.

'*Get them!*' roared Gisburne, and the Brabançons rose and shot their crossbows from their cover among the bushes. As they did so, Robin and Little John fell flat and the deadly bolts passed over them. Gisburne gave an order: Bertrand and his men urged their horses across the stream.

Robin and Little John raced off through the undergrowth, heading for the ambush they had laid, their pursuers close behind them. The Brabançons had been slowed down by the stream, but they were closing in, despite the difficulty of riding down the narrow forest track.

Marion, high above the track with the rest of the outlaws, saw Robin and John leading their pursuers into the trap. Scarlet on a branch, knife in hand, was ready to cut the rope holding up a net. The others were tensed for action.

Down the path raced Robin and John, their pursuers closing the gap fast. 'Ready!' cried Marion, and the outlaws prepared to release their nets. Robin and John ran beneath them and on up the path, but Gisburne suddenly reined his horse, Bertrand and the rest following suit.

'No further!' shouted Gisburne.

'You're crazy!' exclaimed Bertrand angrily.

'Am I? Why only two of them? Why show themselves?'

'An ambush!' said Bertrand.

Gisburne nodded. 'A bloodless one. Don't you understand? It had to be!'

Robin and Little John stopped running. 'Why have they halted?' asked John, gasping for breath.

'Maybe Gisburne's learning to think,' Robin replied. 'That's going to make him dangerous.'

The Brabançons and Gisburne rode back the way they had come.

Will was disgusted. 'The Blessing!' he sneered. 'No blessing for us!'

Gisburne and the Brabançons turned their horses homeward.

'So that was your Robin Hood,' said Bertrand.

'And he's powerless to harm us until after the Blessing!' laughed Gisburne.

'Well, I'm hungry,' said de Nivelles, licking his lips. 'Hunting always gives me an appetite!'

In Wickham, some of the villagers were kneeling in front of the altar to Herne when Gisburne arrived with the Brabançons. Edward saw them coming and got to his feet. While the other villagers rose and cowered away, he stood firm.

'You!' shouted Gisburne at Edward, who strode forward defiantly.

'My lord?'

'Bring us food,' Gisburne ordered curtly.

'All you desire, my lords,' said Edward, 'apart from venison!' And he signalled to the villagers.

Presently the Brabançons were seated round a table, well supplied with food and drink. The interlopers were enjoying themselves. Edward approached the table. 'My lords,' he said, 'the mummers – the maskers – have come!'

'Maskers?' asked Gisburne, and Edward explained that the mummers would present a play.

'Part of your heathen festival, is it?' sneered Gisburne.

'No, my lord,' Edward assured him. 'There's no harm in it.'

'I'll be the judge of that,' said Gisburne pompously.

Suddenly the maskers appeared from one of the huts. They jigged along, accompanied by a tabor and pipe. Like all maskers, they had blackened faces and their hair was covered by head-dresses of straw. Their costumes were made of strips of parchment and plaited straw, which effectively disguised them.

Friar Tuck had hitched up his robe to his knees so that it was no longer visible. He was wearing a wig of coarse string with two huge pigtails, and he was also equipped with two enormous false bosoms. Little John was in a hobby horse, and he, like Nasir and Robin, carried a huge wooden sword, which lay on his shoulders. Will Scarlet had a big straw bag with him.

The maskers jogged up to the table and stopped in front of Gisburne and the Brabançons, and Robin swaggered forward, modelling his gait on Bertrand's. Using a country accent, he burst into verse:

'In comes I, Saint George is my name,
With my great sword I mean to win this game!
If I could meet the Saracen Knight here,
I'd beat him and bale him and stick my sword in his ear!'

The Brabançons cheered, but Guy of Gisburne was not amused.

Little John's turn came next. He announced that he was

a Saracen knight and that he had just arrived in England to bash St George about. The pair hurled insults at each other – and steadily drew nearer to the table where the Brabançons sat. Then insults turned to blows as the Brabançons cheered drunkenly, and they cheered even more loudly when Little John ran Robin through and Robin 'died' after much over-acting.

This was Tuck's big moment, and in a high-pitched voice he called for a doctor. Will, complete with bag, ran forward and felt Robin's heart. Then he took an enormous pill from his bag and pretended to put it in Robin's mouth – upon which Robin sat up, blessed the doctor, grabbed his wooden sword – and shouted 'Now!'

At once Nasir, Robin and Little John swung at the Brab-ançons with their wooden swords, knocking three of them out cold. Will took a club from his bag and flattened Bertrand, while Tuck head-butted another Brabançon. So completely were they taken by surprise that the rest of them, including Gisburne, were rapidly overpowered and disarmed by the outlaws. Will produced some lengths of rope from his doctor's bag, while Little John climbed out of his hobby horse. Neither Gisburne nor Bertrand could believe their eyes. The comedy had turned sour ...

Robin looked hard at his old enemy. 'I mean to win this game, Gisburne!' he said. Gisburne stared at him in complete disbelief.

The Brabançons and Gisburne were tied to the fallen ash tree. 'It'll be dark soon, Guy,' said Robin. 'A pity you'll miss the Blessing. You're badly in need of one!'

Guy remained silent. Little John grinned at him and said, 'We'll be back in the morning to decide what to do with you.'

Gisburne watched the outlaws moving away with the vil-lagers, and kept his seething anger and hatred to himself. The struggle was too much for him, however, and he burst out: 'I'll kill the lot of you!' Bertrand, who was testing the strength of the bonds that held him, asked mockingly, 'Singlehanded, my friend?' Gisburne glared at him venomously.

Robin and his men mingled with the deliriously happy villagers, who were lighting torches from one of the fires outside the huts. 'Come, my friends!' called Edward, and a ragged procession started out from the village, Much attaching himself to the village band.

Gisburne and the Brabançons watched the villagers leave. Bertrand was still trying to free himself. 'You're wasting your time,' said Gisburne.

'My dear Guy,' said Bertrand coldly, 'I don't intend to have my throat cut.'

CHAPTER 8

The villagers reached the forest clearing sacred to Herne as dusk was falling. They headed for hiding places among the trees and dragged out large branches and carcases of venison, which they began to prepare for the fire. As the flames shot up, Edward said solemnly, 'Blessed be!' and the villagers repeated the blessing.

Will Scarlet approached Robin. 'What about Gisburne and his crew? You can't let them go!'

Robin shrugged his shoulders. 'I can't kill them. They're prisoners.'

'Then I'll do it.'

Robin stared hard at him. 'Prisoners?'

'We killed every one we captured when I was a soldier,' said Will grimly. 'You've spared Gisburne twice. Ain't exactly proved himself grateful, has he? Of course, you could always smack his rump and send him back to Nottingham. Only if you do he'll hang everyone in Wickham.'

'If we kill Gisburne in cold blood,' said Robin, 'we'd be no better than he is.'

'What makes you think we are?' asked Will. 'What about the men-at-arms we've killed? How do you feel about them? If you kill Gisburne you'll be doing the world a favour. As for that bunch of mercenaries, the sooner we send that scum to hell the better!'

Robin stared at Will, wondering how to get through to him. 'We can't do it,' he said.

'Then you'd better find an answer,' Will warned him. 'If you don't, all these people are going to die.'

As Robin tried to think of an answer that would satisfy them both, some village girls raced over and dragged Will away. Robin was left looking thoughtfully after him.

At the village, Bertrand de Nivelles was still working away at his bonds. Suddenly he grunted with pleasure, having at last managed to fray the rope. He turned to the villagers who were guarding them and feebly called for water. When one of them brought a jug and put it to Bertrand's mouth, he was felled by a blow like a sledgehammer. The second guard rushed at him with a quarterstaff but he was no match for Bertrand, who ducked under the wild blow and leapt on him. He seized the quarterstaff and struck both men violently on the head, and then looked round at Gisburne. 'What would you do without your Bertrand?' he asked.

'De Nivelles! Bertrand de Nivelles!' His men cheered, and their leader bowed gravely before setting about untying them.

'Guillaume,' he ordered, 'get our weapons.'

'We must find the meeting place,' urged Gisburne as Bertrand untied him. 'There'll be fires, dancing, singing, the smell of food – it should be easy!'

In Herne's clearing Robin raised a chalice. He stood beside Edward, both of them crowned with leaves. 'May Herne the Hunter, Lord of the Trees, protect us!' Villagers and outlaws alike responded with the same prayer.

Robin drank, then passed the chalice to Edward. 'This seals the bond between us,' he said, 'between we of the forest and you of the villages. Between the outlaws and the oppressed. Blessed be!'

Then the dancing started again, and the noise grew louder and louder. It was all too easy for Gisburne and the Brabançons to approach unseen. They moved forward to the very edge of the clearing, poised to strike.

Edward called for silence. 'My friends,' he said, 'soon Herne will be here. He will come before us as he has done since the beginning, to bless us and make us fruitful – ourselves, our animals and our crops. So let us sit quietly under the trees to await his coming.'

The villagers began to settle themselves down in hushed groups. Robin and Marion moved across to Will Scarlet, who was leaning drunkenly against an oak tree.

'Robin Hood!' whispered Gisburne.

Bertrand signalled to his men who crawled even closer and aimed their crossbows, but Gisburne said fiercely to him, 'No! Not yet! I'm going to kill their god in front of them. He'll need more than a doctor to bring him back to life!'

Bertrand nodded grimly and settled down to wait. They crouched silently, almost catching something of the mystery of the Blessing, when suddenly Gisburne grew tense. 'Look over there!' he hissed.

Slowly, almost majestically, Herne the Hunter moved into the clearing. The villagers whispered his name in awe, and it sounded like a sighing wind. Gisburne stared at the mysterious figure.

In the stillness, Herne raised his arms for the Blessing. Bertrand took careful aim, released the bolt from his crossbow, and it hummed across the clearing and took Herne in the thigh. He staggered back, dropping his arms.

Everyone rose. Robin looked round as Gisburne and Bertrand led their men towards the villagers. There was uproar as everyone tried to get out of the clearing at once. Women snatched up their children as they ran. The Brabançons hacked down all who stood in their path, and though the outlaws fought back they were hampered by the terror-stricken villagers. Robin fought his way to Herne. Gisburne saw them for a moment, but then a group of villagers blocked his view and he struck out at them savagely. Will Scarlet, too, was in trouble. He tried to send off a huge Brabançon, but stumbled over the fallen villagers and lost his aim. In desperation, Will picked up a fallen child and staggered towards the safety of the trees. Total confusion now reigned as the villagers fled in all directions, pursued by the pitiless mercenaries.

Gisburne reached the spot where Herne had fallen wounded, only to find that he had vanished. 'Bertrand!' he roared. But there was no answer from de Nivelles.

The cries of the villagers could be heard more and more

faintly as they fled deeper into the forest. Gisburne ran on, alone. Suddenly in the distance he saw Herne again, moving away from him. Gisburne crashed after him, stumbling through bushes and briars that seemed to trip and tear at him almost deliberately. As the heat of the fight drained away from him he began to feel a sense of dread. Finally, he stopped for breath. The noise of his breathing seemed immense in the black silence. As if from nowhere, Herne stood in front of him again, and then vanished into the trees, as Gisburne stumbled forward.

Gisburne sweated and panted his way into the forest, Herne appearing and disappearing from view. His legs weak and his lungs straining, his heart was gripped by icy fear. He was beginning to feel he would never catch his elusive foe. Thunder rolled overhead and the wind began to rise. Sweat dripped in his eyes, and he saw shapes appear out of the darkness, a branch, a hollow log, a startled pigeon ... On he went, hardly caring which way he was going, 'Gisburne! Gisburne! Gisburne!' all around him. He lost his balance and fell. Panic seized him. The trees loomed over him and the wind began to moan through the branches: 'Gisburne! Gisburne! Gisburne!'

'Who's there?' he cried, looking round in terror. 'Stop it! Stop it!' he screamed.

Another crash of thunder overhead. 'Herne! Herne!'

Gisburne ran on blindly, sobbing with fear. He seemed to be fighting and struggling with unseen creatures. He fell on all fours, moaning and straining for breath. 'Leave me! Leave me! O God save me!'

Abbot Hugo was in his bedchamber when they brought Gisburne to him, wild, dirty, tattered and exhausted. Abbot Hugo gaped. 'What's happened to you, man?'

'Save me! Save me!' gasped Gisburne.

'Save you? What are you talking about, Gisburne?' asked the Abbot.

'The forest! The forest, my lord! The trees, the trees!' gibbered the unfortunate Gisburne.

'Save you from the trees? Have you been drinking?'

'Herne! Herne!' Gisburne moaned, and covered his ears as if to try and blot out the sound of his own voice. He was shaking with fear and sobbing uncontrollably.

Abbot Hugo began to understand. 'I warned you, didn't I, Gisburne?' he said solemnly.

In the clearing, Bertrand stood with his men, his sword and clothes covered in blood. 'Guy! Guy!' he shouted angrily. 'Where the devil have you got to? Damn the man! He's impossible – this is no place to play hide and seek! He's headed back home – let's go and rout the craven fellow out of his bed!'

The outlaws were gathered in a small hollow in Sherwood. Herne lay on the ground, a bloody cloth wrapped round his leg. Robin crouched beside Marion, who was tending Herne's wound, as Herne looked up at him.

'You played your part well!' he said softly.

'I know the forest,' said Robin. 'Gisburne doesn't, and he's badly lost. I led him a merry dance, and he has enough scratches and scrapes to more than pay for the hurt he caused you!'

'Let me put him out of his misery!' said Will.

Herne shook his head. 'Leave him to the forest,' he commanded. 'You see your god become a man. An old riddle, my children, but there is nothing to fear. The Blessing has been made.'

Early next morning, Bertrand and his Brabançons left Nottingham, heading south on the coast road. Their path lay past the inn at the crossroads they had visited so brutally a few days before. Bertrand dismounted, and led the rest of the men towards the door.

'It's just as well we were paid in advance, my friends,' said Bertrand over his shoulder. 'The Lord knows what's happened to Gisburne.'

'Perhaps the outlaws got him,' suggested one. 'Maybe he fell in a bog!' said another, and they all laughed.

'Poor employment, anyway,' Bertrand lamented. 'A hundred marks to kill a few serfs. If he hadn't been a friend of mine

I'd never have taken it on. By St Christopher, I need a drink!'

As they swaggered into the ale-house, the innkeeper came towards them nervously. 'Remember us?' asked Bertrand. The man nodded. 'Then bring us some ale!'

The Brabançons sat down noisily. 'New benches, I see!' said Bertrand, and his companions roared with laughter.

The innkeeper returned and with him came Much, carrying ale in an earthenware pot.

Wearing a battered hat pulled down to hide his face, Robin also came in and sat alone, some distance from Bertrand and his men. Sensing sport, Bertrand looked across and drew his men's attention to the stranger. Two of them winked broadly, got up and went over to Robin, and one peered at Robin's ale. Robin picked it up. 'What's that?' asked the Brabançon. 'Ale, is it?' he asked jeeringly. 'English ale?'

Robin ignored the two men and after drinking, put the cup down in front of him. One of them picked it up and sniffed at it. 'Smells bad to me!' he said. Then, very deliberately, he poured the ale all over the table. Robin remained motionless, as the rest of the Brabançons began to snigger. 'Here! Try some of mine!' suggested one, and poured his ale over Robin's head. It dripped from the brim of his hat, but Robin did not move an inch. 'What do you think of it? Taste any better?' Robin still said nothing and his face was expressionless. 'I don't think he liked it!' said the first man, laughing. 'But he'll still have to pay for it, won't he?' answered his fellow clown.

The rest of the Brabançons guffawed, and Bertrand advised him: 'Go on, pay, my friend!'

Robin still sat unmoving, saying nothing at all.

'Are you deaf?' inquired one of his tormentors. Robin slowly shook his head.

'Are you dumb, then?' said another. 'Yes! That's it! Maybe he's dumb.' Once more Robin shook his head.

'Stand up then,' ordered the first mercenary.

'No,' said Robin quietly.

'It can talk!' said the other in mock amazement. 'The ape can talk.' And he held his hand out for the money.

'Pay my friend, eh?' sneered the first. 'While you're about it, all my friends would like a drink as well!'

Bertrand was feeling impatient. The game had gone on long enough. 'Your money!' he ordered, and when Robin remained silent one of the Brabançons grabbed him. 'I said *your money*!' he roared.

Without warning Robin leapt to his feet and hit the man in the stomach. As he doubled up, Robin struck him again. Yet another came at him, and Robin picked up his stool and smashed it on his head. Then he tipped up the table, sending the first mercenary flying. He moved so swiftly that the two Brabançons were left sprawling on the ground before the rest had taken in what was happening.

As they charged towards Robin, Scarlet and Nasir burst through the door and Little John and Tuck came from the kitchen, followed by Much. In the full-scale rough-house that ensued, surprise gave the outlaws the upper hand. Bertrand drew his sword and Robin did likewise, forcing the Brabançon leader out of the door and into the open.

'You've brightened my day,' Bertrand shouted as Robin brandished Albion.

Marion and Tuck watched the duel tensely.

'Where's Gisburne?' cried Bertrand as he fought.

'Sherwood Forest has him!' Robin replied.

Another Brabançon came tottering out of the ale-house, to be hit over the head with a cooking pot brandished by Tuck. Will drove a Brabançon before him out of the back door, finally running him through with a savage laugh.

Bertrand's breathing was becoming laboured. 'You're dead, peasant!' he sneered, with the sweat pouring off his face.

'I don't feel dead!' said Robin, and swept Bertrand's sword from his hand.

Desperately, Bertrand looked round for some means of escape. He leapt towards Marion, surprising her with a dagger held to her throat. He forced her to mount a horse and then he sprang up behind her. 'Try to stop me and she dies!' he called in triumph, galloping off.

But he had reckoned without Marion. She bared her teeth and bit deep into Bertrand's wrist. Cursing, he released his hold on the dagger and she slipped from the saddle, rolling away from the horse's hooves as she landed.

Robin grabbed Little John's bow and swiftly sent an arrow whistling after the Brabançon leader. The arrow took Bertrand between the shoulders and he tipped sideways off the horse, one foot still caught in the stirrup. His body bowled along the track, dragged behind the terrified horse as it galloped away.

The outlaws came racing towards Robin, marvelling at his skilful shot. He went over to where Marion still lay in the dusty path.

'Are you all right?' he asked, and she nodded.

'He was a murderer,' said Tuck.

'They're all murderers,' said Will Scarlet.

The remaining Brabançons were stripped of their finery and trussed up across their horses.

'Listen to me,' Robin said, 'and mark what I say. If any Brabançons ever come to Sherwood again, I swear by Herne the Hunter they'll be buried here!'

CHAPTER 9

Two roads led to Nottingham from the south, and Robin had divided his little band to keep watch on both of them. With Marion and Much he was keeping an eye on one road while the rest of the outlaws watched the other.

The reason for this double watch was that Robin had heard a rumour that the Sheriff was returning from London, and he was determined to give him a warm welcome. Nottingham boasted a royal castle and it was thought that the Sheriff would be bringing part of the King's treasure to it for safe keeping. It was one of several royal treasuries.

High ground separated the two roads, and a signal arrow was to be shot by whichever group spotted the Sheriff's force first. But as the days went by the outlaws' spirits began to droop. Marion, looking up at Robin on a branch high in a tree, called: 'I don't think he's ever coming! It was only a rumour anyway.'

'It's more than that,' Robin called back. 'William says he will. He should know. He works in the castle.'

'Why are you so certain he won't come through Sherwood?' asked Marion.

'Sherwood's ours,' Robin reminded her. 'He daren't risk it!' Then he grinned to himself and asked Herne to send him a rich Sheriff with his wagons groaning with money.

Morale among the other group of outlaws was lower, and in one case downright mutinous. 'Eight days and not a sign of him,' muttered Little John bitterly, and Will and Nasir nodded in agreement. But it was Will who erupted.

'We're always on the move,' he shouted angrily. 'Now we're out here and anyone can take us!'

'Robin says –' Little John started to say, but Will broke in furiously. 'I don't give a jot what he says! We're always doing what Robin says!' he exploded, and walked away.

Tuck started after him, but Nasir stopped him.

'You're right, Nasir,' said Tuck. 'He'll get over it.'

'Maybe,' said Little John, 'but he's getting itchy feet. Might even leave us. Things aren't right between him and Robin. Unless it's sorted out we'll lose him.'

At the other lookout point Much climbed up to Robin and asked, 'Is he coming yet?' Robin shook his head.

'How'll we let the others know?' asked Much, and Robin patiently reminded him that he would shoot a single arrow into the sky over the hilltop, and that they would shoot one if they saw the Sheriff on the other road.

Much frowned. 'I forgot! I often forget, don't I?' Then he took his flute from his belt and started to play it.

'You're thinking of Will, aren't you?' said Marion to Robin. 'Why don't you say something?'

'It's for him to speak first.' Robin frowned.

'But he won't.'

'No,' said Robin, 'he's too stiff-necked. He questions everything. There can't be two leaders.'

'Then tell him so,' Marion replied.

It was Nasir who first spotted their prey – the Sheriff and a strong force of mounted men-at-arms, plus foot soldiers with crossbows surrounding a cart. They were in open country with almost no cover.

'I'll signal Robin,' said Little John.

'We can do without him,' Will scoffed. 'They'll see a signal.'

'Don't be daft! We've got to signal,' said John.

Tuck looked at Will in amazement. 'Four of us against that lot!' he gasped.

'Four or seven, what's the difference?' said Will defiantly.

'Robin!' answered Little John.

'Come on, John!' said Will. 'We can do it. Think of riding that cart over the hill. What a surprise for him!'

Thinking success might restore Will's good humour and

reconcile him with Robin, Little John agreed, but Nasir had doubts. 'It's no game,' he said.

'Kill 'em all, eh, Nasir?' said Will. 'Take the Sheriff's head to Robin along with the money. That should cheer him up!'

'Not if they surrender,' Tuck said firmly.

'*If* they surrender,' said Will grimly.

The Sheriff was getting angry as he and his men crawled slowly along. 'Where the devil's Gisburne?' he complained to the rider beside him, only to see the man knocked out of his saddle by an arrow. 'We're attacked,' shouted the Sheriff. 'Spread out and keep moving!' Then he rode forward, trying to locate the foe. The cart halted and the crossbowmen crouched by it, looking for targets.

'Over there!' shouted the Sheriff, spotting Will and Little John, who had found some cover on the ground. Three mounted men raced towards them. One of them fell, but the other two kept on, lashing out at the outlaws as they sped by.

The Sheriff spotted Nasir and Tuck and sent four riders to deal with them. They rose from their flimsy cover and shot their arrows, but the riders came on, one of them cutting at Tuck who spun round and collapsed as he was hit, Nasir crouching over his motionless body, which lay face down.

Will and Little John rolled out of the way of the riders, then sprinted for their friends. The three on their feet stood over Tuck as the riders bore down on them. Little John unseated one of them with his quarterstaff, wielding it like a lance; the others defended themselves against the swords of the mounted men, who were going too fast to pull up.

'*Get out of it!*' roared Little John, starting to pick Tuck up. 'Help me!' he cried and Will did so, muttering, 'You'll never lift him!'

The riders had regrouped and the crossbowmen were taking aim as Little John carried Tuck towards the trees. Crossbow bolts whined towards Will and Nasir who dived to the ground, then scrambled up after Little John as the riders headed for them.

Sweat poured off Little John's face as he neared the trees, while Will and Nasir turned to face the riders, who circled them, stabbing down with their swords. Will pulled one to the ground and Nasir killed another, then glanced back. Little John had reached the trees!

As the riders hacked down at them, and with the crossbow-men running towards them, the outlaws zigzagged their way to safety.

The Sheriff was not amused by his men's performance. 'You fools!' he shouted as his intended victims disappeared.

When the fugitives reached Robin and the rest of the outlaws, his attitude was a replica of the Sheriff's. 'Fools!' he shouted angrily. 'Why? You knew the plan! You had plenty of time to signal – you must have done!' And he looked hard at Will Scarlet. 'It was your idea, wasn't it?'

Will glared at him, hardly able to control himself. 'We were unlucky,' he muttered.

There was a pause, Robin hardly able to believe what Will had just said. Then Robin coldly and harshly repeated the word 'unlucky'. 'Is that all you can say, Scarlet?' he asked fiercely. 'You're wrong. *Tuck* was unlucky, not you. But if he dies . . .'

'Are you threatening me?' asked Will.

'I'm telling you,' said Robin quietly but with menace, and he turned and went to where Marion and Much were kneeling by Tuck.

For a moment Will stood tensely and then he stalked off. Little John approached Robin, saying, 'We're all to blame!' but Robin ignored him, asking Marion how Tuck was.

'Bad,' she said. 'Brother Tuck – it's Marion here!'

'He won't die, will he, Robin?' Much asked timidly.

Little John turned away and went over to Will.

'Why don't you admit we were wrong?' he asked.

Will's face darkened and for a moment it seemed that he would throw himself at Little John. But he managed to control himself and simply spat out: 'I said we were unlucky!'

*

Meanwhile, with the Sheriff away, Gisburne was enjoying – as he always did – the time he was in charge at Nottingham. At the moment he was staring at a tall and aristocratic-looking Jew named Joshua de Talmont, whose sunken eyes betrayed the pain of an illness that racked him. With him stood his beautiful daughter Sarah, whom he had seen before with her father. He found her so attractive that it was all he could do to concentrate on what her father was saying.

De Talmont had business with the Sheriff and wanted to know when he would be back. 'Tomorrow,' Gisburne told him, enviously noting the fact that father and daughter were more richly dressed than he.

'Are you certain?' asked de Talmont, and Gisburne snorted. 'You're becoming a nuisance,' he told the Jew. 'He will be here tomorrow. And I have the authority to deal with whatever it is you want to see him about.'

'My business is with the Sheriff, the *Sheriff*,' said de Talmont coldly.

'Then come back tomorrow,' Gisburne spat at him. 'And blame yourself for another wasted visit.'

A spasm of pain shot through de Talmont and his daughter supported him. 'What's the matter?' asked Gisburne. 'Are you still sick?'

Sarah pleaded with Gisburne to let her father rest awhile. He was very attracted to her, and so he agreed. 'If he must,' he said. 'This isn't a hospital.' Sarah thanked him.

The Captain of the guard came in with his men and a prisoner.

'A poacher, my lord,' he said, and Gisburne managed to tear his eyes away from Sarah. He noted that the man's hands were bloody.

'Red-handed!' he grunted.

'And soon one-handed!' answered the Captain.

'Do it now,' Gisburne ordered, and the guards took the poacher away. 'Any news of Robin Hood?' he went on.

'Nothing,' replied the Captain.

It was not the most accurate of answers, for as he spoke the

Sheriff was riding through the castle gateway with the two riders who had survived the ambush. Crossbowmen led the horses of the dead riders, their bodies strapped across the saddles. The Sheriff, pale and frowning with suppressed anger, looked straight ahead. The rest of the dead and the wounded men were in a cart.

The Sheriff was told where Gisburne was and hastened to the Great Hall of the castle. 'Gisburne!' he roared as he strode into the hall. Everyone froze: servants, foresters, monks and soldiers ceasing whatever they were doing and looking at their angry leader.

Gisburne rose from a chair as if he had seen a ghost. 'My lord – I thought! I thought . . . !' he said in a strained voice as the Sheriff continued to stride down the hall.

'You thought, did you, Gisburne?' asked the Sheriff sarcastically. 'What a pity I wasn't here! When did you have this thought of yours? While I was in London, or more recently? Surely such an earth-shattering event would linger in the memory. Was it today, perhaps? *While I was being attacked?*'

'Attacked, my lord?' asked Gisburne as the Sheriff reached the dais where his nervous deputy stood.

'Ten miles from Nottingham. Robin Hood's men,' said the Sheriff harshly. 'That was when I had my *thought*, Gisburne. Do you know what it was? It was: Where is *Gisburne*? *Where is the escort I asked for in my letter?* A simple, uncomplicated thought.'

There was dead silence in the hall as everyone stared at Gisburne. 'Your letter, my lord,' he said nervously, 'er – your letter said that you would be here in four days' time – dated the eighth, my lord.'

He produced the letter, which was snatched from him and at once torn up. 'On the seventh, Gisburne. Don't try to get out of it,' said the Sheriff peevishly.

'But my lord –'

'But!' shouted the Sheriff. 'Yes, the butt of everyone in Nottingham, aren't you?'

'You insult me!' shouted the unfortunate Gisburne with spirit.

'I do!' the Sheriff replied. 'And will continue to do so as long as you give me cause.'

'I'm not your whipping boy,' complained Gisburne, and the Sheriff detected a note of real defiance.

'Aren't you? Anyway, I drove them off. Had you been there I'd have finished them off.'

Joshua de Talmont, who had been listening to the angry scene, came forward with Sarah. The Sheriff took a drink from his goblet and asked what he wanted. De Talmont expected the money that the Sheriff owed him and calmly said, 'Payment, my lord.'

'Do you know what you remind me of?' asked the Sheriff. 'A leech, a blood-sucking leech!'

'Your sickness, my lord,' answered de Talmont calmly, 'needs more than a leech. Envy is hatred without a cure.'

'Envy? Why should I envy you?'

'Why indeed!' replied de Talmont. 'It often puzzles me.'

The Sheriff looked hard at him. 'A moneylender!'

'Moneylending is the price of our existence,' said de Talmont, 'the only trade we are permitted to follow. You were willing enough to borrow.' And he quoted: 'Retire without supper and rise without debt.'

'What nauseating hypocrisy! How could a Jew thrive without debtors?' asked the Sheriff with disgust.

'Debtors won't make me thrive,' replied the Jew. 'That's why I'm standing here.'

'Aren't you forgetting who I am?' roared the Sheriff, jumping up.

'Not at all,' said de Talmont. 'You are my servant.'

'Your *what*!' exploded the Sheriff.

'You borrowed money from me,' explained de Talmont. 'Every borrower is a servant to the lender.'

'I'll have you whipped!'

'That won't discharge your debt,' de Talmont pointed out. 'It would be more honourable for you and much less painful for me to let me have the money. However,' he went on, as the Sheriff shouted for the guards, 'if you continue to withhold what is legally mine, I shall have to inform the King.'

The Sheriff stopped the advancing guards as de Talmont said, 'My people are answerable to the King alone. I would advise you not to lose sight of that. Come, Sarah.'

They walked away, the Sheriff noting that Gisburne, despite his anger, was clearly interested in the girl.

'He's made his own rope, Gisburne,' said the Sheriff. 'It only remains to put it round his neck.'

CHAPTER 10

As Joshua de Talmont and Sarah approached their house, they were watched by a small crowd of townspeople. One of them moved towards them and spat at them, but they took no notice: they were used to it. Soon they were safely indoors.

They went straight to the main room of the house, splendidly furnished, rich in tapestries and fine carpets. De Talmont's younger children, Esther and Samuel, ran to embrace their father, who asked them if they had been good. They assured him that they had. 'But not too good lest you be eaten up!' said their father, and they all laughed.

A servant took de Talmont's cloak and Sarah helped him to his seat. 'Run along, now!' Sarah told the children. 'Father is tired.' They scampered off.

'You made an enemy today,' said Sarah with a frown.

'The man who never made an enemy never made anything,' de Talmont replied, but Sarah had not finished.

'I saw how he looked at you,' she said in a worried voice.

'I belong to the King,' de Talmont reminded her. 'That's why the Sheriff hates me. Oh, he'll wriggle and threaten, but in the end he'll pay.'

'I wonder,' said Sarah unhappily.

'We are God's flies, and time will free the fly and cage the eagle.'

He looked lovingly at his seventeen-year-old daughter and said, 'Now I'm going to read the Cabala.'

As he spoke, Samuel and Esther bounded back into the room, pursued by the servant. 'Can't we see the Cabala?' the boy asked eagerly.

'It's not meant for little children or the ignorant,' smiled their father. 'It is ancient wisdom handed down from the time of Moses and it is said that if evil men look at its secrets, the power of the book would overwhelm them. Now, off you go!'

Their father picked up the beautifully ornamented book, many of whose words were decorated with gold leaf and intricate designs. Sarah kissed her father and left him. She felt frightened, and she was right to be, for at the castle events were moving fast.

As soldiers carried to the castle vaults the chests of silver that the Sheriff had brought back from London with him, he was sitting examining documents spread over his table while Gisburne stood sullenly by him.

'It all seems rather a muddle,' said the Sheriff, 'but I suppose I can cope with it.' He leant back in his chair. 'You're too young to remember King Richard's coronation, aren't you?' he asked Gisburne.

'No, my lord, I was there with my father.'

'Splendid affair, wasn't it?' said the Sheriff. 'The people went mad with joy – and killed most of the Jews. One way to celebrate, I suppose! It was attributed to crusading mania at the time, but I think it went deeper than that, don't you? Look what happened in York a year later.'

He rose and turned to Gisburne. 'And it could very well happen in Nottingham, couldn't it?' he suggested. Gisburne supposed it could. 'I propose that it will,' smiled the Sheriff.

Gisburne thought the idea a splendid one, but his mind went back to the Jewish beauty. Let the rest of Nottingham's Jews perish, but not her. He had better send a warning to the family. With a little care he should have the best of both worlds.

The beautiful object of his thoughts could not relax. She feared the Sheriff and had heard about riots against Jews in other English towns. She went over to the window, pulled the curtains across and shivered, though it was warm. Then she went into another room to join Samuel, who was asking to be told the story of his namesake in the Bible, but they were interrupted by Esther. She handed a note to Sarah, who became very frightened; she asked Esther who had brought it, and Esther told her that an unknown man had delivered it.

'What man?' asked de Talmont as he came into the room.

'He had a hood on his face,' said Esther, as Sarah handed her father the note.

'I warned you,' Sarah reminded him.

'It says "Leave Nottingham",' he read out.

'It's a trick to get us outside,' said Sarah.

'No, the danger is real enough. I've seen it,' her father admitted. 'It goes on: "The Sheriff means to kill you".'

As Sarah comforted the frightened children, her father said: 'We must go to my brother's house in Lincoln. And to the family of Aaron, your betrothed. Come, let us prepare at once.'

They were not a moment too soon, for already there was trouble in the streets. A gang of louts were chasing an unfortunate Jew and shouting, 'Get him! Kill him! Punish the filthy Jew!' They caught up with him and he fell, surrounded by a crowd who beat him savagely with sticks. A chant of 'Jew! Jew! Jew!' rent the night air.

Watching the ghastly scene were Gisburne, the Captain and two of his men, all dressed in peasant clothes. 'We spread a rumour that the Jews used the blood of a Christian child to smear on the door posts of their houses,' Gisburne told his companions. Then they ran to join a crowd who were battering down a door with a wooden bench.

'Kill them all! Kill the Jewish pigs!' the mob shouted.

'No wonder they won't eat pork,' said the Captain. 'That'd make them cannibals.'

The rioters laughed raucously. The door gave way and the mob cheered as some of the rioters went in. 'Devil worshippers! Blasphemers! Murderers!' shouted Gisburne as a man and his wife were dragged into the street and surrounded by the crowd. Once again the sticks rained down.

In de Talmont's house the family was preparing to leave, all of them now dressed in simple clothes. De Talmont prayed, then gasped as the pain of his illness shot through him. He picked up the Cabala. 'If anything should happen to me,' he said, 'let no one except my brother open this book. It is the book of power, the Sepher Yetzirah – sacred and secret knowledge not meant for profane eyes.'

Screams and the shouts of the rioters made the family look up in alarm. De Talmont put the Cabala in a bag with other precious belongings and, as the rioters started battering at the front door and chants of 'Jew! Jew' rent the night air, Sarah looked round the lovely room for the last time and followed her father and her brother and sister, sobbing as she ran.

Outside, bodies lay in the street; the rioters were now using a heavy beam to attack de Talmont's front door. The lock gave way and they poured in, but by now the family were hurrying down a narrow street at the back of the house. Inside, the mob smashed bowls, tore tapestries down and ripped up papers. With them was Gisburne. 'They've gone! They've fled!' he raged. 'The one person we wanted. They were warned. They must have been warned!'

He grabbed the Captain. 'Listen to me,' he seethed. 'They all died, understand. *All of them.* If the Sheriff learns they escaped –'

'I understand, my lord,' said the Captain.

Gisburne swung round on the mob. 'There's no one here!' he shouted. '*Let's kill the rest of them!*'

They hurried away, the Captain bringing up the rear. He halted suddenly and picked up a note, which he read; then, tucking it securely into his belt, he followed the rest of the mob. His only prize was de Talmont's servant. The family had got away.

The next morning the Sheriff questioned Gisburne about the riots. 'And de Talmont?' he asked.

'There's not one Jew left alive in Nottingham,' said Gisburne cunningly.

'Good. You'd better hang some of the rioters. Just to demonstrate my anger at this atrocity. And I'll write a suitably outraged letter to the King. Was there much silver?'

'It is being brought here under guard,' Gisburne replied.

'Most of it will go to the Royal Treasury,' said the Sheriff. 'That'll please him!'

'Most of it?'

'Yes, Gisburne, most of it,' said the Sheriff smoothly. 'I must have something for my trouble, surely?'

'And what about me, my lord?'

The Sheriff stopped in his tracks and turned to him. 'I can see I've been away too long!' he said, then went into his chamber and, without turning, slammed the door in Gisburne's face.

In the woods Tuck was being looked after by Marion and Much. Robin came over to find out how he was and left looking grim. He strode over to where the rest of the band stood talking, Will Scarlet moving away as he approached.

'We'll have to get back into Sherwood before Gisburne comes after us,' said Robin. 'We'll take Tuck to Calverton. It's only a couple of miles. We'll need a cart. Much, go into Calverton and get one. We've helped them often enough. Nasir you keep watch.'

Much at once ran off and Nasir chose a good position. Robin, ignoring Will, went back to Marion and Tuck. Soon the outlaws were carrying Tuck to Calverton on a roughly made stretcher, the mutinous figure of Will Scarlet bringing up the rear.

As they reached the village, they saw the villagers lined up to greet them – as they thought. Tuck was lowered to the ground and Robin asked the village headman why they hadn't sent a cart.

'We can't have you here,' he said, and the other villagers nodded. 'It's too dangerous.' The other villagers chimed in with cries of 'Too much of a risk' and 'We'd be punished!'

Robin stared at them in disbelief. 'Where's Edward?' he asked.

'Gisburne's questioning him,' the headman said. 'That's what happens, see?'

'We'll be gone by morning,' said Little John.

The headman shook his head. 'You're outlaws!' he muttered.

'We've helped you often enough,' Robin told him. 'That has to mean something.'

'Something, but not enough,' replied the headman. 'Anyway, what's wrong with going to Sherwood?'

'It's hours from here,' Robin pointed out. 'Tuck needs rest now.'

'Well, he can't rest here,' said the headman firmly.

Robin stared at the villagers, all of whom were carrying stones. Bitterly, he turned to Marion. 'How is he?' he asked, but she only shook her head.

'We'll go,' Robin told the villagers. 'Nothing's forgotten. Nothing's ever forgotten.'

The outlaws picked up the stretcher and started on their way. 'The poor, the oppressed – and the gutless!' sneered Will Scarlet. Robin looked at him angrily, but said nothing.

In a forest clearing that night the outlaws sat silent beside a fire. There was a groan from the sleeping Tuck, and Marion went over to him. His eyes opened.

'Where am I, little flower?' he asked.

'We're back in Sherwood,' she told him.

Tuck stirred himself. 'My head feels like a pumpkin!'

'Lie still and rest,' Marion urged him.

Little John squatted down beside Robin. 'Don't take it to heart,' he said. 'Those villagers were frightened.'

'We risked our lives for them,' Robin replied, 'time and again, and they turned us away. We could have been strangers!'

Will seized his chance. 'You see now, don't you?' he said to them all. 'It's been for nothing, hasn't it? They're not worth fighting for. They're serfs and always will be. We could have all been rich, but no! you had to believe that Herne had chosen you – that you were going to put heart into people – give them hope and maybe the will to fight. Why can't you be honest? You're just an outlaw – and always will be!' Then he turned away and walked slowly into the forest.

Later that day Robin confronted Herne. His feelings were bitter, his hopes dashed, as the strange horned figure came towards him carrying a torch. Herne climbed up a mound so that he looked down on Robin who stared at him bleakly, no longer believing in his mission.

'Why have you come?' asked Herne.

'To break faith with you,' said Robin, feeling dead inside.

'You cannot. You were chosen!' said Herne, but Robin quietly told him that he must find someone else to carry out his task.

'There is no other!' thundered Herne. 'The little ones will hide in terror. The book of power will take revenge. Your arrows must be ready.'

'The target's too far,' Robin groaned wearily; then almost shouted: 'I've lost my aim!'

'Then aim again,' commanded Herne.

'For what purpose?' pleaded Robin. 'To what end?'

'There is no end and no beginning,' Herne the Hunter intoned. 'It is enough to aim.' Then he turned away into the mist that had gathered round him and was gone.

The sun was shining in Sherwood as Tuck lay propped against a tree, his head bandaged with strips of sacking. Much, Little John and Nasir were keeping him company, John angrily cursing the villagers for their cowardice.

'Curse away!' said Tuck. 'It won't bring Scarlet back.'

'It's not Scarlet I'm thinking about,' said Little John, gazing at Robin and Marion who were walking beside a stream.

Robin sat down gloomily. 'I'm tired of Herne's riddles,' he said to Marion. 'He told me it was enough to aim. I might as well shoot at the moon!'

Marion looked at him anxiously, but said nothing.

'I thought they believed in us,' Robin went on. 'I did think they'd begun to take heart ... And the first time – the

–89–

very first time that we need their help – they drive us away.'

After a strained silence, Marion said sadly: 'They did more than the Sheriff and Gisburne with all their men-at-arms could do!'

Robin looked up at her questioningly and she continued. 'They killed Robin Hood – just by rejecting him,' she said quietly but with great emphasis.

Robin stared at her and a cloud seemed to lift from him. He looked lovingly at Marion and slowly walked to her, taking her in his arms gently and kissing her. 'And you brought him back to life,' he said joyfully.

The fugitives, too, were in Sherwood, walking along a path, the children taking it in turn to ride the donkey. De Talmont was supporting himself with a stick. Sarah looked at her father and urged him to rest, but he shook his head and told her they must keep going.

'Why do they hate us?' asked Sarah, as much puzzled as hurt.

'Because it is easier to hate than to understand,' said de Talmont. 'They hate each other for the same reason. No – for the same *lack* of reason!'

'How far is it to Lincoln?' Sarah asked then, to be told that it was more than a day's journey. When she inquired where they would sleep, her father said simply, 'Under the stars. God and his angels will guard us!'

Meanwhile, Robin was feeling more himself. Watched by his friends, he was shooting at a spinning target with four aiming points on it. Much set it spinning and Robin took four arrows from his quiver in swift succession – and hit each mark.

'Witchcraft!' exclaimed Tuck, who was sitting propped against a tree. 'You'll burn in hell!'

'He's getting better!' laughed Robin, then, after a pause, 'We're going after Will!'

'What? To beg him to come back?' asked Little John, as the target was spun once again and Nasir began shooting.

'To settle things between us,' said Robin. 'Once and for all. Then what he does is up to him.'

Not far away from the outlaws' camp the de Talmont family were wending their way through the forest when they were suddenly confronted by a man who leapt from a tree. The man drew his sword and made his demand. 'Your money!' It was Will Scarlet.

'Give it to him, Sarah!' said her father in Hebrew.

'You're Jews!' exclaimed Will.

'We are,' said de Talmont quietly. 'What are you?'

'Lucky, I reckon,' replied Will.

Sarah brought a bag of silver coins from one of the packs on their donkey. Will took it, hid it in his clothing and demanded to know what else they had.

'Nothing you would want,' Sarah said angrily.

'We'll see, shall we?' Will began to search the packs.

Sarah and her father both pleaded with Will, who suddenly came on their sacred book. They implored him to let it alone, and Will shamefacedly put it back in the pack. Then he found their Menorah – their sacred candlesticks.

'No! Not that – not that!' cried Sarah desperately. She pulled her betrothal ring from her finger and held it out to Will. 'Take it!' she said, 'but leave the Menorah!'

With the children's eyes on him, Will felt shamed – and angry in a way he did not understand. 'I don't want your rings or your candlesticks,' he shouted. 'I've got what I want! Go on – be on your way!'

They stood looking at him in silence until finally Will could bear it no longer. He turned away from them and ran off into the forest. After a moment Sarah burst into tears and her father did his best to comfort her.

They continued their journey until Sarah suddenly glanced behind them. 'What is it?' asked her father.

'There's someone following us,' Sarah replied nervously.

De Talmont looked back. 'I can't see anyone,' he said.

'No, I can hear people – horsemen!' she said.

They hurried on as fast as they could, Samuel doing his best to urge the donkey on. Esther, who was riding it, looked round anxiously, and so did Sarah.

Suddenly they saw three horsemen bearing down on them, one of them leading a packhorse. There was no chance of escape. They stopped.

The riders were Gisburne and two of his men. 'Well, de Talmont,' said Gisburne as he rode up to them. 'And where do you think you're going?'

CHAPTER 11

In the Great Hall of Nottingham Castle the Sheriff was calling for Gisburne – without success.

The Captain came forward and informed him that Gisburne had gone.

'Gone?' said the Sheriff, and the Captain handed him a note that he had found in de Talmont's house.

The Sheriff read it, then asked the Captain where he had found it.

'In the house of Joshua de Talmont, my lord,' said the Captain.

The Sheriff raised his eyebrows. 'Are you telling me that de Talmont has escaped?' he asked grimly. The Captain said that he was.

'I was told otherwise,' said the Sheriff.

'Sir Guy wanted it kept from you,' the Captain told his lord.

'I can see that he would,' replied the Sheriff. 'You say that *you* found this?'

'Yes, my lord.'

'But kept it from Sir Guy?'

'I know his hand, my lord,' said the Captain.

The Sheriff looked at the note again. 'Yes, Captain, so do I!' he said, his thoughts elsewhere.

The object of his thoughts was at that moment taking Sarah some way from her father and the children, who were being guarded by Gisburne's men. Gisburne himself had just informed Sarah that he had written the note. 'Why?' Sarah asked.

'Because – it's not easy to put into words,' said Gisburne. 'But – well – you came into the castle several times with your father. You – er – must have noticed my – my interest!'

Sarah felt herself going cold as she realized what Gisburne meant. 'Your – interest?'

Gisburne assured her that in fact it was more than interest.

'I saw you looking at me, if that's what you mean,' said Sarah.

'I find myself attracted to you,' said Gisburne heavily.

'Do you,' replied Sarah. 'And did you tell the Sheriff you were interested in a Jewess?'

'I've left the Sheriff,' Gisburne announced. 'I've taken enough of his insults. Why should I go on being belittled? Why should I serve him, knowing that I'm the better man? I mean to take service with the Earl of Chester. You're coming with me. I don't mind if you're a Jewess. That can be changed when I marry you.'

Sarah gasped. 'But I'm betrothed to Aaron of Lincoln!'

'That's unimportant,' Gisburne told the startled girl. 'It can be dealt with.'

'The way you dealt with my people in Nottingham?'

'That was a riot –'

'Which you knew was going to happen, didn't you?' said Sarah accusingly. Gisburne did not answer.

'You must have done,' Sarah continued, 'because you warned us. Why didn't you warn the others?'

'That wasn't part of the plan,' explained Gisburne, as always totally insensitive. 'Besides, there was nothing I could do. I was only obeying orders.'

'But you didn't. You decided who should die and who should live. You. *You* decided!'

'But I saved you – and your family,' exclaimed Gisburne. 'Don't you understand?'

'I understand,' said Sarah icily. 'Now listen to me. Everything about you disgusts me – your cruelty, your arrogance, your ignorance, your deceit. How could you think I would marry you – with my people's blood on your hands? To be your wife – to renounce everything I believe in! I despise you! I *loathe* you. I'd rather die than have anything to do with you!'

'You're hysterical,' said Gisburne. 'It's been an ordeal, but I know you need a man to match your spirit.' Then he forced her to kiss him as she struggled to escape his embraces.

Her father tried to go to her, but Gisburne's men held him back. 'Do you want your family dead?' he asked her, and she shook her head and began to weep.

'Where are you taking her?' called her desperate father, as she was led to Gisburne's horse.

'She's to be mine, de Talmont,' Gisburne told him.

'You cannot do this. It is forbidden!' called de Talmont, but his guard pushed him to the ground. Esther ran to her father, and young Samuel raced towards Gisburne, now on his horse, and beat his fists against Gisburne's leg. Gisburne kicked him to the ground and rode away, with Sarah trapped in front of him and with de Talmont running vainly after them in a frenzy of grief. He kept on running until a pain shot through him and he tumbled unconscious down a bank.

Samuel and Esther had been told to wait by their father, but were now bewildered, frightened and uncertain what to do.

'We must wait here,' said Esther. 'He'll come back. I know he will! Oh, Sarah! Sarah!' And she burst into tears.

'Don't cry,' said Samuel, trying to comfort her. 'We must be brave. Like Daniel in the lions' den!' They started to pray. Then Samuel heard a noise and ran to see what was making it. The shadowy forms of the outlaws appeared in the trees and he raced back to his sister. 'We must hide quickly,' he said.

The outlaws had heard a sound ahead of them and Robin halted the party.

'What is it?' said Marion

'Voices, coming from over there,' said Robin, pointing at the trees. The outlaws were very much on their guard.

Suddenly they saw the donkey standing on the edge of the path. There was no one to be seen, but Nasir spotted some footprints. 'Horsemen. Two. Maybe three,' he said.

Marion heard another faint sound and went towards it. There, crouching down and peering through the leaves, were Esther and Samuel.

'It's all right. I won't hurt you,' said Marion with a smile, and the others came across to look. 'Poor little devils,' said Little John.

'We're your friends. We want to help,' Marion told the children. Nasir said they were Jews and Robin asked if they could speak English. When he found that they could, he asked them where their mother was.

'Mother is dead,' said Esther.

'And your father?' asked Marion.

'He's looking for – the man who – who took Sarah. She's our sister.'

Marion tried to comfort Esther. 'Stay here with them,' Robin ordered Marion, Tuck and Much, then turned to Little John and Nasir. 'We're going hunting,' he said grimly.

They came upon de Talmont first, lying at the bottom of the steep slope down which he had fallen. After Little John had checked that he was alive, Robin told him to get the injured man back to the others.

Gisburne, Sarah and the two soldiers were still moving fast through the forest. Unbeknown to them, one of the outlaws saw them pass by. It was Will Scarlet . . .

Some way on Gisburne's horse went lame, and he called a halt and dismounted. He ordered Sarah to get down. She did so and stood silently.

'What's the matter with you?' Gisburne asked her, coming close to her. 'Listen. Your old life is over. I can give you everything you want. Don't you understand?'

'I'll kill myself before I marry you,' Sarah vowed.

'Don't be stupid!' Gisburne rasped. 'We'll rest. We've a long journey ahead.'

After seeing Gisburne, Will headed on through the forest, just off the path along which Gisburne had ridden. Robin and Nasir heard a sound in the trees and Nasir shot an arrow into them. Seconds later Will appeared, shouting: 'You could have killed me!'

There was a long pause as Robin and Will stared hard at each other; then Will asked, 'Are you after Gisburne?' Seeing

Robin look surprised, he said: 'He's got the Jew-girl! Come on!'

Others, too, were after Gisburne that day, for the Sheriff, the Captain and their men were riding through Sherwood. The wretched Guy of Gisburne was in serious trouble.

Robin, Will and Nasir reached him first, spreading out and slowing closing in just as Sarah was warning her hated suitor that her father would certainly appeal to the King.

'Let him!' said her would-be lover scornfully. 'All Jews belong to the King. You're his property. I'll buy you!'

There was a roar of 'Gisburne!' and he turned to see Robin walking towards him, flanked by Nasir and Scarlet. Gisburne and his men drew their swords.

'I want the girl, Gisburne!' said Robin.

'She's mine, wolf's-head!' cried his old enemy. Then Robin and his two men drew their swords and charged their three adversaries.

It was a vicious fight at close quarters, watched by a terrified Sarah, and it ended with both Gisburne's men dead and with Robin's sword at Gisburne's throat. Meanwhile, Nasir walked over to Sarah, bowed to her, and greeted her with the Hebrew words, 'Shalom Alecheim.'

'We were looking for you,' said Robin to Will.

'You found me, didn't you?' replied Will tensely, as Robin finished tying Gisburne's hands behind his back. Will now crossed to Sarah and returned the money bag he had taken from her.

'You robbed them?' Robin asked.

'Yes, well – I've been wrong about other things, haven't I?' said Will with a rueful grin. 'Not that you're always right – 'cos you ain't. But – well, you brought us all together and – well – you're the one to lead us – that's all!'

The black days were over . . .

Elsewhere in the forest things seemed to be improving, too. De Talmont was able to sit up and watch Little John, who had Samuel on his shoulders and was holding Esther's hand.

'He knows every tree in Sherwood, does Robin,' said the big man to Samuel. 'He'll find 'em, you'll see!'

As he spoke, the Captain and his men were preparing to attack, watched by the Sheriff and his horsemen. The soldiers, armed with crossbows, ran forward. Little John lowered Samuel to the ground and Much and Marion sprang to their feet, but there was nothing they could do. The row of crossbowmen faced them and behind the bowmen were the mounted soldiers.

There was a moment's silence, then the Sheriff cantered forward. 'I can't approve of your company, de Talmont,' he said. 'Though there's not much to choose between outlaws and outcasts, is there? *Don't move!*'

He looked around, a smug expression on his face. 'Where's Gisburne?' he asked.

'He – he took my daughter,' stammered de Talmont.

'Yes, I thought that must be it,' mused the Sheriff. 'He's very susceptible. Where's the King of Sherwood?'

There was no answer and the Sheriff pointed at Samuel. 'Captain!' he ordered, and the Captain raised his crossbow and aimed it at the boy.

Marion rushed in front of Samuel and cried, 'He's hunting Gisburne.'

'How ironic!' said the Sheriff with a harsh laugh. 'So am I! But I seem to have done better than I hoped.'

'How did you find us?' asked de Talmont wearily.

'We found your servant,' the Sheriff answered. 'And after ... a little persuasion, she told us that you were heading for Lincoln. Keeping off the roads, of course.'

Robin and the outlaws with him were approaching the spot where the Sheriff and his prisoners were. They were unaware of any danger, but suddenly Robin halted. 'Down!' he ordered.

Will pushed Gisburne roughly to the ground and Nasir pulled Sarah down beside him. 'What is it?' asked Will.

Robin peered ahead. He could just see two crossbowmen

menacing the outlaws and de Talmont. He inched his way forward.

Will put his mouth to Gisburne's ear. 'Make one sound, Gisburne,' he whispered, 'and I'll cut your throat.' Robin watched for a moment longer, then came carefully back.

He crawled to Will and Gisburne and whispered: 'The Sheriff! He's got them all.'

Will got to his feet, but Robin pulled him down. 'We can't!' he hissed.

The Sheriff had just noticed the donkey and the packs it carried, and ordered the Captain to search them. He went to the packs and began emptying them, scattering everything on the ground. He found the Menorah and held it up for the Sheriff to inspect, while de Talmont groaned miserably. 'What beautiful workmanship, de Talmont,' he said. 'Must be priceless, I imagine.' De Talmont said nothing.

'Any other treasures?' asked the Sheriff, and the Captain produced the book. 'Let me see it,' ordered the Sheriff.

'I warn you –' de Talmont started to say, but the Sheriff swung round on him. 'Warn me?' he laughed.

'What's this?' he went on. 'A book of spells? How to turn lead into gold, perhaps?'

'Do not open it,' ordered de Talmont in a voice of sudden thunder.

'How absurd!' said the Sheriff, mockingly.

He crossed to where the Captain stood uncertainly, and took the book from him. '*No!*' commanded de Talmont.

The Sheriff took no notice and slowly opened the book. He stared at it intently and his expression began to change. A strange sound filled the air building in intensity until it reached a deafening peak. Then it suddenly stopped.

The book fell from the Sheriff's nerveless hands and he stood trembling until the whole of his body shook with fear. His face twitched, his eyes stared wildly, and terror seemed to seize every part of him. Suddenly he clapped his hands to his face and started to scream.

'No no no no no no no no!' he cried. 'Keep away! Keep

away from me!' he shouted. 'The serpents! See how they curl like smoke! Thicker! Thicker!'

The Captain ran forward and the Sheriff drew his sword. The men-at-arms stared at the Sheriff, lowering their weapons and looking at each other. They were completely unnerved.

'He's bewitched!' said Robin in awe. With Will and Nasir he moved forward, all drawing their swords. The Sheriff started to retreat, jabbing the air with his sword. 'There! There! There!' he cried.

The Captain attempted to take the Sheriff's sword from him, while Little John grabbed his quarterstaff and laid about the soldiers with it. Much got his sling into action, and several soldiers became so demoralized that they hurled down their weapons and fled. Nasir shot down another soldier who was levelling his crossbow at Marion, and Robin swung the Captain round and knocked him out. Meanwhile, Will pulled one of the mounted soldiers from his horse. And all the while the Sheriff continued to rant and rave.

'They mean to bury me alive!' he cried. 'My hands are rotting. Look! See! See the leeches – the leeches! They're plotting against me, pulling me down! Dragging me under the slime! I can't breathe! Fingers – fingers at my throat! The dead are coming from their graves!'

He collapsed on his knees, howling like a dog. 'Get them away from me!' he screeched. 'The breath – the stinking, stinking breath! They'll come for me when I'm asleep and the daggers will *stab – stab – stab – stab! Ahhh!*' And he collapsed in a heap.

By now the outlaws were in charge; Marion, Tuck and Much collected the fallen crossbows while Will and Nasir kept an eye on what was left of the terrified opposition. Robin walked over to the Sheriff, lifted his head and slapped him hard across the face. The Sheriff stared back at him, his eyes dead.

After some moments he scrambled unsteadily to his feet and looked blankly around him. Everyone stared back at him.

'Sheriff,' said Robin. 'Do you know me?'

The Sheriff nodded his head vaguely.

'Will,' said Robin, and Scarlet brought Gisburne forward. The Sheriff looked at his subordinate with loathing. 'Tie the Sheriff up,' Robin ordered Little John, and moments later he and Gisburne stood beside each other, each with their arms tied tightly behind their backs.

'Are you going to hang us?' asked Gisburne in a flat voice.

'You haven't been judged,' Robin said sharply. 'Who accuses these men?'

Sarah stepped forward. 'I accuse them!' she said fiercely. 'They plotted to kill my father – to kill all of us. The murdered the Jews in Nottingham! An eye for an eye and a tooth for a tooth! They must die!'

De Talmont got slowly to his feet and came forward with great dignity. 'And I say let them live!' he said solemnly.

Everyone was startled by his words, and Sarah said: 'Father!'

De Talmont looked at her lovingly. 'The most beautiful thing anyone can do, Sarah, is to forgive,' he said with a smile. 'It is also the sweetest form of revenge.'

Robin looked at Will Scarlet and then turned to the Sheriff. 'You've been sentenced,' he said. 'On your way!'

The defeated soldiers and their dejected leaders moved off down the road towards Nottingham.

Robin looked round at the reunited family. 'You'll be our guests until you are ready to leave for Lincoln,' he told them. 'Nasir will take you there.'

Much went to where the book lay on the ground and gingerly picked it up. He carried it to de Talmont.

'Sir,' he asked him, 'what did he see in this book that drove him mad?'

'His own wickedness,' said Joshua de Talmont.

CHAPTER 12

Little John shifted his weight uncomfortably and leaned back against the cold, dank wall of the dungeon. His eyes were gradually becoming accustomed to the gloom, but the stench of the place still stung sharp in his nostrils. All around him the vague shapes of his fellow prisoners moved and muttered to themselves, while an occasional scuffling, scampering sound reminded him that the dungeon held more than just its human prisoners. John stared into the darkness and cursed the twist of fate that had led him to be captured alone and weaponless on the edge of Sherwood. Not that the Sheriff's men had had it all their way, though. He grinned at the remembrance of the satisfying blows which had laid out two men-at-arms before he was overpowered. There would be several sore heads being nursed in Nottingham Castle tonight! But how was he to escape? His mind raced through many improbable schemes before sinking back into despair.

Suddenly, a scraping noise came from above, accompanied by loud cursing, and the dungeon grille was thrown back. A youth, tall, tough and cheery, tumbled into the dungeon to a chorus of roars of laughter from the guards. The new prisoner sprang to his feet and yelled back up at his captors.

'Hey you! This floor hasn't been swept for weeks!' The grille slammed shut and he roared, 'I'm talking to you, you ugly swine!'

An old prisoner shuffled forward, carrying a rat. 'Say hullo to Arthur,' he said.

'What's your name?' Little John asked the newcomer, ignoring the old man.

'What's yours?' asked the young man cockily, and seemed impressed when Little John told him.

'You'll never get out of here,' croaked the old man to no one in particular.

'You're with Robin Hood,' the young man said. 'You're an outlaw.'

'Feet first – it's the only way!' mumbled the old prisoner conversationally.

'My name's Mark,' the newcomer announced. 'I didn't think they'd ever catch any of you.'

'Arthur knows – don't you, Arthur?' said the old man to his talented rodent.

'What are you in here for?' Little John asked Mark, who confessed to being caught carrying a bow. 'A poacher, eh?' said John.

'Poacher, peddler, sailor – I've been a lot of things in my time,' Mark told him. 'What'll they do to you?'

'Hang me – when they've finished,' said Little John with a bitter laugh, and the old prisoner intoned: 'Only way out of here!'

'Gisburne wants the lot of us,' Little John explained, 'and all the people who help us.'

'Think Robin will try to get you out?' Mark asked.

'I know he will,' said Little John quietly, 'that's the trouble.'

When the news of Little John's capture reached Sherwood Forest, the outlaws immediately sprang into action. Weapons were checked, new strings fitted to bows and runners sent to nearby villages, gathering information. At the centre of this bustling activity Robin stood thinking furiously, trying to work out a plan of attack.

'We'll go to Nottingham tomorrow,' said Robin.

'Why not tonight, Robin?' asked Marion.

'Gisburne knows we'll try for John,' Robin explained. 'He'll expect us at night. He'll mount extra patrols, double the guard. It's market day tomorrow. The town'll be full of people. It gives us more of a chance.'

As the details of the rescue were thrashed out, Robin's

thoughts fled back to his strange encounter with Herne that morning. He had found Herne huddled over a fire at the back of his secret cave, shivering uncontrollably, even though the day was already quite warm. At Robin's gentle touch, Herne had sprung round, snarling like a cornered animal, and Robin had realized that he was in the grip of a trance. As he watched and waited, Herne's eyes had closed, while a strange muttering came from deep within his throat, only rarely bursting through as coherent speech.

'Herne,' said Robin softly.

His voice had seemed to penetrate the mists of the trance and Robin could see that his master was struggling to regain the power of speech.

'From the Devil they came,' groaned Herne, 'and to the Devil they will return . . . The lion!' His voice cracked as he shouted again. 'The lion!'

'The lion?' Robin had asked, as Herne's voice died away once more. 'Do you mean the King?'

'He falls . . . dies!' breathed Herne.

Suddenly, the shuddering had returned and Herne had gripped Robin's arm fiercely.

'Lackland!' he had hissed. 'Some call him Softswood. He comes!'

'Prince John!' breathed Robin.

'A prisoner from the dead – a prisoner,' Herne continued. 'Once close to you. Save him!'

He began twitching uncontrollably and Robin had tried to calm him, without much success. 'Who is this prisoner?' he had asked. '*Who is he?*'

But the power of Herne's trance was already on the wane and Robin had got nothing more from him. He had wrapped his master in furs and waited patiently until the last traces of the trance had left him before returning to the camp. Now, of course, it seemed only too obvious that Herne's vision had been a warning about Little John's capture. And Robin threw himself into the plans for a rescue that would be both spectacular and effective.

*

Gisburne, too, was plotting. The capture of Little John was a real feather in his cap, but the defeat of Robin and his annoying band of outlaws would undoubtedly make him famous. Barely suppressing his excitement, he gleefully began to dictate a message to the monk at his side, who sat scratching noisily with a pen.

'Guy of Gisburne to Robert de Rainault, High Sheriff of Nottingham, greetings!' Gisburne proclaimed, relishing the sound of his own voice. 'Know that this day, John Little of Hathersage, called by others Little John –'

A servant appeared and Gisburne rounded on him, angry at being interrupted. 'What is it, man?' he asked.

Before the servant could answer, Peter de Leon, Seneschal to Prince John, came into the hall. Young, smooth and charming, he was every inch a courtier, though he had an arrogance which irritated Gisburne immensely.

'My master is at Newark,' de Leon announced, 'and commands that you prepare for his arrival here tomorrow.'

'Prince John?' said Gisburne, raising his eyebrows. 'But I thought –' He stopped.

'That he was with his brother the King in Normandy?' asked de Leon, and Gisburne nodded.

'But the High Sheriff's at Westminster,' said Gisburne.

'Aren't you acting for him?' asked de Leon.

'Yes, but I'm a soldier, not a courtier,' said Gisburne, 'and I've no –'

'The Prince is also a soldier,' de Leon cut in.

'Yes, I know,' Gisburne said, 'but – don't misunderstand me – I'm honoured to receive him. It's just that all the details of – of – you know!'

'That's why he sent me,' explained de Leon. 'Although I'm sure you'd manage perfectly well on your own.'

'Exactly,' said Gisburne. 'It's the personal things. What he eats, for example.'

De Leon assured him that the King's cook travelled everywhere with him, that he prepared every dish – and tasted it first! 'Of course,' said Gisburne. 'Er – does the Prince like music?'

'Not particularly,' de Leon told him. 'He has other diversions – but they'll be coming with him!'

'Why is he visiting Nottingham?' asked Gisburne.

'I expect he'll tell you that,' said the youthful courtier, 'and if he doesn't, don't ask. Oh – he has a bath every two days.'

Gisburne was staggered by the news. 'Whatever for?' he asked, and was told that it was his custom.

'How extraordinary!' mused Gisburne.

'He's an extraordinary man,' de Leon said, with a kind of sarcasm in his voice. 'By the way, if he – how shall I put it? – if he becomes irritated, then leave him!'

'Leave him?' said Gisburne.

'Immediately,' he was told. 'Simply bow and go!'

'But why?' asked Gisburne and de Leon smiled. 'It's safer,' he said meaningly.

Peter de Leon had done what he came to do and, escorted by Gisburne, went down to the courtyard and mounted his horse.

'One final thing, Sir Guy,' he said. 'The castle walls.'

'The walls?' repeated Gisburne.

'Parts appear to be crumbling away,' explained de Leon. 'It would be politic to begin repairing them before Prince John arrives. He tends to notice things like that. I'll see you tomorrow then!' And he rode out of the castle.

Gisburne stood staring indecisively for a moment before turning to where the Captain was crossing the courtyard. 'Captain!' he shouted.

Unnerved by this turn of events and furious that his plans for trapping Robin would have to be postponed, Gisburne stood staring indecisively after the royal Seneschal for a moment. Then he snapped into action and issued a rapid list of instructions for the repair of the walls, riding roughshod over his Captain's complaints.

'Use the servants! Use the prisoners! Use every man, woman and child in the castle! I don't care how you do it – just get it done!' he roared.

By the following morning the courtyard was in chaos. Carts

were drawn up laden with stone, scaffolding was being hastily erected by workmen, the prisoners were lined up under heavy guard, ready to leave for a nearby quarry, and there was an overwhelming air of panic. The work on the walls had begun but it was painfully slow, and even Gisburne was forced to realize that it would never be completed in time.

Pandemonium broke out as the news reached the castle that Prince John's procession was in sight. Things weren't helped by a string of contradictory orders from Gisburne, who was still desperately trying to clear the courtyard as de Leon rode in. Behind him was Prince John, whose way was almost blocked by wagons and workmen. He and his nobles looked round in astonishment.

Prince John's servants started unloading his throne, his bath, his chest and baskets of clothes, while a group of men-at-arms brought a hooded prisoner from one of the wagons.

Prince John whispered to de Leon, who gave orders to the men-at-arms. 'Take him to the west tower!' Meanwhile the Prince looked round the courtyard, cold with anger at the obvious inefficiency of the deputy Sheriff.

He dismounted and went into the castle, watched curiously by the line of chained prisoners. 'Who was that?' asked Little John, and was rewarded by a stinging blow across his shoulders from the Captain's whip. 'That was Prince John, you villain!' the Captain told him, and ordered his men to herd the prisoners towards the gate-house.

Inside the Great Hall, Gisburne was squirming with embarrassment at having been caught so unprepared for his royal visitor. However, Prince John, an impressive figure despite his lack of inches, affected not to have noticed and summoned Gisburne to his side. 'I have a prisoner with me. No one must speak to him. Yes?'

'I understand, my lord,' said Gisburne solemnly.

'Aren't you curious?' asked John.

'My lord?' answered Gisburne, not sure how to take this. Prince John inclined his head and whispered the prisoner's identity in Gisburne's ear. Gisburne recoiled, astonished.

'But he's dead . . .' he began.

The Prince cut in swiftly. 'The guards will admit no one to see him, except me. Understood?' With a slight wave of the hand he dismissed Gisburne.

Gisburne rose, backed down the steps and knelt again at the very moment that John gestured everyone to rise. The wretched Gisburne was stranded on his knees and staggered to his feet as he realized his predicament.

'You're a fool, Gisburne,' Prince John announced, and left with de Leon. As he passed the ranks of servants, he noticed a very pretty maid and stopped in the doorway to whisper to de Leon before going out. De Leon beckoned the girl, who nervously came over to him. Then they left the hall.

Everyone started chattering except Gisburne, who stood brooding at the prospect of having the Prince in Nottingham for any length of time.

While Prince John was making his presence felt at Nottingham Castle, the prisoners were entering Sedgeham Quarry, not far away. Several small boys were playing there, and one of them recognized Little John as he marched along chained to Mark. With a word to his friends, he raced off to the forest and soon arrived breathless at the outlaws' camp. He was just in time, as Robin's original plan was about to be put into action. The news that Little John was out in the open suddenly made everything simpler and the outlaws swiftly made their way out to the quarry. Skilled woodsmen, they had no trouble in surrounding the quarry unheard and unseen by the guards on lookout duty. There was a breathless moment as the outlaws waited, listening to the sounds of the forest above them and the noise of the prisoners working below, before Robin leapt to his feet, an arrow at his bowstring, and called out to the Captain of the guards.

'Lay down your weapons and release the prisoners!'

The Captain swung round in his saddle. The sun was in his eyes as he gazed at the figure on the edge of the quarry.

'Did you hear me?' shouted Robin.

'I heard you,' the Captain shouted back.

'Then release all the prisoners!'

Instead, the Captain shouted: 'Attack them!' A guard levelled his crossbow at Little John, but Mark hurled a large stone at him, which struck the guard in the chest and sent him crashing backwards, the arrow from his crossbow shooting harmlessly into the air.

'Now!' ordered Robin. Moments later, after a brief skirmish, only the Captain remained alive.

'You were warned,' Robin told him. 'Go and tell Gisburne.' The Captain turned his horse and galloped from the quarry.

The outlaws ran to Little John. 'Sometimes you're more trouble than you're worth!' laughed Robin.

'Not often!' grunted Little John with a chuckle.

Striking the chains from the prisoners' feet took time and, while the outlaws worked, Little John and Mark told Robin about the arrival of Prince John and the mystery of his masked prisoner.

Later, back at the outlaws' camp, the subject came up again. 'He must be the prisoner that Herne spoke of,' said Robin.

'But why was he masked?' asked Marion.

'It's obvious that he's no ordinary prisoner,' Robin replied. 'He's clearly to do with Prince John.'

'What's it matter to us then?' asked Will gruffly.

'Because that must be the man Herne said we were to save – not Little John,' Robin explained.

Will asked why they should save him and Tuck complained that they didn't know who he was. Robin turned to Little John.

'In the west tower?' he asked him.

'That's where they took him,' Little John said and looked at Mark for confirmation.

'Aye,' said Mark. 'He could hardly stand.'

The outlaws lapsed into silence, until Robin said angrily, 'There must be a way!'

'You're mad!' Will told him.

Silence descended for several minutes, then Mark suddenly spoke out. 'I know! I'll betray you!'

Little John spluttered out the drink that he was just about to swallow, and the rest stared at Mark as if he was demented.

'I go to Gisburne, see,' he explained, 'and tell him I'm with you. That I can lead him and his men here if he'll pay me and give me a pardon. That way I'll bring him into Sherwood while you get into the castle.'

There was another silence as the outlaws considered the scheme. Will gave his approval. 'That's not bad!'

'They wouldn't leave the castle unguarded,' Little John pointed out.

'Yes, but with Gisburne out of the way we'll have a real chance,' said Robin.

Marion looked at Mark. 'What about you?' she asked.

'I'm a poacher, don't forget. I'll bring 'em deep into the forest and then just disappear.'

'And by then we'll be out of Nottingham again,' said Will.

'With the prisoner,' Marion added.

'But what if Gisburne doesn't go for it?' asked Tuck.

'He's got to,' Mark explained. 'His name will be mud after this morning. The thought of catching all of you will be too much for him, I reckon.'

Robin agreed. 'But it's a risk for you,' he said to Mark.

'That's why I want to do it.'

'How will we know if Gisburne's taken the bait?'

'Because I'll come back and tell you,' Mark promised. 'And anything else I've learnt. Reckon I'll be back first light tomorrow. Don't any of you worry!'

'We'll be waiting,' said Robin.

In Nottingham Castle the outlaws' old enemy, Gisburne, was not at his ease. Prince John was examining his collection of jewels while speaking softly to him.

'Are you excusing what happened?' the Prince inquired silkily as he stared at the ruby he was holding up to the light. He had heard about the incident at the quarry.

Gisburne said nothing, so the Prince went on. 'I have heard of the wolf's-head, Gisburne, and of your pathetic attempts to catch him.'

'But my lord!' protested Gisburne eagerly, 'I shall catch him. Even now –'

Prince John gave him a look so chilling that Gisburne's voice trailed away into a stifled gasp.

'The King pardoned him. Yes?' said John.

'He did, my lord,' Gisburne agreed. 'But Robin Hood broke faith. He tried to murder me, my lord!'

'I'm really not interested in your personal feud,' said John coldly. 'And the fact that you're de Rainault's protégé – if that's all you are – means nothing to me. But because of your incompetence you've lost prisoners from the dungeons of a royal castle.'

He paused for a moment and gestured to the Captain, who stood by Gisburne. 'He is the only survivor from the men supposed to guard them,' John continued. 'Now you may think that your position protects you from the consequences of this fiasco, but I am the King's brother and one day – who knows what I may be? So know this. I forgive nothing! And I pardon no man. *Guards!*'

Two men-at-arms came in at the double and Prince John rose and pointed at Gisburne. 'Take him away and put him in the dungeons he emptied so successfully!'

'But my lord,' cried Gisburne frantically, 'the plan – my plan! Even now there is –'

'God's teeth! Do you *dare* to speak?' screamed Prince John.

'You must listen to me, my lord!' cried Gisburne piteously.

'Out! Out! Out!' screeched Prince John hysterically, and Gisburne was dragged away. The Captain bowed and beat a hasty retreat after the men-at-arms.

In a rage, Prince John returned to his jewel box and picked over the rings, muttering to himself. His courtiers, recognizing the symptoms, kept well out of his way and prayed that the mood would pass.

Unfortunately for Abbot Hugo, who arrived in response to

an urgent summons from de Leon, the Prince was still petu-
lant several hours later and was merely toying with the
sumptuous meal prepared for him by his cooks.

'You're late, Abbot!' he snapped as the cleric reached the
High Table. Hugo started and looked around nervously for
Gisburne.

'Don't waste your time looking for the so-called deputy
Sheriff,' said the Prince with a nasty little laugh. 'I've had him
removed.'

'Removed!' said the Abbot in alarm.

'Not from this world, Abbot,' John said with a glint in his
eyes, 'though I confess I was tempted!'

The Prince's companions sniggered appreciatively as he
continued. 'Till I leave Nottingham, Gisburne's safer where
he is.' Then he glanced round the table and became very
serious.

'Now my lords, the security of this kingdom and of its
Crown has brought me from the war in Normandy. As you
know, each province of the Angevin empire has its own laws
with regard to the succession. It's a very complicated matter
– the hereditary principle has never been clearly established,
and many of the English barons are at best – undecided.
Quite frankly, I'm worried that should my brother the King
fall in battle through his own recklessness – and lately the risks
he has taken have been absurd – should he fall, I say, without
naming his successor, this country could face another civil
war. And that would split the empire!'

He turned suddenly to Abbot Hugo. 'That is why I have
sent for you, Abbot,' he said. 'The Church has great influence
over the barons. Yes?'

'It sometimes does, my lord.' Hugo was uneasy.

'Sometimes? You don't sound very convinced.'

Hugo started sweating. He felt himself being driven into a
corner.

The Prince stared hard at him. 'Then I'll convince you,'
he said with a chilly smile. He led Hugo to a small room in
the west tower of the castle. Inside at a table sat a masked
prisoner, his hands manacled.

'We could play a guessing game, couldn't we, Abbot?' suggested Prince John, but Hugo simply went on staring in horror at the masked man.

'Hugo!' the prisoner whispered.

'Who is he?' asked Hugo fearfully. '*Who is he?*'

Prince John walked round the table and placed himself behind the prisoner. He looked at Hugo keenly and said: 'Someone who will ensure that you support me in persuading certain barons that I am the rightful heir to the throne.' Then he pulled off the hood.

'By heaven!' said Abbot Hugo, staring in amazement as he realized who the prisoner was. 'Sir Richard of Leaford! But he's been dead for years!'

Fully restored to good humour by the trick he had played, the Prince led the shattered priest back to the Great Hall.

'You see, Abbot, everyone *thinks* Sir Richard died in the Crusade. But he didn't. He was merely wounded and kept prisoner for years. When he was finally released and returned to these shores, I had him arrested before he could contact his family or any of his other disloyal friends. He's been my prisoner ever since.' His face drew closer to Hugo's. 'But now *you* are going to help *me* use *him* against his friends. Aren't you?' he said nastily. 'There's David, Earl of Huntingdon,' the Prince continued, 'the Earls of Derby and Warwick – and William de Mowbray. They're the main dissidents. None of them likes me and they've all got an eye on the main chance. You will enlighten them, won't you, Abbot? Yes!' And he took him by the hand.

'Yes, my lord,' said the Abbot quietly. 'I will.'

'Good!' said John, taking a fine ring from the Abbot's finger and putting it on his own.

A Captain came up to the table and whispered something to de Leon. Then he came over to John.

'One of the escaped prisoners has returned, my lord,' he said, indicating where Mark stood under guard. 'He wants to see Sir Guy.'

'Then he shall,' smiled the Prince. 'Take him to the dungeon!'

Protesting furiously, the hapless Mark was bundled across the courtyard and thrown unceremoniously into the black pit of the dungeon again.

'I must see Sir Guy!' he screamed, as the grille slammed shut. 'Let me see Sir Guy! It's a matter of life or death!' The guards merely laughed coarsely and spat, before sauntering casually away.

Raging with frustration Mark turned on his heel, his eyes glittering with fury, only to be brought up short by the sight of the prisoner at the far end of the dungeon.

'Sir Guy! What in heaven . . .'

'Never mind that,' snapped Gisburne. 'Why are you in here? What did you learn? God's blood, Henry, can't you do anything right?'

Shocked by the use of his real name, Mark could only stammer a reply.

'It . . . it's all gone wrong!' he moaned.

'Stop snivelling!' roared Gisburne. 'Tell me what happened! Did you learn anything from Little John?'

'No, my lord – nothing!' said Mark. 'But I saved his life when Robin Hood rescued us and they've let me join them.'

'Have they now?' mused Gisburne.

'If you'd been free we could have caught them all,' Mark told him. 'I wasn't expecting this.'

'Then blame Prince John,' Gisburne said bitterly. 'When the mood takes him he'll listen to no one.'

'He'll wish he had,' Mark said with a frown.

'What do you mean?' asked Gisburne.

'They're planning to get his prisoner.'

'They know who he is?' asked Gisburne.

'No, my lord.'

'They must,' muttered Gisburne. 'Now listen, Henry, if they come for him, they'll come for you as well. You're one of them now!'

Mark nodded.

'Now then – if they succeed, with me powerless down here –

go with them, wait your chance and when you can – silence him!'

Mark looked puzzled.

'Do you want to be rich?' Gisburne asked him. 'Do you want power, Henry? Prince John will reward us both. The one thing he can't afford is to let that man reach King Richard in Normandy!'

CHAPTER 13

In the cold light of the misty dawn, the Abbot Hugo and his monks left Nottingham Castle to return to their home at St Mary's Monastery. Burdened by his thoughts, Hugo barely noticed his surroundings as the cart which carried him jolted its way along the road through Sherwood Forest. The implications of Prince John's secret ambitions lay heavy on his soul and he groaned as he realized that he would have no option but to obey.

As the procession reached the ford, two lithe figures dropped from a tree and called for the Abbot to halt. Hugo's blood boiled as he recognized Robin and Marion.

'You villain!' roared Hugo. 'Have you no respect for the Church?'

'Not while you're in it!' laughed Robin.

'Break your journey, Abbot Hugo,' suggested Marion.

The rest of the outlaws seemed to Hugo to appear from nowhere. 'Game pie? Jugged hare? Venison?' asked Tuck.

'And then I pay through the nose for it,' grunted the Abbot.

'Why not?' asked Much. 'You've got the right nose for it.'

'You'll all burn in hell!' proclaimed the Abbot.

Later, the Abbot sat uncomfortably on a log while venison was being cooked over a simple spit, turned by Much. All the outlaws were gathered around the spit except Nasir, who was keeping watch.

'Aren't you going to bless the meat?' Robin asked Hugo.

'Listen to me, wolf's-head,' erupted Hugo. 'When Prince John learns that I'm your prisoner –'

'It'll be too late,' cut in Will Scarlet.

Hugo went white. 'Too late?'

'That's what I said.' Will leered at him.

Will looked as if he was about to attack the Abbot, who shouted fearfully to Robin, 'Keep him away from me!' The outlaws guffawed.

'We've got some questions for you, Hugo,' he said, 'and when we get the answers we'll tell Gisburne we've got you. We'll shoot a message over the castle wall.'

'It won't get to Gisburne,' said Hugo with contempt. 'Not while he's –' He stopped, mentally kicking himself.

'Not while he's what, Hugo?' said Robin. 'What's happened to him?'

As Hugo remained silent, Will decided a little encouragement was needed. He drew his dagger and bent close to the Abbot. 'What's happened to Gisburne?' he asked menacingly, and when there was no answer, he spat out: 'I'll give you one more chance. *What happened to Gisburne?*'

'He's been dismissed,' Hugo screeched fearfully.

There was total silence as the outlaws tried to take in the Abbot's statement. Then Will asked: 'Where is he then? I said, *where is he?*'

'*In the dungeons!*' howled Hugo, quaking with fear. 'He is! He is!' he went on, as Scarlet menaced him with his dagger, then withdrew it with a harsh laugh.

'It's too good to be true,' exclaimed Little John.

Marion decided that Prince John had done the amazing deed because he didn't trust anyone.

'But why lock Gisburne up?' asked a bemused Will.

'Because of what happened at the quarry, perhaps,' said Robin. He turned back to Hugo. 'Prince John has another prisoner, too, hasn't he?' he asked.

Abbot Hugo stared hard at him. Did this wretch know everything?

'Who is he?' Robin asked sharply, but the Abbot claimed he knew nothing of a prisoner.

'I've seen him,' Little John announced. 'Don't lie, Abbot – that's a sin.'

'Did Prince John send for you?' Robin asked. 'Was it to show you his prisoner?'

Abbot Hugo's eyes gave him away.

'That's it,' said Marion. 'Why, Abbot? What exactly does he mean to you?'

'And why do they hide his face?' asked Robin.

'Leave him to me!' grinned Will, winking at Robin and drawing his dagger. 'All right, Abbot, now I'll ask you a straight question. Which ear's your favourite, the right or the left?'

'Keep away, you villain!' rasped Hugo hoarsely, his voice strained from tension and from shouting.

'Don't you call me a villain, you swivel-eyed old hypocrite,' said Will with an evil glint in his eyes. 'Hold him, John!' And as John did so Will asked once again, 'Who's the prisoner?' Then, as Hugo screamed, Will grabbed his ear and prepared to slice it from his head. *'Who is it?'* he shouted for the last time before using the dagger.

Abbot Hugo looked at Marion and moaned. 'Her father! Her father! Sir Richard of Leaford!'

That night Robin galloped towards Nottingham Castle in the uniform of one of Abbot Hugo's guards. It was a dark, moonless night and the sound of the horse's hooves echoed the pounding of his heart. As he sped along his mind raced over the incredible story Abbot Hugo had revealed. Poor Marion was distraught at the thought that her father might be alive after all, yet in danger. To a man, the outlaws had thrown themselves into this daring plan to free him.

When Robin reached the castle gate with his horse badly lathered, he tumbled off and collapsed at the feet of the guards on duty.

John was drinking in the Hall with his companions when Robin was brought in, filthy, and with blood on his face and neck. He appeared to have survived a desperate fight.

'It's one of Abbot Hugo's guards, my lord,' said de Leon.

'What happened?' asked the Prince, looking irritated.

'He's been ambushed by Robin Hood and the Abbot's his

prisoner,' said de Leon, after listening to Robin's mumbled account of what had happened in the forest.

As Robin swayed and almost collapsed, Prince John exploded in a fury. 'God's teeth!' he screamed. 'I've heard of nothing but Robin Hood ever since I came to Nottingham.'

Everyone tried to keep out of his way as he raged on.

'What's wrong with everyone in this miserable county?' he asked bitterly. 'Are they all sheep? *De Leon!*'

De Leon, who had been edging away from his furious master, stopped dead in his tracks. 'My lord?' he inquired.

'Hunt him down!' shouted Prince John wildly.

'But – but, my lord?' asked the nervous de Leon.

'You're beginning to sound like Gisburne!' sneered John. 'Do you want to join him?'

'No, my lord,' whispered de Leon, 'but at night, my lord!'

'Yes, at night, de Leon,' rasped the Prince, 'when they least expect you. Show me some spirit! Prove yourself! Catch him or kill him! *Kill them all!*'

De Leon bowed deeply to him and Prince John, his rage spent for the moment, leant over a chair trying to recover himself. De Leon hurried to Robin, who lay slumped on the floor. 'Where was the ambush?' he asked crisply.

Robin looked up at him and mumbled, 'Close by Dark Mere.'

De Leon swung round on the Captain and asked if he knew the place. The Captain nodded and de Leon snapped: 'Get your men ready.' Then he told a couple of monks to see to Robin's wounds.

De Leon bowed to John and followed the Captain out of the hall at the double. The monks half carried Robin out with them. Suddenly Prince John's rage returned and he screamed hysterically: 'Don't fail me, de Leon!'

Soon the war party was streaming through the gateway of the castle, watched from cover by Will Scarlet, Nasir and Little John.

Swiftly, silently, the outlaws shinned up the scaffolding on the outer wall and despatched the remaining, unsuspecting guards. In moments they were over the dungeon grille in the courtyard, peering down into the blackness below.

'Are you there, Mark?' Little John called.

Mark gestured to Gisburne to remain silent and stepped forward into the light that came down from above.

'Little John?' called Mark, his voice sounding very excited.

'Is that Gisburne down there?' asked Little John.

'Yes,' said Mark.

'Lay him out!' ordered Little John.

The ladder descended. 'Come on, lad! Come on!' urged Little John, and Mark swiftly climbed up it apparently having flattened Gisburne.

In the west tower, Robin was also busy. He kicked open the door of the room that held Marion's father, catching the two guards by surprise. He killed one and disabled the other before turning to Sir Richard. The knight had risen to his feet, his face gaunt with suffering.

'Who are you?' asked the knight.

'A friend,' said Robin simply, and led him out of the room.

Tuck was waiting in the forest with horses, and the outlaws were soon speeding towards their camp. There was a touching reunion between Marion and her father, watched by Abbot Hugo and the other captives, as well as by the outlaws.

'Don't cry!' said Sir Richard huskily, wiping the tears from her cheeks. 'I could never bear to see you cry!'

'I thought you were dead!' sobbed Marion.

'There were times when I was certain I was dead,' said her father, embracing her. 'And you were nothing more than a dream, and so was England.' He looked round at the outlaws. 'These serfs of yours fought like lions,' he said.

'Father, they –' Marion started to say, but Sir Richard interrupted her.

'You must free them, Marion,' he told her. 'They deserve it. All of them – even the Saracen.' He stared keenly at Nasir.

'John was more cruel than any Saracen,' he went on. 'I knew too much about his treachery to the King.'

He then went towards Abbot Hugo. 'Another traitor!' he said. 'You robbed my daughter of her inheritance.'

'I made her my ward,' pleaded Hugo.

'Yes, that was clever of you,' Sir Richard admitted. 'Put her in a nunnery and took my lands. And now you'll do anything to keep them, won't you? Even help John get the Crown.'

He turned away in contempt and once more addressed Marion. 'They told me you were living with outlaws – that you were married to one of them! Is that true?' he asked.

Marion paused for a moment, then went to him and knelt, taking his hands in hers. 'Father, it is true,' she said simply.

There was a long moment of silence; then Robin came and knelt beside her. Sir Richard stared at him.

'A fine son-in-law, Sir Richard!' Hugo called sarcastically. 'Son-out-of-law, more like. The bloody-handed Robin Hood.'

Sir Richard stared keenly at Robin. 'But you're not a cruel man,' he said. 'Your eyes are kind. You saved me. You take no pleasure in killing. Who are you?'

'The son of Ailric – of Locksley,' said Robin. 'Murdered by his brother.' He pointed at Hugo.

'I knew Ailric,' Sir Richard said. 'He was a rebel, too.' He turned to Marion. 'And you – even when you were little – were always a tiresome child.' He looked at them both and sighed. 'What can I do but give you my blessing?' he said.

Marion kissed him as the outlaws gathered round the happy pair.

Later that morning, Sir Richard asked for a fresh horse. Intrigued, Abbot Hugo wandered over to watch his preparations.

'How long am I to be kept here?' asked Hugo crossly.

'Until Sir Richard's safe in Normandy,' Robin told him.

'You're not going to the King?' asked the terrified Hugo.

'Yes, Hugo, I'm going to him,' said Sir Richard coldly. 'I'm going to lay Prince John's treachery before him and demand the return of my lands.'

Little John patted Hugo on the head. 'Don't worry,' he said kindly. 'We'll look after you.'

'Like you was gold!' sneered Will Scarlet.

'With any luck he will be,' Tuck said. 'If they pay the ransom.'

'I'll play to you,' Much promised the quivering Abbot.

'You won't want to leave in the end,' Tuck prophesied.

Abbot Hugo looked at his tormentors. 'One day,' he threatened, 'one day – I'll –'

Tuck came right up to him and shook his finger at him. 'Now you don't want to be nasty after all that venison,' he said.

Robin had been thinking. 'Someone must go to France with Sir Richard,' he said.

'I'm no sailor, Robin,' said Little John.

'None of us is,' Robin replied.

'He is,' said Little John, pointing to Mark.

Mark, looking suitably eager, said he would willingly go. 'You can't leave Marion and they'd kill Nasir. It's got to be me. Anyhow, I owe it you!'

Robin strode over to him and clasped his hand, while Tuck blessed him – and told him to watch out for Prince John! Then they all rode off, leaving Will and Much guarding the Abbot.

Hugo sat down glumly and watched while Much played a tune on his pipe. 'Tell me,' said the downcast prelate to Will after a while, 'when was Henry outlawed?'

'Who?' asked Will.

'Henry of Skipton,' said Hugo. 'When was he outlawed?'

Will became very alert. He looked quickly at Little John, then stared at Hugo. 'Do you mean Mark?' he asked in alarm.

'Is that what he calls himself now?' said Hugo. 'It was Henry, when he worked for me.'

'He worked for you?' said Will, his heart skipping a beat, and he leapt to his feet. 'Some poacher! He's tricked us all! Much – you get after them. Head for Fairlight Cove.'

Much jumped up, ran to a horse and was soon galloping out of the clearing.

The evening sun was glinting on the water of a rocky inlet

as Robin rode up a path to where the others were waiting for him. Behind him was a boat with a large square sail.

He came to Sir Richard's side. 'The captain will take you,' he said, 'but we'll have to wait for the tide.'

Robin and his party moved down on to the shore and huddled in the shelter of some rocks. Suddenly the fisherman waved to them. 'The tide has turned,' said Robin. 'It's time.'

Sir Richard got up and Marion threw her arms around him. 'Take care of her,' he told Robin warmly.

Robin shook his hand and said he would. He wished him a safe voyage.

Sir Richard nodded and walked out towards the boat with Mark. 'May Herne protect them both!' said Robin, putting an arm round Marion comfortingly.

They watched as Mark and Richard reached the boat and clambered aboard. The sail was hoisted by the fisherman and the boat put out to sea.

'Pray for a calm sea!' laughed Sir Richard, as he waved farewell.

Marion waved back, a lump in her throat at the thought of the dangers her father would face on his long journey to find King Richard.

All at once there was a shout from the cliffs. Everybody turned and watched in astonishment as the exhausted Much yelled and signalled frantically at the departing boat.

'Robin! Robin! Stop . . . Mark! Stop . . . Mark!'

As the implication of Much's despairing cry sank in, Robin whirled round and saw to his horror that Sir Richard was already struggling with Mark in the boat. A knife flashed and Sir Richard fell.

Robin dived into the water and swam for the boat, his strong arms cutting smoothly through the waves. Nasir remained fuming impotently on the beach because of his inability to swim. He and Marion watched with their hearts in their mouths as Robin hauled himself into the boat and caught Mark's arm as he thrust downwards to stab the stunned Sir Richard in the heart. There was a brief, ferocious struggle, but Gisburne's man was no match for the strength of Herne's son and soon Mark's lifeless body was floating away on the tide.

When Sir Richard had recovered somewhat, the boat set out again.

'Twice you saved me,' said Sir Richard warmly. 'I shan't forget!'

'Take care, father,' cried Marion. 'God speed!'

'I will,' he replied. 'We shall meet again!'

And the frail little boat sailed into the setting sun.

That same sunset saw Prince John in one of his notorious tantrums, an even worse one than usual. De Leon stood nervously watching and listening.

'D'you think this would have happened in my father's time, de Leon?' he roared. 'Where's Abbot Hugo? With Robin Hood! *Robin Hood!* He's laughing at me. The whole of Nottingham's laughing at me. I should never have sent you, de Leon. You're a talker!'

At that moment two guards brought in Gisburne. Prince John looked at him and managed to control himself a little. 'I'm giving you one last chance, Gisburne,' he said. 'If Sir Richard reaches the King –'

'He won't!' Gisburne broke in wildly. 'He won't, my lord!'

Before Gisburne could continue, a messenger burst into the Great Hall.

'News! News from Normandy!' he shouted. 'King Richard is dead!'

Prince John grabbed the parchment from the messenger and opened it with trembling hands. He read its contents slowly, while everybody waited with bated breath. Suddenly the Prince looked up, a triumphant glitter in his eye.

'Killed by an arrow,' he cried. 'Killed by an arrow, fighting for Chalus! And he named *me* his heir! He named me his heir! His heir!' His voice rose hysterically and then he broke into peals of laughter.

'The King is dead! God save King John!' shouted Gisburne. The cry was taken up by the crowd as they sank to their knees.

'God save King John!'

CHAPTER 14

A small, ramshackle barn surrounded by dense undergrowth and tall trees stood in the heart of Sherwood. At first sight it looked derelict, but a thin column of smoke could be seen coming from a hole in the centre of the roof. Moss and ivy clung to the decaying walls, and mists rising from the forest floor made the mysterious-looking barn seem sinister – even evil.

Round the door posts magical signs had been scratched, and rams' horns, entwined with ivy, hung on the door. Beyond the door, in the interior of the barn, the feeling of mystery deepened, with magical talismans hanging from the roof and a fire smouldering in a circle of stones.

Crouched by the fire was a young woman with long, straight hair. She was staring at a small doll that stood on a three-legged stool in front of her, a home-made doll – that looked like her!

She was busily making another doll and was putting a small hood over its head. This doll bore a striking resemblance to Robin Hood!

The woman, whose name was Lilith, was putting the final touches to her work, and all the time she whispered. 'By the air which I breathe, by the breath which is within me, by the earth which I touch, I conjure you. And by the names of the spirits who are princes residing in you I conjure you that you send down to obsess, torment, and harass the body, spirit, soul and five senses of he whom I desire, and that he shall have no friendship for anyone in this world other than I, Lilith, your servant. So shall he be obsessed, tormented, and look on no one nor find comfort nor love in any but me. I conjure you to accomplish this and promise to satisfy you duly. By Hermes the thrice great, by the Shield of Solomon and by the power of the Lord of Darkness – creatures of Earth, I name thee Herne's son – Robin Hood – now thou art he!' And Lilith, beautiful and sensual, lifted up the doll in dedication.

She then bound the two dolls together with a plaited scarlet cord with nine knots in it. She had formed a witch's ladder . . .

In another part of the forest, Robin, who had been enjoying watching some comic fighting between Little John and Will Scarlet, stopped laughing abruptly as Lilith's enchantment started to take effect. As Lilith passed the two dolls to and fro through the smoke from the fire, he clutched his head, unable to understand what was happening to him. Marion turned to say something and her face fell.

'What is it?' she asked, and Robin turned to her and looked at her as if she were a complete stranger. She reached out to touch him and he backed away. The outlaws had ceased their horseplay and all were now staring at their leader.

'Come with me! Come with me!' intoned Lilith as she again passed the two dolls through the smoke, and Robin, who was becoming more and more agitated, put his hands over his ears as if trying to blot out the sound of hidden voices.

His friends all started asking what was the matter with him and Marion went up to him. He pushed her away violently and she nearly fell. As the outlaws stared at him, he looked at them with fear in his eyes, turned, and disappeared into the trees.

'What's up with him?' asked Tuck.

'I – I don't know!' said Marion. She ran after Robin but could not catch him.

Robin walked through the forest totally oblivious of his surroundings, moving as if he was in a dream. Lilith was anointing her arms, shoulders and neck with oil, slowly and languorously, and Robin as he walked heard music that was mysterious and inviting.

He came to a small clearing and there on the other side of

it was Lilith. He walked towards her and took her in his arms and kissed her.

'I knew you would find me,' said Lilith.

Robin asked her who she was and she told him; then put her fingers against his mouth as he started to speak. She took his hand and led him away.

They reached the barn, which was now a place of enchantment, garlanded with flowers. A harp played softly and Lilith vanished, to return in a beautiful gown of silk. She carried a goblet and they both drank from it.

Robin sank down on to a divan covered in pale-coloured silks and strewn with soft cushions. Lilith bent down and kissed him, whispering, 'Will you stay with me – stay and be my love? And never leave me?'

'Why should I ever leave you?' asked Robin.

'Marion!' said Lilith with venom, but Robin had no memory of her.

'Don't you remember me?' asked Lilith seductively.

'There's no one in the world but you,' whispered Robin and reached out for her.

Moving away, she asked, 'How can I be sure? If you want me, you must prove your love.'

'Ask me. I'll do anything!' promised the bewitched Robin.

'I wonder,' said Lilith and kissed him. 'If this is true, then bring me the Silver Arrow!'

There was a moment of silence. Despite his enchantment Robin was troubled.

'Bring it to me and prove your love,' breathed Lilith.

'But . . . the Arrow?'

'Then I'll be yours,' said Lilith very softly. 'Isn't that what you want? Bring me the Arrow!'

Robin had a last moment of hesitation, then the enchantment totally overwhelmed him. 'I will!' he said eagerly. 'I'll bring it to you!' Lilith had driven every doubt from his mind.

CHAPTER 15

Marion returned dejectedly through Sherwood to the out-laws' camp.

'I've searched everywhere,' she said. 'He's in danger. I'm sure of it.'

'He sees things, does Robin. Always has,' said Much. 'Things that happen.' Marion told him that this was different. 'Then maybe Herne called to him,' Much went on.

'No. It wasn't Herne,' said Marion and confessed that she was frightened.

'We'll find him, lass!' said Little John. 'Nasir'll track him down.'

Nasir nodded, and Little John went on: 'Best there is. He can find anyone!'

'He's still in Sherwood, little flower,' said Tuck. 'He must be!'

'And Sherwood's why we've survived,' Will chimed in.

Tuck asked him what he meant and Will explained. 'Twenty miles wide, thirty miles long, ain't it? And some parts so thick you have to hack your way through. And we're looking for a man who knows every inch of it.'

'You're such a hopeful beggar, aren't you?' said Little John, then, turning to Marion, 'We'll find him.' Soon they were moving through the forest, led by Nasir.

It was now evening, and for Nasir at least the trail was clear as he stared down at broken twigs and freshly bruised leaves. They reached the clearing where Robin had first seen Lilith, and Nasir stood where they had first embraced.

'What do you make of it, Nasir?' asked Little John.

'One comes and they meet,' he said.

'Who comes?' asked Marion, but Nasir merely shrugged, even though he knew it was a woman.

Robin was watching them from cover as Little John asked, 'Who could it be?'

Tuck said: 'It's a right mystery, ain't it?' but as he spoke Will, hearing something, raced across the clearing. Robin saw him coming, broke cover, and fled into the forest with Will after him. 'It's Robin!' cried Will.

All the outlaws gave chase, Tuck and Marion bringing up the rear. Robin reached a tree and leant against it as if panting for breath. But as Will reached him, Robin swung round and knocked him to the ground. Then he ran on.

Little John caught up with him, they struggled and Robin was pinned to the ground. Soon all the band were gathered round their leader, who was no longer capable of struggling.

He looked at them through dulled eyes. 'Don't you know us?' asked Little John, but Robin looked away – then tried to make a break for it. Nasir and Will grabbed him.

'He's mad,' said Tuck sorrowfully.

'No, he's bewitched!' cried Marion.

They tied him tightly to a tree and Marion went up to him. 'Look at me!' she said.

Robin looked up, his expression blank. He had no idea who she was.

'Who am I, Robin?' Marion asked, and Robin stared at her, shuddered and turned away. *'No!'* he shouted violently.

Little John put his arm round Marion and said, 'He doesn't know you. He doesn't know any of us!'

'What can we do?' poor Marion sobbed and Will answered grimly, 'Find whoever's done this to him.'

'You don't know what you're up against,' said Little John.

'Don't I?' said Will. 'Do you want him to stay in their power? Whoever it is we've got to find 'em and make 'em release him.'

That night, as the outlaws sat round a fire, Marion said decisively, 'We must go to see Herne. He made Robin his son – sent him to lead us. We must go to him.'

'There's no one else,' Little John agreed. 'Only Herne can help us.'

Much got up and took a goblet of water to Robin. When he proffered it to him Robin turned away. Poor Much lowered his head and turned to go, but Robin said commandingly: 'Let me loose!' Much turned and stared at him and Robin's eyes seemed to pierce him as he said once again: 'Let me loose!'

Much, to whom Robin seemed a stepbrother, came close to him, hating to see him tied up like an animal.

'Please! I beg you!' said Robin, but after a pause Much replied, 'I can't – the others! – I can't!'

'I shall die if you don't free me!'

'You won't die. Why should you?' said Much. 'I want to help you. We all do.'

'Then free me,' said Robin, looking as if his heart would break.

Much glanced round, took out his knife and cut Robin's bonds. A moment later he was racing off like an animal freed from a cage.

Little John was the first to reach Much. 'By St Thomas!' he shouted, and Much started to weep. The other outlaws gathered round him and he said, 'I had to let him go. He said he'd die.'

In Nottingham Castle the Sheriff was hurrying down a dark passage followed by Ralph of Huntingdon and Gisburne.

'Where did you find her?' he asked Ralph.

'Close by Castle Belleme, my lord,' he replied.

'What about the other one?' said the Sheriff, but Ralph had seen nothing of her. The Sheriff thought that curious.

They reached an iron-studded door and Ralph unlocked it. Inside, a young woman was chained to the wall by her wrists, and her feet were also chained. Like Lilith, she was sensuously attractive. She stared at the trio malevolently.

'You know who I am, don't you?' said the Sheriff, and the young witch spat at him.

'She's possessed,' Gisburne said.

'Then we'll whip the devils out of her, won't we?' said the Sheriff, and the witch turned her head away.

'Yes, she understands,' continued the Sheriff. 'If you want to spare yourself a considerable amount of physical pain, you'd better listen carefully. I'm aware that you and your so-called sister-in-magic served the late Baron de Belleme – and assisted in his revolting practices. There's no point in denying it.' Without taking his eyes off the witch, he went on: 'What was the man's name? Ah, yes, Waldric,' said the Sheriff, noting how the witch's eyes blazed when she heard the name. 'You remember the Baron's steward? Told us quite a lot before he died – his memory improved dramatically. For example, he told us that after his master had been killed by Robin Hood – before the castle was pillaged and set on fire by the local mob – two women were seen running away carrying certain instruments of magic, together with a casket. Perhaps you'd care to confirm that?'

The witch remained silent and the Sheriff continued. 'I've spent two years looking for that casket. Where did you hide it?'

The witch still said nothing and the men moved away. 'Yes. The jewels are safe,' said the Sheriff. 'Still there to be taken!'

'The jewels, my lord?' said Gisburne, puzzled.

Later, when the three had eaten, the Sheriff began to speak.

'The Baron was a Crusader,' he said, 'and it's known that his custom was to trade distinguished prisoners for precious stones. As the Saracens put great value on their commanders, Belleme returned to England with a considerable fortune.'

'I'll make the woman talk, my lord,' promised Gisburne.

'I doubt it,' said the Sheriff. 'Waldric, yes, but not her. She's one of an evil sisterhood who worshipped the Baron and would do anything for him. His power still dominates them from the grave.'

'Then it's likely the treasure's cursed, my lord,' said Ralph.

'Very likely,' the Sheriff replied. 'So Abbot Hugo will exorcise each emerald. Wash 'em in the font if necessary. But we still have to find them, don't we?'

'We'll find them,' Ralph promised.

'And soon,' the Sheriff stressed. 'I need to placate the King. They *must* be found!' Then he stalked away, frowning.

Gisburne and Ralph wasted no time. After conferring briefly, they summoned the Torturer and a monk with parchment, ink and pen, and made their way to the Torture Chamber. Gisburne threw open the door and the trio entered as the witch looked up in sudden fear. 'Prepare her!' Gisburne ordered the masked Torturer, and made ready to enjoy himself.

Word reached the Sheriff later about what was going on and he angrily made his way to the Torture Chamber. 'Did I say you could question her?' he roared at Gisburne as Ralph stood as far away as he could.

'My lord, I thought –' started Gisburne.

'You thought you'd enjoy yourself for a few hours, didn't you?' sneered the Sheriff.

'No, my lord!' Gisburne pleaded. 'I hoped to surprise you by discovering the whereabouts of Baron de Belleme's jewels.'

'I don't like surprises. I never have,' the Sheriff said icily. 'Especially when you are involved. Did she tell you anything?'

'Curses and blasphemy mainly,' Gisburne told him. 'I've got it written down. Shall I read it?'

He went to get the report from a monk who sat at a table nearby, but the Sheriff snatched it from him and scanned it quickly to find the part that interested him.

'"Where is the treasure of Simon de Belleme?"' he read out. '" No, I will not speak. No! No! Azael protect me!"' There was more in the same vein, including pleas for mercy.

'Then she swooned, my lord,' said Gisburne.

'Did she?' said the Sheriff. 'Where was I? Ah, yes. "Question: Where is the treasure? Can you understand me?" "Kill me! Kill me. The eye. Take – No – Say."'

'The rest was unintelligible, my lord,' said Gisburne.

The Sheriff put down the interrogation report, but Ralph picked it up with a 'May I, my lord?' The Sheriff nodded.

Ralph read slowly ' "The eye. Take. No. Say." Say – Satan! The Eye of Satan!'

'What are you babbling about?' yawned Gisburne.

'The jewels are still at Castle Belleme,' he said, and the Sheriff raised his eyebrows.

'On the north wall of the castle, my lord, high above the river, there's a gargoyle – a one-eyed devil. It's known to the local people as Satan. "The Eye of Satan".'

'My dear Ralph,' said the Sheriff, putting his arms round the young man's shoulders. 'Something tells me you're going to go far!'

Gisburne, racked with rage and jealousy, could have killed them both on the spot.

Meanwhile, the outlaws had reached Herne's lake and cave. Tall trees fringed the lake and mist hung over the water as Marion stepped into a dugout and started poling herself across the lake.

'Let one of us come with you!' called Little John, but Marion called back that she must see Herne alone. Unbeknown to any of them, Robin was hiding above the entrance to the cave.

Herne appeared on a promontory and waited for Marion, while Robin crept down into the cave. A small fire was burning on the altar – on which lay the Silver Arrow. Sweating, he slowly approached it.

On the shore Herne greeted Marion. 'I know why you have come,' he said, 'but the Hooded Man is hidden from me by a cloud of darkness. He is slave to another – bound by sorcery. You alone can and must find him, for soon he must face the greatest of his enemies – and know himself in the white flame of his power. Then he will truly be Herne's son. Come to me.'

Marion left her boat and walked to him. He gave her a small earthenware bottle and, feeling puzzled, she took it.

'Listen well,' Herne told her and when he had explained what she must do, her spirits lifted a little.

In the cave, Robin had reached the Arrow. It was an effort to take it, but he finally succeeded and slipped away.

As Robin was running from the cave, Herne was escorting Marion to her boat. 'The Powers of Light and Darkness are with you,' he told her. 'Farewell, Marion.'

When she returned to the outlaws, they questioned her eagerly.

'What did he tell you?' asked Little John.

'He spoke in riddles,' said Marion. 'Robin is hidden from him by a cloud of darkness, he said. So we must find him.'

'We must go back to that clearing and pick up the trail again,' Little John said. 'Can you lead us there, Nasir?' Nasir nodded gravely.

Poor Much looked away, but Little John comforted him. 'We're not blaming you, lad. We'll get him back, so cheer up!'

'Will there be demons?' asked Much.

'You and your demons!' laughed Little John. 'Herne'll protect us.'

'And not only Herne,' said Tuck.

The man they sought was standing in Lilith's barn looking at Lilith with love in his eyes – and she was looking lovingly at the Silver Arrow.

'Now do you believe that I love you?' asked Robin.

'Oh yes,' Lilith said softly. 'I believe you now. You have betrayed Herne for me.'

'The Arrow is yours and I am yours,' said Robin, moving towards her to try and take her in his arms, but she evaded him gently. 'Not yet, my love,' she said. 'First we must go from here.'

She came close to him and looked deep into his eyes, saying softly, 'I need you to help me.'

Robin said: 'You know I will!' and she told him to come

with her. Then she picked up the Arrow and said: 'You're Herne's son no longer. Now you must serve Azael.'

They journeyed towards Castle Belleme, but when they had almost reached it the witch looked anxiously at Robin, who was becoming uneasy.

'I – I know this place!' he said.

Lilith looked into his eyes and purred. 'Here you slew Baron Simon!'

Robin stared and breathed, 'Castle Belleme!'

They reached the gateway and stared at the desolation.

'They came that night,' said Lilith, 'came from miles around. The people who had feared the Baron de Belleme plundered the castle – set it ablaze. It was an evil place, they said. What did they know, my love?' And she led him into the castle.

They walked together along the crumbling battlements, gazing around them as a bright sun shone down on the unholy place; then they went deep into it down steps lit – to Robin's surprise – by a torch burning on the wall. They reached the crypt that served as a tomb, its door charred and blackened by fire. There were cobwebs everywhere, yet again a torch was burning.

'They stole everything they could,' said Lilith harshly. 'And still they take the very stones.'

Robin pushed the door and it fell from its hinges. They went through the gap into the crypt – which was lit by two more torches. Yet it was a place of shadows, just as it was when Robin long ago had released Marion from the great iron pentacle that was still on the wall. Rats scurried away from the altar where rams' horns lay in thick dust, and in the middle of the altar stood a plain stone coffin, its lid bearing a magical sign.

'Do you remember,' said Lilith, looking at Robin intensely.

'Oh yes, I remember,' said Robin.

Lilith took the torch from him and lit four candles which stood north, south, east and west. All were black. The tomb stood in the midst of two concentric circles and there were magical writings between the circles.

'The Baron's body was never found,' Lilith recalled softly. 'We brought it here.'

'But the tomb?' asked Robin, and Lilith said: 'It lies in a circle of power. He prepared it. Help me!'

She tried to move the slab and Robin went to help her. They slid the lid from the tomb and saw Simon de Belleme – looking exactly as he did when he was alive.

'See!' whispered Lilith. 'Death has left no mark on him. Azael has protected his servant. See, Robin! Are you afraid?'

'No, I'm not afraid,' Robin replied, completely under her spell.

'I've dreamed of this moment,' Lilith said in ecstasy. 'Waited till the time was right – the day of Mercury, the hour of his death, the man who killed him and the means by which he died!' And she held up the Arrow in one hand and began to speak, her whisper echoing round the tomb.

'I conjure thee, by Hermes the Thrice Great, by the Shield of Solomon and by the power of the Lords of Darkness. *Venite! Venite!*'

A dull rumble of thunder seemed to come from below them. Lilith placed the Arrow in Belleme's hands and intoned: '*Palas aron azinomas!*' Then, as the thunder continued, she bent down and kissed Belleme. His eyelids trembled, then opened . . .

Lilith ran to him and knelt, kissing the hem of his gown.

'I knew you would not fail me,' said Belleme.

'Oh, my lord, my lord!' breathed Lilith in adoration.

'By the power of this Arrow and by Azael's command I have returned to do his bidding,' exulted the Baron, helping Lilith to her feet and turning to Robin. 'Now you know that everything Herne told you was a lie. He forced you to become his champion, but Lilith has freed you. Your fighting days are over.'

Robin nodded and stared at Lilith adoringly.

'Look at the fool,' sneered Belleme. 'He's powerless. You've done well, Lilith.' Then he turned to Robin. 'Did you really believe you could overthrow me?' he exulted. 'I who have stood before the bloodstained altars of Babylon? I who worshipped Rhadamanthus in the Temple of the Sun, and conjured the spirits of the dead in the catacombs of Alexandria? Slave – know that I am the messenger of the Lord Azael, Prince of Demons, and that with his aid I shall bring war, famine and pestilence to the world until all men turn to evil and bow down before the Lords of Darkness!'

He drew Lilith to one side. 'At midnight you will bring me his heart,' he said. Lilith curtsied and went to Robin, smiling at him and taking his hand.

'Come!' she said.

Little knowing the nightmare scene that was awaiting them, Gisburne and Ralph were nearing the castle, both with coils of rope on their saddles.

'You'd better be right about this,' said Gisburne. 'There's no proof, is there?'

'The Eye of Satan,' Ralph said. 'That's where it's hidden!'

'It'll be a real feather in your cap, won't it?' Gisburne said coldly.

'In both our caps, Sir Guy,' insisted Ralph, and they rode on, Gisburne inwardly fuming at the confidence of the young Captain.

When they reached the castle they were amazed at the desolation. 'It's been said that the dungeons lead straight down to Hell,' Gisburne muttered. 'The whole place smells of evil.'

'I see it's a convenient quarry for the local villagers,' Ralph replied.

'They'll bring it down round their ears one of these days,' Gisburne answered, leading the way to a door.

They hurried to a room with a window that looked over the river, and stared down on the gargoyle, some ten feet below. 'It's impossible,' said Gisburne, but Ralph was not so sure.

'It's dangerous,' he said, 'but not impossible.'

'Then you can prove me wrong,' Gisburne said intensely.

Ralph was getting ready to climb down to the gargoyle, a

rope round him which Gisburne was belaying round a pillar. He climbed out and was slowly lowered until he was level with the gargoyle. 'That's far enough!' he shouted, and Gisburne tied off the rope and looked down.

Ralph searched the wall behind the gargoyle. He pulled a stone away and saw a hole behind it. Dropping the stone, he put his hand into the hole and drew out a dirty leather bag. 'It's here!' he shouted. 'Pull me up!'

Gisburne drew him up the wall and Ralph threw the bag into the room to give himself the use of both hands on the rope.

'The Sheriff was right,' Gisburne told him. 'He said you'd go far!' Then he drew a dagger and cut the rope, sending Ralph to his death.

Gisburne hastily opened the bag, which was full of jewels, some set in rings and small ornaments. 'I'm free of you, Sheriff!' he exulted. And moments later he was hurrying down the steps.

Soon he lost his way in a maze of dark passages and began to feel nervous; then he came to a corner and turned it. In front of him were stairs to the crypt – and at the top of the stairs stood a dead man, the terrible Baron de Belleme.

'I see you remember me!' sneered the Baron. 'No. I'm no spirit. I breathe as you breathe – as your companion breathed before you killed him. *Give me the jewels!*'

Sobbing, Gisburne handed the bag to Belleme. 'You are fortunate,' said Belleme. 'I shall spare you – to tell the Sheriff. I command his presence here. Now *go!*'

Gisburne stood paralysed with fear for a moment. Then, uttering a choked cry, he fled from Belleme, who watched him with amused contempt.

CHAPTER 16

Edward had been poaching in Sherwood and was wandering through the forest with a brace of rabbits. Suddenly he stopped in amazement: walking together not far away from him were Robin and Lilith and, sensing something was wrong, he followed them . . .

Later, shadows were darkening the clearing as Marion and Much reported back that they had not found Robin. Much threw himself miserably on the ground.

Marion asked where the others were, and Little John told her that they were searching the woods above the valley. They heard a whistle and Little John said, 'That's Scarlet!' Much whistled back.

'Six of us!' said Marion. 'We need six hundred!'

'He has to be somewhere, little flower,' said Tuck.

'But if he's hiding from us . . .' Marion sighed.

'Or being hidden,' said Little John.

Will and Nasir appeared, both shaking their heads, and she turned away from them to hide her unhappiness.

Will looked at her and quietly said: 'We'll eat, sleep and start again at sun-up,' and she hid her face against him and sobbed, Will doing his best to comfort her. She stopped crying and took her place by the fire, then raised a drinking vessel and said softly, 'Herne protect us!' The rest repeated her words and the bowl was passed round the circle in silence.

'Why do I feel so cold?' asked Marion. 'Who are they? Who's done this to him? Why?'

'Because he's Herne's son,' said Little John. 'He once said that the whole world was a battlefield – not just Sherwood! A never-ending war between the powers of good and evil.'

Suddenly, Nasir gestured warningly to John and pointed

to the darkness. But as the outlaws took up defensive positions, there was a whistle. Much whistled back and said: 'It's Edward.'

Edward and Marion exchanged blessings and Edward said: 'Didn't expect to find you here!' Little John explained that they were looking for Robin.

'I'd leave him alone if I were you,' said Edward.

'What do you mean?' asked Marion. 'Why do you say that?'

'Because I've seen him,' Edward replied. 'Not an hour since – with a girl.'

Marion asked: 'With a girl! Where?' but Edward told her to let him be. 'He'll come to his senses,' he said.

'Where were they, Edward?' asked Marion, but Edward was embarrassed.

'It isn't what you think,' said Little John. 'He's been be-witched. Doesn't know us. He's like a stranger!'

'And there was a look in his eyes as if he was in torment,' said Marion.

Edward drew in his breath. 'I'll take you to him,' he said.

Something was also wrong at Nottingham Castle, or so it seemed as Guy of Gisburne rushed into the Great Hall, shout-ing, 'My lord Sheriff!' Not finding him, he raced up the stairs to the Sheriff's chamber.

He burst in, to find two serving girls giving the Sheriff his bath. He looked up. What had Gisburne done now? he won-dered. 'Something tells me I'm in for a surprise,' he said. 'Are you going to surprise me, Gisburne?'

He held out his hand and shut his eyes, but nothing hap-pened. Then he saw Gisburne's face and became quiet – and deadly.

'Where are they? Where's Ralph?' he asked.

'He's dead, my lord. He fell,' said Gisburne.

'Fell? How careless! Where are the jewels?' asked the Sheriff.

'I don't know how to tell you, my lord ...' Gisburne hesitated.

'I'm sure you'll find a way,' said the Sheriff evenly. 'You usually do.'

Gisburne remained silent and began sweating.

'They weren't there, were they?' said the Sheriff. 'A wild goose and a dead duck!'

'They were there, my lord,' Gisburne assured him, and, as if he was talking to a child, the Sheriff asked where they were now.

'The Baron took them,' announced Gisburne. 'The Baron de Belleme!'

Grabbing a towel and pulling himself out of the tub, he said: 'Listen to me, Gisburne. It's been a long day and I'm not in the mood for your feeble attempts at humour. Where are the jewels?'

'I tell you Belleme has them!' said Gisburne desperately 'I swear it! Fetch me a Bible.'

'You don't need a Bible, you need a turn or two on the rack!' threatened the Sheriff.

'*He spoke to me!*' shouted Gisburne.

'*He's dead!*' roared the Sheriff.

'*I know!*' erupted Gisburne.

The Sheriff stared at Gisburne, then said quietly, 'I don't know what you're trying to do, Gisburne, but whatever it is I've had enough of it!'

'He stood there,' burbled Gisburne, 'and took the jewels from me. Then he said: "Tell the Sheriff I command his presence here."'

'Is that all?' inquired the Sheriff. 'Have you shot your bolt? Or must I stand freezing to death while you continue with this ludicrous rigmarole?'

'It *was* Belleme!' Gisburne pleaded.

The Sheriff sighed. 'All right. You were robbed by a ghost! So tomorrow we'll go to the castle and if this – this thing fails to appear, I'll send you to hell to fetch it!'

*

In Lilith's barn the witch was looking at herself in a mirror. Robin came up and kissed her. 'I could never leave you,' he said.

'What if I made you leave me?' she asked. 'I could, so easily! Suppose I told you that tomorrow would never come?'

'Even if that was true, we'd still be together,' said Robin.

'Would we?' asked Lilith, and Robin swore that nothing could ever part them.

Lilith picked up a goblet and slowly approached him. 'No. Nothing!' said Robin.

Lilith paused, then gave the goblet to Robin. 'Drink!' she said.

As he raised it to his lips the outlaws erupted into the barn, Little John and Nasir grabbing Robin and Lilith being seized by Edward and Nasir. '*No!*' cried Robin in anguish. Marion ran up to Robin and hurled the fluid from the little flask that Herne had given her straight at Robin's face. It hit his eyes and his expression began to change.

The barn was no longer a place of enchantment to him. There was no harp music, there were no garlands of flowers, Lilith, who was fighting like a wild cat, was dressed once more in a plain, russet-coloured garment, not a beautiful silk gown. 'Swine! Swine!' she shrieked.

Robin stopped struggling, but his friends were taking no chances and still held him firmly. Tuck brought the two dolls to Marion. 'Look at this!' he said.

Marion took them and ripped them apart as Lilith screamed: 'He'll kill you all. All! You'll burn in hell – all of you!'

She freed herself from Edward and tore Nasir's face with her nails, forcing him to let go of her. Then she rushed out of the barn screaming 'Azael! Azael!' as she raced into the forest. Edward and Nasir were about to follow her, but Little John said, 'Let her go!'

Robin looked at Marion with love in his eyes once more and they fell in each other's arms.

Now he was their leader again, and he urgently tried to

convince them that Belleme was alive. 'How can he be?' asked Will, and Much looked scared.

'I stole Herne's Arrow,' Robin told them. 'And she used its power to bring him back to life.'

The following dawn saw the Sheriff and Gisburne ride up to Castle Belleme with a bodyguard of twelve men-at-arms. Gisburne was still trying to convince the Sheriff that he was telling the truth.

'So you still say that you saw him,' he said, 'and that Ralph "fell"?'

Gisburne remained silent, and the Sheriff went on. 'You're such a liar, Gisburne. But, as you see, I've come prepared for any treachery you might have planned.'

They rode into the castle and the Sheriff and Gisburne dismounted. 'Stand guard!' ordered Gisburne.

'Well, where is the late and unlamented Baron?' asked the Sheriff, and Gisburne told him he was inside. He led the way into the ruins.

The atmosphere of the place began to have its effect on the Sheriff, whose morale was lowered still further when there was a low rumble from the foundations, causing stones to come tumbling down. 'Why are you doing this, Gisburne?' he asked. 'What do you hope to gain?' Then, as Gisburne remained silent, he shouted: 'I'm here, Baron!'

His voice echoed and faded into the distance. Gisburne looked frightened, and the Sheriff told him he was pathetic. 'Shall we go on?' he suggested, and led the way down to the crypt.

Reaching it, they looked round, and when the Sheriff spoke he lowered his voice, so oppressive was the atmosphere.

'All the magical paraphernalia,' he said. 'Just as it was the day he died. The day he *died*, Gisburne!'

Suddenly he drew his dagger and pressed it against Gisburne's throat. 'You murdered Ralph, didn't you?' he accused him. 'You have the jewels. Why the elaborate and bizarre story, Gisburne? *Why?*'

But Gisburne was staring over his shoulder, and when the Sheriff saw the look on his face, he turned.

There stood Belleme, watching them from the shadows, an evil smile on his face. The Sheriff's dagger clattered to the flagstones as he stared at Belleme in disbelief. 'You're – you're dead!' he exclaimed fatuously, if understandably.

'You speak of something of which you have no knowledge,' said Belleme contemptuously. 'What is death, de Rainault? When does a man die? When the last breath leaves his body? Or when he rots? And if he doesn't rot, de Rainault? If the frozen hours stretch on for ever, his blood a silent river of ice, waiting – waiting! What then, de Rainault?'

The Sheriff crossed himself and Belleme looked at him with contempt. 'You cross yourself when you believe in nothing,' he said. 'You doubted my powers and mocked my sorcery, yet something in you feared me. See!' And he held up the Silver Arrow.

'The Arrow!' gasped the Sheriff.

'Yes, mine at last!' Belleme exulted. 'I am the real power. You are nothing.'

He looked up, knowing that other intruders were entering the castle – Robin and his men, and Edward. The outlaws saw the two tethered horses, and at that moment one of the men-at-arms saw them and raced to warn the Sheriff. The outlaws followed cautiously.

In the crypt Belleme cried, 'He is coming. His anger scalds him. He must have that arrow. He's reckless – desperate!'

'Who is coming?' asked the Sheriff.

'Our enemy,' proclaimed Belleme, excitement mounting in him. 'The Hooded Man!'

The man-at-arms broke in on them, crying, 'Sir Guy! My lord Sheriff! *Robin Hood!*'

Both men turned to Belleme, who said quietly and menacingly, 'Perhaps now you will believe?'

The pair hesitated, then rushed up the steps.

Robin led the outlaws on to the battlements, and at once the men-at-arms guarding the door down to the crypt opened fire with their crossbows, then rushed at the outlaws. The Sheriff and Gisburne appeared on the battlements, Gisburne drawing his sword. He started towards his men, but the Sheriff held him back.

A ferocious fight began, soon on two levels as some of the men-at-arms climbed down charred timbers to reach the ground. And below in the crypt that housed his tomb Baron de Belleme stood in the centre of his circle and with his dagger traced a pentacle in the air in front of him. Then he spoke.

'Lord of Lightnings! Great Prince of the Powers of Fire and Ruler of tempests, storms and whirlwinds – smite thou mine enemies!'

A howling wind shot through the castle like a tornado and an earthquake shook the ground, hurling the combatants backwards. Gisburne and the Sheriff, though hit by the wind, argued furiously, Gisburne screaming that he must help his men, the Sheriff determined to flee. The Sheriff's arguments prevailed and the pair made their escape through the battle, clawing their way over piles of rubble in their haste to get away.

The outlaws re-grouped. They had killed several men-at-arms and the rest were cowering on the ground or rushing from the castle. 'He's raising a storm!' Robin shouted above the howling wind. Then he led his men through the crypt door.

In the crypt Belleme was calling out, 'Destroy them, Dark Lord! Rend their flesh with the cruel talons of thy terror!'

A titanic rumbling continued, as did the howling of the wind. Belleme's eyes gleamed in ecstatic triumph.

Robin was leading the outlaws down towards the crypt. He hesitated for a moment, uncertain which way to go, but the outlaws and Edward raced on. Suddenly the floor above collapsed, cutting them off from Robin, who frantically started to clear the rubble, and then swung round at the sound of demonic laughter.

It came from Belleme, who stood at the top of the steps holding the Silver Arrow. Robin rushed towards him, but the Baron vanished into the swirling mist that had begun to seep into the castle.

Robin reached the battlements only to see Belleme standing by the ruins of the Great Hall. He was holding the Arrow high above his head for Robin to see.

With his sword drawn, Robin sprinted along the battlements, but Belleme suddenly pointed the Arrow at him. As if struck by a blow, Robin was lifted bodily off the battlements and fell some fifteen feet to the ground. He was uninjured, though badly winded – and he had lost his sword. Belleme stood laughing at him, but Robin climbed painfully back on to the battlements.

Now Belleme could be seen in the window of the ruined Great Hall, his eyes blazing fire. Robin began to climb towards him, but a force like a hurricane seemed to beat him back as Belleme looked down, mocking the mere mortal who dared challenge him. He held out the deadly Silver Arrow, placing it between his palms, and opening them so that the Arrow lay on them pointing at Robin's heart.

Robin could not move. He felt transfixed by Belleme, whom he heard speaking quietly as if within his own head. 'Nothing can save you. How fitting that Herne's Arrow should kill his son!'

Belleme stared at the Arrow as if it was a living thing. 'Azael!' he commanded. The Arrow flew from his hand as if shot from a bow, speeding through the window of the Great Hall towards its target with an unearthly rushing sound. But in mid flight a great hand clasped it – the hand of Herne the Hunter, who stood beside Robin, his arm protecting him from the hellish Arrow that was inches from his breast.

Belleme stared at his enemies, his diabolic eyes blazing hatred at the human symbols of goodness that confronted him. Then the swirling mists enveloped him.

Herne turned to Robin and gave him the Arrow, and Robin ran forward to where Belleme had stood. But the mists rolled back . . . and Belleme had disappeared. He looked back and found that Herne, too, had vanished.

Robin remembered his comrades and ran to where they had been buried in rubble. As he approached the pile of stones, the head of Little John suddenly appeared through a large hole in the fallen masonry. 'Well, don't just stand there,' said Little John, grinning broadly. 'Get us out!'

Robin laughed with relief and began pulling away the stones, and so one by one all the outlaws and Edward climbed out through the hole.

Soon they were leaving the castle, watched by the terrible Baron Simon de Belleme. There was a sardonic smile on his face.

CHAPTER 17

The golden late-summer sun filtered gently through the arching branches of the trees, deep in the heart of Sherwood. As it reached the floor of the massive forest, it touched and warmed the clear waters of the deep pool which lay trapped beneath a thin, splashing waterfall tumbling from the rocks above.

Floating gently in the water, barely moving, Marion watched Robin dive from a large rock by the waterfall and reflected, with a sigh, that this was possibly one of the most beautiful places in the forest. As Robin's head broke the surface of the water, she swam over to him

'I wish that summer would never end,' she said as she reached him. Robin rolled over and floated on his back.

'There'll be ice on this pond, come the winter.'

'And dead leaves,' Marion replied. 'If we were hedgehogs, we could curl up and sleep all winter – or bats, or squirrels. They've more sense than we have!'

'You can be a hedgehog if you want to,' Robin laughed, splashing her face playfully. 'I'd rather be me and shiver!'

'Oh, you!' Marion dodged, half cross, half laughing, and swam noisily away. Robin turned to swim after her, knowing that he could catch her easily, when his eye was suddenly caught by a shadowy figure standing by a clump of holly bushes at the side of the pool. His heart quickened as he recognized the horned head of Herne the Hunter.

He swam swiftly over to Herne and hauled himself out of the water, waiting to discover why his master had chosen this moment to appear to him. To Marion, watching anxiously from the middle of the pool, it seemed that the figure of Herne was laden with doom and she repressed a shudder at this sudden premonition of danger.

As Robin had come to expect, the message Herne brought was cloaked in mystery.

'Who is the greatest enemy?' he asked Robin in his quiet voice. Robin stared and could not answer.

'He's always been near you. Sometimes at your shoulder.' Herne stopped, watching a growing realization in Robin's face.

'I've always known he was there,' said Robin eventually.

'You must face him. The time has come,' Herne paused. 'Listen! Each man travels along one path and, at the end of it – if he has the courage – he will meet himself and know his power.'

'Will you be there?' asked Robin.

'No.' Herne's voice was laden with sadness. 'But we cannot be parted. There's another riddle for you! Go now! One comes, one goes, and you are needed.'

Robin stood deep in thought long after Herne slipped back into the darkness of the forest, until recalled by an anxious cry from Marion, who was dressing at the far edge of the pool. She ran round to where he stood and watched with troubled eyes as he dried and dressed himself.

'Come! We're wanted at the camp,' he said, taking her hand. 'Something's happened.'

The news that Nasir had been seen riding out towards Nottingham on his own had come as a shock to the outlaws remaining at the camp. None of them would ever risk revealing himself so foolishly without a disguise. In Robin's absence, Will had decided to follow Nasir. He had mounted his sure-footed horse and ridden off to find the Saracen, while the rest waited eagerly for his return. But the news Will brought back with him was not good. He had tracked Nasir for a while and watched as he met two strangers, who were mounted and heavily armed. Expecting a fight to break out, Will had readied himself to leap into the fray; he had been extremely surprised to see Nasir ride off quietly with the strangers. As they passed his hiding place, he had seen that Nasir's new companions were Saracens, like Nasir himself.

Will was puzzled.

'I can't put my finger on it. But there was something strange about that meeting. It's not like Nasir to ride off and leave us without a word.'

'Do you think he'll be back?' Little John asked.

'Of course he will,' said Tuck, looking up from the goat he was milking. 'Nasir won't betray us. He's one of us, now, whatever his past has been. He'll come back.'

'Then what is he up to?' asked Will.

'He'll come back,' repeated Tuck.

'I hope you're right,' said Will gloomily. 'But I can't help feeling that there's trouble brewing!'

Trouble was certainly brewing at Nottingham Castle but for the moment the Sheriff's anger was directed solely at the trembling figure of the barber behind his head, who was attempting to shave off his beard.

'If you cut me again, you'll lose your fingers,' he told the terrified man. 'You're shaving your Sheriff – not skinning a rabbit!'

Gisburne watched the barber's fumbling efforts with a little smile playing round his lips. The smile disappeared as the Sheriff turned to him and asked, 'I hope I'm doing the right thing?'

'Oh yes, my lord,' said Gisburne encouragingly. 'A great improvement!'

The Sheriff glared at him, then told the barber to get on with it.

A servant suddenly came running in. 'A messenger from the King, my lord!' he said, which caused the Sheriff to swing round and nick himself on the barber's knife. He howled with pain and slapped his hand to the cut, leaping up and raging: 'You palsied butcher!'

He grabbed a small towel from the barber's quivering arm and pressed it to the cut, then looked at the evidence. There was hardly any blood to be seen. '*You've mutilated me!*' he roared.

He lashed out at the barber, who at first did his best to fend off the blows and then, at a nod from Gisburne, fled – and bumped straight into the messenger.

The Sheriff was too busy shouting at Gisburne to realize that the messenger had appeared. 'I want him flayed alive, Gisburne – flayed alive!' he exploded. 'Hell's teeth – I'm lacerated! Out! Out! Get the villain out!' And he collapsed in his chair, holding the towel against his face.

By this time the King's messenger, a fresh-faced youth with no more than a blond down on his chin, had reached the Sheriff. 'This cannot wait, my lord,' he said coldly.

'Can't it!' replied the Sheriff, puce with rage.

'I am Hubert de Guiscard, Herald to the King,' said the newcomer. 'What I have to say is for your ears only.'

The Sheriff looked at Guiscard and pulled himself together. He dismissed Gisburne, who glared at Guiscard, then left.

'I'll come directly to the point,' Guiscard said. 'The King wishes you to put an end to the wolf's-head, Robin Hood – immediately!'

'Immediately?' repeated the Sheriff. 'Excellent. How?'

'The method hardly concerns him,' said Guiscard haughtily. 'What does concern him is that the name Robin Hood has become a symbol of resistance to the authority and governance of King John.'

'I am aware of that!' started the Sheriff, but Guiscard cut in.

'Let me finish! You are entirely responsible for this situation and the King will no longer tolerate it. Unless this wolf's-head dies within the month you will be stripped of your office and sent to fight the King's enemies in Normandy. Your successor has already been chosen.'

'Then I'll endeavour to obey,' said the Sheriff sulkily.

'You will obey, my lord, or lose everything,' said Guiscard icily. 'Do you understand me?'

When the Sheriff indicated that he would do his best,

Guiscard wished him good hunting, bowed insolently and then stalked out.

'Hunting!' mused the Sheriff thoughtfully. 'Yes! That's it. We'll go hunting!'

Laughing happily at the beautiful simplicity of the idea that had come to him, he snapped out órders to Gisburne, who hurried to do his bidding. A boy was sent scampering round to the kennels while Gisburne and a small band of armed men rode out towards the unsuspecting and peaceful village of Wickham, which lay on the edge of Sherwood.

Within a matter of hours, the Sheriff's plans were well laid, the dog-handlers had their vicious and ravenous hounds prepared and all that was needed was the bait which would draw the outlaws from the safety of Sherwood Forest. The Sheriff paced impatiently in front of the huge fire in the Great Hall. He stopped as the sounds of Gisburne's return reached him and waited until his second-in-command appeared in the hall escorting two villagers, one a well-built man, the other a small, frightened boy.

'Edward of Wickham, my lord, and his son,' Gisburne announced. 'I've left men at the village. No one can leave.'

The Sheriff nodded and sat on the table, his feet on a stool. He looked at Edward and Matthew. He was enjoying himself.

'You're wondering what I'm up to?' he said. 'I'll tell you! You're a trouble-maker, Edward. You support Robin Hood, you and everyone in your village. You've been helping that wolf's-head and his gang for months.'

'Don't lie to me, scum!' he roared as Edward tried to interject. 'I know. Who tells him when the dog-handlers are near or when Sir Guy's patrols are getting a little close? You do, you filth! And you do it for venison – and grain – don't you? Grain he's robbed from wagons on their way here.'

He got up and put his face close to Edward's, who stared back at him. 'Remember Loxley?' he said. 'A rebel village! And now it's just a name and a tangle of undergrowth.'

He went back to the map and jabbed it with his finger. 'I've had my eye on Wickham for some time, and tonight I'm clearing it of every man, woman and child. I'm selling the men to Ranulph of Chester – he wants more soldiers; the rest can beg, for all I care.'

Edward muttered that it was shameful, and the Sheriff sneered. 'Yes, it is, isn't it? Monstrous! And you're to blame. It's going to haunt you. I'm going to let you live!'

He pointed at Matthew. 'He can live, too,' he said, 'provided you do as I say. Nice little boy, isn't he?'

'He's done you no harm,' said Edward bravely.

'He's your son and he lives in Wickham,' roared the Sheriff. He took an apple and threw it to the boy, and then came closer to him. 'I'm sure you love your father,' he said to Matthew. 'And you wouldn't want anything to happen to him, would you?'

Matthew shook his head, and the Sheriff continued, 'What an intelligent child! So you're going to take a message to him, aren't you? To Robin Hood!'

CHAPTER 18

In the early morning of the next day Robin and his five companions were making their way down the shady forest track towards Wickham. All were armed and moved warily. There was a hint of autumn in the chilly air. The leaves would soon be falling.

'What could they want?' asked Marion.

'The boy didn't know,' said Robin, sensing trouble.

In Wickham every hut concealed its quota of crossbowmen. Others were waiting behind cover in the village and on its outskirts. Edward and Gisburne were the first to see the outlaws and Edward came out of his hut to greet them, his heart almost broken. 'I've got you this time!' said the Sheriff in his hiding place as they reached the centre of the village.

'Get ready!' Gisburne whispered to his men. The outlaws stopped a few yards from their friend, who was a little to one side of his doorway.

'Good morning, Edward!' said Robin cheerfully.

It was Will who saw something wrong in the villager's eyes. Swinging round, he scanned the huts and bushes desperately. Sunlight gleamed on the helmet of a concealed soldier.

'*Ambush!*' he roared.

The outlaws scattered back towards the trees as the startled crossbowmen opened fire. Men-at-arms poured out of hiding with Gisburne at their head, racing to block the outlaws' retreat. Robin drew Albion to defend himself. 'To the forest!' he shouted.

The Sheriff was on his horse, watching the flight from a vantage point. It did not matter that the trap had been sprung too soon. If any got away, there would be fine sport in the woods to follow. He saw Little John charge, staff swinging, into a sea of men-at-arms and disappear. Nearby, Will struck out at the knot of soldiery that surrounded him, burning with panic and fury that he had allowed himself to be caught.

Tuck was at Robin's elbow, lashing out gamely at those within reach. Marion and Much were close behind, busy with bow and sling as Robin lead the rush for where the men-at-arms were thinnest. Albion swung, stone and arrow hummed past his ear and men ahead staggered. Suddenly the way was open.

'Come on!' Robin shouted.

Gisburne barred the way, hacking. Robin parried, stepped inside his opponent's swing and clubbed him to the ground with the pommel of his sword. They rushed for the trees.

In the shelter of the woods they paused, Marion shot a final arrow and Robin looked back. Will was pinned against the wall of a hut and more men-at-arms were coming at them. Retreat was the only course, and Robin led Marion, Much and Tuck away from the village where Little John lay sprawled unconscious on the ground.

The four fugitives ran through the forest they knew so well. No pursuers could ride through such close country. Surely they could evade armoured men on foot in their own woods! But they had covered only a few hundred yards when they heard the hounds baying and knew that another factor had entered the game. Tuck was already lagging behind.

In front of him, Robin panted: 'We'll be back for Little John and Will.' He looked left and right, then gasped: 'We'll make for the stream.'

Some way beyond the water the four outlaws came to a small hollow and fell exhausted to the ground, poor Tuck unable to speak.

'Why don't we fight them?' Marion asked Robin, but he told her there were too many to fight. 'Did Edward betray us?' she went on.

'No. He was forced,' Robin said, and Marion remembered Edward's son.

The outlaws lay listening, then Much cried: 'They're coming!' They scrambled up and started running again, all of them still panting and Tuck beginning to suffer greatly.

The hounds were at the water now and finding where the fugitives had crossed. It did not take them long, and soon the Sheriff and his men and animals were striking out across the stream.

Back in Wickham, Will and Little John stood bound and heavily guarded as Gisburne, shaking his head, came over to them from one of the huts.

'Where's the Saracen?' he asked, but got no answer. 'Where is he?' he asked again. 'Why isn't he with you?'

'Wouldn't you like to know?' said Will, and Gisburne hit him in the mouth. Will smiled defiantly.

'It's the end for all of you! You're finished!' said Gisburne, and pointed towards Edward's hut. 'Put 'em in there!' he rasped.

From a tree-covered hill overlooking the village Nasir the Saracen stared down from his horse at the scene below. He saw the last of the hunt disappearing into the forest, and the two prisoners being thrown into one of the huts. With a sigh he slipped from his horse and begun the long stalk down to the village.

He reached the first huts unobserved, and settled down in cover to watch Gisburne talking to a group of his men. Silently he unslung his bow and set an arrow to the string.

Two men-at-arms spotted Nasir and started creeping towards him. The outlaw was in the act of drawing on Gisburne when they rushed him with a yell. He spun and shot half over his shoulder at his attackers, then dropped his bow and broke cover as the second man dashed past his wounded comrade and chased him into the village.

The place was alive with soldiery. Trapped, Nasir set his back against a hut wall and drew his sword, but the odds were hopeless. Men-at-arms crowded around, and crossbow-men were scrambling on to nearby roofs for a clear shot. Staring at Gisburne, he dropped his sword.

'Tie him up,' ordered Gisburne.

Little was being said by the three prisoners slumped down in Edward's hut. All at once Nasir was hurled inside and, as he struggled to sit up, he asked where Robin and the rest were. Will told him they'd got away. 'Leastways, we hope they did,' said Little John.

Ashamed of his failure to rescue his friends, Nasir said nothing.

'Who were those men you went off with?' asked Will suspiciously.

'So it was you that followed me?' said Nasir. 'They were Hashishiyun – in your tongue "Assassins".'

'Killers!' said Will and Nasir nodded.

'They kill – yes,' he explained, 'for their – their *belief*!'

'So what did they want with you?' asked Will.

'I am one of them,' said Nasir quietly. 'They were sent to take me back.'

'Why didn't you tell us all this?' asked John.

'It was my quarrel, not yours,' Nasir replied. 'But now I have washed my hands of it.'

'And they let you?' asked Will.

'They had no choice,' said Nasir softly.

Deep in the forest Tuck was in trouble. The long chase was proving too much for him, and he was slowing his friends down. Now they had reached a small marshy area in the forest, thick with reeds and evil-smelling pools, where Robin hoped to throw the hounds off the scent and gain a breathing-space. As they surged into the clutching mud a mist swam before Tuck's eyes. His feet stuck in the mire and no fear of man, hound or Sheriff could move them again. In his misery the prospect of being caught seemed no worse than that this hopeless, nightmare flight should continue. He swayed, and fell full-length in the marsh.

'Leave me,' he muttered. 'I'm done for!'

'We must hide him,' said Robin. 'Quickly!'

With the crashing sounds of pursuit ringing closer and

closer in their ears, they dragged the sopping Tuck to the nearest bed of reeds and left him lying there, hidden from view, as they ran for cover. The pursuers reached the marsh a moment later. Tuck crossed himself and lay still as the shouting and baying mob cast around for the point at which the fugitives had taken to firm ground again. Yelling soldiers passed within feet of his hiding-place, then the sounds of the hunt slowly faded.

For a long while the exhausted Tuck lay where he was, but the discomfort of his position and the cold mud clinging to his gown finally forced him to make a move. He climbed slowly out of the marsh and leaned against a tree. At that moment three men-at-arms emerged limping from the undergrowth, stragglers for whom the pace of the hunt had proved too hot. The four men glared at each other, panting. At length Tuck, still leaning against the tree, brandished his sword.

'Be off!' he growled.

The soldiers spread out and circled him slowly. Tuck skipped clumsily to one side, aimed a blow at the nearest, and fell over a tree root. Two soldiers landed heavily on his back, and he lay helpless while the third tied his hands with his own cassock cord.

CHAPTER 19

Robin, Marion and Much were now on the edge of the forest. They were running down a narrow track with high ground on either side, and getting very tired.

Their enemies were not far behind, and suddenly the Sheriff shouted: 'There! Do you see them?' The pursuers stepped up the pace.

The fugitives stumbled across open ground towards a group of boulders that offered some cover. Even as they reached them, the hounds and their handlers came into view among the last of the trees. Robin drew an arrow and loosed it at the leading man, who fell with a cry. The other handler pulled his hounds back into cover. The Sheriff and his men joined him and looked out across the open ground. Two arrows that were both a warning and a challenge flew from the boulders, and a man fell from the saddle he had just climbed into.

'Damn the man!' said the Sheriff as they led their horses back into the trees. He turned to one of the captains standing near him. 'Hood can always outshoot us with those cursed longbows,' he said. 'Take some of your men and work round the back of him.'

Robin, however, had chosen his spot well. The open ground provided pitifully inadequate cover for stalking. Much saw the Captain and his four men before they were half way. Coolly Robin picked his target and shot, snatched his next arrow as Marion loosed at the fleeing soldiers, and was able to shoot again before the survivors dived behind the nearest cover. Silence fell. Three men lay still on the grassy slope, while the Captain and one man-at-arms crouched behind their small boulder and the Sheriff's men watched from the trees.

Suddenly the two men got to their feet and dashed for the forest. The outlaws shot, and the man-at-arms stumbled and fell as two arrows pierced him through his body. The Captain ran on towards the first trees, until a last arrow from Robin came dipping under the low branches to catch him in the thigh. He crumpled in a heap, and two men-at-arms rushed out to drag him into cover.

Robin, Marion and Much continued to watch the open ground in front of them. 'Well shot!' said Robin without looking at Marion, who asked him what he thought would happen next.

'It depends how many they are,' he said grimly. 'We're out of range of any crossbows and we've shown that he can't outflank us. How many horsemen has he got, I wonder?'

Marion watched Robin calmly thinking things out, then said quietly, 'Are we going to die?'

'Everyone dies,' he replied, looking directly at her.

'That isn't what I said,' Marion replied, very seriously.

'I know,' said Robin. He paused before adding, 'It's not over yet.'

He moved a little way from Marion and beckoned Much to him.

'We'll beat them, won't we?' asked Much.

Talking very quietly so that Marion would not hear, Robin said to Much: 'Now when I tell you to, you're to go with Marion up there to the top of the hill. It'll be safe: I'll cover you.' As Much looked puzzled, he went on, 'You're to go deep into Sherwood and lie low until it's dark. Do you understand?'

Much nodded and Robin continued, 'Then I want you to make your way to Kirklees Abbey and ask for sanctuary.'

'What about you?' Much asked, and Robin said that he'd follow them – later ...

For the first time Much began to realize the extreme danger they were in. 'Robin, I don't –' he started, but Robin cut in. 'I'm putting all my trust in you, Much,' he said with great feeling. 'You won't fail me, will you?'

'If that's what you want,' Much said, 'but what if –'

'It'll be easy,' Robin told him. 'And I'll join you at Kirklees – I promise.' Then, as Much looked reassured, Robin went on: 'Now keep your eyes on our friends over there and sing out if anyone moves. And when I give the word – go as fast as you can.'

Robin had made it sound easy and Much believed him. Robin patted him reassuringly and went back to Marion. They sat down together and Robin put his arms round her. 'I'm going to ask you to do something you won't want to do, but it's the –'

'I'm not leaving you!' Marion cut in. 'I'm staying *here*!'

There was a pause, and then Robin said, 'I thought you had more courage.'

'Courage?' Marion asked in surprise.

'To stay alive.' Then he looked at her for a long moment and, speaking very quietly, said, 'Dying's easy!'

Marion sobbed and he held her close, stroking her hair.

'No! No! You're a Crusader's daughter!' said Robin, wiping away her tears, and Marion managed to control herself.

'You see?' said Robin. 'I'm asking you to live. Not just because I love you but because it's meant to be.'

'Nothing's meant to be!' said Marion.

'It is. It is!' Robin told her. 'And one day you'll know it.'

'Let me stay with you! Please!' said Marion.

'There are so many things I want to say to you,' Robin told her, 'but time's caught up. Now I can only say that I've loved you since the first moment I saw you.'

Marion pleaded with him not to make her go, but he only replied, 'Do you want them to win?'

'I don't care about them,' she said bitterly.

'But you must!' Robin insisted. 'For the sake of everything we've meant to each other. You must care – because that way you'll keep alive all we believe in. And I can't die then, can I?'

Marion became calmer and Robin went on, 'Now, listen.

He's sent men down the valley. They'll encircle us and cut off your escape. You must go now!'

'Hold me!' said Marion.

Instead, Robin unbuckled his sword-belt and placed Albion, scabbard and all, in Marion's hands.

'Take this,' he said. 'And this,' as he kissed her lightly on the cheek.

'Robin!' called Much from his look-out post. Two cross-bowmen were climbing round to their left, seeking a position from which they could shoot down among the boulders. If they came much closer they would be able to prevent Marion escaping. Each outlaw loosed an arrow, and a man fell. The other dropped down behind his comrade.

'You must go now!' said Robin.

'I love you!' cried Marion. Then she and Much were gone, scrambling for the brow of the hill behind as Robin laid his last half-dozen arrows out before him. A crossbow bolt from the hillside came humming in and skipped among the boulders, the man was firing at extreme range across his comrade's body.

A voice was yelling orders in the wood – the Sheriff had realized that the outlaws were escaping. A line of horse and foot emerged from the trees, hurrying towards the boulders. Robin stood up in full view, setting his foot on the rock on which his arrows lay.

He must take the horsemen first, or they would run his friends down before they reached the forest. He loosed, snatched his next arrow, and saw a man drop slowly from the saddle as his first shot struck. The Sheriff was shouting orders from behind his men as he grasped that the outlaw he wanted most was still among the boulders. The foot soldiers broke into a run. The horsemen began to circle, aiming for the point at which Much and Marion had crossed over the hill. Still ignoring the oncoming men-at-arms, Robin aimed shot after shot at the small group of knights, sending them reeling from their saddles with desperate accuracy. One remained, bending low in his saddle and riding full stretch for the ridge. The shouts of the infantry were coming closer, and another bolt from the hillside clattered among the boulders. Robin loosed again and heard the scream of a wounded horse. The fugitives were safe.

The men-at-arms were murderously close now, just a few yards short of the first boulders as Robin set his last arrow on the string. The Sheriff was nowhere to be seen – hiding behind his men while they brought down the outlaw. The great bow bent and sprang, sending the arrow flying high over the forest in a salute to all that had been. In the last moments that were left to him, Robin unstrung his bow and broke it on his knee. Then the soldiers charged forward and he was lost from sight as swords flashed down, glinting in the sun.

CHAPTER 20

It was evening in Sherwood, and the lonely figure of a hooded man, staff in hand, was walking slowly through the trees. He heard horses and men approaching and hid his staff. Then he swung himself lightly up into a tree beside the track. Moments later the Sheriff and his men rode by.

As they disappeared from view, the hooded man swung down and went on his way, coming at last to a lake where a boat lay waiting in the mists that were starting to rise from the water. He could see a horned figure standing motionless on the far bank and stepped back in surprise, staring. The figure beckoned.

The hooded man poled himself across and stepped out on to the far bank.

'Do you know me, boy?' asked the one who waited for him. 'I am Herne the Hunter and you are a leaf driven by the wind.'

The hooded man stopped. 'Herne is a spirit and you –'

'And I am a man,' said Herne. 'What brought you here?'

'I don't know. There was a voice – and I was dreaming!'

'My voice?' asked Herne and, when the newcomer shook his head, asked, 'And what did it say to you, this voice?'

'The same thing over and over again,' said the hooded man. 'It was a dream. It said "Nothing's forgotten. Nothing is ever forgotten."'

'Then he is free,' said Herne.

'Nobody's free!' the other replied. 'What does it mean?'

'It means you are a messenger,' Herne told him. 'Perhaps something more.'

'No, you're wrong! I'm just a fugitive!'

'"And the hooded man shall come to the forest, there to

meet with Herne the Hunter",' said Herne, '"to be his son – and do his bidding."'

'I want nothing to do with you!' said the hooded man.

'He brought you here,' Herne told him, and held out a longbow. 'String it.'

'Why?'

'To give it purpose.'

The hooded man took the bow and set the bowstring in its notch. Herne looked at him keenly. 'You also have a purpose,' he said. 'You must prove yourself. Come!' He walked away and the hooded man followed him.

Gisburne watched the Sheriff enter his tent, and walked, grinning, to Edward's hut.

Edward and the captive outlaws were crouched on the ground, all of them tied up.

'I've some interesting news for you,' Gisburne told them. 'Your precious leader is dead, killed by the Sheriff's men. What do you say to that?' There was no reply.

'I am surprised,' said Gisburne. 'Not that it matters very much. This time tomorrow you'll have joined him.'

He went out and there was a long silence, finally broken by Little John, who burst out: 'I don't believe it! He wants us to die thinking that Robin's dead!'

'Then what about Marion and Much?' asked Will quietly.

'What do you mean?' said Tuck.

'Why not say they're all dead? We'd never know any different, would we?' Will pointed out. 'I think it's true!' he went on. 'Look, we've got to face it! He's gone! And I reckon that somehow, before he died, he got the others away.'

'Will's right,' said Tuck. 'He'd do anything to save them! Poor little flower . . . It'll break her heart!'

He was right. Marion was sitting in the darkness in the outlaws' camp, staring straight ahead, as a nightingale sang above her. She was forcing herself not to break down, but suddenly she started to shiver. Much looked at her and said he'd light a fire. Marion said no, but Much argued that she was cold. 'No fire,' she told him.

'I thought Tuck would be here by now,' he said. 'Do you think Nasir has gone for good?' But Marion remained silent.

'Anyway,' Much went on, 'Robin'll meet us at Kirklees. He said so. He promised. They'll never catch him.'

Marion wept.

'Remember how he fought the Templars?' said Much. 'And that time he jumped from the cliff at Ravenscar?'

'Yes, I remember,' Marion replied. 'I remember everything.'

Much took his jerkin off and put it round Marion's shoulders. 'He'll be back,' he said. 'Then we'll rescue Will and Little John. He won't let the Sheriff have them.'

Marion turned slowly and said calmly and almost remotely, 'Robin's dead. He said goodbye to me.' And when Much went on arguing with her she cut in gently, 'He's dead, I tell you. Why do you think he gave me Albion?'

'Because –' Much said, and stopped. A moment later he asked, 'Dead?' and Marion nodded, looking tenderly at him. Much buried his face in his hands.

In Wickham the Sheriff and his men were feasting and drinking to celebrate their victory, with only Gisburne looking sour-faced.

'Don't pull such a long face, man,' said the Sheriff. 'It's not every day we put paid to a dangerous bunch of rebels. The men are entitled to celebrate.'

Gisburne kicked at the dying embers of the fire.

'All the same, my lord, I wish we had the body to show the people of Nottingham.'

The Sheriff leered in the firelight. It was a measure of his mood that he permitted such criticism to pass unrebuked.

'It was unrecognizable, Gisburne. The fools would only claim it was a trick.' He laughed. 'Drink, man, and think of the crows at work on his bones!'

'When are we leaving for Nottingham, my lord?' asked Gisburne.

'When I'm ready,' the Sheriff said with a scowl. 'Why are you so on edge? Do you think Marion's going to attack?'

'The outlaws have many sympathizers,' Gisburne reminded him.

'Sympathizers don't do anything but sympathize, Gisburne,' the Sheriff said heartily, and patted Gisburne on the back. 'Relax, my friend. We've won!'

In the trees the hooded man was watching. He could see the Sheriff and Gisburne, and the men-at-arms carousing round the fire. He had no sword, but he carried the longbow that Herne had given him. He started creeping towards the village.

Two men-at-arms were talking loudly, and both laughed as they drank. After toasting each other, one moved away. The hooded man rose up from the darkness and knocked the other soldier senseless, dragged him into cover and took his sword from him. He worked his way to a spot behind Edward's hut, hid in the undergrowth, then moved forward and started to break in through the wattle with his stolen sword.

The outlaws listened to the sound. 'What's that?' asked Little John.

'Well it ain't mice!' said Will.

'It's Robin!' whispered Little John. 'Gisburne was lying.'

The hooded man suddenly broke through and Little John repeated, 'Robin!'

The newcomer gestured for silence, then went over to Nasir and cut his bonds. 'They said you were dead,' Tuck whispered.

The hooded man began to cut Little John free.

Outside, the Sheriff turned to Gisburne. 'Back to Nottingham!' he ordered. 'Get the prisoners.'

Gisburne went over to the soldiers and ordered: 'Prepare to leave. You three, come with me.' And he led the way to Edward's hut.

'Gisburne!' whispered Nasir, seeing the four men advancing.

'Go!' ordered the hooded man, and Nasir slipped through the hole, followed by Will and John, and then Tuck. The hooded man went over to Edward, but he said: 'Leave me! They'd kill my boy.'

'Get them out!' ordered Gisburne at the door of the hut as the hooded man joined the rest outside. Three men-at-arms entered and found Edward smiling, and a large hole in the back wall.

The outlaws, led by the hooded man, raced into the forest.

Gisburne came into the hut and dashed out again, catching sight of the last of the outlaws racing for cover. 'Stop them!' he roared.

The Sheriff, who had been preparing to mount with his knights, looked across the village just as the hooded man sent an arrow into one of Gisburne's men. Gisburne drew his sword and started towards the hooded man, who loosed an arrow that pierced Gisburne's arm, forcing him to drop his sword. He stared in disbelief at the hooded figure.

'Kill that man!' roared the Sheriff, but his men feared the hooded man with his terrible bow. Slowly the man backed away towards the trees as the Sheriff exploded: 'Kill him! Kill him!'

Nobody moved. Two soldiers crossed themselves. Then the hooded man vanished into the trees. The Sheriff stared into the darkness, immobile as a statue.

The outlaws headed for their camp, smiling in greeting when they saw Marion and Much. But they began to sense that something was wrong.

'Where's Robin?' asked Little John. Marion showed him Albion and their mood changed as they realized what it signified.

'But he came to rescue us at Wickham!' said Little John, staring at the sword.

'No, John,' said Marion quietly. 'He's dead.'

In the Great Hall of Nottingham Castle the Sheriff was sitting moodily in his chair, attended by Gisburne.

'Well, whoever he is, Gisburne, he isn't Robin Hood!' he said.

'It hardly matters, does it?' Gisburne replied. 'Because of him the outlaws are back in Sherwood.'

'But who is he?' the Sheriff asked. 'Who *is* he, Gisburne?'

'I don't know, my lord,' Gisburne said slowly. 'But I know who the men thought he was.'

'Oh, my God!' cried the Sheriff. 'Are we starting again?'

EPILOGUE

It was sunset, and the outlaws were walking away from a grave at the foot of a dead oak tree in Sherwood Forest. They headed for the lake and there they paid their last tribute to their friend with fire arrows.

One by one they shot their arrows, each of them remembering their beloved leader. Nasir's arrow was the first, and in his mind's eye he recalled that moment, before he joined the outlaws, when he had his two swords at Robin's throat. Now his arrow fell in fiery tribute into the waters of the lake.

Tuck was the next to shoot. His was a more recent memory – of how, when he was at his last gasp, Robin had said tenderly, 'We must hide him!'

Next came Will Scarlet, who mused on how he had fallen out with Robin and how he had been welcomed back to the band. His arrow flashed in the sunset.

Little John remembered how Robin had set him free when he had been bewitched by the Baron de Belleme; how Robin had asked him his name, and he had said, 'John Little. I'm from Hathersage!' – and how Robin had replied, 'Little John, more like!' He, too, shot his arrow, memories crowding his mind.

Now it was Much's turn. He heard Robin saying, 'I'm putting all my trust in you, Much. You won't fail me, will you?' He wept as he sent his arrow flaming into the sky.

And last of all Marion raised her bow. She heard Robin's voice long ago in Nottingham Castle, as she had stood looking at him in her bedroom, and he said: 'You are like a May morning.' She watched her arrow vanish into the waters.

Then another arrow flamed into the lake, and the outlaws all looked round. The hooded man stood some way from them at the edge of the trees.

NASTY!

Michael Rosen

Seven stomach-churning, flesh-crawling, spine-chilling stories that give a new meaning to the word 'nasty'. Whatever your weakness, be prepared for some nasty turns as you read Michael Rosen's first collection of stories for Puffin.

THE CLOCK TOWER GHOST

Gene Kemp

Addlesbury Tower is haunted by Rich King Cole, a mean old man who fell off it long ago in mysterious circumstances. Its newest terror is Mandy – feared by her family and eventually by the ghost too. In the war they wage to dominate the tower, Mandy and King Cole do frightful and funny things to each other, little guessing how much they really have in common.

THE GHOST OF THOMAS KEMPE
Penelope Lively

Strange messages, fearful noises and all kinds of jiggery-pokery! It began to dawn on James that there was probably a ghost in the house. But what kind of ghost was it that had come to plague the Harrison family in their lovely old cottage? James sets out to find the answer in this delightfully funny story.

KEPT IN THE DARK
Nina Bawden

Clara, Bosie and Noel all found the big, strange, isolated house and the grandparents they'd never met before rather daunting. And when David turned up and claimed he belonged there too, things got even more disturbing. There were so many secrets to find the answers to.

Heard about the Puffin Club?

... it's a way of finding out more about Puffin books and authors, of winning prizes (in competitions), sharing jokes, a secret code, and perhaps seeing your name in print! When you join you get a copy of our magazine, *Puffin Post*, sent to you four times a year, a badge and a membership book.

For details of subscription and an application form, send a stamped addressed envelope to:

The Puffin Club Dept A
Penguin Books Limited
Bath Road
Harmondsworth
Middlesex UB7 ODA

and if you live in Australia, please write to:

The Australian Puffin Club
Penguin Books Australia Limited
P.O. Box 257
Ringwood
Victoria 3134